FROM THE JOURNAL OF CANDIDIA SMITH-FOSTER:

"By now reader probably wondering what *H. post hominem* might be. Or (at very least) me. Viewed in that light, introductions are in order:

"Name: Candidia Maria Smith-Foster. Born 11 years ago to Smiths; orphaned 10 months later; adopted by Dr. and Mrs. Foster—'Daddy' and 'Momma.' Been known as 'Candy' since first breath.

"*Homo post hominem* is new species, apparently immune to all 'human' disease, plus smarter, stronger, faster, etc., emerging to inherit Earth after *H. sapiens* eliminated selves in short, efficient bionuclear war. Am myself *Homo post hominem*. Rode out war in Daddy's marvelous shelter, now engaged in walkabout, searching for fellow survivors. Of which reader must be one. . . .

"Tomorrow morning, though not now. Tired. disappointed. Perhaps just bad day: too long, too many expectations. Too much letdown.

"Never mind. Tomorrow is another day—Pollyanna *lives!*"

Portions of *Emergence*, published in *Analog* magazine, earned David R. Palmer a Nebula Award nomination, two Hugo Award nominations, and two John W. Campbell award nominations for best new writer. Now, with the publication of his first full-length novel, Palmer takes his place as one of the most exciting new voices in science fiction.

EMERGENCE

David R. Palmer

BANTAM BOOKS

TORONTO · NEW YORK · LONDON · SYDNEY · AUCKLAND

EMERGENCE

A Bantam Book / November 1984

3 printings through July 1985

*Volumes I and II of this novel have
appeared in somewhat different form
in Analog Science Fiction/Science Fact
magazine.*

ISBN 0-553-25519-3

Published simultaneously in the United States and Canada

---

*Bantam Books are published by Bantam Books, Inc. Its trademark,
consisting of the words "Bantam Books" and the portrayal of a
rooster, is Registered in U.S. Patent and Trademark Office and in
other countries. Marca Registrada. Bantam Books, Inc., 666 Fifth
Avenue, New York, New York 10103.*

PRINTED IN THE UNITED STATES OF AMERICA

H   12   11   10   9   8   7   6   5   4   3

This book is dedicated, with love, to
Sherry,
my wife,
without whose patience,
understanding, support, and unerring feel
for what's right and what isn't, this
book would never have seen print;
and who never, ever doubted.

With deepest gratitude to Stanley Schmidt, Ph.D., who bought my first (and second) sales; Betsy Mitchell, who copyedited them; March Laumer, who offered my first professional encouragement; and Russell Galen, my agent.

With thanks to all the patient folk who indulged and aided me in the necessary research, including (but not limited to): Bill Tjalsma, Russian Language Department, University of Florida. Ralph T. Guild III, M.D.; Frances Boulus Guild, R.N.; Allan W. March, M.D. (all of Shands Teaching Hospital, University of Florida). John J. Boyle, M.D., Gainesville, Florida. Joseph Green, Education and Awareness Branch, NASA. Joe Angelo, Ph.D., USAF, Eastern Space and Missile Center, Patrick Air Force Base. Kerry Mark Joels, Gregory P. Kennedy, David Larkin, authors of *The Space Shuttle Operator's Manual*. Jane Beckham, Law Librarian, Marion County, Florida. Sarah Willard, Tulane University.

And special thanks to Lou Aronica at Bantam Books, Inc.: an editor whose exemplary taste and literary discrimination is matched only by his courage . . . !

Contents

VOLUME I
Emergence

Nothing to do? Nowhere to go? Time hangs heavy? Bored? Depressed? Also badly scared? Causal factors beyond control?

Unfortunate. Regrettable. Vicious cycle—snake swallowing own tail. Mind dwells on problems; problems fester, assume ever greater importance for mind to dwell on. Etc. Bad enough where problems minor.

Mine aren't.

Psychology text offers varied solutions: Recommends keeping occupied, busywork if necessary; keep mind distracted. Better if busywork offers challenge, degree of frustration. Still better that I have responsibility. All helps.

Perhaps.

Anyway, keeping busy difficult. Granted, more books in shelter than public library; more tools, equipment, supplies, etc., than Swiss Family Robinson's wrecked ship—all latest developments: lightest, simplest, cleverest, most reliable, nonrusting, Sanforized. All useless unless—correction—until I get out (and of lot, know uses of maybe half dozen: screwdriver for opening stuck drawer; hammer to tenderize steak, break ice cubes; hacksaw for cutting frozen meat . . .).

Oh, well, surely must be books explaining selection, use.

Truly, surely are books—thousands! Plus microfilm library— even bigger. Much deep stuff: classics, contemporary; comprehensive museum of Man's finest works: words, canvas, 3-D and multiview reproductions of statuary. Also scientific: medical, dental, veterinary, entomology, genetics, marine biology; engineering, electronics, physics (both nuclear and garden variety), woodcraft, survival, etc., etc.; poetry, fiction, biographies of great, near-great; philosophy—even complete selection of world's fantasy, new and old. Complete Oz books, etc. Happy surprise, that.

Daddy was determined Man's highest achievements not vanish in Fireworks; also positive same just around corner. (Confession: Wondered sometimes if was playing with complete deck; spent incalculable sums on shelter and contents. Turns out was right; is probably having last laugh Somewhere. Wish were here to needle me about it—but wouldn't if could; was too nice. Miss him. Very much.)

Growing maudlin. Above definitely constitutes "dwelling" in pathological sense as defined by psychology text. Time to click heels, clap hands, smile, Shuffle Off to Buffalo.

Anyhow, mountains of books, microfilm of limited benefit; too deep. Take classics: Can tolerate just so long; then side effects set in. Resembles obtaining manicure by scratching fingernails on blackboard—can, but would rather suffer long fingernails. Same with classics as sole remedy for "dwelling": Not sure which is worse. May be that too much culture in sudden doses harmful to health; perhaps must build up immunity progressively.

And technical is worse. Thought I had good foundation in math, basic sciences. Wrong—background good, considering age; but here haven't found anything elementary enough to form opening wedge. Of course, haven't gotten organized yet; haven't assimilated catalog, planned orderly approach to subjects of interest. Shall; but for now, can get almost as bored looking at horrid pictures of results of endocrine misfunctions as by wading through classics.

And am rationing fantasy, of course. Thousands of titles, but dasn't lose head. Speedreader, you know; breach discipline, well runs dry in matter of days.

Then found book on Pitman shorthand. Changed everything. Told once by unimpeachable source (Mrs. Hartman, Daddy's secretary and receptionist) was best, potentially fastest, most versatile of various pen systems. Also most difficult to learn well. (Footnote, concession to historical accuracy: Was also her system; source possibly contaminated by tinge of bias.) However, seemed promising; offered challenge, frustration. Besides, pothook patterns quite pretty; art form of sorts. Hoped would be entertaining.

Was—for about two days. Then memory finished absorbing principles of shorthand theory, guidelines for briefing and phrasing; transferred same to cortex—end of challenge. Tiresome being genius sometimes.

Well, even if no longer entertaining for own sake, still useful, much more practical than longhand; ideal for keeping journal, writing biography for archeologists. Probably not bother if limited to longhand; too slow, cumbersome. Effort involved would dull enthusiasm (of which little present anyway), wipe out paper supply in short order. Pitman fits entire life story on line and a half. (Of course helps I had short life— correction: Helps brevity; does nothing for spirits.)

Problem with spirits serious business. Body trapped far underground; emotional index substantially lower. Prospects not good for body getting out alive, but odds not improved by emotional state. Depression renders intelligent option assessment improbable. In present condition would likely overlook ten good bets, flip coin over dregs. Situation probably not hopeless as seems; but lacking data, useful education, specialized knowledge (and guts), can't form viable conclusion suggesting happy ending. And lacking same, tend to assume worst.

So journal not just for archeologists; is therapeutic. Catharsis: Spill guts on paper, feel better. Must be true— psychology text says so (though cautions is better to pay Ph.D.-equipped voyeur week's salary per hour to listen. However, none such included in shelter inventory; will have to make do).

First step: Bring journal up-to-date. Never kept one; not conversant with format requirements, Right Thing To Do. Therefore will use own judgment. One thing certain: Sentence structure throughout will have English teachers spinning in graves (those fortunate to have one).

English 60 percent flab, null symbols, waste. Suspect massive inefficiency stems from subconsciously recognized need to stall, give inferior intellects chance to collect thoughts into semblance of coherence (usually without success), and to show off (my $12 word can lick your $10 word). Will not adhere to precedent; makes little sense to write shorthand, then cancel advantage by employment of rambling academese.

Keep getting sidetracked into social criticism. Probably symptom of condition. Stupid; all evidence says no society left. Was saying:

First step: Bring journal up to present; purge self of neuroses, sundry hangups. Then record daily orderly progress in study of situation, subsequent systematic (brilliant) self-extrication from dire straits. Benefits twofold:

First, will wash, dry, fold, put away psyche; restore mind to customary genius; enhance prospects for successful escape, subsequent survival. Second, will give archeologists details on cause of untimely demise amidst confusing mass of artifacts in shelter should anticipated first benefit lose rosy glow. (Must confess solicitude for bone gropers forced; bones in question *mine!*)

Enough maundering. Time to bear down, flay soul for own good. Being neurotic almost as tiresome as being genius. (Attention archeologists: Clear room of impressionable youths and/or mixed company—torrid details follow:)

Born 11 years ago in small Wisconsin town, only child of normal parents. Named Candidia Maria Smith; reduced to Candy before ink dried on certificate. Early indications of atypicality: Eyes focused, tracked at birth; cause-effect association evident by six weeks; first words at four months; sentences at six months.

Orphaned at ten months. Parents killed in car accident.

No relatives—created dilemma for baby-sitter. Solved when social worker took charge. Was awfully cute baby; adopted in record time.

Doctor Foster and wife good parents: Loving, attentive; very fond of each other, showed it. Provided good environment for formative years. Then Momma died. Left just Daddy and me; drew us very close. Was probably shamelessly spoiled, but also stifled:

Barely five then, but wanted to *learn*—only Daddy had firm notions concerning appropriate learning pace, direction for "normal" upbringing. Did not approve of precocity; felt was unhealthy, would lead to future maladjustment, unhappiness. Also paternalistic sexist; had bad case of ingrown stereotypitis. Censored activities, reading; dragged heels at slightest suggestion of precocious behavior, atypical interests.

Momma disagreed; aided, indulged. With her help I learned to read by age two; understood basic numerical relationships by three: Could add, subtract, multiply, divide. Big help until she had to leave.

So sneaked most of education. Had to—certainly not available in small-town classroom. Not difficult; developed speedreading habit, could finish high school text in 10, 20 minutes; digest typical best-seller in half, three quarters of hour. Haunted school, local libraries every opportunity (visits only; couldn't bring choices home). But town small; exhausted obvious resources three years ago. Have existed since on meager fruits of covert operations in friends' homes, bookstores; occasional raids on neighboring towns' libraries, schools. Of course not all such forays profitable; small-town resources tend to run same direction: slowly, in circles. Catalogs mostly shallow, duplicated; originality lacking.

Frustrating. Made more so by knowledge that Daddy's personal in-house library rivaled volume count of local school, public libraries put together (not counting shelter collection, but didn't know about that then)—and couldn't get halfway down first page of 95 percent of contents.

Daddy pathologist; books imperviously technical. So far over head, couldn't even tell where gap lay (ask cannibal fresh off plane from Amazon for analysis of educational deficiencies causing noncomprehension of commercial banking structure). Texts dense; assumed reader already possessing high-level competency. Sadly lacking in own case—result of conspiracy. So languished, fed in dribbles as tireless prospecting uncovered new sources.

Single bright exception: Soo Kim McDivott, son of American missionary in Boxer Rebellion days, product of early East-West alliance. Was 73 when retired, moved next door two years ago. Apparently had been teacher whole life but never achieved tenure; tended to get fired over views. Did not appear to mind.

Strange old man. Gentle, soft-spoken, very polite; small, seemed almost frail. Oriental flavoring lent elflike quality to wizened features; effect not reduced by mischief sparkling from eyes.

Within two weeks became juvenile activity focus for most of town. Cannot speak for bulk of kids, but motivation obvious in own case: Aside from intrinsic personal warmth, knew everything—and if exception turned up would gleefully drop everything, help find out—and had *books*. House undoubtedly in violation of Fire Code; often wondered how structural members took load.

Fascinating man: Could, would discuss anything. But wondered for a time how managed as teacher; never answered questions but with questions. Seemed whenever I had question, ended up doing own research, telling *him* answer. Took a while to catch on, longer before truly appreciated: Had no interest in teaching knowledge, factual information—taught learning. Difference important; seldom understood, even more rarely appreciated. Don't doubt was reason for low retirement income.

Oh, almost forgot: Could split bricks with sidelong glance, wreak untold destruction with twitch of muscle. Any muscle. Was Tenth Degree Master of Karate. Didn't know were such; thought ratings topped at Eighth—and heard rumors *they* could walk on water. (But doubt Master Mac would bother. Should need arise, would politely ask waters to part—but more likely request anticipated, unnecessary.)

Second day after moving in, Master was strolling down Main Street when happened upon four young men, early 20s, drunk, unkempt—Summer People (sorry, my single ineradicable prejudice)—engaged in self-expression at Miller's Drugstore. Activities consisted of inverting furniture, displays; dumping soda-fountain containers (milk, syrup, etc.) on floor; throwing merchandise through display windows. Were discussing also throwing Mr. Miller when Master Mac arrived on scene.

Assessed situation; politely requested cease, desist, await authorities' arrival. Disbelieving onlookers closed, averted eyes; didn't want to watch expected carnage. Filthy Four dropped Mr. Miller, converged on frail-looking old Chinese. Then all fell down, had subsequent difficulty arising. Situation remained static until police arrived.

Filthies taken into custody, then to hospital. Attempted investigation of altercation unrewarding: Too many eyewitness accounts—all contradictory, disbelieving, unlikely. However, recurring similarities in stories suggested simultaneous stumble as Filthies reached for Master; then all fell, accumulating severe injuries therefrom: four broken jaws, two arms, two legs, two wrists; two dislocated hips; two ruptured spleens. Plus bruises in astonishing places.

Single point of unanimity—ask *anyone:* Master Mac never moved throughout.

Police took notes in visibly strained silence. Also took statement from Master Mac. But of dubious help: Consisted mostly of questions.

Following week YMCA announced Master Mac to teach karate classes. Resulted in near-riot (by small-town standards).

Standing room only at registration; near fistfights over positions in line.

Was 16th on list to start first classes but deserve no credit for inclusion: Daddy's doing. Wanted badly—considering sociological trends, self-defense skills looked ever more like required social graces for future survival—but hesitated to broach subject; seemed like probable conflict with "normal upbringing" dictum.

So finally asked. Surprise! Agreed—granted dispensation! Was still in shock when Daddy asked time, date of registration. Showed article in paper: noon tomorrow. Looked thoughtful maybe five seconds; then rushed us outdoors, down street to Y. Already 15 ahead of us, equipped to stay duration.

Daddy common as old slipper: warm, comfortable, folksy. But shared aspects with iceberg: Nine-tenths of brains not evident in everyday life. Knew was very smart, of course. Implicit from job; pathologist knows everything any other specialist does, plus own job. Obviously not career for cretin—and was *good* pathologist. Renowned.

But not show-off; was easy to forget; reminders few, far between. Scope, foresight, quick reactions, Command Presence demonstrated only in time of need.

Such occurred now: While I stood in line with mouth open (and 20 more hopefuls piled up behind like Keystone Cops), Daddy organized friends to bring chairs, cot, food, drink, warm clothing, blankets, rainproofs, etc. Took three minutes on phone. Was impressed. Then astounded—spent whole night on sidewalk with me, splitting watches, trading off visits to Little Persons' room when need arose.

Got all choked up when he announced intention. Hugged him breathless; told him kismet had provided better father than most workings of genetic coincidence. Did not reply, but got hugged back harder than usual; caught glimpse of extra reflections in corners of eyes from streetlight. Special night; full of warmth, feelings of belonging, togetherness.

After Daddy's magnificent contribution, effort to get me into class, felt slight pangs of guilt over my subsequent misdirection, concealment of true motivation. True, attended classes, worked hard; became, in fact, star pupil. But had to—star pupils qualified for private instruction—yup!—at Master's home, surrounded by what appeared to be 90 percent of books in Creation.

Earned way though. Devoted great effort to maintaining favored status; achieved Black Belt in ten months, state championship (for age/weight group) six months later. Was considered probable national championship material, possibly world. Enjoyed; great fun, terrific physical conditioning, obvious potential value (ask Filthy Four), good for ego due to adulation over ever-lengthening string of successes, capture of state loving cup (ironic misnomer—contest was mock combat: "killed" seven opponents, "maimed" 22 others for life or longer).

But purely incidental; in no way distracted from main purpose:

With aid of Master (addressed as "Teacher" away from *dojo*) had absorbed equivalent of advanced high school education, some college by time world ended: Math through calculus, chemistry, beginnings of physics; good start on college biology, life sciences—doing well.

Occasionally caught Teacher regarding me as hen puzzles over product of swan egg slipped into nest; making notes in "Tarzan File" (unresolved enigma: Huge file, never explained; partially concerned me, as achievements frequently resulted in entries, but was 36-inches thick before I entered picture), but definitely approved—and his approval better for ego than state cup.

Regarding which, had by then achieved Fifth Degree; could break brick with edge of hand, knee, foot. But didn't after learned could. Prospect distressed Daddy. Poor dear could visualize with professional exactitude pathological consequences of attempt by untrained; knew just what each bone splinter would look like, where would be driven; which tendons torn from what insertions; which nerves destroyed forever, etc. Had wistful ambition I might follow into medicine; considered prospects bleak for applicant with deformed, callused hammers dangling from wrists.

Needless concern; calluses unnecessary. With proper control body delivers blow through normal hands without discomfort, damage. Is possible, of course, to abuse nature to point where fingers, knuckles, edge of hands, etc., all turn to flint, but never seen outside exhibitions. Serves no purpose in practice of Art; regarded with disdain by serious student, Master alike.

So much for happy memories.

Not long ago world situation took turn for worse. Considering character of usual headlines when change began, outlook became downright grim.

Daddy tried to hide concern but spent long hours reading reports from Washington (appreciated for first time just how renowned was when saw whom from), watching news; consulting variety of foreign, domestic officials by phone. Seemed cheerful enough, but when thought I wasn't looking, mask slipped.

Finally called me into study. Sat me down; gave long, serious lecture on how bad things were. Made me lead through house, point out entrances to emergency chute leading down to shelter (dreadful thing—200-foot vertical drop in pitch dark, cushioned at bottom only by gradual curve as polished sides swing to horizontal, enter shelter). Then insisted we take plunge for practice. Although considered "practice" more likely to induce psychic block, make subsequent use impossible—even in time of need—performed as requested. Not as bad as expected; terror index fell perhaps five percent short of anticipation. But not fun.

However, first time in shelter since age three. Scenic attractions quickly distracted from momentary cardiac arrest incurred in transit. Concealed below modest small-town frame house of unassuming doctor was Eighth Wonder of World. Shelter is three-story structure carved from bedrock, 100 feet by 50; five-eighths shelves, storage compartments. Recognized microfilm viewer immediately; identical to one used at big hospital over in next county. Film-storage file cabinets same, too—only occupied full length of two long walls; plus four free-standing files ran almost full length of room. Rest bookshelves, as is whole of second floor. Basement seems mostly tools, machinery, instrumentation.

Hardly heard basic life-support function operation lecture: air regeneration, waste reclamation, power production, etc. Was all could do to look attentive—books drew me like magnet. However, managed to keep head; paid sufficient attention to ask intelligent-sounding questions. Actually learned basics of how to work shelter's vital components.

. . . Because occurred to me: Could read undisturbed down here if knew how to make habitable. (Feel bad about that, too; here Daddy worried sick over my survival In The Event Of—and object of concern scheming about continued selfish pursuit of printed word.)

Tour, lecture ended. Endless spiral staircase up tube five

feet in diameter led back to comfortable world of small-town reality. Life resumed where interrupted.

With exception: Was now alert for suitable opportunity to begin exploration of shelter.

Not readily available. As Fifth was qualified assistant instructor at formal classes; took up appreciable portion of time. Much of rest devoted to own study—both Art (wanted to attain Sixth; would have been youngest in world) and academics, both under approving eye of Master. Plus null time spent occupying space in grammar school classroom, trying not to look too obviously bored while maintaining straight-A average. (Only amusement consisted of correcting textbooks, teachers—usually involved digging up proof, confrontations in principal's office.) Plus sundry activities rounding out image of "normally well-rounded 11-year-old."

But patience always rewarded. If of sufficient duration. Daddy called to Washington; agreed was adult enough to take care of self, house, Terry during three days' expected absence. Managed not to drool at prospect.

Terry? True, didn't mention before, by name; just that had responsibility. Remember? First page, fourth paragraph. Pay attention—may spring quiz.

Terry is retarded, adoptive twin brother. Saw light of day virtually same moment I emerged—or would have, had opened eyes. Early on showed more promise than I: Walked at nine weeks, first words at three months, could fly at 14 weeks. Achieved fairly complex phrases by six months but never managed complete sentences. Peaked early but low.

Not fair description. Actually Terry is brilliant—for macaw. Also beautiful. Hyacinthine Macaw, known to lowbrows as Hyacinth, pseudointellectuals as *anodorhynchus hyacinthinus*— terrible thing to say about sweet baby bird. Full name Terry D. Foster (initial stands for Dactyll). Length perhaps 36 inches (half of which is tail feathers); basic color rich, glowing, hyacinth blue (positively electric in sunlight), with bright yellow eye patches like clown, black feet and bill. Features permanently arranged in jolly Alfred E. Neuman, village-idiot smile. Diet is anything within reach, but ideally consists of properly mixed seeds, assorted fruits, nuts, sprinkling of meat, etc.

Hobbies include getting head and neck scratched (serious business, this), art of conversation, destruction of world. Talent for latter avocation truly awe-inspiring: 1500 pounds pressure available at business end of huge, hooked beak. Firmly believe if left Terry with four-inch cube of solid tungsten carbide, would return in two hours to find equivalent mass of metal dust, undimmed enthusiasm.

Was really convinced were siblings when very young. First deep childhood trauma (not affected by loss of blood parents; too young at time, too many interesting things happening) induced by realization was built wrong, would never learn to fly. Had stubbornly mastered perching on playpen rail shortly before began walking (though never did get to point of preferring nonchalant one-legged stance twin affected—toes deformed: stunted, too short for reliable grip), but subsequent step simply beyond talents.

Suspect this phase of youth contributed to appearance of symptoms leading to early demise of Momma Foster. Remember clearly first time she entered room, found us perched together on rail, furiously "exercising wings." Viewed in retrospect, is amazing didn't expire on spot.

(Sounds cold, unfeeling; is not. Momma given long advance notice; knew almost to day when could expect to leave. Prepared me with wisdom, understanding, love. Saw departure as unavoidable but wonderful opportunity, adventure; stated was prepared to accept, even excuse, reasonable regret over plans spoiled, things undone—but not grief. Compared grief over death of friend to envy of friend's good fortune: selfish reaction—feeling sorry for self, not friend. Compared own going to taking wonderful trip; "spoiled plans" to giving up conflicting movie, picnic, swim in lake. Besides, was given big responsibility—charged me with "looking after Daddy." Explained he had formed many elaborate plans involving three of us—many more than she or I had. Would doubtless be appreciably more disappointed, feel more regret over inability to carry out. Would need love, understanding during period it took him to reform plans around two remaining behind. Did such a job on me that truly did not suffer loss, grief; just missed her when gone, hoped was having good time.)

Awoke morning of Daddy's trip to startling realization—didn't want him to go. Didn't like prospect of being alone three days: didn't like idea of *him* alone three days. Lay abed trying to resolve disquieting feeling. Or at least identify. Could do neither; had never foreboded before. Subliminal sensation: below conscious level but intrusive. Multiplied by substantial factor could be mistaken for fear—no, not fear, exactly; more like mindless, screaming terror.

But silly; nothing to be scared about. Mrs. Hartman would be working in office in front part of house during day; house locked tight at night—with additional security provided by certain distinctly nonsmall-town devices Daddy recently caused installed. Plus good neighbors on all sides, available through telephone right at bedside or single loud scream.

Besides, was I not Candy Smith-Foster, State Champion, Scourge of Twelve-and-Under Class, second most dangerous mortal within 200-mile radius? (By now knew details of Filthy Four's "stumble," and doubt would have gotten off so lightly had I been intercessor.)

Was. So told feeling to shut up. Washed, dressed, went down to breakfast with Daddy and Terry.

Conduct during send-off admirable; performance qualified for finals in stiff-upper-lip-of-year award contest. Merely gave big hug, kiss; cautioned stay out of trouble in capital, but if occurred, call me soonest—would come to rescue: split skulls, break bones, mess up adversaries something awful. Sentiment rewarded by lingering return hug, similar caution about self during absence (but expressed with more dignity).

Then door of government-supplied, chauffeur-driven, police-escorted limousine closed; vehicle made its long, black way down street, out of sight around corner.

Spent morning at school, afternoon teaching at Y, followed by own class with Master. Finally found self home, now empty except Terry (voicing disapproval of day's isolation at top of ample lungs); Mrs. Hartman done for day, had gone home. Silenced twin by scratching head, transferring to shoulder (loves assisting with household chores, but acceptance means about three times as much work as doing by self—requires everything done at arms' length, out of reach).

Made supper, ate, gave Terry whole tablespoon of peanut butter as compensation for boring day (expressed appreciation by crimping spoon double). Did dishes, cleaned house in aimless fashion; started over.

Finally realized was dithering, engaging in busywork; afraid to admit was really home alone, actually had opportunity for unhindered investigation of shelter. Took hard look at conflict; decided was rooted in guilt over intent to take advantage of Daddy's absence to violate known wishes. Reminded self that existence of violation hinged upon accuracy of opinion concerning unvocalized desires; "known wishes" question-begging terminology if ever was one. Also told self firmly analysis of guilt feeling same as elimination. Almost believed.

Impatiently stood, started toward basement door. Terry recognized signs, set up protest against prospect of evening's abandonment. Sighed, went back, transferred to shoulder. Brother rubbed head on cheek in gratitude, gently bit end of nose, said, "You're so bad," in relieved tones. Gagged slightly; peanut-butter breath from bird is rare treat.

Descended long spiral stairs down tube to shelter. Ran through power-up routine, activated systems. Then began exploration.

Proceeded slowly. Terry's first time below; found entertaining. Said, "How *'bout* that!" every ten seconds. Also stretched neck, bobbed head, expressed passionate desire to sample every book as pulled from shelf. Sternly warned of brief future as giblet dressing if so much as touched single page. Apparently thought prospect sounded fun, redoubled efforts. But was used to idiot twin's antisocial behavior; spoiled fun almost without conscious thought as proceeded with exploration.

Soon realized random peeking useless; was in position of hungry kid dropped in middle of Willy Wonka's Chocolate Factory: too much choice. Example: Whole cabinet next to microfilm viewer was *catalog*!

Three feet wide, eight high; drawers three feet deep, six inches wide (rows of six); ten titles per card (*thin* cards) —72 cubic feet of solid catalog.

Took breath away to contemplate. Also depressed; likelihood of mapping orderly campaign to augment education not good. Didn't know where to start; which books, films within present capacity; where to go from there. Only thing more tiresome than being repressed genius is being ignorant genius recognizing own status.

Decided to consult Teacher; try to get him to list books he considered ideal to further education most rapidly from present point, cost no object. (Was giving consideration to Daddy's ambition to see me become doctor; but regardless, no education wasted. Knowledge worthwhile for own sake.) Didn't feel should report discovery—would be breach of confidence—but could use indirect approach. Not lie; just not mention that any book suggested undoubtedly available on moment's notice. Ought to fool him all of ten seconds.

Started toward switchboard to power-down shelter. Hand touching first switch in sequence when row of red lights began flashing, three large bells on wall next to panel commenced deafening clangor. Snatched hand back as if from hot stove; thought had activated burglar alarm (if reaction included thought at all). Feverish inspection of panel disclosed no hint of such, but found switch marked "Alarm Bells, North American Air Defense Command Alert." Opened quickly; relieved to note cessation of din, but lights continued flashing. Then, as watched, second row, labeled "Attack Detected," began flashing.

Problem with being genius is tendency to think deep, mull hidden significance, overlook obvious. Retrieved Terry (as usual, had gone for help at first loud noise), scratched head to soothe nerves. Twin replied, "That's *bad*!" several times; dug claws into shoulder, flapped wings to show had not really been scared. Requested settle down, shut up; wished to contemplate implications of board.

Impressive. Daddy must be truly high-up closet VIP to rate such inside data supplied to home shelter. As considered this, another row flashed on, this labeled "Retaliation Initiated." Imagine—blow-by-blow nuclear-war info updates supplied to own home! Wonderful to be so important. Amazing man. And so modest—all these years never let on. Wondered about real function in government. With such brains, was probably head of supersecret spy bureau in charge of dozens of James Bond types.

Don't know how long mindless rumination went on; finally something clicked in head: Attack? Retaliation? *Hey* . . . ! Bolted for steps. Terry sunk in claws, voiced protest over sudden movements.

Stopped like statue. Daddy's voice, tinny, obviously recording: "Red alert, radiation detected. Level above danger limit. Shelter will seal in 30 seconds—29, 28, 27 . . ." Stood frozen; listened as familiar voice delivered requiem for everything known and loved—including probably self. Interrupted count once at 15-second mark to repeat radiation warning, again at five seconds.

Then came deep-toned humming; powerful motors slid blocks of concrete, steel, asbestos across top of stairwell, did same for emergency-entry chute. Sealing process terminated with solidly mechanical clunks, thuds. Motors whined in momentary overload as program ensured was tight.

Then truly alone. Stood staring at nothing for long minutes. Did not know when silent tears began; noticed wet face when Terry sampled, found too salty. Shook head; said softly, "Poo-oor bay-bee...."

Presently found self sitting in chair. Radio on; could not remember turning switch, locating CONELRAD frequency. Just sat, listened to reports. Only time stirred was to feed, water Terry; use potty. Station on air yet, but manned only first three days.

Was enough, told story: Mankind eliminated. Radiation, man-made disease. International quick-draw ended in tie.

Final voice on air weakly complained situation didn't make sense: Was speaking from defense headquarters near Denver—miles underground, utterly bombproof, airtight; self-contained air, water—so why dying? Why last alive in entire installation? Didn't make sense....

Agreed, but thought objection too limited in scope. Also wondered why *we* were still alive. Likewise didn't make sense: If invulnerability of NORAD headquarters—located just this side of Earth's core under Cheyenne Mountain—proving ineffective, how come fancy subcellar hidey-hole under house in small town still keeping occupants alive? And for how long? Figured had to be just matter of time.

Therefore became obsessed with worry over fate of retarded brother. Were safe from radiation (it seemed), but plague another matter. Doubted would affect avian biochemistry; would kill me, leave poor baby to starve, die of thirst. Agonized over dilemma for days. Finally went downstairs; hoped might turn up something in stores could use as Terry's Final Friend.

Did. Found armory. Thought of what might have to do almost triggered catatonia; but knew twin's escape from suffering dependent on me, so mechanically went ahead with selection of shotgun. Found shells, loaded guns. Carried upstairs, placed on table. Then waited for cue.

Knew symptoms; various CONELRAD voices had described own, those of friends. Were six to syndrome. Order in which appeared reported variable; number present at onset of final unconsciousness not. Four symptoms always, then fifth: period of extreme dizziness—clue to beginning of final decline. Was important, critical to timing with regard to Terry. Desperately afraid might wait too long; condemn poor incompetent to agonizing last days. And almost more afraid might react to false alarm, proceed with euthanasia; then fail to die—have to face scattered, blood-spattered feathers, headless body of sweetest, jolliest, most devoted, undemandingly loving friend had ever known.

Which was prospect if acted too soon—intended to stand 20 feet away, blow off head while engrossed in peanut butter. Pellet pattern expansion sufficient at that distance to ensure virtually instantaneous vaporization of entire head, instant kill before possibility of realization, pain. Would rather suffer own dismemberment, boiling in oil, than see innocent baby suffer, know was me causing.

Thus, very important to judge own condition accurately when plague sets in.

Only hasn't yet. Been waiting three weeks, paralyzed with grief, fear, apprehension, indecision. But such emotions wearisome when protracted; eventually lose grip on victim. I think perhaps might have—particularly now that journal up-to-date, catharsis finished. Book says therapy requires good night's sleep after spilling guts; then feel better in morning. Suspect may be right; do feel better.

Okay. Tomorrow will get *organized*...!

Good morning, Posterity! Happy to report I spent good night. Slept as if already dead—first time since trouble began. No dreams; if tossed, turned, did so without noticing. Appears psychology-text writer knew stuff (certainly should have; more letters following name than in). Catharsis worked—at least would seem; felt good on waking. Wounds obviously not healed yet, but closed. A beginning—scabs on soul much better than hemorrhage.

Situation unchanged; obviously not happy about fact (if were would know had slipped cams). But this morning can look at Terry without bursting into tears; can face possibility might have to speed birdbrained twin to Reward before own condition renders unable. Thought produces entirely reasonable antipathy, sincere hope will prove unnecessary—but nothing more.

Despairing paralysis gone; mind no longer locked into hopeless inverse logarithmic spiral, following own tail around ever closer, all-enveloping fear of ugly possibility.

Seems have regained practical outlook held prior to Armageddon; i.e., regard worry as wasteful, counterproductive if continued after recognition, analysis of impending problem, covering bases to extent resources permit. Endless bone-worrying not constructive exercise; if anything, diminishes odds for favorable outcome by limiting scope of mind's operation, cuts down opportunities for serendipity to lend hand. Besides, takes fun out of life—especially important when little enough to be had.

Time I rejoined world of living (possibly not most apt choice of words—hope do not find am in exclusive possession). First step: consider well-being. Have sadly neglected state of health past three weeks; mostly just sat in chair, lay abed listening to airwaves hiss.

And speaking of physical well-being—have just noticed: am ravenous! Have nibbled intermittently, without attention to frequency, content—mostly when feeding, watering Terry. (Regardless of own condition, did *not* neglect jovial imbecile during course of depression. Even cobbled up makeshift stand from chair, hardwood implement handle; found sturdy dishes, secured firmly to discourage potential hilarity. Granted, diet not ideal—canned vegetables, fruits, meat, etc.—but heard no complaints from clientele, and would be no doubt if existed: Dissatisfaction with offerings usually first indicated by throwing on floor; if prompt improvement not forthcoming, abandons subtlety.)

Have also noticed am *filthy*! Wearing same clothes came downstairs in three weeks ago. Neither garments nor underlying smelly germ farm exposed to water, soap, deodorant since. (Can be same fastidious Candy Smith-Foster who insists upon shower, complete change of clothing following any hint of physical exertion, contact with even potentially soiled environment? Regrettably is.) And now that am in condition to notice—*have*! Self-respecting maggot would take trade elsewhere.

So please excuse. Must rectify immediately. Bath (probably take three, four complete water changes to do job); then proper meal, clean clothes. Then get down to business. Time to find out about contents of shelter—availability of resources relevant to problems.

Be back later. . . .

Apologies for delay, neglect. But have been so *busy*!

Bath, resumption of proper nutrition completed cure. Spirits restored; likewise determination, resourcefulness, curiosity (intellectual variety; am not snoop—rumors to con-

trary). Also resumed exercises, drills (paid immediate penalty
for three-week neglect of Art—first attempt at usual *kata*
nearly broke important places, left numerous sore muscles).

Have systematically charted shelter. Took pen, pad downstairs to stores, took inventory. Then went through bookshelves in slow, painstaking manner; recorded titles, locations
of volumes applicable to problems. Project took best part of
three days. Worth effort; variety, volume of equipment simply
awesome. Together with library, probably represents everything necessary for singlehanded founding of bright new
civilization—from scratch, if necessary. (Not keen on singlehand-
ing part, however; sounds lonely. Besides, know nothing
about Applied Parthogenesis; not merit-badge topic in scouts.
[Only memory of subject's discussion concerned related
research—was no-no; leader claimed caused myopia, acne,
nonspecific psychoses.] Oh, well, considering age, prospects
for achieving functional puberty, seems less than pressing
issue.)

Speaking of pressing issues, however—found *food*. Foun-
der of civilization certainly will eat well in interim. Must be
five-year supply of frozen meat, fruit, fresh vegetables in
deep-freeze locker adjoining lower level (huge thing—50 feet
square). Stumbled upon by accident; door wasn't labeled.
Opened during routine exploration expecting just another
bin. Light came on, illuminating scenery—almost froze tip of
nose admiring contents before realized was standing in
50-degree-below-zero draft. Also good news for Terry: Daddy
anticipated presence; lifetime supply of proper seed mix in
corner bin. Will keep forever; too cold to hatch inevitable
weevil eggs, etc.

Actually haven't minded canned diet; good variety
available—but sure was nice to drop mortally-peppered steak
onto near-incandescent griddle, inhale fumes as cooked; then
cut with fork while still bleeding inside charred exterior. Of
course, had to fight Terry for share; may be something likes
better, but doesn't come readily to mind.

Is regrettable this could be part of Last Words; means
must exercise honesty in setting down account. Bulk of
organized theologies I've read opine dying with lie upon lips
bodes ill for direction of departure. Since can be no doubt of
Terry's final Destination, must keep own powder dry. Twin
would be lonely if got There without me—besides, without

watching would announce presence by eating pearls out of Gate.

So despite self-serving impulses, must record faithfully shameful details of final phase in monumental inventory: assault upon card file. Intended to make painstaking, card-by-card inspection of microfilm catalog (vastly more extensive than bound collection), recording titles suggesting relevance to problems. Grim prospect: 72 cubic feet holds dreadful quantity of cards—each with ten titles. Even considering own formidable reading speed, use of Pitman for notes, seemed likely project would account for substantial slice of remaining lifespan—even assuming can count upon normal duration.

However, could see no other way; needed information. So took down first drawer (from just below ceiling, of course; but thoughtful Daddy provided rolling ladder as in public stacks), set on table next to notepad. Sighed, took out first card, scanned—stopped, looked again. Pulled out next 20, 30; checked quickly. Made unladylike observation regarding own brains (genius, remember?). Reflected (after exhausted self-descriptive talents) had again underestimated Daddy.

Humble healer, gentle father was embodiment of patience—but had none with unnecessary inefficiency. Obviously would have devised system to locate specifics in such huge collection. Useless otherwise; researcher could spend most of life looking for data instead of using.

First 200 cards index of *index*. Alphabetically categorized, cross-referenced to numbered file locations. Pick category, look up location in main file; check main file for specific titles, authors; find films from specific location number on individual card. Just like downtown.

So after settled feathers from self-inflicted wounds (ten well-deserved lashes with sharp tongue), got organized. Selected categories dealing with situation; referred to main index; decided upon specific films, books. Cautioned Terry again about giblet shortage, dug out selections. Settled down to become expert in nuclear warfare, viral genocide; construction details, complete operation of shelter systems.

Have done so. Now know exactly what happened. Every ugly detail. Know which fissionables used, half-life durations; viral, bacterial agents employed; how deployed, how long remain viable threats without suitable living hosts. Know what they used on us—vice versa. Found Daddy's papers dealing with secret life.

Turns out was heavyweight government consultant. Specialty was countering biological warfare. Privy to highest secrets; knew all about baddest bugs on both sides. Knew how used, countermeasures most effective—personally responsible for development programs aimed at wide-spectrum etiotropic counteragents. Also knew intimate details of nuclear hardware poised on both sides of face-off. Seems had to: Radiation level often key factor; in many cases benign virus, bacteria turned instantaneously inimical upon exposure to critical wavelengths. Only difference between harmless tourist and pathogen: Soothing counsel transmitted from pacific gene in DNA helix to cytoplasmic arsenal by radiation-vulnerable RNA messenger. Enter energy-particle flood, exit restraint; hello Attila the Germ. Clever, these mad scientists.

Undoubtedly how attack conducted—explains, too, fall of hermetically sealed NORAD citadel. Entire country seeded over period of time with innocuous first-stage organisms until sufficiently widespread. Then special warheads—carefully spaced to irradiate every inch of target with critical wavelength— simultaneously detonated at high altitude across whole country. Bombs dropping vertically from space remained undetected until betrayed by flash—by which time too late; radiation front travels just behind visible light. Not a window broken but war already over: Everybody running for shelter already infected, infectious with at least one form of now-activated, utterly lethal second-stage plague. Two, three days later—all dead.

Supposed to be another file someplace down here detailing frightful consequences to attackers; haven't found yet. Only mention in this one suggests annihilation even surer, more complete among bad guys—and included broken windows.

Tone of comment regretful. Not sure can agree. True, most dead on both sides civilians—but are truly innocent? Who permitted continuing rule by megalomaniacs? Granted, would have been costly for populace to throw incumbent rascals out, put own rascals in—but considering cost of failure in present light . . .

Must give thought before passing judgment.

Enough philosophy.

Have learned own tactical situation not bad. No radiation detectable on surface, immediate area (instrumentation in shelter; sensors upstairs on roof of house—part of TV antenna). Not surprising: According to thesis, nuclear stuff to be used almost exclusively as catalyst for viral, bacterial invaders. Bursts competely clean—no fallout at all—high enough to preclude physical damage. Exception: Direct hits anticipated on known ICBM silos, SAC bases, Polaris submarines, bomber-carrying carriers, overseas installations—and Washington. . . .

Where Daddy went. Hope was quick, clean.

Plague another question entirely. Daddy's opinion holds infection self-curing. No known strain in arsenals of either side capable of more than month's survival outside proper culture media; i.e., living human tissue (shudder to contemplate where, how media obtained for experiments leading to conclusion). Odds very poor such available longer than two, three days after initial attack; therefore should be only another week before is safe to venture outside, see what remains of world.

However, wording "should be" erodes confidence in prediction; implies incomplete data, guesswork—*gamble*. Considering stake involved is own highly regarded life, placing absolute reliance on stated maximum contagion parameters not entirely shrewd policy.

So shan't. Now that can get out whenever wish, no longer have such pressing need to; claustrophobic tendencies gone. Shelter quite cozy (considering): Dry, warm, plumbing, furniture; great food (brilliantly prepared), safe water; good company, stimulating conversation ("Hello, baby! What'cha doin'? You're so bad! Icky *pooh*!"); plus endless supply of knowledge. Delay amidst such luxury seems small price for improved odds. So will invest extra two months as insurance.

Figure arbitrary; based on theory that treble safety factor was good enough for NASA, should be good enough for me. (Of course theory includes words "should be" again, but must draw line somewhere.)

And *can* get out when ready. Easy: Just throw proper switches. All spelled out in detailed manual on shelter's systems, operation. Nothing to it. Just pick up book, read. After finding. After learning exists in first place. (Daddy could have reduced first three weeks' trauma had bothered to mention, point out where kept—on other hand, had learned how to get out prior to absorbing details on attack, doubtless be dead now.)

Makes fascinating reading. Shelter eloquent testimonial to wisdom of designer. Foresight, engineering brilliance embodied in every detail. Plus appalling amount of money, shameless level of political clout. Further I got into manual, more impressed became. Is NORAD headquarters miniaturized, improved: hermetically sealed; air, water, wastes recycled; elaborate communications equipment; sophisticated sensory complex for radiation, electronics, detection, seismology, medicine. Power furnished by nuclear device about size of Volkswagen—classified, of course (talk about clout?). Don't know if works; supposed to come on automatically when municipal current fails. But according to instruments, am still running on outside power.

Let's see—nope; seems to be about everything for now. Will update journal as breathtaking developments transpire.

Hi. One-month mark today. Breathless developments to date:

1. Found stock of powdered milk: awful. Okay in soup, chocolate, cooking, etc., but alone tastes boiled.

2. Discovered unplugged phone in hitherto-unnoticed cabinet. Also found jack. Plugged in, found system still working. Amused self by ringing phones about country—random area codes, numbers. But no answers, of course; and presently noticed tears streaming down face. Decided not emotionally healthy practice. Discontinued.

3. Employed carpentry tools, pieces of existing makeshift accommodation to fabricate proper stand for brother. Promptly demonstrated gratitude by chewing through perch (which had not bothered for whole *month!*). Replaced with thick, hardwood sledge handle; sneered, dared him try again. Thereby gained temporary victory: Fiend immediately resumed game but achieving little progress. Wish had stands from upstairs in house. Are three, all eleven years old—still undamaged (of course, perches consist of hard-cured, smooth-cast concrete—detail possibly relevant to longevity).

Guess that's it for now. Watch this space for further stirring details.

Two months—hard to believe not millennia. Einstein correct: Time *is* relative. Hope doesn't get more so; probably stop altogether. Have wondered occasionally if already hasn't.

Not to imply boredom. Gracious, how could be bored

amidst unremitting pressure from giddy round of social activities? For instance, just threw gala party to celebrate passing of second month. Was smash, high point of entombment, sensation of sepulchral social schedule. Went all out—even invited Terry (desperately relieved to find invitee able to squeeze event into already busy whirl of commitments).

First-class event: Made cake, fried chicken thighs; broiled small steak; even found ice cream. All turned out well. Preferred steak, cake myself; honored guest chose ice cream (to eyebrows), chicken bones (splits shafts, devours marrow—possibly favoritest treat of all). No noisemakers in inventory (gross oversight), but assemblage combined efforts to compensate. At peak of revelry birdbrain completed chewing through perch. Was standing on end at time, of course; accepted downfall with pride, air of righteous triumph. Then waddled purposefully in direction of nearest chair leg. Had to move fast to dissuade.

Replaced perch.

Also have read 104 microfilmed books, regular volumes. Am possibly world's foremost living authority on everything.

As if matters.

Later.

Ever wanted something so bad could almost taste, needed so long seemed life's main ambition? Finally got—wished hadn't?

You guessed: three months up—*finally*!

Went upstairs, outside. Stayed maybe two hours. Wandered old haunts: familiar neighborhood, Main Street shopping area, Quarry Lake Park, school, Y, etc.

Should have quit sooner; would, had understood nature of penalty accruing. By time got back was already too late; trembling all over, tears running down face. Scabs all scraped from wounds; worms awake, gnawing soul. In parlance of contemporaries-past, was bad trip.

However, conditions outside are fact of life, something must face. Must overcome reaction unless intend to spend balance of years simulating well-read mole. Nature works slowly, methods unesthetic; tidying up takes years. Inescapable; must accept as is; develop blind spot, immunity. Meanwhile will just have to cope best I can with resulting trauma each time crops up until quits cropping.

Well, coping ought be no problem. Catharsis worked before, should again. But wish were some other way. No fun; hurts almost as much second time around. But works—and already learned cannot function with psyche tied in knots. So time to quit stalling. "Sooner started, sooner done; sooner outside, having fun."—Anon. (Understandably.)

Only just *can't* right now. Not in mood; still hurting too bad from initial trauma. Guess I'll go read some more. Or pound something together with hammer.

Or apart.

Later.

Okay. Feel no better yet, but feel less bad. Is time got on with therapy.

Suspect current problems complicated by *déjà vu*. Still retain vivid mental picture of body of Momma Foster minutes after pronounced dead. Bore physical resemblance to warm, wise, vital woman whose limitless interests, avid curiosity, ready wonderment, hearty enjoyment of existence had so enriched early years.

But body not person—person *gone*. Resemblance only underscored absence.

So too with village: Look quick, see no difference. Bears resemblance to contentedly industrious, unassuming small farm town of happy childhood. Same tall, spreading trees shade same narrow streets; well-kept, comfortably ageless old homes. Old-fashioned streetlights line Main Street's storefront downtown business district, unchanged for 50 years, fronting on classic village square. Hundred-year-old township building centered in square amidst collection of heroic statues, World War One mementos, playground equipment; brightly painted, elevated gazebo for public speakers. Look other direction down street, see own ivy-covered, red-brick school at far end, just across from Y. Next door, Teacher's house looks bright, friendly, inviting as ever in summer-afternoon sunshine.

But open door, step out onto porch—illusion fades. Popular fallacy attends mystique of small towns: Everyone knows are "quiet." Not so; plenty of noise, but right kind—comfortable, unnoticed.

Until gone.

Silence is shock. Is wrong, but takes whole minutes to

analyze *why* wrong; identify anomalous sensation, missing input.

Strain ears for hint of familiar sound: Should be faint miasma of voices, traffic sounds drifting up from direction of Main Street; chatter, squeals, laughter from schoolyard. Too, is truly small town; farmlands close at hand: Should hear tractors chugging in fields, stock calling from pastures. Should catch frequent hollow mutter as distant semisnores down highway past town; occasional, barely perceptible rumble from jet, visible only as fleecy tracing against indigo sky. Should be all manner of familiar sounds.

But as well could be heart of North Woods; sounds reaching ear limited to insect noises, bird calls, wind sighing through leaves.

Visual illusion fades quickly, too. Knee-deep grass flourishes where had been immaculately groomed yards; straggly new growth bewhiskers hedges, softening previously mathematically exact outlines. Houses up, down street show first signs of neglect: isolated broken windows, doors standing open, missing shingles. Partially uprooted tree leans on Potters' house, cracking mortar, crushing eaves, sagging roof. Street itself blocked by car abandoned at crazy angle; tire flat, rear window broken, driver's door hanging open. Closer inspection shows Swensens' pretty yellow-brick Cape Cod nothing but fire-gutted shell; roof mostly gone, few panes of glass remain, dirty smudge marks above half-consumed doors, windows; nearby trees singed.

And the *smell* . . . ! Had not spent last three months sealed in own atmosphere, doubt could have remained in vicinity. Still strong enough outside to dislodge breakfast within moments of first encounter. And did. Happily, human constitution can learn to tolerate almost anything if must. By time returned to shelter, stench faded from forefront of consciousness—had other problems more pressing:

Learned what knee-deep lawns conceal. Three months' exposure to Wisconsin summer does little to enhance cosmetic aspects of Nature's embalming methods: Sun, rain, insects, birds, probably dogs too, have disposed of bulk of soft tissues. What remains is skeletons (mostly scattered, incomplete, partially covered by semicured meat, some clothing). Doubtless would have mummified completely by now in dry climate, but Wisconsin summers aren't. At best, results unappealing; at worst (first stumbled over in own front yard), dreadful shock.

Yes, I know; should have anticipated. Possibly did, in distant, nonpersonally-involved sort of way—but didn't expect to find three bodies within ten feet of own front door! Didn't expect to confront dead neighbors within three minutes after left burrow. Didn't expect so *many*! Thought most would be respectably tucked away indoors, perhaps in bed. That's where I'd be. I think.

Well, lived through initial shock, continued foray. Was not systematic exploration; just wandered streets, let feet carry us at random. Didn't seem to matter; same conditions everywhere. Peeked into houses, stores, cars; knocked on doors, hollered a lot.

Wasn't until noticed twin digging in claws, flapping wings, protesting audibly, that realized was running blindly, screaming for somebody—*anybody*!

Stopped then, streaming tears, trembling, panting (must have run some distance); made desperate attempt to regain semblance of control. Dropped where stood, landed in Lotus. Channeled thoughts into relaxation of body, achievement of physical serenity; hoped psyche would heed good example.

Did—sort of. Worked well enough, at least, to permit deliberate progress back to shelter, deliberate closing door, deliberate descent of stairs, deliberate placing of Terry on stand—all before threw screaming fit.

Discharged lots of tension in process, amused Terry hugely. By end of performance fink sibling was emulating noises. Ended hysteria in laughter. Backward, true, but effective.

Recovered enough to make previous journal entry. Granted, present (therapeutic) entries beyond capacity at that point; but after spent balance of day licking wounds, night's rest, was fit enough to make present update, discharge residual pain onto paper.

Amazing stuff, therapy: Still not exactly looking forward to going outside again; but seem to have absorbed trauma of dead-body/deserted-city shock, adjusted to prospect of facing again. Forewarned, should be able to go about affairs, function effectively in spite of surroundings.

Which brings up entirely relevant question: Exactly what *are* my affairs, functions...? Now that am out, what to do? Where to go? What to do when get there? Why bother go at all?

Okay, fair questions. Obviously prime objective is find Somebody Else. Preferably somebody knowing awful lot about Civilizations, Founding & Maintenance Of—to say nothing of where to find next meal when supplies run out.

Certainly other survivors. Somewhere. So must put together reasonable plan of action based on logical extension of available data. Sounds good—uh, except, what *is* available data?

Available data: *Everybody* exposed to flash, to air at time of flash, to anybody else exposed to flash or air exposed to flash or to anybody exposed to anybody, etc., either at time of flash or during subsequent month, anywhere on planet, is dead. Period.

Shucks. Had me worried; thought for moment I had problem. Ought be plenty survivors; modern civilization replete with airtight refuges: nuclear submarines, hyperbaric chambers, spacelabs, jet transports, "clean assembly" facilities, many others (not to forget early-model VW beetles, so long as windows closed). Ought be many survivors of flash, initial contagion phase.

But—loaded question—how many knew enough; stayed tight throughout required month? Or got lucky; couldn't get out too soon despite best efforts? Or, with best of intentions, had supplies, air for duration? Or survived emotional ravages; resisted impulse to open window, take big, deliberate breath?

Could employ magnet to find needle in haystack; easy by comparison. Real problem is: *Is needle in there at all?*

Well, never mind; leave for subconscious to mull. Good track record heretofore; probably come up with solution, given time.

Other, more immediate problems confronting: For one, must think about homestead. Can't spend balance of years living underground. Unhealthy; leads to pallor. Besides, doubt is good for psyche; too many ghosts.

Where—no problem for short term; can live just about anywhere warm, dry. Adequate food supplies available in shelter, stores, home pantries, etc.; same with clothing, sundry necessities. Can scavenge for years if so inclined.

However, assuming residential exclusivity continues (and must take pessimistic view when planning), must eventually produce own food, necessities; become self-sufficient. Question is: Should start now or wait; hope won't prove necessary?

Not truly difficult decision: Longer delayed, more difficult transition becomes. Livestock factor alone demands prompt attention. Doubtless was big die-off over summer. Too stupid to break out of farms, pastures, search for water, feed, most perished—"domestic" synonym for "dependent." And even of survivors, doubt one in thousand makes it through winter unaided. Means if plan to farm, must round up beginning inventory before weather changes. Also means must have food, water, physical accommodations ready for inductees beforehand.

Means must have farm.

However, logic dictates commandeering farm relatively nearby. Too much of value in shelter; must maintain reasonable access. Availability of tools, books, etc., beneficial in coming project: provisioning, repairing fences, overhauling well pumps, etc.

Plus work needed to put house in shape for winter. Wisconsin seasons rough on structures; characteristic swayback rooflines usually not included in builders' plans, zoning regulations. After summer's neglect, buildings of farm selected apt to need much work—none of which am qualified to do. Expect will find remainder of summer, fall, highly educational, very busy.

So perhaps should quit reflecting on plans, get move on. Best reconnoiter nearby farms. Be nice to find one with buildings solid, wells pumping, fences intact, etc. Be equally nice to meet jolly red-dressed, white-bearded gentleman cruising down road in sleigh pulled by reindeer.

Hi, again. Surprised to see me? Me, too. Thinking of changing name to Pauline, serializing journal. Or maybe just stay home, take up needlepoint. Seems during entombment character of neighborhood changed; deteriorated, gotten rough—literally gone to dogs. Stepped out of A & P right into—

Nope, this won't do. Better stick to chronology; otherwise sure to miss something. Might even be important someday. So:

Awoke fully recovered—again (truly growing tired of yo-yo psychology). Since planned to be out full day, collected small pile of equipment, provisions: canteen, jerky, dried apricots, bag of parrot mix; hammer, pry bar (in case forcible investigation indicated). Went upstairs, outside.

Retained breakfast by force of will until accustomed to aroma.

Took bike from garage, rode downtown (first ride in three months; almost deafened by twin's manic approval). After three months' neglect, tires a tad soft (ten-speed requires 85 pounds); stopped at Olly's Standard, reinflated. And marveled: Utilities still on, compressor, pumps, etc., still working—even bell rang when rode across hose.

Started to go on way; stopped—had thought. Returned, bled air tanks as had seen Big Olly do. Had explained: Compression, expansion of air in tanks "made water" through condensation; accumulation bad for equipment. Found was starting to think in terms of preserving everything potentially useful against future need. (Hope doesn't develop into full-blown neurosis; maintaining whole world could cramp schedule.)

Set about conducting check of above-ground resources: Eyeball-inventoried grocery stores, hardware, seed dealers; took ride down to rail depot, grain elevators. Found supplies up everywhere; highly satisfactory results. Apparently business conducted as usual after flash until first symptoms emerged. No evidence of looting; probably all too sick to bother.

And since power still on, freezers in meat markets maintaining temperature; quantity available probably triple that in shelter. If conditions similar in nearby towns, undoubtedly have lifetime supply of everything—or until current stops.

(Personally, am somewhat surprised still working; summer thunderstorms habitually drop lines, blow transformers twice, three times a year—and *winter* . . . ! One good ice storm brings out candles for days; primary reason why even new houses, designed with latest heating systems, all have old-fashioned Franklin-style oil stoves in major rooms, usually multiple fireplaces. Doubt will have electricity by spring.)

OH HELL! Beg pardon; unladylike outburst—but just realized: Bet every single farm well in state *electrically* operated. I got *troubles . . .* !

Well, just one more problem for subconscious to worry about. Can't do anything about it now—but must devote serious thought.

Back to chronology: Emerged from A & P around ten;

kicked up stand, prepared to swing leg over bike. Suddenly
Terry squawked, gripped shoulder so hard felt like claws met
in middle. Dropped bike, spun.

Six dogs: Big, lean, hungry; visibly exempt from "Best
Friend" category.

Given no time to consider strategy; moment discovered,
pack abandoned stealth, charged. Had barely time to toss
twin into air, general direction of store roof, wish Godspeed.
Then became very busy.

Had not fought in three months but continued *kata;* was
in good shape. Fortunate.

First two (Shepherd, Malamute) left ground in formation, Doberman close behind. Met Malamute (bigger of two)
in air with clockwise spin-kick to lower mandible attachment.
Felt bones crunch, saw without watching as big dog windmilled
past, knocking Shepherd sprawling. Took firm stance, drove
forward front-fist blow under Doberman's jaw, impacting high
on chest, left of center. Fist buried to wrist; felt scapula,
clavicle, possibly also humerus crumble; attacker bounced
five feet backward, landed in tangle. Spun, side-kicked Shepherd behind ear as scrambled to rise; felt vertebrae give.
Took fast step, broke Malamute's neck with edge-hand chop.
Spun again, jumped for Doberman; broke neck before could
rise.

Glanced up, body coiling for further combinations—relaxed;
remaining three had revised schedule; were halfway across
parking lot.

Looked wildly about for Terry; spotted twin just putting
on brakes for touchdown on shopping-cart handle 20 feet
away. Wondered what had been doing in interim; seemed
could have flown home, had dinner, returned to watch outcome.

Retrieved; lectured about stupidity, not following orders—
suppose had been flankers? Would have been lunch before I
got there.

Birdbrain accepted rebuke; nuzzled cheek in agreement,
murmured, "You're so icky-poo!"

Gave up; continued sortie.

Wondered briefly at own calmness. First blows ever
struck in earnest; halfway expected emotional side effects.
But none; only mild regret had not met attackers under
favorable circumstances. Doberman in particular was beautiful specimen, if could disregard gauntness.

Decided, in view of events, might be best if continued

explorations in less vulnerable mode. Decided was time I soloed. Had driven cars before, of course; country kids all learn vehicular operation basics soonest moment eyes (augmented by cushions) clear dashboard, feet reach pedals.

Question of which car to appropriate gave pause. Have no particular hang-ups: Familiar (for nondriver) with automatics, three-, four-speed manuals, etc. But would be poking nose down vestigial country roads, venturing up driveways more accustomed (suitable) to passage of tractor, horses; squeezing in, out of tight places; doubtless trying hard to get very stuck. Granted, had been relatively dry recently; ground firm most places. But—considering potential operating conditions, physical demands. . . .

Would take Daddy's old VW. Happy selection: Answered physical criteria (maneuverable, good traction, reliable, etc.); besides, had already driven—for sure could reach pedals, see out. Did give thought to Emerson's Jeep, but never had opportunity to check out under controlled conditions. Further, has plethora of shift levers (three!). True, might be more capable vehicle, but sober reflection suggested unfamiliar advantages might prove trap; seemed simpler, more familiar toy offered better odds of getting back.

Pedaled home quickly, keeping weather eye out for predators (can take hint). Arrived without incident. Found key, established blithe sibling on passenger's seatback; adjusted own seat for four-foot-ten-inch stature, turned key.

Results would have warmed ad writer's heart: After standing idle three months, Beetle cranked industriously about two seconds, started.

Gauge showed better than three-quarters full, but wanted to make sure; lonely country road frequented by hungry dog packs wrong place to discover faulty gauge. So backed gingerly down drive (killed only twice), navigated cautiously to Olly's. Stuck in hose, got two gallons in before spit back. Beetle's expression seemed to say, ". . . *told* you so," as capped tank, hung up hose.

Went about tracking down suitable farm in workmanlike fashion, for beginner. Picked up area USGS Section Map from sheriff's office. Methodically plotted progress as went; avoided circling, repetition. Drove 150 miles; visited 30, 35 farms; marked off on map as left, graded on one-to-ten basis. Were many nice places; some could make do in pinch. But none rated above seven; nothing rang bell until almost dark.

Found self at terminus of cowpath road. Had wound through patchy woods, hills; felt must go somewhere, so persevered to end, where found mailbox, driveway. Turned in; shortly encountered closed gate. Opened, drove through, resecured. Followed drive through woods, over small rise, out into clearing, farmyard. Stopped abruptly.

Knew at once was *home* . . . .

To right stood pretty, almost new red-brick house; to left, brand-new, modern steel barn, hen house; two silos (one new), three corn cribs—all full.

Got out, walked slowly around house, mouth open, heart pounding. No broken windows, doors closed, shingles all in place—*grass cut!* For glorious moment heart stopped altogether; thought had stumbled on nest of survivors. Then rounded corner, bumped into groundskeepers—sheep.

Owners quite dead. Found remains of man in chair on porch. Apparently spent last conscious moments reflecting upon happy memories. Picture album in lap suggested four impromptu graves short distance from house were wife, three children; markers confirmed. Fine-looking people; faces showed confidence, contentment, love; condition of farm corroborated, evidenced care, pride.

Grew misty-eyed looking through album. Resolved to operate farm in manner founders would approve. Had handed me virtual "turnkey" homestead; immeasurably advanced schedule, boosted odds for self-sufficiency, survival. Least I could do in return.

Farm nestles snugly in valley amidst gently rolling, wooded countryside. Clean, cold, fast-running brook meanders generally through middle, passes within hundred yards of house; and by clever fence placement, zigs, zags, or loops through all pastures. Perimeter fence intact; strong, heavy-gauge, small-mesh fabric. Probably not entirely dogproof, but highly resistant; with slight additional work, should be adequate.

Contents of silos, cribs, loft, product of season's first planting; second crop still in fields—primary reason stock still alive, healthy. Internal gates open throughout; allowed access to water, varied grazing (including nibbling minor leakages from cribs, silos). Beasties spent summer literally eating "fat of land"; look it.

Besides five sheep are nine cows (two calves, one a *bull*), two mares, one gelding, sundry poultry (rooster, two dozen chickens, motley half dozen ducks, geese). No pigs, but no tears; don't like pigs, not wild about pork either.

From evidence, losses over summer low. Found only three carcasses: two cows, one horse. Bones not scattered; doubt caused by dogs. More likely disease, injury, stupidity—salient characteristic of domestic ruminants: Given opportunity, will gorge on no-no, pay dearly later.

Wandered grounds, poked through buildings until light gone. Found good news everywhere looked. Nothing I can't use as is, put right with minor work.

Clocked distance on return: 17 miles by road. Not too bad; can walk if necessary—should breakdown occur while commuting—but perhaps wiser to hang bike on bumper.

Still, machines can't last forever; only matter of time before forced back to horseback technology. Will have occasion to visit shelter often. Map shows straight-line distance only nine miles; guess better learn bulldozer operation, add road-building to skills. (Goodness—future promises such varied experiences; may vary me to death. . . .)

Was late when finally got back to shelter, tired but glowing all over at prospect. Can hardly wait for morning, start packing, moving in; start of new life.

Demented twin shares view; hardly shut up whole time were at farm. Or since. Lectured stock, dictated to poultry, narrated inspection tour throughout. Hardly took time out for snack, drink. Must be country boy at heart. So urbane, never suspected.

Hey—am really *tired*!

Good night.

Oh! Hurt places didn't even know I had. Suspect must have come into being just for occasion.

Six trips to farm. Count 'em.

Light failed just before self. Packing stuff from house no problem: Eight, ten trips to car; all done. Stuff in shelter is rub. Aye.

Two hundred feet straight up, arms loaded. Repeatedly.

Must be better way.

Good night.

This is embarrassing; guess is time quit posing as genius. Proof in pudding. What matters 200-plus IQ if actions compatible with mobile vegetable?

Occurred this morning to ponder (after third trip upstairs) how excavated material removed during construction. Hand-carried in buckets...?

Counting stairwell, material involved amounts to 200,000 cubic feet plus. At half cube per bucket, assuming husky lad carrying doubles, 15-minute round trips, that's 32 cubic feet every eight hours. Would take ten-man crew 625 days—not counting down time due to heart attacks, hernias, fallen arches....

And what about heavy stuff? Doubt nuclear generator carried down by hand—must weigh couple tons.

Okay. Obviously done some other way. But how? Oh—shelter manual; had forgotten. Thumbed through quickly, found answer: *elevator*! Of course. Missed significance of small, odd-shaped, empty storeroom during first inspection. Other things on mind; didn't notice controls.

Balance of day much easier. Still tired tonight but not basket case.

Tomorrow is another day...!

STOP THE PRESSES! Strike the front page! Scoop! I'm not me—I'm something else. No—we're not us—no— Oh, bother; not making *any* sense. But can't help it; hard to organize thoughts—so *DAMNED* excited...! Will try, *must* try. Otherwise will end up leaving out best parts, most important stuff. Then, by time get feathers settled, blood pressure reduced, will have forgotten *everything*! *Oh*, must stop this *blithering*. Must get back to chronology. So...

Deep breath...release slo-o-ow-ly...heart slowed to normal. Physical tranquility...serenity...ohm-m-m...

Amazing, worked again.

Okay. Resumed packing this morning. Took two loads over, returned for third. Finished; everything in car, at farm, that felt would need. But still fidgeting; couldn't decide why. No question of something forgotten; farm only short drive away; omission not crisis.

Finally recognized source of unscratchable itch: Was time I did duty. Had avoided at first; knew couldn't face prospect. Then got so busy, slipped mind. But now remembered: Soo Kim McDivott. Teacher. Friend.

To friend falls duty of seeing to final resting place.

Generally inured now to face of death per se; unaffected last few days by myriad corpses have stepped over during course of running errands. Had no problem, for instance, removing Mr. Haralsen from porch to proper place beside wife, children; even finished job with warm feeling inside. (Suspect original trauma caused by sudden shock of events; enormity, completeness of isolation.) Condition improved now; felt could perform final service for old friend—more, felt need to.

Went next door, looked for body. Checked entire house: upstairs, downstairs, basement—even stuck head in attic.

Finally returned to library. Teacher had used as study; desk located there, most of favorite dog-eared references close at hand. Hoped might find clue regarding whereabouts amidst clutter.

First thing to catch eye was "Tarzan File" standing on desk. Large envelope taped to top, printing on face. Glanced at wording. Blood froze.

Was addressed to me!

Pulled loose, opened with suddenly shaking fingers. Teacher's meticulous script, legible, beautiful as Jefferson's on Declaration, read:

> *Dearest Candidia,*
> *It is the considered opinion of several learned men familiar with your situation, among them Dr. Foster and myself, that you will survive the plague to find and read this. The viral complex employed by the enemy cannot harm you, we know; it was created as a specific against* Homo sapiens.

Almost dropped letter. Surely required no genius to note implications. Took deep breath, read on:

> *I know, my child, that that statement must sound like the ramblings of an old man in extremis . . .*

Ramble? *Teacher?* Ha! True, was old; condition intrinsic to amount of water over dam—of which lots (all deep, too). Probably also in extremis; lot of that going around when wrote this. But ramble? *Teacher?* Day Teacher rambles will be day Old Nick announces cooling trend, New Deal, takes up post as skiing instructor on glorious powder slopes of Alternate Destination. *I* ramble; Teacher's every word precise, correct.

Precise, correct letter went on:

*...but please, before forming an opinion, humor
me to the extent of reading the balance of this letter
and reviewing the supporting evidence, which doc-
uments 25 years of painstaking investigation by me
and others.*

*Note that of the 1,284 incidents wherein wild
animals of varying descriptions "adopted" human
children, none (with the exception of the very
youngest—those recovered from the wild below age
three) developed significantly beyond the adoptive
parents. They could not be taught to communicate;
they evinced no abstract reasoning; they could not
be educated. IQ testing, where applicable, produced
results indistinguishable from similar tests performed
on random members of the "parents'" species. Further, except for the 29 cases where the adoptive
parents were of a species possessing rudimentary
hands (apes, monkeys, the two raccoon incidents; to
a lesser degree the badger and the wolverine), the
children possessed no awareness of the concept of
grasping, nor did it prove possible to teach them
any manual skills whatever.*

*Finally, most authorities (note the citations in
the file) are agreed that Man is born devoid of
instincts, save (a point still in contention) suckling;
therefore, unlike lesser animals, human development
is entirely dependent upon learning and, therefore,
environment.*

*This principle was deeply impressed upon me
during the years I spent studying a number of these
children; and it occurred to me to wonder what effect
this mechanism might have within human society—
whether average parents, for instance, upon producing a child possessing markedly superior genetic potential, might raise such a child (whether through
ignorance, unconscious resentment or envy, deliberate malice, or some unknown reason) in such a
manner as to prevent his development from exceeding
their own attainments; and if such efforts took place,
to what extent the child would in fact be limited.*

Then followed narrative of early stages of investigation,
solo at first, but producing preliminary findings so startling

that shortly was directing efforts of brilliant group of associates (including *Daddy!*), whole project funded by bottomless
government grant. Object of search: reliable clues, indicators
upon which testing program could be based enabling identification of gifted children (potential geniuses) shortly after
birth, before retardation (if such truly existed) began operation.

Efforts rewarded: Various factors pinpointed which,
encountered as group, were intrinsic to genetically superior
children. Whereupon study shifted to second phase. As fast
as "positives" found, identified, were assigned to study group.
Were four:

AA (positive/advantaged), potentially gifted kids whose
parents were in on experiment; guided, subsidized, assisted
every way possible to provide optimum environment for
learning, development. AB (positive/nonadvantaged), potential geniuses whose parents weren't let in on secret; would
have to bloom or wither, depending on qualities of vine. BA
(negative/advantaged), ordinary babies, random selection, whose
parents were encouraged (for which read "conned") to think
offspring were geniuses; also received benefit of AA-type
parental coaching (and coaches didn't know whether dealing
with AA or BA parents), financial assistance. And BB
(negative/nonadvantaged), control group: ordinary babies raised
ordinary way. Whatever that is.

As expected, AAs did well in school; average progress
tripled national norm. Further, personality development also
remarkable: AA kids almost offensively well-adjusted; happy,
well-integrated personalities. BAs did well, too, but beat
national figures by only 15 percent. Were also generally
happy, but isolated individuals demonstrated symptoms
suggesting insecurity; perhaps being pushed close to, even
beyond capabilities.

ABs also produced spotty results: Goods very good,
equaling AA figures in certain cases. However, bads *very* bad:
ABs had highest proportion of academic failures, behavior
problems, perceptibly maladjusted personalities.

BBs, of course, showed no variation at all from national
curves; were just kids.

Study progressed cozily; all content as confirming evidence of own cleverness emerged from statistical analysis,
continued to accumulate (Teacher, in particular, basking in
glow emanating from vindication of theory), when suddenly
Joker popped from deck:

It became obvious that AA and AB children lost vastly less time from school through illness. Further breakdown, however, showed that approximately one third of the positives never had lost any time, while the balance had attendance records indistinguishable from the norm. Detailed personal inquiry revealed that these particular children had never been sick from any cause, while the balance had had the usual random selection of childhood illnesses. It was also determined that these unfailingly healthy positives were far and away the highest group of achievers in the AA group and constituted the best, worst, and most maladjusted of the AB group.

At that time study blessed by convenient tragedy: AA "healthy" child died in traffic accident. Body secured for autopsy.

Every organ was examined minutely, every tissue sample was scrutinized microscopically and chemically, and chromosome examination was performed. Every test known to the science of pathology was performed, most three, four, and five times, because no one was willing to believe the results.

And thereafter, quickly and by various subterfuges, complete physicals, including x–rays, and biopsy samples of blood, bone, skin, hair, and a number of organs, were obtained from the full test group and compared.

The differences between "healthy" positives and the balance proved uniform throughout the sample, and were unmistakable to an anthropologist . . .

Shock upon shock: Folksy, humble, simple Teacher was Ph.D.—three times over! Physician (double-barreled—pediatrician, psychiatrist) plus anthropologist. Predictably, renowned in all three—qualities leading to Tenth Degree not confined to Art.

. . . but none of themselves were of a character to attract the notice of a physician not specifically and methodically hunting for an unknown "common denominator," using mass sampling techniques and

a very open mind; nor would they attract notice by affecting the outcome of any known medical test or procedure. The single most dramatic difference is the undisputed fact, still unexplained, that "healthy" positives are totally immune to the full spectrum of human disease.

Difference proved independent of race, sex: Makeup of AA, AB "healthy" kids 50 percent female; half Caucasoid, one-third Negroid, balance apportioned between Oriental, Hispanic, Indian, other unidentifiable fractions. Breakdown matched precisely population area from which emerged.

The conclusion is indisputable: Although clearly of the genus Homo, AA and AB "healthy" children are not human beings; they are a species distinct unto themselves.

Quite aside from the obvious aspect of immunity and the less obvious anatomical characteristics which identify them, these children possess clear physical superiority over Homo sapiens children of like size and weight. They are stronger, faster, more resistant to trauma, and demonstrate markedly quicker reflexive responses. Visual, aural, and olfactory functions operate over a broader range and at higher levels of sensitivity than in humans. We have no data upon which to base even a guess as to the magnitude, but all evidence points toward a substantially longer lifespan.

A study was begun immediately, a search for clues which might help to explain this phenomenon of uniformly mutated children being born to otherwise normal, healthy human couples. And these couples were normal: To the limits of our clinical capabilities to determine, they were indistinguishable from any other Homo sapiens.

However, it was only very recently, after years of the most exhaustive background investigation and analysis, that a possible link was noticed. It was an obvious connection, but so removed in time that we almost missed its significance, due to the usual scientific tendency to probe for the abstruse while ignoring the commonplace.

The grandmothers of these children were all of a similar age, born within a two-year span: All were conceived during the rampage of the great influenza pandemic of 1918–19.

This "coincidence" fairly shouts its implications: Sweeping genetic recombination, due to specific viral invasion, affecting either of the gametes before, or both during, formation of the zygotes which became the grandmothers, creating in each half of the matrix which fitted together two generations later to become the AA and AB "healthy" children.

Personally, I have no doubt that this is the explanation; however, so recently has this information come to light that we have not had the time to study the question in detail. And suspecting that something may be true—even a profound inner conviction—is not the same as proving it. I hope you will one day have the opportunity to add this question to your own studies. It needs answering.

After much reflection we named this new species Homo post hominem, *meaning "Man Who Follows Man"; for it would appear that the mutation is evolutionary in character, and that, given time and assuming it breeds true (there is no reason to suspect otherwise—in fact, chromosome examination suggests that the mutation is dominant; i.e., a* sapiens/hominem *pairing should unfailingly produce a* hominem), *it will supplant Homo sapiens entirely.*

Wonderful thing, human nervous system; accustoms quickly to mortal shocks. Didn't even twitch as other shoe landed—or perhaps had anticipated from buildup; just wondering how would be worded.

Very nice; no fanfare, just matter-of-fact statement:

You, my child, are a Homo post hominem. *You are considerably younger than your fellows among the study group, and were never involved in the study itself. Your identification and inclusion in our sample came about late and through rather involved and amusing circumstances.*

The Fosters, as you know, had long desired a child and had known equally long that they never

*could have one. When your natural parents died, it
was entirely predictable that they lost no time securing your adoption (which is certainly understandable; you were a most winning baby).*

Neither Daddy nor rest of staff thought to have me
tested; had been exposed to ten months' "unmonitored parentage"; was "compromised subject." Besides, Daddy wasn't
interested in studying me; wanted to enjoy raising "his little
girl." Professional competence crumbled before gush of atavistic
paternalism. Most reprehensible.

Momma disagreed; felt determination of potential would
provide useful child-rearing information. In keeping with
formula long established for maintaining smooth marriage,
kept disagreement to self; however, took steps: Prevailed
upon staff to test me—all unbeknownst Daddy.

Tests proved positive, but follow-up determination as to
"healthy" status not performed—didn't occur to discipline-
blindered scientists, and Momma didn't know any better so
didn't insist.

*You were a genius; she was content. And she
thereupon took it upon herself to see that you were
raised in the same "advantaged" manner as the rest
of the AAs—with the exception of the fact that the
doctor did not know this was taking place. He
continued to enjoy his "daddy's little girl" as before,
prating endlessly about the advantages of "sugar
and spice," etc. And as for the rest of us, after
swearing each other to secrecy about your test
results and our involvement, we forgot you. You
were, after all, a "compromised subject."*

Was almost five when next came to their attention. Had
soured "sugar and spice" by glancing up, commenting living-
room wall ". . . looks awful hot." Was, too—result of electrical
fault. Would have burned down house shortly.

Remember incident clearly. Not that caused any particular immediate fuss, but Daddy spent balance of evening
trying not to show was staring at me.

*The doctor had spent much time during the
previous few years observing children whose visual*

perception extended into the infrared and ultraviolet; and as shortly thereafter as possible, without letting Mrs. Foster know, he had you examined and tested.

Oho! Finally—explanation of what triggered Daddy's reaction that day—and of friends' inexplicable night-blindness, even during summer. Of course, could understand difficulty seeing at night during winter; is *dark* outside on cold night. Only perceptible glow comes from faces, hands; and after short exposure to cold, cheeks, noses dim perceptibly.

And remember also that testing session. Salient feature was expressions of other staff as repeated tests done on previous (conspicuously unmentioned) occasion: utterly deadpan.

It was only after the tests (performed fully this time) identified you as a Homo post hominem; *after the doctor had diffidently broached this fact to Mrs. Foster and she, giggling helplessly, confessed to him; and, finally, we also came clean, that further testing demonstrated that you were substantially more advanced in intellectual development than the profile developed by our studies suggested you should be at that age.*

How nice. Even as superkid can't be normal; still genius. Is no justice.

Detailed analysis of this phenomenon brought forth two unassessable factors: One, you had experienced ten months of unmonitored parentage; and two, your subsequent upbringing had been AA from your mother but BB from your father. Since we could neither analyze nor affect the first of these, we chose to continue the second factor unaltered, observing you closely and hoping that in some way, then unknown, the whipsaw combination of indulgent spoiling and accelerated, motivational education you had received to this point would continue to produce these outstanding results.

Momma's death terminated experiment; but before she left, made Teacher promise would take over overt management of education, keep pushing me as hard as would accept while Daddy (apparently) continued classic BB father rôle. Momma felt hunger for knowledge already implanted; abetted by Daddy's careful negative psychology, seeding of environment with selected books (*Ha!*—always suspected something fishy about circumstances surrounding steady discovery of wanted, needed study materials, always just in time, just as finishing previous volume [not complaining; just wish planting had gone faster]), would carry on through interim without lost momentum. Was right, too—but now know how puppet must feel when wires too thin to discern.

Phase Two of scheme hit snag, though; was not anticipated would take four years for Teacher to extricate self from complications attendant profession(s), "retire."

Fortunately the delay appeared to be without consequences. Mrs. Foster's opinion of you was borne out: Dr. Foster reported that you located every book he planted—and not a few that he didn't. He said it was rarely necessary to "steer" you; that you were quite self-motivated, distinctly tenacious, and could be quite devious when it came to tracking down knowledge in spite of the "barriers" he placed in your way.

By the time I managed to delegate all my other responsibilities to my successors and devote my entire attention to you, your advantage over other AAs had increased impressively. There were only a very few individuals showing anywhere near as much promise. And by the time the blunderings of our late friends behind the Iron Curtain put an end to all such research, you were—for your age—quite the most advanced of our hominems.

If I seem to harp on that point, it is because you must remember that this study was initiated some 20 years ago. You are ten years younger than the next youngest in our group; and as advanced as you are for your age, you still have considerable catching up to do—see that you keep at it.

Yes, I know; the exigencies of solo survival will occupy much of your time, but do not neglect your studies entirely. Cut back if you must, but do not terminate them.

Now, if I may presume to advise a singularly

gifted member of an advanced species, there is security and comfort in numbers. You will doubtless find the preservation and extension of knowledge more convenient once a group of you has been assembled. Within the body of the Tarzan File you will find a complete listing of known Homo post hominems. *I can anticipate no logical reason why most should not be alive and in good health.*

Pawed through File with shaking hands. Found listing referred to: collection of minidossiers. One had small note attached. Read:

Dear Candy,

It is now almost time for me to leave, and a number of things still remain undone, so I must be brief.

The subject of this dossier, Peter Bell, is the direct, almost line-bred descendant of Alexander Graham Bell (would that I could have tested him). A measure of his intellect is the fact that he, alone of our hominems, deduced the existence and purpose of our study, the implications regarding himself, and most of the characteristics of his and your species.

To him, not long ago, I confided your existence, along with my impressions of your potential.

As well as probably being your equal (after you reach maturity, of course), he is also nearest to your own age, at 21; and of all our subjects, I predict he is the most likely to prove compatible with you as you continue your unrelenting search for knowledge in the future—in fact, he may give you quite a run for it; he is a most motivated young man.

However, I was unable to reach him following the attack; therefore he does not know that you are alive and well in the shelter. The burden is upon you to establish contact, if such is possible—and I do urge you to make the attempt; I feel that a partnership consisting of you two would be most difficult to oppose, whatever the future may bring you.

Love,
Teacher

Hands shook, blood pounded in head as turned back to first letter. Balance consisted of advice on contacting other hominems—AAs from study.

Cautioned that, based on (terribly loose) extrapolation of known data, should be perhaps 150,000 of us on North American continent—but virtually *all* must be considered ABs, replete with implications: high proportion of maladjusteds, discontents, rebels, borderline (or worse, after shock of depopulation) psychotics, plus occasional genius. Plus rare occurrences of surviving *Homo sapiens*.

Teacher suggested moving very deliberately when meeting strangers. Evaluate carefully, rapidly, selfishly. If decide is not sort would like for neighbor, hit first; kill without hesitation, warning. No place in consideration for racial altruism. Elimination of occasional bad apple won't affect overall chances for lifting species from endangered list; are enough of us to fill ranks after culling stock—but only one *me*. Point well taken.

Letter continued:

> Well, time grows short. So much remains to be accomplished before I leave, so I had best hurry.
>
> I leave with confidence; I know the future of the race is in hands such as yours and Peter's. You will prosper and attain levels of development I cannot even envision; of that I am certain. I hope those heights will include much joy and contentment.
>
> I might add this in parting: When your historians tell future generations about us, I hope they will not be unduly severe. True, we did not last the distance; also true, we did exterminate ourselves, apparently in a display of senseless, uncontrolled aggression; equally true, we did many other things that were utterly wrong.
>
> But we did create a mighty civilization; we did accumulate a fund of knowledge vast beyond our capacity to absorb or control; we did conceive and aspire to a morality unique in history, which placed the welfare of others ahead of our own self-interest— even if most of us didn't practice it.
>
> And we did produce you!
>
> It may well be that we were not intended to last more than this distance. It may even be that your

coming triggered seeds of self-destruction already implanted in us for that purpose; that our passing is as necessary to your emergence as a species as was our existence to your genesis.

But whatever the mechanism or its purpose, I think that when all are Judged at the end of Time, Homo sapiens will be adjudged, if not actually a triumph, then at least a success, according to the standards imposed by the conditions we faced and the purposes for which we were created; just as the Cro-Magnon, Neanderthal, and Pithecanthropus—and even the brontosaur—were successful in their time when judged in the light of the challenges they overcame and the purposes they served.

Single page remained. Hesitated; was final link with living past. Once read, experienced, would become just another memory. Sighed, forced eyes to focus:

Candy, my beloved daughter-in-spirit, this is most difficult to bring to a close. Irrationally I find myself grieving over losing you; "irrationally," I say, because it is obviously I who must leave. But leave I must, and there is no denying and little delaying of it.

It will be well with you and yours. Your growth has been sound, your direction right and healthy; you cannot fail to live a life that must make us, who discovered and attempted to guide you this far, proud of our small part in your destiny, even though we are not to be permitted to observe its fulfillment. I think I understand something of how Moses must have felt as he stood looking down that last day on Nebo.

Always know that I, the doctor, and Mrs. Foster could not have loved you more had you sprung from our own flesh. Remember us fondly, but see that you waste no time grieving after us.

The future is yours, my child; go mold it as you see the need.

Good-bye, my best and best-loved pupil.

Love forever,
Soo Kim McDivott

P.S.: By the authority vested in me as the senior surviving official of the United States Karate Associa-

*tion, I herewith promote you to Sixth Degree. You
are more than qualified; see to it that you practice
faithfully and remain so.*

Read, reread final page until tears deteriorated vision,
made individual word resolution impossible. Placed letter
reverently on desk, went upstairs, outside onto balcony porch.
Was Teacher's favorite meditation setting. Settled onto ve-
randa swing, eased legs into Lotus.

Terry understood; moved silently from shoulder to lap,
pressed close, started random-numbers recitation of vocabulary in barely audible, tiny baby-girl voice. Held twin nestled
in arms as pain escalated, tears progressed to silent, painful,
wracking sobs. Sibling's uncritical companionship, unques-
tioning love all that stood between me and all-engulfing
blackness, fresh awareness of extent of losses threatening to
overwhelm soul.

Together we watched early-afternoon cumulonimbus form
up, mount into towering thunderheads, roil and churn, finally develop lightning flickers in gloom at bases, arch dark
shafts of rain downward to western horizon; watched until
fading light brought realization how long had sat there.
Brighter stars already visible in east.

Reviewed condition with mounting surprise: eyes dry,
pain gone from throat, heart; blackness hovering over soul
mere memory. Apparently had transcendentalized without
conscious intent, resolved residual grief. All that remained
was sweet sadness when contemplated Daddy, Momma, Teacher;
were gone along with everything, everybody else, leaving
only memories. Suddenly realized was grateful being permitted to keep those.

Cautiously moved exploratory muscle, first in hours.
Terry twitched, fretted; then woke, set up justifiable protest
over starved condition. Arose, shifted twin to shoulder; went
inside, downstairs.

Picked up Tarzan File, Teacher's letter, went back to
Daddy's house. Fed birdbrain, self; settled down, skimmed
File's contents.

Presently concluded Teacher correct (profound shock,
that): Peter Bell doubtless best prospective soulmate of lot.
Very smart, very interested, very conscious; educational cred-
its to date sound like spoof (*nobody* that young could have
earned that much, except, uh . . . perhaps me—okay); very

strong, quick; very advanced in study of Art (Eighth Degree!); plus (in words of Teacher): "Delightfully unconcerned about his own accomplishments; interested primarily in what he will do *next*." And, ". . . possessed of a wry sense of humor." Sounds like my kind of guy. Hope turns out can stand him.

Sat for long moments working up nerve. Then picked up phone, deliberately dialed area code, number. Got stranded after a few moments' clicking, hissing when relay somewhere Out There stuck. Tried again; hit busy circuit (distinct from busy number; difference audible—also caused by sticky relay). Tried again, muttering in beard. Stranded again. Tried again. Failed again.

"That's *bad*!" offered Terry enthusiastically, bobbing head cheerfully.

Took deep breath, said very bad word, tried again.

Got ring tone! Once, twice, three times; then: "Click. Hello, is that you, Candy? Sure took you long enough. This is Peter Bell. I can't come to the phone right now; I'm outside taking care of the stock. But I've set up this telephone-answering machine to guard my back. It's got an alarm on it that'll let me know you've called so I can check the tape.

"When you hear the tone at the end of my message, give me your phone number if you're not at home—*don't forget the area code* if it's different from your home—and I'll call you back the moment I get back and find your message. Boy, am I glad you're all right."

"Beep!"

Caught agape by recording. Barely managed regroupment in time to stutter out would be home; add if not, would be at farm, give number before machine hung up, dial tone resumed.

Repeated bad word. Added frills tailored specifically for answering machine.

Did dishes, put away. Refilled twin's food dish, changed water; moved stand into study, placed next to desk, within convenient head-scratching range.

Settled into Daddy's big chair, opened journal, brought record up-to-date. Have done so. Now up-to-date. Current. Completely. Nothing further to enter. So haven't entered anything else. For quite a while.

Midnight. Might as well read a book.

Stupid phone.

*   *   *

Awoke to would-be rooster's salute to dawn's early light. Found self standing unsteadily in middle of study, blinking sleep from eyes, listening to echoes die away. Glared at twin; received smug snicker in return.

Took several moments to establish location, circumstances leading to night spent in chair with clothes on. When succeeded, opened mouth, then didn't bother—realized bad word wouldn't help; no longer offered relief adequate to situation.

Casual approach had worn out about one A.M.—by which time had read possibly ten pages (of which couldn't remember single word). Featherhead snored on stand; nothing within reach to disassemble, had lost interest.

Yawning prodigiously myself by time abandoned pretense, grabbed phone, dialed number.

Got through first try. But was *busy*!

Repeated attempt at five-minute intervals for two hours or until fell asleep—whichever came first.

Have just tried line again. Still busy. Better go make breakfast.

Contact problem no longer funny. In two months since last entry have averaged five tries daily. Result: Either (usually) busy signal or transistorized moron spouts same message. One possible explanation (among many): Recorded message mentions no dates; could have been recorded day after Armageddon, yesterday—anytime.

Not that am languishing, sitting wringing hands by phone, however; have been *busy*. Completed move to farm; padded supply reserves; shored weaknesses; collected additional livestock, poultry. Have electrified fences, augmented where appeared marginally dogproof; trucked in additional grain (learned to drive semi, re-re-re-replete with 16-speed transmission—truly sorry about grain company's gatepost, but was in way; should have been moved long ago); located, trucked in two automatic diesel generators, connected through clever relay system so first comes on line (self-starting) if power fails, second kicks in if first quits. So far has worked every time tested, just as book said.

Have accumulated adequate fuel for operation: Brought in four tankers brim full of diesel (6,000 gallons each); rigged up interconnecting hose system guaranteeing gravity feed to generators—whichever needs, gets. At eight gallons hourly (maximum load), should provide over four months' operation if needed. (However, farm rapidly taking on aspect of truck lot. Must think about disposing of empties soon; otherwise won't be able to walk through yard.)

Overkill preparations not result of paranoia. Attempting to make place secure in absence; improve odds of finding habitable, viable farm on return, even if sortie takes longer than expected. Which could; is over 900 miles (straight-line) to File's address on Peter Bell. And he's only first on AA list; others scattered all over.

Have attempted to cover all bets, both home and for self on trip. Chose vehicle with care: four-wheel-drive Chevy van. Huge snow tires bulge from fenders on all four corners, provide six inches extra ground clearance, awesome traction. Front bumper mounts electric winch probably capable of hoisting vehicle bodily up sheer cliff. Interior has bed, potty, sink, stove, sundry cabinets—and exterior boasts dreadful baroque murals on sides.

Though might appear was built specifically to fill own needs (except for murals—and need for buildups on pedals), was beloved toy of town banker. When not pinching pennies, frittered time away boonies-crawling in endless quest for inaccessible, impassable terrain. Bragged hadn't found any. Hope so; bodes well for own venture.

Personal necessities, effects aboard. Include: ample food, water for self, Terry; bedding, clothing, toiletries; diverse tools, including ax, bolt cutters, etc.; spares for van; siphon, pump, hose for securing gas; small, very nasty armory, including police chief's sawed-off riot gun, two magnum revolvers, M-16 with numerous clips and scope. Not expecting trouble, but incline toward theory that probably won't rain if carry umbrella.

Leaving this journal here in shelter for benefit of archeologists; keep separate book on trip. Can consolidate on return; but if plans go awry, this account still available for Posterity.

Well, time to go: Unknown beckons.

But have never felt so small. Awfully big world waiting out there.

For me.

VOLUME II
Seeking

Hi again, Posterity. Happy to see me? Or just surprised? Wish could be happier to see you. Should be, of course, and perhaps one day will be again. But just now view prospect of commencing this record with less than enthusiasm.

Appreciably less: Present overdue status not question of mere sloth, inefficiency; delay is product of sober consideration, sound reasoning. Entirely deliberate: been stalling.

But before condemning dilatory scribe out of hand, please attend, one, all; explanation follows, to wit:

Scared. No, not shaking-in-boots scared, not blood-turns-to-cottage-cheese scared; more an ominous-disquiet scared, two shivers qualmier than knock-on-wood scared. Leery of tempting fate.

See: commensurate with tenacious optimism expected of journeyman-grade Pollyanna, intend this record (together with previous journal [Vol. I], plus all subsequent memoirs) for future study by, ultimate benefit of, future generations—if any—tended in respectful, unhurried fashion by historians, students, archeologists in suitably dignified setting: Smith-Foster Post-Armageddon Historical Library & Archives.

Fond aspirations envision *lots* of subsequent volumes, eventually amassing truly impressive collection covering very long time span; accumulated in orderly manner by Library courtesy of Yours Truly through regular donations, personal delivery. (Key words here are *regular* and *personal:* Want no gaps—and especially don't want final volume dropped off by unwashed, travel-weary, buckskin-clad, intrepid explorer-of-unknown, plucked from God-knows-where.)

Foregoing tidy scenario intrinsic to present emotional well-being; implying, as does, long-range goals; own demise postponed many, many years hence; arriving (if ever) long after achieving revered status as beloved silver-haired *old* counselor; authentic sage, oracle *senectutis causa*, expiring gracefully in own bed amidst tearful mob of properly devoted descendants, admirers.

However (follow logic closely now): Longer journal commencement deferred, longer am able to ignore alternate possibilities—perhaps even probabilities—that impending events may interrupt record midchapter. Even midsentence. Until begun, this volume cannot be last in series. (Cannot be discovered incomplete amongst own bones somewhere on depopulated planet.)

Which is uncomfortable notion at best. Much prefer waiting until events justify more positive outlook, reasonable expectation of survival, living Happily-Ever-After.

(Curious behavior, must admit, for certified genius.)

However, personal problems are no excuse to compromise record; responsible histographer must face darkest prospects squarely, do job. True, this journal meant for proper delivery to proper audience; and if such be assured, could be prepared as well after the fact, at leisure, as minor adjunct to activities comprising Happy Ending. But if not—assuming worst: found under grisly circumstances by fellow involuntary ragtag explorer—even he entitled to complete account, within limits imposed by conditions.

Not least of which: very real doubt typical Bold Wanderer able to decipher Pitman shorthand. But would *be* no record in longhand: So inefficient, agonizingly slow; results bulky, burdensome to carry.

Besides, not my problem: shorthand system identified on cover, together with author, subject matter. Texts available at any library (most should stand, protect contents for centuries). My notes clear, straightforward; without unusual briefs, nonstandard phrase linkages. Given time, motivation, legible to anyone.

And must demand *some* effort from Posterity (regardless of whom may consist). Being furnished, after all, valuable detailed information on End of World. Not available at every corner newsstand.

As may be.

Peter Bell, trustworthy, reliable, responsible (according

to Tarzan File—along with brilliant, sensitive, witty, handsome). Distinctly not sort to ignore constantly ringing phone. Or 50 messages on answering machine. To say nothing of known damsel (distress or otherwise quite immaterial; evidence suggests ain't many of us). Would have returned call had been home, gotten message. Since didn't, wasn't.

Certainly. I knew that.

But human—pardon, mean *Homo post hominem*—psyche surely most perversely useless corner of entire mind. Unreasonable beastie, downright illogical. Makes no sense at all for naked-eye confirmation of months-ago deduced fact to precipitate funk.

Move-out deliberate, unhurried, thorough; signs unmistakable: Doors, windows neatly shut; closets emptied, personal effects removed; utilities switched off at fuse box. Obviously had business elsewhere, went; had ample time to. Nothing about absence to create ominous doubts, assumptions, speculations. Simply moved. Period.

Granting which, enigma remains: Candidia Maria Smith-Foster, superkid, prize intellect in or out of research project—coldly analytical, logical, rational, etc., etc.—agitatedly pacing through Peter Bell's empty house; repeatedly peeking into empty closets, endlessly ransacking empty drawers; playing back empty answering-machine tape over, over again; wringing hands, streaming tears, sniffling, blubbering—

For almost three solid hours . . . !

Disgraceful performance: Behaving like maiden forsaken at altar. Atavistic. No justification.

Terry endured in relative silence, occasionally moving from one shoulder to other, shifting weight, intermittently shrugging to settle feathers. Comments limited to single low whistle when we entered obviously vacant premises, occasional "How 'bout that" as time passed. No doubt embarrassed for me.

Wait. *No* justification?

Correction, please: Atavistic, true, but partially justified. . . . Justified.

Entirely justified.

Justi-damn-fied all to pieces!

Why *not* upset? Months of hopes, anticipations, expections; long, hard trip—for *nothing!* Nary a clue—not even faintest hint remains to suggest destination, whereabouts.

Some superman . . . ! Inconceivable could go off without

leaving note—self-respecting five-year-old *human* would expect me on doorstep eventually (if alive), leave forwarding address.

But perhaps being too harsh.... Should take comfort instead from apparent discovery that certain fundamental behavioral principles transcend interspecies gulf; continue unchanged, intact, eternal; intrinsic to new race as was old. Datum no doubt scientifically fascinating in own right; of great satisfaction to researcher. But frankly, until now never troubled head over whether new species might boast thoughtless, self-centered, imbecilic male *twits*!

Oh, dear. Just look—ink hardly dry following wallow through well-intentioned (if debatable) solicitude for plight of hypothetical NonScheduled Reader (NSR) and already hip-deep in tirade comprehensible *only* to proper audience. So sorry; will try to do better. Really.

By now NSR probably wondering what *H. post hominem* might be. Or Tarzan File. Or perhaps who Peter Bell is. Or Teacher. Or Terry. Or (at very least) me.

All right. Fair questions; deserve straight answers. So shall endeavor to bear in mind possible audience other than intended: Fellow survivor, perhaps—but demonstratedly better at it—someone lacking vantage of orderly progression from Vol. I (left in shelter library beneath address on cover, Index No. 1.1.1). Viewed in that light, however reluctantly, introductions are in order:

Name: Candidia Maria Smith-Foster. (Note: Nothing "sinister" about "bar"; used here proudly to honor adoptive parents together with kin.) Born eleven years ago to Smiths; orphaned ten months later; adopted by Dr. and Mrs. Foster— Daddy and Momma. Been known as Candy since first breath.

Beyond that (briefly): *Homo post hominem* is new species; originating during great influenza pandemic of 1918–19 through viral recombination of unborns' genes; apparently immune to all "human" disease, plus smarter, stronger, faster, etc.; discovered accidentally by researchers headed by Teacher (next-door neighbor, genius), aided by Daddy, while hunting for clues identifying genius-level children as newborns; emerging to inherit Earth after *H. sapiens* eliminated selves in short, efficient bionuclear war. Tarzan File Teacher's record of said research; identifying, profiling, locating all known hominems. Peter Bell *H. post hominem* associated with Teacher's research project; closest of project hominems to own age;

best prospect of lot for future soulmate, according to matchmaking Teacher in letter constituting Last Words. Terry is own adopted twin brother (full name Terry D. Foster—initial stands for Dactyl); identical but for mental retardation and being Hyacinthine Macaw. Am myself *Homo post hominem*. Rode out war in Daddy's marvelous shelter; now engaged in walkabout, searching for fellow survivors. Of which reader must be one.

There. Clear enough?

No? Complaints—from NSR? Too brief? More confused now than before explanation?

'Some *nerve*! If reader truly nonscheduled, then writer almost certainly *dead* . . . !

Wait, please don't sulk; surely can't expect sympathy from corpse—should be grateful for simple courtesy. . . . True, could repeat entire background each time begin new journal—of course, volumes soon rival Tarzan File's bulk even before commencing new entries. But then why bother writing Vol. 1 in first place? So shan't; have better things to do.

Now: Tarzan File lists names, addresses of all AA, known AB hominems. But specifically, Teacher referred me to Peter Bell—AA superkid, smart as me (intimated might be smarter; hurled gauntlet to prove him wrong). Had told him about me, too. Suggested I get in touch.

Now, current scope of interest in "future soulmate" limited to practical matters: food, shelter, protection, survival—short-term essential stuff; deferring obvious racial continuity issue until puberty, completion of glandular development, make pertinent. (And probably unavoidable—have no valid basis to doubt will be just as tiresomely boy-crazy, once plumbing commences normal function, as next ingénue. But can *hope*.)

However, long experience (relativistic expression, of course, considering modest life span thus far) amply justifies habit of equating Teacher's least hint with Revelation From On High. Certainly adequate incentive to make attempt. Phone system still functioning in many portions of country (according to aural evidence: Ring tone obtainable using most area codes, random numbers); so tried number listed in Tarzan File.

No luck. True, answering machine camped on line picked up phone, spouted message for me; but Peter never returned calls.

For two and a half months!

(Oversensitive soul might, by this time, ponder reciprocity of interest. Might even [given modest encouragement] contemplate feeling neglected, unattractive; launch into spate of mouthwash, deodorant changes; file teeth, fluff nails, polish hair, etc.)

Nonsense, of course. Endless possible explanations: Defective answering machine, talking but not recording; phone system itself finally disintegrating (not unreasonably: six months without maintenance—even in system based on hydroelectric power, with computerized call routing automatically diverting calls around trouble spots, time must come when trouble spots constitute *norm*, system collapses). Perhaps, too—certainly equally likely—Peter simply not home, for own good purposes. No more reason now to wallow in morbid speculation than during months since initial contact attempt frustrated.

Though, granted, too busy then to spare attention for proper moping. Not easy, in only two and a half months, to locate suitable farm convenient to Daddy's house (and shelter treasures beneath); catch up all chores necessary to improve chances that livestock, structures survive Wisconsin winter's ravages.

Nor did trip from Dairy State heartland to Peter's Cornell campus (New York State) residence provide much time to reflect unsettling possibilities, generally inequitable nature of life. Physical fragility of human civilization becoming evident after only six months' neglect: Road system in sorry state, getting rapidly worse. Trees down here, there; poles broken, lines draped elegantly in inconvenient places; surprising numbers of washed-out culverts, impassable bridges.

Four-wheel-drive Chevy van wonderfully capable, easy to drive—with lifts on pedals to accommodate own modest stature. High ground clearance, awesome traction make easy work of marginal terrain. Solved many blockages simply by driving around—through fences; across fields, small streams; up hill, down dale, etc.—but spent fully as much time on shanks' mare, cutting, prying, winching, digging, etc., as driving. (Educational travel mode: Really get "feel" for countryside—feel it under nails, in shoes, tangled in hair, embedded in clothing. . . .)

Well, journal commencement, however belated, yielding usual result: Hurt, rage, disappointment discharged on paper; blood pressure lowered, practical state of mind restored—

along with perspective: Crying over spilled milk null exercise; benefits neither spiller nor spillee.

Okay. So Peter Bell not here. Elsewhere. Gone. Now what?

Prime objective obviously unaffected; unchanged from very first day we stuck nose outside shelter following expiration of predicted maximum contagion factor after World Ended: Find *somebody else*.

Somebody smarter, bigger, stronger; with broad shoulders, laughing eyes, windblown blond hair; font of wisdom concerning all aspects of establishing bright new civilizations for fun and profit. (Be nice, too, if knows location of Yellow Brick Road.)

But Teacher's statistics project only 150,000 hominems on North American continent. (*Entire* continent—8,795,052 square miles [National Geographic World Atlas figures].) Another perspective, same problem: 58.63 square miles per person.

One solution: Rule off continent graph-paper style, in squares 7.6575 miles per side; pick square at random; stand at center; yell through bullhorn. Then repeat—150,000 times.

However viewed, awful lot of elbow room. Population spread terribly thin. Accidental meeting probability effectively zilch—which fact may, upon reflection, be disguised blessing. . . .

Don't really *want* to meet ABs; not until securely ensconced within bosom of AA community. Hate to sound prejudiced, but am; can't forget Teacher's opinion that majority laboring under some form of emotional problem, high percentage downright pathological. Not unreasonable, then, to assume every contact but AAs, absent convincing evidence to contrary, possibly hauling unsecured payload—potentially dangerous.

Which revives burning issue: Peter Bell not here; no hint of how long gone, where to. May even be dead—from available data, likely as not. Speculation pointless.

But I'm alive. Very much so. Firmly resolved to maintain trend. Ergo, logical next step: Pick another AA from File. Doesn't matter which; only Peter Bell personally recommended, described. Others only represented by impersonal File entries. Okay, but faceless.

However, close to 100 AAs recorded, scattered all over U.S. No assurance any address still valid and random visits could take forever, or longer. Only reasonable procedure: Plot

locations on map; lay out most efficient meander touching all
bases, shortest time, distance—reserving, of course, right to
fly off on wild tangent should events offer even most tenuous
clue.

Intend just that. Tomorrow morning, though; not now.
Tired. Disappointed. Probably still vexed, too, if had energy.
Even Terry subdued—for him. Perhaps senses mood. Perhaps just bad day: too long, too many expectations. Too much
letdown.

Never mind. Tomorrow is another day—Pollyanna *lives*...!

Good morning, Posterity! Night's sound sleep; huge,
well-balanced, delicious breakfast (prepared by gourmet chef,
with—or despite—intensive assistance of manic twin [laugh-
ing hugely, grabbing at everything in sight]) produced usual
result: Energy, optimism restored—along with independence:
Who *needs* Peter Bell...!

Plenty of fish in sea; Tarzan File full of alternatives—or
failing that, might well be more fun to go out, locate, stalk,
capture indigenous AB buck in native habitat; then house-
break, domesticate, teach rudiments of coherent thought,
civilized speech. Why not? Might work. (And if not, gently
separate cervical vertebrae [to discourage kiss-and-tell; wouldn't
want to acquire "reputation"], throw back, try again.)

True, simpler to find AAs, settle again into secure little-
girl/student rôle; allow others to make important decisions,
feed, clothe, house, protect. (Sometimes wearisome, being
master of own destiny. Worse than being genius. Lonely, too.
Need hug.)

Enough! Used up whole year's sniveling ration yesterday. Brace up chin! Square off shoulders! Forward *ho*!

So this morning, following breakfast, scrounged campus
(carrying crowbar, sledge hammer; implements intrinsic, these
days, to serious pursuit of scrounging trade); located large-
scale U.S. map, plotted AA locations, connected with straight
lines.

And discovered predictable trend: All grouped about
top-line schools, leading research centers. Harvard, M.I.T.,
Johns Hopkins, etc., on East Coast. UCLA, U. of California
(Davis), etc., on West. Kansas State U., U. of Minnesota, U.
of Colorado, U. of Illinois, U. of Chicago, etc., etc., about
Midwest. Plus AEC, NASA, JPL facilities all over country.

Appears nation's recent progress muchly traceable to AAs. (Hope didn't also figure in downfall.)

Okay. So much for short-term strategy: Hunt proceeds hence by-the-numbers.

But what about long-term? Good point. What if, at last, search comes up dry? As might. . . .

Indeed—what *if* . . . ? Not most comfortable premise for dyed-in-wool Pollyanna to contemplate, but valid. Every coin has two sides. Rankest stupidity to ignore possibility might lose toss; fail to plan for exigencies lurking on dark side.

Very well. Reflecting as pessimist, grimly: Wise to leave notes all over, wherever might stop, pass through, visit; where other survivors (of whatever stripe) might find. True, probably—*certainly*—come to attention of itinerant ABs. Can't be helped.

But so what? Candy Smith-Foster, youngest-ever wearer of Sixth Degree Black Belt, uneasy at prospect of meeting strangers? Even potentially dangerous strangers? Yes. (But pretty potentially dangerous own self; harbor no genuine doubts about ability to cope with aberrant behavior as necessary. *Will* reach peaceful understanding, accommodation with fellow survivors; *will* live in altruistic, gentle harmony with neighbors, whomever may be, whatever background. Or else.)

College utilities still working; administration building well stocked with modern communications media marvels: electric typewriters, photocopiers, etc. Convenient opportunity; shall take advantage, spend next few days here; compose most utterly bare-bones, boiled-down condensation possible: message to leave about countryside during travels.

Content giving pause. Should identify self—but within limits. (No point, for instance, mentioning age, sex, dimensions. Teacher's caution firmly in mind; well aware that whatever response in numbers, substantial percentage bound to be maladjusted. No point slanting advertising toward weirdos.) Should describe resources, advantages of hometown area, farms (omitting shelter mention; my little secret for now, until familiar with recruitees, confident of intentions). Must include invitation to visit, partake in mutual deliberation over whether acceptance into community advantageous both ways.

Have also concluded, after initial hesitation, message must contain explanation of *H. sapiens/post hominem* situation, etc. Facts, evidence clearly documented; Teacher's conclusion unaffected by scoffers—but doubt will care much for neighbors lacking minds sufficiently open to appreciate data, understand implications, and (most of all) accept *necessity* of next step:

Central industry in *my* community to be AA-type upbringing, education of children (to degree possible in ruined world). All else secondary, supportive. No compulsion, pressure; volunteers only. But dissenters need not apply. Big world; can live elsewhere.

Granted, noble resolve most conveniently parallels own selfish desires (*so* much to learn!); but if Dark Ages follow collapse of *H. sapiens*' civilization, won't be *my* fault.

There! Not so tough: Mere three days' full-time, unremitting labor—writing, rewriting, trimming, condensing, paring, slashing, distilling, rooting out, re-rewriting, etc., etc. —and leaflet complete.

Masterpiece of brevity: single page (legal size, double-sided; uniform 1/10-inch margins top, bottom, left, right; 15-pitch type) says everything necessary in only 5,768 well-chosen words—plus metaphoric extra thousand implied by tiny map sketched at end.

Initial small stock produced on nifty both-sides-at-once Xerox. (Wonderful machine; some benefits of old civilization *must* be saved for Posterity—10,000 copies, *three hours!*)

Shall affix to doors of food, hardware, sporting goods, clothing stores, etc., as ride along. Pass hundreds every day; been taking local roads rather than interstates. (Esthetic choice; admittedly not logical: Interstates doubtless better condition, easier driving; but somehow lonelier [*said* wasn't logical], more depressing.)

Not terribly original plan, but *I* forage constantly, almost daily; reasonable inference holds other survivors do likewise. And certainly have generally similar needs, "shop" same places.

Final analysis—becomes question of numbers: Post enough leaflets, bound to catch eye. Somebody's eye. Someplace. Sometime. Probably.

Tomorrow leave for Boston. Harvard-M.I.T. area, home for five AAs: Herman Smith, Mario Ling, Gayle Kinnart, Theron Parker, Rex Hollister.

Parker, Ling, Smith deeply involved (according to File)

in project combining M.I.T.'s space research center, computer center, nuclear reactor, magnetics lab; Harvard's medical school, biochemical facility, seismographic station. Wouldn't discuss objective, but spin-off breakthroughs, inventions, products so numerous, administration declined to push it.

Hollister working at Harvard only, but at medical research, anthropology, biophysics, geology, political theory.

Kinnart's Ph.D.'s in nuclear physics, oceanography, computer science, meteorology, astronautics. Worked when, where, with whom, on what she chose. Taught, researched, invented at will. Delighted in shaking up Establishment's institutions, the crustier the better; C.L.E.P.ed *Juris Doctor* in spare time, over organized opposition of Bar (disapproved failure to utilize proper law-school channels). Sued *pro se*, won, obtained J.D. by Supreme Court decree. Also holds Seventh Degree Black Belt. (If consciously, actively seeking role model, girl could do lots worse—hope she likes me.)

Enough woolgathering. To bed now. Far to go tomorrow; much to do.

But calmly, coolly; optimistically but with caution, discipline. No more paralytic disappointment, hysteria, tears—*no matter what*. If trail proves cold, will play hand as dealt: Study facts as materialize; proceed logically, efficiently as indicated.

But can *hope.* . . .

Silly me. To think, really expected to make Boston in single day (seemed reasonable goal while studying map: only 275 miles, straight-line distance).

But not crow, not flying. Driving. Slowly, cautiously. Through heavily wooded, very hilly (almost mountainous) terrain; numerous small towns, villages; over narrow, winding, bumpity road obviously surveyed, installed by larcenous paving contractor whose sole ambition (well and truly realized) was smothering in concrete most expensive distance between any two points.

Together with previously observed uniform deterioration of highway system, conditions generally less than ideal for rapid transit: Downed trees, abandoned vehicles, landslides, etc., do little to speed progress.

Then final unexpected barrier: Hudson River. Not anticipated as problem; maps show bridges all up-, downstream.

True, are many bridges; however, those encountered

thus far quite impassable: Some blocked by horrendous traffic jams; some visibly unsafe, spans sagging, etc.; some actually collapsed, lying in, under water. Several boast combinations of all of above. (Prefer not to think what must have been like when refugee-laden bridges, loaded beyond designers' worst nightmares, came down.)

Camping tonight on romantic west bank, at lush forest's edge, under clear, star-studded, moonlit sky. Doubtless be more favorably impressed if conducting appraisal from other side.

Tomorrow will head south along river. Bridge frequency increases as approach New York City. Bound to get across sooner, later.

Delete previous pearl of wisdom. Written by idiot, without consideration of facts, human nature. Indeed, bridges more frequent to south. Also bigger, wider, more capacious. However, increased population more than made up difference.

Drove south all the way to Newark, Verrazano Narrows Bridge to Brooklyn. All blocked, damaged, or both.

Jams on surviving spans exceed belief. Example (not worst): Faced with immovable crush of vehicles parked on George Washington Bridge, obsessed beyond reason, control, someone elected to leave Manhattan—in large bulldozer, *over top*. And so tightly packed together were cars in path that most occupants unable to open doors, squeeze through windows, etc., flee in time. Predictably dreadful results. (But *someone* coped: Operator, crawler both dead; stopped halfway across, perched like giant carnivore on mashed vehicles beneath.)

Camping again tonight on romantic west bank of Hudson River, same place as night before last—same lush forest, under same clear, star-studded, moonlit sky, etc.

(Bah . . . !)

Tomorrow will head *north* along river. Population density decreases considerably that direction. Bound to get across sooner, later. Or drive *around* damned thing.

Murphy would have snickered, said, ". . . *told* you so." And been right: Very first bridge north of where quit exploring, three days before, stood wide open, unobstructed, safe.

Crossed without incident; continued through New York State, into Vermont, east-southeast across Appalachian Mountain spine into Massachusetts—into more bridge trouble: Connecticut River.

Pretty stream. But wide, impassable due to bridge damage. Lots of bridges, lots of damage. Appears to have been heavy flooding earlier: Barges flung about like toys; presence of bridge supports in paths presented little hindrance.

None daunted but wiser now, headed north immediately, upstream. Mere 150 miles sufficed to bring us to intact span.

Across and flushed with confidence, headed again southeast—toward Boston, with no potential geographical obstacles visible ahead on map.

Be there by noon tomorrow, barring untowardnesses.

(And *not* getting excited. Waiting to see what lies ahead. Calmly, coolly, objectively.)

Nothing lies ahead! Or sits, stands, hops, skips, jumps. And getting mighty fed up with whole business.

Once is nothing more than random incident, dice cast, crumbled cookie, flopped mop. Twice probably coincidence, without statistical significance; no doubt concerning to pessimist, but not alarming to rational intellect. Three times could still be coincidence, but scary coincidence; probability laws bent way out of shape.

Four times is trend. No doubt about it; worry is appropriate response.

And *six* times—conclusive. Utterly so.

Nobody home. Again. All signs point to orderly move-out. *Again*. No clues suggesting possible destination, whereabouts. *Again!*

Performed most thorough going-through of homes, offices, labs of all five M.I.T.-Harvard-area AAs. Turned up nothing. Simply vanished. Carefully, efficiently, without loose ends.

AGAIN!

Kinnart's house first stop; then office. Scene at house duplicated Peter Bell's; office equally barren: Everything personal, if even faintly portable, gone. Results at Smith's, Ling's, Parker's, Hollister's similar, equally dismaying. No affirmative data; all evidence negative, inferential, based on what not found.

Returned to Kinnart's house for night. Lovely place:

Even stripped of personal touches, still homey; retains comfortably feminine ambience.

Great relief after weeks of living in van, sleeping on bunk, cooking with charcoal, Sterno. Electric power out, but gas, water still work. Easy enough to run extension cord in for evening's lighting.

Decision to spend night under civilized roof met twin's approval. Loves travel, but *bon vivant* at heart; wallows in luxury at every opportunity (believes anything worth doing worth overdoing). And apparently concluded time ripe for good wallow: Hurled self into project with glee (mere fraction of which, publicly displayed in times past, sure to result in involuntary hospitalization). Participation included: assisting carrying tee stand in from van (me carrying; manic sibling gripping crossbar with toes, wings flapping at max); unpacking food (container-opening one of brother's pettest passions—problem arises confining enthusiasm to appropriate time, place, object); setting table (loves this part: Waddles joyously about tabletop, seizing plates, utensils—anything not nailed down—laboriously carries/drags to edge; surreptitiously peeks around to see if observed yet; then heaves over side, watching fall, bobbing head, chortling under breath as impact occurs—then back for more).

In especially rare mood today; having wonderful time: talking, warbling like trained chainsaw, assisting until seemed must be three of him. Finally became necessary—to retain own sanity—to banish him to stand, order him, "Stay!"

Feelings unruffled by rebuff, of course. Within moments had discovered refrigerator handle within reach. While doing sideways chin-ups, indicated continuing willingness—nay, eagerness—to help clear table. Before meal was over.

Had turned on gas first thing on arrival, lit water heater. Have put clean sheets on firmest bed in house. Looking forward to indescribable pleasure of hot shower, followed by best night's sleep in weeks.

Looking forward *intensely*—helps keep mind off AAs' disappearance. Impossible six people could vanish so utterly, without *any* clue.

Well, perhaps morning will bring inspiration: Maybe subconscious noticed something so-called "conscious" missed while worrying.

Good night.

*   *   *

Eureka! (Sort of.)

Upon waking this morning, realized search not thorough as should have been. Oh, thorough enough regarding not missing single drawer, looking under beds, examining every inch—but was looking *for* things; paying no attention to what might be missing. Stated in yesterday's entry, ". . . all evidence negative, inferential, based on what not found." But made no effort to determine *what* not found; haven't inferred worth darn.

So following breakfast (found old-fashioned campfire waffle iron in basement, works equally well on kitchen gas range—results *wonderful* with maple syrup after so long); adjourned back to Kinnart's office; conducted repeat search, this time with eyes, perception, *mind* open. And learned:

Remaining lab contents limited to stock equipment, scientific goodies available anywhere. Nothing visible appropriate to work of most brilliant researcher in five (un?)related fields. Vacant table space suggests missing equipment, but not much. And no clues as to what.

However, one artifact obvious by absence—her First Microscope. (Every student scientist and/or doctor receives as gift or purchases in school a First Microscope. Sometimes powerful, sophisticated instrument; sometimes Woolworth's Student Special—but always treasured for life; always prominent in office, whether used or not.) Absence significant.

But not as glaring as lack of any scrap of work notes, memoranda, programs, floppy disks, photographs, printouts, results—in short: irreplaceable stuff, without which any research reverts back to square one.

Went back then; reinspected homes, offices of other four Boston-area AAs; confirmed similar conditions. Physical gear remaining wondrously varied but limited to catalog stock; nothing custom-made, no records. And *no* First Microscopes!

So much for available facts; now for inferences: Left, probably as group; went somewhere already physically equipped to continue studies, taking more specialized, irreplaceable tools, notes, records, etc.

(Granted, premise requires quantum leap past logic; but given reasonable parallel between their thinking and mine—assuming also work in progress [and opportunity]—only tenable conclusion.)

Besides, was *necessary:* Had, while ruminating, forgotten Armageddon side effects. No possibility hominems, with olfactory sensitivities far transcending *H. sapiens'*, could have remained in population-dense Boston area during months immediately following species' end. Or any large, heavily peopled area. Own experience in tiny Wisconsin hometown proof enough: Had not spent first three months sealed in shelter, breathing own recycled air, would have been driven away.

So—again—what now? Conclusions interesting, probably valid—almost certainly valid. Also, in practical terms, next to useless. Even were conclusions confirmed—all Tarzan File AA addresses in fact obsolete—so what? Who cares? Equally pointless is speculation over why gone. Ringing question is *where*!

Without *some* hint—positive data, not accumulation of negatives—search deteriorates to pure exploration. Futile on face of it; continent simply too big for random poking about. Too much area; too few targets—and even methodical search won't improve odds. Not really. AAs might well move into section just covered, remain undiscovered forever.

Besides, what (beyond wishful myopia) limits scope of search to North America? Whole planet now available (excepting only several extremely radioactive areas in Asia, where [according to Daddy's secret papers] U.S.'s displeasure over attack most intensely expressed). Surprising if AAs failed to capitalize on all available resources, natural or man-made, wherever extant, to found, secure, develop community from which to gather, store, preserve, ultimately extend knowledge base accumulated during *H. sapiens'* sway on Earth.

Hmm. . . . Uninformed observer might suspect pattern developing here: Seems every time central question ("What now?") crops up, somehow vanishes again beneath welter of irrelevant detail, philosophy, speculation.

Goodness. . . . Candy Smith-Foster subconsciously refusing to face facts? Perhaps because answers unpalatable?)

Nonsense! Nothing subconscious about it. Plain as day: scared to death. And with best of reasons: answers *stink*!

Consider remaining options: One, can assume—not unreasonably after six consecutive strikeouts—Tarzan File truly dead end; set off blindly into wilderness, playing entirely by ear; distributing leaflets widely, collecting ABs catch-as-can, if at all.

Or, two, ignore six-ply coincidence; play out hand as dealt by Tarzan File, follow through to conclusion; not so much expecting dramatic results as sticking to scientific method, ensuring resultant fine-tooth examination of homes, offices overlooks not least clue suggesting whereabouts.

Then set off blindly into wilderness.

Or silly-season stuff, among which least hairbrained notions include: Acquiring necessary knowledge (not impossible, considering formidable reading speed, comprehension/retention level); constructing, activating powerful omniband radio station; broadcasting endless worldwide appeal for company.

Or how about skywriting? Attention-getting, certainly; and effective each time over huge chunks of geography. Given *H. post hominem* mind, reflexes (far quicker, better integrated than predecessors'), how difficult can be to learn aircraft operation basics? Memorize book, absorb theory; then apply practical. (Shucks, Wrights only human, managed *without* theory.)

Probably neither truly silly-season ideas. Farfetched, yes. But not totally beyond pale, given sufficient impetus (i.e., desperation—cornered rat apt to try anything).

No, not really silly—*silly* is debating whether might be possible very quickly to breed special strain of mosquito (limited to drinking hominem blood); securing very small notes to very tiny collars, sending out to spread word.

Now, *that's* silly. . . .

And demonstrates lengths will go to avoid facing "What now" question. Not that have any real choice: Big world; only information even potentially helpful is Tarzan File, whether current or not. Must be verified, unto bitter end if necessary. As well might be.

So. Six down, 93 to go. Next stop: Baltimore, Johns Hopkins University; Barbara, James, Frederick Harper. No, not related—*family*: Idyllic *ménage à trois* of several years' standing. Harpers, according to file, enjoyed benefits, protections of marriage laws, without violating them but without common-law togetherness risks, by simply *co*habitating; defining responsibilities toward one another, to heirs, regarding assets, etc., by forming corporation, incorporating into bylaws useful provisions from marital, probate law. Reported very happy. Perhaps all three being doctors, dovetailed specialties, helps.

Discovery piqued curiosity. Checked further through File. And learned plural living arrangements not uncommon amongst AAs: Fully one-third involved in family units of more than two. Largest such encompasses five.

Intriguing. But not sure my cup of tea. Earliest memories pervaded with gently intense love emanating from, between, all around Daddy, Momma Foster. Couldn't have spent formative years basking in glow always surrounding, enveloping them, anyone near them, without being imprinted to some extent with bias toward general wonderfulness of twosome life—joy of being single most important thing in life of Someone Wonderful.

Certainly hope Harpers home. Apart from obvious, interested in observing daily workings of family life; see whether they glow together. (If so, at what intensity in which combinations.)

Off tomorrow to Baltimore—or perhaps "toward" more realistic preposition: Though only 427 miles, according to map, *know* about map distances now (been through that before, haven't we). So don't expect to make it in single day. Or even two, three.

For one thing, must retrace path around much of Connecticut, Hudson rivers—doubles distance right there. Additionally, frequent stops to post leaflets in promising locations takes time. Finally, map shows two additional major rivers between here, there (Delaware, Susquehanna); both so convenient to large populations, almost certain downstream bridges useless.

Can't take less than week. Maybe two.

If possible at all—for very different reason: While hasn't been hint of residual radiation heretofore; Baltimore very close to Washington. Capital one of few targets across land scheduled for broken windows: According to Daddy's secret papers, favored with many direct hits. Quite conceivable D.C. area still hot. Equally probable, Baltimore unsafe as well.

Been testing ambient background radiation periodically with geiger counter from shelter (recent design: lightweight, quite sophisticated [nine-tenths of capabilities completely over head]). Will step up checking frequency as approach Baltimore area.

Bedtime again—after another deliciously hot shower. Then to that firm, cool bed.

Tomorrow beckons. . . .

* * *

Yes, Posterity, derelict again—sorry. Trying to do better, really. Sometimes difficult to muster energy. But trust me: Missed nothing through failure to enter daily progress from Boston on regular basis. Omissions, if any, not substantive in nature—*events* not substantive; absence from history books not world-shaking.

Because mostly dull. Indescribably so. Hundreds of miles. Some on roads, some not. Thoroughfare varied from expressways to pasturelands; passability from utterly not to unobstructed. Myriad get-out-and-copes. Engaged four-wheel-drive lots. Cleared path with winch frequently. Doubled back often.

First break in routine came while working southward through rural portion of Pennsylvania, apparently egg-farming region. Accidentally rediscovered old source of fresh meat: Hit chicken. Happily, not going very fast; killed cleanly with bumper instead of mashing flat with tire. Stopped, cleaned immediately; roasted over charcoal for early dinner.

Delicious—thought so myself—but Terry transported beyond ecstasy: Waded in with gusto; split, pulverized bones; cleaned out every scrap of marrow, gristle. Long time since last chicken dinner; poor baby probably in throes of withdrawal.

Experience profitable long-term as well as short. That night switch clicked in brain, disturbing sleep. Old switch. Primitive circuit.

Found self suddenly awake, staring into darkness. Pictured clearly in mind's eye was tee shirt seen on tourist several years back: cartoon of hungry vulture glaring down from tree branch, muttering, "Patience, *hell*—I'm going to go *kill* something . . . !"

H. sapiens not scavenger. Was, in fact, puny physique notwithstanding, deadliest predator on planet. Any reason for successor to be less forthright about satisfying appetite? Moral issue, perhaps? Should *H. post hominem* be vegetarian, as philosophical principle?

No . . . ! Nothing philosophical about vitamin deficiency, creeping malnutrition. Granted, probably entirely possible for hard-working, full-time agrarian to raise sufficiently diverse crop to constitute balanced meatless diet. But for explorer, nomad, simply not practical.

So next day, again feeling carnivorous (anticipating brother's vote if asked), stopped van, caught chicken in footrace. Issue considerably in doubt at first. Prey ran to, fro, dodged about squawking. Wondered for time if might have to resort to gun.

But finally zigged when smart money all on zag; fell victim to feral pounce to gladden heart of primalest hungry raptor ever admitted to guild—which, in fact, by then apt self-description (though neither growled during chase nor stood with foot on kill afterward, beating chest, screaming mangani victory cry).

Dinner that night especially tasty. Perhaps calories expended in pursuit honed appetite; perhaps enjoyment on more atavistic level. Hard to say—and don't much care: If reverting, will enjoy it.

Began edging westward to flank Delaware River while still far enough north that detour of little consequence. Finding passable bridge never became issue.

But same not true of Susquehanna; another matter entirely: long, extending far northwest, very wide. Bridges encountered during initial exploration all collapsed. Began to think might have to circumnavigate after all. Until came to railroad trestle.

Stopped van abruptly. Stared. Deliberated at length, with distaste. Reconnoitered on foot, all the way across. Took careful measurements.

Yes, was possible—probably not even actually dangerous. But uncomfortable notion: Span between tread centers and track separation identical; giant mud/snow flotation tires fully 15 inches across tread face, providing perhaps four inches' grace either way before risk mounted. And even if did allow vehicle to slip off rails, wooden ties sufficiently closely spaced to permit crossing completion by bump-bump-bump method, assuming care, deliberate progress.

(Rather *not* slip off rails, though, thank you. True, walked entire span; inspected structure for apparent faults. But layperson; key word is "apparent": Not versed, personally, in abstruse skills required to determine at single glance which tie sound, which rotten. And cantilever loading provides severest test of strongest member; little doubt that bump-bump-bumping whole way across surefire system for substandard tie detection. Quick, positive detection.)

However, longer debated matter, less attractive became alternative. Judging by map, dearth of bridges upstream, mountainous contours of land, can't-get-there-from-here character of roads, less appealing became prospect of driving around Susquehanna. Looking at thousand miles at minimum; probably more, considering present-day road conditions. Did not care to spend another two weeks getting past dumb river.

Therefore backtracked to last small town. Located hardware store; scrounged to good effect, assembling components necessary for Rube Goldberg device intrinsic to rash solution: Mirror, mounted out at end of tripodish boom secured to front end of roof rack, both ends of bumper; with control rod permitting accurate positioning from driver's seat—lash-up enabling direct observation of front tires' actual ground-to-tread contact point, removing seat-of-pants element from precision driving required to remain on tracks.

With mirror boom in place, control rod tested, working properly, next step was getting van perched on tracks. Accomplished well back from trestle, on solid right-of-way.

Front wheels easy; went where pointed. Mostly. Were, of course, encountering rails at fairly acute angle. With four-wheel-drive engaged, transmission in first gear, transfer box in low-low, released brake, eased out clutch, crept forward inch by inch. Right front wheel climbed first rail effortlessly, dropping to roadbed between tracks. Double contact next; doubled weight also—and doubled resistance, as smooth steel/rubber coefficient attempted to hoist weight of van's entire front end. Progress first limited to sideways, tires glancing off rails' shoulders, sliding along tracks without mounting. But finally corners of big mud/snow treads caught, drew front end upward. Moments later, following careful steering adjustments, front tires centered on rails.

Rears another matter, however: Right rear stubbornly dragged against left track for 30 feet before bumping up, over onto roadbed between rails. Then for good hundred feet both rears clawed ineffectually, unable to gain purchase.

Finally, with bare hundred yards remaining before commencing trestle ascent, gave up. Set brake, exited. Employed shovel to pile up small gravel ramp against rail ahead of each rear tire. Primitive solution (employing engineering principles well regarded in Pharaoh's day) but serviceable: Five feet beyond, all four wheels poised neatly on rails.

Astonishing, after all that effort, how quickly enthusiasm for project (product of own cleverness) waned:

Ten feet out on span, to be precise. Just far enough for hitherto-unnoticed breeze, unimpeded now by aught but

trestle's cobweb structure, to seize ample sail area presented
by van's slab sides and nudge. Gently but perceptibly.

(In retrospect, doubt actual chassis movement [limited,
of course, to slight suspension yield, tire sidewall squirm]
exceeded quarter inch in any direction. Then, however, felt
like major tectonic adjustment.)

Was suddenly conscious how very different trestle had
looked from on foot: wider, solider, *much* more secure.

And wooden ties projecting from under tracks on either
side appeared shorter now when viewed through windshield
from driver's seat, with river as background beyond, below—
far below. Tie ends not visible, for instance, through side
windows—*nothing* visible through side windows. Except distant ground, river.

Noticed van had stopped. Wondered briefly if due to
wind also, until discovered (looking past white-knuckled hands
gripping steering wheel) both feet apparently trying to push
brake pedal through floorboard. Had forgotten clutch; engine
dead.

(Probably just as well. With engine dead, could not yield
to rash impulses: Could not attempt to back up. Mirror not
placed to permit observation of exact rear-tire/rail relationship, nor could envision any practical means of doing so.
Further, geometry inherent in reverse steering precluded
making attempt to regain solid ground astern: Small angular
changes at rear are product of large lateral displacements at
front. Would have led to immediate bump-bump-bumping.
Or worse.)

Became aware was perspiring all over. Felt spontaneous
aching sensation in soles of feet, palms of hands. Eyes began
to burn, tear. Noticed also mounting sense of suffocation.

Memory chose that moment to call up, play back life-
long accumulation of admonishments concerning Bridges,
Premature Burning Of; Corners, Painting Oneself Into; Leaping Before Looking, etc. Cheeks grew hot; glad Teacher
couldn't see star pupil then, frozen at wheel amidst predicament created solely by own failure to consider all aspects of
problem before charging in.

But wait—what if Teacher *were* watching...? From
Above. Wouldn't do to let him see funk continue. Momentary
startlement probably barely excusable, considering circumstances, provided not carried beyond limits of good taste. If

watching, Teacher would expect to see constructive signs of recovery soon. Or would look sorrowful; make entry in notebook.

(Said recovery no doubt expected to include movement of portions of completely paralyzed body—that would be hard part.)

With effort almost physical in character, managed to wrench gaze from river below. Turned perceptions inward, initiating code sequence leading to transcendental state. And reaped prompt dividends: Upon closing eyes, cause of optic discomfort immediately evident—probably hadn't blinked for whole minutes! Likewise, shortness of breath alleviated by resumption of respiration. . . .

And as meditative discipline took hold, thought processes again began to acquire semblance of coherence; acted to clamp down, brake churning emotions, restore control. Heartbeat slowed, perspiration subsided.

Opened eyes; focused on point at which rail disappeared under tire. Noted was perfectly centered under tread. Directed attention to left hand. Tried three times before fingers unclenched from wheel, shifted grip to mirror control rod. Readjusted mirror to inspect other tire, rail. Also centered.

Okay. Everything. Under. Control.

Returned mirror to left tire, rail. Without angles to allow for, offered more direct observation, clearer perspective.

Returned left hand to wheel. Eased right hand's grip to point where feeling returned to fingers; moved to ignition switch. Took longer to get left foot from brake pedal, depress clutch. Turning key required act of raw will.

After being clutch-killed, engine started raggedly, settling into lumpy, galloping idle as gas-soaked plugs shorted, fired, shorted again. Torque reaction, transmitted through engine mounts to chassis, produced motion almost as scary as wind.

Ignored it. Moved right foot from brake pedal; placed gently on accelerator. Eased clutch out (had never taken out of gear); applied hint of gas. Forward motion resumed.

Applied fraction more power. Small fraction. Proceeded deliberately. About two-thirds mile across trestle, but in no hurry. Plenty of time.

Quickly learned driving not that difficult: Merely question of keeping eyes fixed on rail disappearing beneath tire tread; steering precisely to keep centered; ignoring van's frequent wind-induced shrugs. (Ignoring also scenery and own position relative thereto.)

No, not difficult at all. But rather tense work. And as initial session dragged on, began to feel effects of prolonged concentration; decided might be wise to stop, take breather. Did so, looked around—discovered had come barely hundred yards!

No, wasn't difficult. But took best part of three hours to complete crossing.

And when finally cleared trestle, solid ground under rails beneath all four wheels (waited until could confirm in rear-view mirrors to ensure wasn't being fooled by optical-mistic illusion; do something silly while rear end still overhung void), wasted no time turning sharply off tracks, bumping over rails, driving down embankment to level ground.

Stopped, got out; walked back to cliff edge, breathing hard. Suddenly rubbery legs seemed to suggest another time-out. Sat abruptly. And as stared out over valley, down at river, up at bridge, found was reviewing incident in detail: Had saved minimum of week's travel; and barring ever-present potential for untoward development arising out of mechanical failure (and despite recurring apnea episodes during crossing), probably not *inherently* dangerous. Reflected at length, totaling pluses, minuses.

Finally concluded: *stupidest damnfool stunt have ever pulled . . . !* What was all-fired rush? So *might* have had to spend another week circling river. Or month, for that matter. So *what . . . !* Not as if on *schedule . . . !*

Mechanical-failure risk *real;* but only then, sitting at brink, contemplating vistas conquered, did practical implications sink in: What would have done had tire gone flat midspan? Or engine quit? Or *steering* come adrift . . . ?

Sum of potential failure through which could have been stranded or pitched into space at least equals, probably exceeds, total number of parts of which van constructed. Madness to hazard position in which ten-cent part's failure could cause other than fleeting botheration.

Now, loss of van not disaster per se; replacements endlessly available, one form or another. But inconvenient; much semi-irreplaceable equipment aboard. (To which considerations might be added inconvenience attendant to dropping self, Terry into river, some bunchteen dozen feet below.)

However, when scrutinized under gimlet microscope of

hindsight, incident not entirely devoid of redeeming aspects (apart from obvious: Yes, am across *that* river). No question now: Been blundering along, gripped by curious form of mental myopia. Tight grip, too: Even when glimmer of sense raised head (in form of blithering panic ten feet from safety), never entered head to abort—set brake, seize Terry, abandon ship through rear doors.

Few bridges thus far encountered standing actually physically impassable—to pedestrian. But for blinder-mindedness regarding van, could have *walked* across, carrying gear; then picked new vehicle on far side. Certainly no dearth of replacements.

Sure, would take several trips to move whole inventory. Probably hard work. But quicker than driving around each river found sprawled across path. (And surely easier on nerves than emulating Wallendas.)

But, incredibly, was first time concept crossed mind, even as most fleeting of notions. (Curious behavior for certified genius—perhaps should just resign gracefully; avoid humiliation intrinsic to being found out, summarily drummed from corps.)

Okay! *Was* stupid—lesson learned. But water over dam; no benefit accrues from brooding over mistakes (besides, sackcloth itchy; ashes hard to shampoo from hair). On notice now—van expendable; shall keep fact in mind.

(But perhaps, in exercise of reasonable foresight, new policy implementation unnecessary. Ever. Because not truly fond of idea—not through fuzzy sentimentality, irrational attachment to inert mechanism, of course; practical considerations only: supremely capable on/off-road vehicle; quirks, limitations of which now second nature. Also capacious: lots of gear aboard, stowed neatly; everything in its place, readily at hand. Further, after pedal-lift installation, shift-lever extension, seat relocation, fits me—not insignificant factor from four-foot-ten-inch perspective. Besides, finally have galley in shape: cabinets, drawers organized; stove, oven properly broken in. Hate to go through that again.)

So van expendable, true. Fact now in mind. But "expendable" not synonymous with "consumable": that fact in mind, too. Next question, please.

Which (from *serious* historian, student) must be: Did you find anyone, anything, in Baltimore?

Answer: Of *course* not. Yet—just got here. (Apart from

happy discovery that, proximity to Washington notwithstanding, ambient radiation still reads within normal limits.)

Harpers not home; no surprise there. House displays usual signs (which have come to know, hate) of methodical move-out seen elsewhere. No clues immediately apparent; fine-tooth search must await morrow—been long day.

But first, another wallow in civilized decadence. Power out along much of East Coast, but Harpers' house totally solar powered, plus has own deep well—utterly independent of local utilities. Flip switch, electricity restored. Water standing in system already hot from automatic convective functioning of calorie collector on roof; with electricity working again, pump stands ready to replenish water as used. In brief: *Hot shower time again!*

Which is practically first thing did upon investigating house. Supper preparation, consumption next; only then turned to present journal update. (Sorry, Posterity; itchy, smelly skin and empty belly come first.)

And delays aside, now appears have done duty: Noteworthy observations, activities memorialized. Time for evening's revels to peak:

Three beds to choose from. Not difficult decision, though: King-size unsuitable (truly, have walked on marble floors with more resilience). Queen-size fitted with ten-inch foam mattress (into which unwary sleeper might sink beyond hope of rescue). Twin bed, however, is Just Right.

Good night, Posterity.

Goodness . . . ! Hard to know where to begin. So *much* to relate, but must keep tight rein on impulses lest record become even less coherent than usual. Strictly, therefore, by chronology:

Arose well rested. Indulged in another long, hot shower. Prepared breakfast with usual hilarious difficulty; fending off, with effort, assistance intensively volunteered by jovially ravenous sibling (surely most trying aspect of relationship: Seems the earlier the hour, more unbearably cheerful becomes).

Performed usual half-hour *kata* to settle breakfast, loosen up musculature.

Thereafter went through house. Thoroughly. Negative-result pattern confirmed suspicions previously formed: Deliberate, preplanned exodus; whether prior to *H. sapiens'* demise or immediately thereafter, unknown, immaterial. Lingering question still *where*.

Finished house examination; time to extend sweep to offices, general work environs. Packed, adjourned to van. Dug address list from Tarzan File, placed on dash next to wheel. Cleaned, refilled Terry's water, seed dishes—

Of *course* bringing twin: Wouldn't *dream* of leaving birdbrained innocent alone, unprotected. Besides, what if failed to return? *Ever*. Food, water soon run out. Consequences inevitable; details (how end arrives, how long takes) simply don't bear thinking about! Yes, retarded brother's constant companionship high in nuisance value (often downright maddening), but *necessary* to peace of mind.

Found city map at nearby drugstore, oriented self, located destination; set forth in general direction of Hopkins campus; specifically, doctors' office park adjacent to teaching hospital.

Never got there.

Everything happened at once, in slow motion: One moment was driving west (had overshot, going first to Harpers' home) down medium-wide downtown arterial (four lanes, no parking; high-rise buildings jutting from sidewalk edges to form concrete canyon), slowing to turn north at next corner. Next moment, just as moved wheel to begin turn, caught glimpse (same instant heard engine's bellow, tires' shrieking) of gold-trimmed, shiny black blur already entering intersection from north, turning east: Full-race Trans Am (wide wheels, tires; unmuffled chrome headers; heaven knows what else) flailing into corner almost sideways, on radius which, requiring entire width of both streets, terminated somewhere between own vehicle's headlights.

No time for cleverness—instinctively stamped on brakes, threw hand up to brace Terry, stiffened other arm on steering wheel to brace me, gritted teeth, awaited outcome.

Trans Am driver did react, somehow: Sensed, rather than saw, front wheels twitch outward; heard engine's thunder falter, almost gasp, then redouble. Hurtling vehicle's sideways approach around corner abruptly changed radius, momentarily flattening curve, missing van's left front corner by merest fraction of flinch.

Progress thereafter less clear: Observation limited to what could make out in mirrors.

Trans Am apparently completed slide around corner (and

own frail self) by slapping right rear wheel into curb, with front wheels still pointed sharply to right. Sliced immediately across sidewalk into storefront.

Vehicle, building, both erupted in shower of fragments, dust, sudden plume of flame. Remnant of car ricocheted from impact cloud, spinning like dervish, shedding parts en route, to recross street. Smote that building tail first with horrendous thump, triggering yet another debris explosion, considerably more flame; from which emerged still spinning, appreciably smaller, still shedding parts, now gushing fire in earnest; recrossing street to crash again. And still again. And—oh, never mind.

Would be nice to report own reaction at this point cool, efficient, intelligent. Can't. Wasn't. Intellect momentarily shut down completely. Forgot existence of large, fully charged CO_2 extinguisher; forgot about Gel-Coat (flame-retardant, wet-chemical-soaked blanket with whose protection could have *bathed* in burning gasoline for five minutes without discomfort); forgot about Hurst gasoline-engine-hydraulic rescue equipment (capable of ripping open any door, shearing off roof posts, unpeeling vehicle crumpled like ball of foil to extract occupants); crowbar, sledge—all languishing in lockers in rear of van. Even forgot to set brake, shift transmission to neutral before taking action. (Didn't matter; had killed engine again in heat of moment.)

Only knew had finally found *somebody*—possibly very last other soul on Earth—and might be dying before own disbelieving eyes.

Sprang from driver's seat while accident still unwinding (seemed to take *forever*). Landed in dead run. Forced to hurdle several gasoline trails left burning as careening wreckage crossed, recrossed street between impacts.

Overtook accident at Trans Am's ultimate resting place, half-buried in display window some hundred yards beyond van. Arrived as building-material cascade tapered off; rubble piling high on roof, hood, trunk, littering nearby pavement.

And since kamikaze slide's final yards were backward, vehicle now resting on own gasoline track; flame pond spreading slowly about wreckage, storefront, as contents gurgled from ruptured fuel tank (rescue growing more complicated even as stood there, shielding face from heat [painful even at ten yards], squinting through inferno for glimpse of occupant).

But not last-desperate-second, screaming-crisis emergency; merely grim. No flames yet visible in interior; reasonable to assume passenger compartment intact (underneath, at least; topsides a mess: Glass gone, along with bumpers, fenders; front windshield posts both torn loose; roof at angle never contemplated by styling engineers).

Cooked occupant inevitable but not imminent; had time to secure from van equipment appropriate for crossing gasoline lake safely, forcing probably jammed door, extracting victim, retreating in good order.

(Never mind exploding gas tanks—exist only in fevered imaginations of sensation-oriented, irresponsible Hollywood screenwriters: Fire Marshal Hathaway [Daddy's friend, neighbor; lived just down street] said so. Claimed endless fueling of myth fostered needless widespread explosion-fear. Marshal Hathaway considered filmmakers' behavior quasi-criminal— certainly reckless negligence: Public saw so many crashes-followed-by-explosions on TV, in films, believed it; and more peoples' injuries compounded when unprofessionally dragged from wrecked cars—burning or not—by Good Samaritans fearing explosions following accidents than recordable. *Liquid* gasoline doesn't explode; only gasoline vapor, *correctly mixed with oxygen,* explodes—and only if ignition delayed until precise moment ideal mixture achieved. Burning cars *don't* explode.)

None of which rambling bears on fact driver in fair way to roast if not gotten out promptly—gasoline fires *hot!*

Therefore steeled heart, clamped down emotions, blocked from mind distracting awareness of real stakes at issue; concentrated dispassionately on tactical evaluation, selected tools, commenced organized rescue effort...

Well, not exactly. (Mind *still* shut off.)

Took short run, dived headfirst. Passage through flames too brief for more than hint of real heat. Felt only momentary, intolerable ovenlike sensation; had barely time to be startled as breath sucked from lungs in reaction. More startling was incredible roar as flames licked at face, hair, clothing: From distance imperceptible; at heart of conflagration sounded like freight train.

Sailed through left front side window, fetching up in disarray on far side against door. Raised head to look around, discovered was gasping for breath: Already pretty warm inside.

Untangled limbs, crawled to driver—sprawled under

dash. Examined gently as commensurate with haste, thoroughly as possible under conditions; determined no condition apparent taking precedence over fire: Bleeding from various lacerations ranged from inconsequential to serious, but no fracture grossly evident—though spine distinctly separate question, not determinable under present conditions. Would have to cross fingers.

(Of *course* qualified to render opinion: Fair-haired only baby girl of best doctor in whole world! Thoroughly, properly instructed in advanced first aid; more knowledgeable in emergency medicine than paramedic.)

Once assured rescue itself probably wouldn't kill him (him?—*HIM*...!) turned attention to getting us *out*: Really getting hot in there.

Especially floorboard, now that had moment to notice; not ideal storage environment for victim while figuring out next step. Braced self, hauled limp body up one end at a time, dumped on seat.

Cast about interior for inspiration. At first found little cause for optimism. Then attention fixed on rear seat cushion: Ripped from moorings, lay skewed across interior, one end almost protruding from rear window. Recognized possible solution.

Tried left door. Not surprised when refused to budge. (But disappointed.) Didn't bother with right door; solidly wedged against wall in which vehicle embedded.

Indulged in moment's worry: Required little imagination to visualize consequences of attempting to push cushion through window, positioning to bridge pooled gasoline; climb through window dragging victim—amidst 20-foot-high flames...!

Options (few at outset) evaporated as gasoline lake outside spread, temperature inside mounted. In fact, as practical matter, single avenue remained. But regarded with disquiet: somewhat risky.

No—*damned* risky. For self (until now personal safety never at issue; could have aborted, exiting same way arrived, exposure limited to possible superficial scorching, crisping around edges) as well as for rescuee: If failed, both dog meat. (Well done.)

Indeed might fail: Strength required far beyond that usually at command. Plus considerable endurance.

Now. Strength available. But endurance most iffy.

Surely everyone remembers stories of 92-pound house-wife who, witnessing car fall off bumper jack onto husband, performs hundred-yard dash in three seconds flat, lifts car with one hand, extracting hubby with other. Or hiker, confronting grizzly without warning, who subsequently finds self standing 30 feet above ground; on lowest limb of tree too big to have encircled with arms, legs; with no memory of how got there. Etc.

Less widely known: Many such stories true.

Solution arcane but not supernatural. Straightforward biochemistry: Given protein machine (assuming well-toned musculature, ample lung capacity, sound heart, circulatory system in good repair), energy expenditure limited to rate at which fuel metabolized; muscle cells nourished; heat, waste removed. Reserve stored in muscle tissues negligible.

Cells of which muscles composed contract not in unison but take turns; work in relays. System allows each cell a rest period to recharge during even most strenuous exercise; also means only tiny fraction actually participate at any moment.

Now, if stimulus encountered which triggers substantial majority of cells in given muscle simultaneously, awesome feats ensue (along with real potential for popped ligaments, tendons, fractured bones—system *designed* for shiftwork operation).

Own karate training, as with any advanced student, had covered Hysterical Strength, Unleashing & Management Thereof; had gone, in fact, beyond routine analysis, theoretical discussion—into practical: Teacher included hypnosis in curriculum. Planted within psyche posthypnotic code to loose Beast Within at ultimate need.

Present quandary seemed to fall within definition: Needed more strength than possessed; else would die. Clear enough, even allowing for Teacher's dire warnings.

For nothing magic about transaction. Simple arithmetic: X calories produced, available within Y length of time. Rigidly controlled by inverse proportion rule: Double consumption, halve duration.

During tests had seen own strength increase tenfold. Briefly. Followed by crushing fatigue: in strict accordance with *tanstaafl* principle.

But saw no alternative.

Lay back on front seat, fanny close to door. Gripped steering wheel with one hand, seat edge with other. Drew back legs, knees on chest. Concentrated inward. Gathered forces; focused *ki* flow into, through legs. Transformed trigger word utterance into *kiai*, intensity of scream hurting throat, and

    . . . KICKED!

Astounding results: Door burst open, whistled through arc, crashed against hinge limits; welds failed, door flew down sidewalk, bouncing end-over-end.

Instantly air vanished inside vehicle as heat flooded through door opening; searing lungs; dessicating eyes, nasal passages; scalding exposed skin. Smelled burning hair; never doubted was own.

Time of essence now as never before: If couldn't get victim, self, safely beyond flames before metabolic supercharge ran down, likely wouldn't—unconsciousness only seconds away.

Organizing actions to avoid waste motion suddenly acquired desperate importance. Snatched rear-seat cushion over into front; thrust through door opening (through which flames now licked, beginning to char headliner), positioning to bridge infernal moat. (Or *almost* bridge—just lacked length to span, with pond still spreading.)

Seized driver, propped up into approximately seated position, slumped against seat back. Loosened jacket, pulled up over head, zipped shut. Shoved limp arms down into pants; tightened belt to hold in place.

Shrugged own jacket upward, retracting head like turtle. Placed shoulder just below victim's beltline; tugged, felt weight roll onto back as torso collapsed forward. Slid arm under thighs; lifted, jogging shoulder to center load in fireman's carry. (And marveled at own strength—while dreading impending consequences of reckless squandering: Sustained consumption rate surely four, five times norm; probably more.)

Straightened experimentally: Bumped roof to gauge relationship between victim's fanny, own shoulders—crouch needed to clear upper door frame.

Fixed seat cushion's location indelibly in mind's eye. Took deep breath, held it; closed eyes, pinched jacket shut over face. And

    . . . LEAPED!

Time stopped as again felt blast-furnace ambience envelop whole body. Seemed to hang motionless midair; conscious this time of flames probing, digging, seeking access through flimsy coverings. Oppressive heat, pervasive roar blanketed all other sensations.

Feet blindly seeking landing, but impact somehow unexpected, surprise. Cushion yielded underfoot as knees bent, absorbing extra weight; then airborne again, leaping for fire's boundary—and heart stopped as cushion skidded away from legs' thrust, robbing jump of power needed for distance, throwing balance off.

Eyes snapped open, head jerked forward, trying to get clear of jacket; even at risk of optic burns, needed to *see*, reestablish orientation—*mustn't* fall while still within holocaust!

Dragged fabric clear of eyes just as cool air washed jacket, over clothing, into lungs; as landed, stumbling briefly, on flat, dry, *cool* pavement.

Shrugged victim to ground; conducted hasty inspection for burning clothing—mine, his. Used own jacket to smother small blaze on victim's left pants leg.

Then attention riveted by rapidly forming pool of blood under leg: bright red—arterial stuff. Probably femoral, judging by amount. Must have been lying such that position created pressure block, preventing loss in car. Moving eliminated obstruction. If femoral, had as little as 20 seconds left—less whatever time had been bleeding in car since first moved.

Heavy denim parted like cobweb before preternatural strength: Tore pants leg open from ankle to crotch; then ripped entirely free from garment. Turned victim over; confirmed suspicion immediately:

Deep gash from medial upper thigh to anterior knee— *spurting*.

Twisted denim strip into rope; looped about thigh above wound. Looked around briefly, wistfully—no sticks within reach. Slid fingers under bandage, made hard fist; partially stood, stepped three fast turns around body, using own hand as stick, tightening tourniquet very nicely, thank you, but cutting off blood to fingertips in process.

Seized collar with left hand, right still lodged in tourniquet; swung victim back up over shoulder into fireman's carry.

Staggered then, beset by flash of vertigo; suddenly aware of warning twinges as muscles all over body threatened to cramp. Conscious also of perspiration abruptly streaming from body in rivers as autonomic system belatedly noticed calorie-consumption rate, tried to do something about mounting internal temperature. And breathing affected now, too: coming in deep, tortured gasps.

But couldn't complain; not unexpected. In fact, remarkable aspect to condition is why symptoms so long deferred—no idea how was still functioning at all. According to data, painfully garnered through previous supervised (and conservative) experiments, activity level sustained during past few minutes flatly impossible. Should have achieved coma long since through massive fatigue products build-up, with vital organs shutting down from systemic shock; death imminent, barring only most profound life support, treatment.

However, seemed less than opportune moment to question blessing. Set off for van at dead run.

Arrived still conscious but deteriorating: Heartbeat thundering inside skull; lungs afire; cramps attacking in earnest now; black patches flickering across vision; clothing dripping, saturated with sweat.

Terry greeted with "Hello, baby; what'cha doo-in'?"; but couldn't spare breath, time to respond.

Threw open side doors, slung victim into own bunk. Then found couldn't reach tool locker door from bedside. Frantic visual search located crowbar on floor near door (had used earlier to enter drugstore). Made long leg, snagged with foot. Dragged within reach of left hand; substituted for right in tourniquet—with relief.

Stumbled to refrigerator, shaking life back into fingers. Rummaged through stored food; found quart of Gatorade, plastic container of yesterday's chicken soup. Gulped about half Dr. Cade's elixir in single swallow; put away equal portion of Yiddish cure-all.

Worried somewhat over possible consequences: Food, drink not easy travelers in stomach during, right after sustained violent exercise. Especially cold. But knew needed *something* immediately to start replenishment after huge energy drain.

Couldn't *afford* collapse then; didn't have *time* for own problems. Victim about to lose leg—plus certainly in shock, doubtless sinking moment by moment: Even if somehow failed to die as direct result of injuries, shock could finish job—would, untreated.

Returned to bunk. Apprehensively called again upon

unnatural strength. Found, to surprise, enough remained to
lift foot of bunk one-handed; hold elevated while inserting
prop (Gel-Coat kit—flameproofing goodies which should have
been used to eliminate much drama from rescue). Would
have been easier to elevate legs conventionally, with pillow;
unfortunately, supine position unworkable due to wound location: Needed victim prone to treat.

Located Daddy's Number Two black bag, saline I.V. kit
from medical supply locker. Rooted through bag; found stop-
watch, sphygmomanometer. Took pulse, checked blood pressure: fast, strong, respectively.

Lifted eyelids, flicked sunlight across pupils with hand
mirror. Were unequal, nonreactive; plus unmistakeable twitching
movements: nystagmus—concussed certainly.

Then froze, transfixed.

All this time—while examining in car, on sidewalk; lifting,
dragging about, carrying; attaching tourniquet, checking vital
signs—had dealt with discrete anatomical components. Never
connected dots; never mentally assembled into whole person.
Never *saw* face. Until then.

Was kid . . . !

Little, if any, older than self.

Comprehension dawned suddenly: Had thought was dealing with adult; carrying, in addition to own compact tonnage,
perhaps three times again own weight (heft difficult to judge
when heart is pure, strength is strength of ten). In fact, apart
from peak efforts (unsticking door, traversing flaming moat
with piggyback passenger), exertion level hardly more than
doubled. Could have accomplished most heroics almost as
well without metabolic short circuit. Well . . . maybe.)

However, with understanding came chilling realization:
Clinical picture even less rosy than first appeared. Healthy
blood pressure reading but snare, delusion in child when
hemorrhage a factor. Young cardiovascular systems amazingly
resilient when challenged; simply pump faster, harder as
blood volume diminishes, maintaining adequate pressure the
while.

Right up to sudden, catastrophic, final dissolution; total
failure.

Viewed thus, pulse rate most disquieting: Suggested
important fraction of total blood supply already gone. And
quick review of wound confirmed loss still in progress, though
slowed by tourniquet.

Agonized for endless moments, poignantly aware of limitations of own training; indecision compounded by mental processes blunted by physical, mental fatigue. Knew, of course, what needed doing; but shrank from unavoidable conclusion regarding by whom.

(Granted, possessed requisite knowledge. Inescapable, since Daddy [pathologist or not] one of only two doctors in town, often called upon to perform emergency-room care, usually in own home, invariably at odd hours when no one available to assist but Yours Truly. Watched closely then; listened attentively to accompanying lectures. Even, at proud paternal urging, acquired skill at certain limited surgical techniques, practicing on animal cadavers. But *never*—alone, unaided—so much as placed Band-Aid on *person*.)

However, time—blood—wasting. And own condition now serious impediment to concentration, precision work. (Maybe wasn't burning energy at quadruple usual rate; couldn't know what overload factor consisted of. But knew was exhausted; never experienced such fatigue before.) Nor, without long rest, much nourishment, was condition likely to improve. Which ruled out usefully immediate future. Unless . . .

Weighed options carefully—shuddered. But saw no way out. Closed eyes, directed consciousness inward. Took deliberate, deep breath; held briefly; released slowly, exhausting tension with it. Then—for second time in only minutes—triggered hysterical tap.

Like magic, felt vision clear, hands steady, cramps abate. But not fooled: Heart still hammered; was still fountaining sweat; breathing, though no longer paroxysmal (regular now, slowed to point where wouldn't affect dexterity), still amounted to panting. Condition unchanged: Beneath veneer was still totally exhausted. Tried not to dwell on probable cost when came time to pay Piper. Hoped benefits of sufficient duration—surely wouldn't work third time.

Took seat on campstool at bedside. Bent over leg; drew wound lips apart to assess damage extent, severity. Blood volume made visual structure identification impossible. Removed saline baggie from kit; extended I.V. tube, chopped off end. Squeezing bag to provide pressure, used as hose to irrigate, cleanse area. Worked pretty well, but relief only temporary: Adjoining tissues full of slowly oozing bleeders; and at very bottom of gash, visible now, gaped slice in femoral artery, welling gently afresh with each systole, reflooding area with bright red blood.

Which wouldn't do at all; had to see to work. Pondered briefly; then cranked another turn into tourniquet. Uncomfortable about solution: First Law of Tourniquets holds *must* be loosened every 12 minutes, 18 at outside. Failure to comply results in tissue death downstream, autolysis, ultimately gangrene.

But here question less clear: Two-inch rent in artery wall complicated equation; hydraulic principles demanded concern at least equal to other factors. (Probably more than equal, as continued to debate matter: Blood geysering out through least resistant path certainly of negligible value downstream—and even *if* somehow beneficial, advantages accruing to leg moot if body to which attached promptly expires as side effect.)

But knowledge that choice impending if artery repair not completed within time limit acted as incentive to speed work. Fell to; gathered, set out, organized equipment.

Hosed down wound again. Scrutinized closely; breathed sigh of relief: Tourniquet now achieving desired result; arterial flow stopped. Virtually imperceptible seepage remained from vascularity in surrounding tissues, but makeshift lavage spray adequate remedy.

Next juggled odds quickly, unhappily. Time most critical, true; but upon reflection, concluded potential shock consequences justified investing whatever time necessary to start I.V. before undertaking actual repair.

And if Daddy watching from Above, made him proud: Had I.V. inserted, taped in place, saline flowing—all within single minute. (Practice on long-suffering arm simulacrum [paramedic training aid] paid off: Found vein first try.)

Performed necessarily abbreviated scrub, using drinking water, soap, finishing off with alcohol slosh. Squirmed into rubber gloves with difficulty—not easy, solo, while maintaining asepsis.

(Mostly unworried about infection per se; Teacher's opinion holds *H. post hominems* immune to known human disease. But key words, even if Teacher's very own, are "opinion," "known," and especially *"H. post hominem"* [of which victim surely must be one—but don't *know* that]—and would be humiliating to perform repair successfully; then lose patient to toxemia through preventable gross sepsis. So within limits imposed by surroundings, did best to adhere to sterile procedure.)

Tore open first packet, containing prethreaded fine needle, suture (offered up silent thanks for modern medical technology as did so; would never make good stereotypical female—were *own* life at stake, couldn't thread needle in fewer than 20 tries).

Picked up two hemostats. Stared down into wound. Took deep breath. Seized needle with finely-pointed jaw tips of right-hand hemostat. Commenced.

Proved less difficult than feared. Following initial shock (as learned live patients *warm* inside), technical fascination took over, supplanted apprehension; permitted training to emerge, do job properly. Hemostats gripped needle surely; resultant control wonderfully precise, even down in cramped quarters at bottom of wound. Artery cleanly slit; edges straight; stitches went into place neatly, evenly, closely spaced, just as had when practiced similar repair on hog cadaver under Daddy's direction.

(Sure wish had practiced oftener; developed semblance of professional competence, speed—sealing high-pressure artery called for such tiny stitches; so little time remained and seam so long. . . .)

But wasted none glancing feverishly at watch; concentrated on task at hand. Mind already made up, subconsciously at least: Would *not* risk boy's life to save leg. True, be nice if managed to save it, too—indeed, striving mightily to accomplish repair in time to prevent limb death.

(Mightily—but not *quickly*; never realized vascular surgery so time-consuming.)

For one thing, one-legged comrade poses significant liability in present-day survival-oriented environment. For another, despite pretensions toward calloused pragmatism, must confess to certain esthetic prejudice in favor of physically sound partner—perhaps even, should circumstances so devolve, mate.

(But repair was *taking* so *long*.)

Finally, even granting advantages intrinsic to performing amputation at leisure in Hopkins teaching hospital's modern operating theatre, amidst latest, most advanced medical wonders (who cares—lack even faintest notion of how to operate them), odds slim for patient surviving procedure. Above-knee amputation serious business, truly major surgery; approached with due respect by most veteran of doctors—likelihood of happy outcome, given amateur-level ministrations in procedure so intrinsically fraught, seemed less a question for serious assessment than object of gallows humor.

(But not laughing; was going to find out unless got move-on—taking too long!)

And *didn't want to cut kid's leg off!* Even if somehow managed to avoid killing him in process, would never be able to meet eyes without cringing inside. Yes—despite full knowledge that dummy's own maniacal driving brought on disaster; that consequences on his head alone; that own role limited to saving fool life—would still feel guilty....

(*Damn—taking too long ...!*)

Stole glance at watch—at least 16 minutes gone (guestimating from crash) and good half inch yet unrepaired. What to *do* ...!

Discovered mind not made up after all. Convictions wavered, crumbled at moment of truth. Should continue repair, cross fingers for dispensation from immutable metabolic laws? Or gamble on holding blood loss to tolerable minimum with local pressure now that wound largely closed?

(But how much *is* tolerable minimum—considering losses to present; mitigated by, thus far, just under pint of saline? Further, how effective is local pressure apt to be on femoral spurting—even if wound largely closed?)

Wait. Perhaps another way out. Not cornered—maybe. With luck.

Solution required judicious hemostat placement: Was necessary to grip, pinch together remaining open edges of sliced artery walls with curved jaws; lock handles, sealing shut.

Now could ease tourniquet temporarily, safely...

... If hemostat secure.

... If *stitches* adequate.

... If no other significant bleeders in wound.

... If abruptly releasing balance of blood supply into previously substantially drained extremity didn't trigger final shock collapse through major blood-pressure drop....

... If—oh, *hell!* Simply couldn't stand it any longer—released tourniquet, poised to take action as required.

Wasn't. So glad.

Took time then for breather, suddenly aware of first hints of returning fatigue. Peeled off gloves; finished Gatorade, soup.

Removed patient's shoes, socks; inspected toes as circulation resumed. (Should have at outset: color, temperature key clinical signs to circulation status in leg, foot.)

Sat back, eyes closed, relaxed; breathed deeply, modulating oxygen intake just at fringes of hyperventilation symptoms, hoping to get running start on replacing stores before disintegration set in earnest. Knew wouldn't really help, but beat waiting idly for collapse—for which *still* didn't have time.

After five minutes, retightened tourniquet, donned second pair of rubber gloves, released hemostat. Lavaged site again, flushing away seepage accumulated from surrounding tissues. Resumed needlework.

And marveled: Delicate stitchery, tiny knots suddenly easy—now no longer racing clock, impeding own efforts through tight-collar syndrome.

Soon last stitch in place; femoral repaired. Only closing-up chores remained, housekeeping incidentals: Rejoining severed muscles, closing skin layers; assembling, installing homemade pressure bandage incorporating splint to prevent knee flexion during initial healing process. Much easier going—nothing life-or-death. And could use larger stitches.

Then followed quick, apprehensive review of own condition. No serious portents detected; so stripped limp body (yes, completely; potentially fastest bleeding tissues on male body concealed by shorts; no shrinking damsel I—besides, modesty lousy reason to lose patient through negligence); examined head to foot, identified additional serious (relative term, this, compared to femoral) lacerations; closed with stitch here, tuck there, bandage where appropriate. Finished by covering with blanket, slipping pillow under head, connecting fresh saline baggie to I.V.

Whereupon, quite without warning, found self face down next to bunk, viewing world through darkening, flickering mists (viewing two worlds, point of fact), while breathing transformed abruptly into agonizing gasps, heartbeat stabilized at tachycardiac level, every muscle in body knotted into single huge cramp. Couldn't even cry out. And *wanted* to.

Could have ended pain by triggering posthypnotic relaxation sequence; but sleep—akin to coma—sure to follow immediately, and couldn't afford yet; important details remained undone:

Van's right-side double doors gaped wide; driver's door hung open, too, just as had left it when leaping out. Knew must remedy before letting go: Bound to be dogs in area (have not forgotten [will *never* forget] dog-pack encounter shortly after emerging from shelter); pooches would be pleased indeed to discover van standing open—and ready access to three helpless occupants.

Besides, Terry's water, food dishes not filled since leaving Harpers'; no telling how long oblivion might last. Plus urgent need to stoke own fires before going under; nourishment deficit almost as critical as fatigue.

All of which posed problem:

Body on strike. Brain apparently still operating at what passes for normal function, but commands ignored as burnout reaction intensified, symptoms worsened. Try as might, couldn't elicit so much as purposeful twitch from any voluntary muscle, even unto least finger.

Too busy twitching *in*voluntarily; spasming, in fact: Body jerked, convulsed, shuddered in response to multiple random cramps attacking, releasing, attacking again from head to toe. Ravages flopped body about like chicken recently deprived of head (uncomfortably apt simile; brain quite as unable to communicate with body as if physically separated).

Thrashed for timeless, endless interval. Several seconds at least. Then subsided into gently quivering heap, face up, limbs intertwined in Gordian disarray; cramps abated, muscles relaxing, going limp—pain easing toward residual ache. Would have sighed with relief if such possible, but breathing not among voluntary functions then.

Besides, knew relief was only fool's paradise: Could feel heat; knew face was flushed. Could feel perspiration volume increasing, sweat streaming from entire body; dripping where possible, collecting in hollows elsewhere—one pool quickly threatened to overfill valley formed by nose, cheek; invade eye. And breathing rate such that nose began to run.

Suspected was not pretty sight. But not encouraging to realize Terry, intently peering down from stand, actually had nothing to say. Just made big, round, worried eyes; stared first one eye, then other. And *know* what it takes to dismay my brother.

But worry surely nullest of exercises. Understood problem; knew only solution was food, sleep. And knew *must* finish chores first.

So again turned perception inward. Concentrated. Groped for *ki* within soul. Felt it stir. Created channel, felt flow

begin. Gently guided into right arm. Willed dead meat to
move.

Terribly pleased to note response. And not a little amazed.

Expanded control zone. Levered body into sitting position; then rolled over onto hands, knees. Moving most carefully (nothing worked without painstaking, step-by-step supervision), crawled forward to driver's seat.

Where paused momentarily, mulling options, calculating
odds. Shortest route involved climbing into seat to reach door
handle. But never seriously considered as solution (as well
might have been mountaintop). Or could go around; between
seats, past engine cover, under steering wheel. Farther to
travel. But level.

Even so, had to stop en route, rest. Twice.

Eventually, however, fingers closed limply around door
handle. Marshaled forces for effort—pulled doors shut hard
enough to secure latch. Barely. (Noted, gratefully, front windows rolled up far enough for safety; all others swing-out
construction, couldn't open far enough to pose security risk.)

Then—somehow—managed to turn around under steering
wheel, avoiding getting snagged on pedals in process; set off
on return trip amidships.

Arrived in due course within reach of side door handles.
Again assembled energies (what remained), swung door shut—
even remembering to close in proper order: Rear first, then
front, so overlapping latches engaged instead of rebounding,
negating efforts. Experienced profound thrill, sense of accomplishment, from having done it right.

Considered taking brief time-out for rest but realized
wouldn't help. So heaved self upright on knees, ignoring
tendency for surroundings to orbit own vertical axis. Scooped
up saucer full of parrot seed mix from container on counter;
lumbered (still on knees) to stand, prepared to dump contents into sibling's food cup.

And stopped, confused: Was full. As was—now visible at
far end of perch—water cup.

Set down saucer carefully. Tried to think problem through,
but not easy: Data input too fast; of such anomalous, almost
contradictory nature; mind functioning so slowly. Shook head—
regretted at once: No one in such condition should move
head quickly. Ever. Pain obscured vision momentarily. When
receded, found self leaning against side doors, head resting
against window glass, eyes closed.

Solution obvious, but reached only after labored deliberation: Of course food, water untouched: Had embarked from
Harpers' this morning—several lifetimes prior—*something
under an hour ago!* (Indeed, Albert knew whereof spoke:
Time *is* relative; truly flies when having fun. . . .)

Probably smiled as arrived at conclusion. Which expression surely faded as eyes opened, focusing on glare from
holocaust surrounding Trans Am, mere hundred yards behind
van. Building in which vehicle embedded now well involved:
Smoke, fire gushing from windows many stories up, obviously spreading rapidly.

And given shoulder-to-shoulder nature of downtown
concrete-canyon architecture, only matter of hours before
entire block ablaze—in fact, as flames gutted high-rises,
structures' collapse sure to follow; filling, bridging streets
with burning debris, spreading conflagration from block to
block. Only few more hours before entire city engulfed in fire
storm.

Implications percolated slowly but with finality. Knew
taste of defeat: truly bitter—age-old cliché accurate, but
woefully inadequate.

Not that had given up. Though slowed, dulled, mind still
functioning more or less coherently; knew if passed out now
would never wake: Van's destruction, together with frail
contents, guaranteed as blazing walls crashed down to fill
street where parked.

But problem deeper than mere awareness of threat,
unflagging resolve. Body pushed too far; was finished: Utterly
in grip of fatigue-toxin-overdose-induced myasthenialike collapse, paralysis. Not a single cell from voluntary musculo-
skeletal group responsive to brain's commands—doubt house-
current application would have elicited so much as twitch.

Tears began to trickle from under lids as eyes closed,
body slid limply down door, crumpling onto floor to lie
unmoving. Final thoughts were fading jumble fuzzy with
disappointment, regret, outrage: Had come *so* close; felt so
cheated—

"Hel-*lo*, baby . . . !" wailed Terry in anguished tones.

—and horror: Hoped smoke, fumes, big piece of falling
debris would find us before flames; couldn't bear thought of
retarded twin, gorgeous feathers ablaze, rolling about floor,
struggling, screaming. . . .

*   *   *

Waking was nice: gradual, luxurious process, allowing time to revel in same cozy lack of urgent purpose which always attended first awareness on summer mornings during school vacation. Bed was lovely: firm; made up with cool, clean-smelling sheets; light, soft blanket. And from somewhere floated lilting chords of Beethoven's *Pathétique* sonata.

Once got around to opening eyes, saw that surroundings comprised large, cheerful, well-appointed bedroom, simply reeking of restrained good taste.

Had no idea where might be, how got there, or why; and didn't much care. Was sufficient that felt marvelously rested, deliciously comfortable—until essayed first lazy stretch.

Accompanying yawn brought cognizance of tube up nose; a discovery so startling, almost distracted from surprise of learning right arm immobile, apparently strapped down. Deliberate swallow confirmed tube also present in esophagus. Unpleasantly so.

Followed tube with eyes to bottle hanging on stand at bedside. Didn't need to read label to recognize Isocal HCN, first choice amongst medical community for endogastric feeding of comatose patients.

And next to Isocal hung partial baggie of Ringer's lactate— saline with electrolytes added. From it ran tube to I.V. —plugged into right arm.

As pondered these phenomena (with rapidly dwindling enthusiasm), yet another anomalous sensation intruded amongst already churning thoughts. Or perhaps *lack* of sensation more accurate: For first time in living memory, had awakened without awareness of overfull bladder. Which realization flowed without pause into dawning perception that Something Was Amiss in *that* region as well.

Began immediate left-handed exploration to determine quality, extent of damages. Was dismayed to learn attire consisted of overlarge (knee-length) tee shirt—and *diaper* . . . ! Complete with safety pins. And, speaking as expert babysitter, quite professionally executed. (Strategically located slit in crotch of mortifying garment admitted [as suspected] Foley catheter.)

Further exploration revealed substantially absent eyebrows, lashes; head hair appreciably shorter in spots than remembered it. Had obviously been brushed out, breaking off scorched, shriveled ends—

Oh! Memory returned in bewildering rush. Bringing

with it sudden dread, rampant curiosity: *Where was Terry?*
What about *kid?* What happened? More particularly, *who*
happened it?

Reasonable questions, to be sure. When last participated
in events, score was Candy zero, Grim Reaper nine—in
ten-point match. Lethal probabilities abounded; situation,
without exaggeration, dire.

Known on-site cast included Terry; concussed kid (with
stiff leg, profound blood loss, stitches all over hide); and, of
course, Yours Truly—plucky neighborhood zombie. Terry didn't
get us out of fix; get me cleaned up, plugged in, plumbed,
drained. *I* sure didn't—and kid was . . .

No! Enough. . . . Without facts, speculation worse than
nonproductive; downright *maddening* . . . !

Had to find out for self—couldn't lie quietly in bed,
waiting for someone *(whomever!)* to walk in, in own good
time, and fill in blanks (selectively—telling patient "only
what's good for her"). Had to know—*now* . . . !

Doggedly returned to self-examination. Found tender
areas of pinkish skin on forehead, hands, ankles—another few
seconds and would have been serious burns. Determined all
muscles, while weak, again responded to wishes. (Almost
unbearably relieved: Daddy had recited cases where muscle
overuse resulted in permanent burnout.)

Concluded, at length, was sound enough to dispense
with life-support toys; return to transacting personal business
personally. Could eat faster, absorb protein, calories more
efficiently orally than through tube (certainly enjoy it more).
Further, examination demonstrated no clinical evidence of
dehydration; no point, then, to retaining I.V. And could
damn well go potty myself!

Okay, no reason couldn't get up—just matter of unplugging
tubes. (Straightforward-sounding, simple statement of intent:
easy to say.)

Effectuation, however, less so. Sensations accompanying
do-it-yourself nasogastric tube removal unlikely to find place
in catalog of experiences without which life is not complete.
Same for catheter. Neither truly painful coming out. Actually.
Exactly. Quite. But felt *horrid.* . . .

I.V., on other hand, did hurt. But over quickly; slight
bleeding stopped immediately with momentary pressure.

Then addressed question of standing. Knew was weak,

but fairly certain could manage. With care, slowly, taking very short steps.

Question of very short steps, however, proved premature. Spent appreciable interval sitting on edge of bed, head between knees, waiting for room to stabilize. Which did, eventually.

Whereupon, gingerly stood, paused briefly to verify balance in working order; then employed selfsame care, very short steps, to navigate slowly to door.

Hall in which found self was higher-ceilinged, wider than those in houses which constituted experience during formative years. Décor, too, beyond what have come to recognize as norm.

Piano now into first measures of unfamiliar solo transcription of Wagner's *Rienzi* overture. Stood briefly, listened.

(Daddy included in shelter collection essentially entire Andre Perrault international catalog; record collection upstairs in house almost equaled. Have myself spent important fraction of short life exposed to, absorbing, enjoying classical music. Plus Daddy once took me to Horowitz concert in Chicago, where, in three too-short hours, artist demonstrated all he'd learned about playing piano over perhaps 70-odd years of training, practice, dedication. Have, despite youth, acquired discerning ear.)

This pianist good. Possibly even *that* good. But didn't recognize touch. Wondered who might be; when recording made.

Followed music down hall to balcony—from either end of which descended wide, sweeping staircase (of sort on which Cinderella lost slipper), terminating in foyer into which Daddy's whole house would fit without crowding (if tucked to side to miss chandelier).

Glided down nearer staircase, feeling like figure in dream. Music coming from partially open door on far side of foyer. Crossed room, silently pushed door open.

Terry's tee stand stood next to gleaming ebony concert grand at center of library/study whose shelves held books in numbers rivaling perhaps even Daddy's shelter library—and all hardbacks, most leather. Harebrained sibling himself *(alive!)* relaxed on one foot, raptly watching, listening as my erstwhile patient, leg bandaged but now unsplinted, played and music flowed through room, filling heart, crumbling barriers behind which had thought *those* emotions safely locked away forever.

Moved silently into room; held out arm. Twin's eyes snapped wide; almost leaped in eagerness to swarm aboard. Settled in chair just behind, to side of oblivious musician. Terry discharged immediate hysterical gladness over reunion through series of head dives, cheek rubs; then snuggled down in lap, pressed close, sighed, closed eyes. Held my baby brother tight in arms.

And, soundlessly, cried. Cried for Momma, for Daddy; for unknown, unremembered flesh-and-blood parents; for Teacher; for all my friends; for acquaintances; for whole world of strangers—cried for all *dead*.

Cried for Terry, miraculously alive when should have burned to death. Cried for boy—*another person!*—incredibly still alive in spite of crash, terrible wounds, my bumbling treatment, fire—sitting now at piano, playing as composer only might have dared to dream.

Cried for me—for grief, for relief, for joy.

Cried for past. Cried for future. Cried for hope. . . .

Cried while boy finished *Rienzi*, swept into Rachmaninoff, Chopin, Brahms, many others; all from memory, most full orchestral works somehow transcribed for piano alone; all played as if keyboard itself were come to life, complete with soul demanding outlet, expression.

Boy finished Berlioz's *Symphonie Fantastique* with marvelously cacaphonic climax whose violence quite made up for missing orchestra; tiptoed with startling gentleness into Pachelbel's *Canon in D*. And into resultant sweet tranquility he spoke; voice low, tightly controlled: "I thought you were dead."

Didn't reply—correction: Couldn't.

"Terry woke me trying to rouse you—he and I have become friends waiting for you, and I've had time to read your journal. He was down from his stand, scrambling all over you, flapping his wings, pulling at you desperately, nuzzling you, screaming at you. That's what woke me up."

Lapsed into silence for long moments, music flowing without pause. "The whole block next to us was in flames. The heat was incredible and wreckage was coming down all around us. The street was filling up with burning debris and the building on the other side was starting to go as well—it looked like something out of an old movie of London during the Blitz."

Again fell silent, moving bandaged leg restively, but

music never hesitated. "I had a hell of a time getting into the driver's seat with my leg in that splint, not to mention maneuvering the I.V. hose and pouch; and I knew I'd better leave it in place—I was weak as a kitten, and the blood all over the place made it obvious why. Finally I hung the I.V. pouch on the rear-view mirror, stuck the leg out the window, and used my right leg to drive. It wasn't easy, shifting an unfamiliar transmission without using the clutch. I don't think I hurt it.

"I got us out of there and came home. I thought you were dead." Music soared gently, filling lengthening silence with beauty, while boy's breathing rate mounted visibly, settled gradually. Only quarter profile visible from own vantage, but wet cheek's glint unmistakable. Yet when resumed, voice was still almost conversational.

"You *looked* dead. You were grayish-white and you didn't appear to be breathing at all. Terry wouldn't let me touch you at first; he crouched on your body, wings half-spread, feathers fluffed to make him seem three times life-size, neck outstretched, that huge hooked bill open and threatening, and making a *noise* in his throat that..."

Voice trailed off, but fingers never faltered.

"...that reminded me of the sound my mother made when she found my father's body. He was the first to go in the plague." Tendons stood out in neck, but music continued unbroken.

"I thought you were dead; so I concentrated on trying to comfort Terry, soothing him, getting him to accept me, to come to me. Only after that was I able to attend to you—and notice that you were still perspiring. I had never heard of a dead person perspiring—I've never seen anyone *sweat* like that—so I brought you inside, got you cleaned up, and put you to bed.

"You were running an astonishing temperature for a live person—the books I've read suggest that people don't survive at 109 degrees, and it didn't seem very likely that you'd manage it much longer—so I packed you in ice and started an I.V. to put back some of that water sluicing off you. I wired you to our EKG—

"Oh, yes, we have a fully equipped emergency room here in the house. This was the kind of neighborhood, back when we had lots of fussy, hypochondriac old neighbors and relatives, where one couldn't afford to be without one; it would get you talked about, at the very least, and more likely disinherited. All the house staff were required to be fully conversant with the use of all the equipment, just in case.

"And while there was a stigma attached to people who possessed those skills—menial work, you know, performed by the 'servant class'—and even though I've never been sick in my life . . ."

Bingo! Heart skipped a beat—*never been sick . . . !*

". . . I judged that it was the sort of thing that might well come in handy someday. So I kept my eyes open—and bribed several of our retainers, incidentally—and became a pretty fair EMT, if I do say so myself. But *you . . .*" Narrative faltered again; music bridged gap as breathing discipline labored to restore control.

"You were my valedictorian exercise." Declaration followed by long breath, uninterrupted music. "Keeping you alive called for everything I learned from our staff, extensive study on my own, and more luck than anyone has a right to expect—yours or mine, I'm not sure.

"You were a mess."

"Thank you." Blurted reply after boy's last four words but before content registered. Experienced momentary pang of dismay lest he take it wrong, be offended. How could he know how slowly own thoughts functioning; how far behind utterance comprehension lagged.

But mattered not. Hadn't heard. Probably not listening at all; wrapped in own thoughts. Monologue continued without pause:

"Your heart stopped twice. The first time I managed to restart you with CPR alone; the second time it took three jolts with the defibrillator paddles and an injection of adrenaline directly into your heart. *That's* something the staff didn't teach me. . . ."

Without bidding, hand drifted to chest; fingers sought, found tiny bandage just to left of sternum, between fourth, fifth ribs.

"Between the ice—courtesy of the industrial-grade icemaker in the bar in the ballroom—and the I.V., I got your temperature back down somewhere near normal and restored your fluid level. That took most of the rest of the day.

"But still you were fading almost as I watched. For some reason your tissues apparently were consuming themselves, as happens in extreme starvation, but faster—which made no sense to me as you were in good flesh and apparently healthy otherwise. So I intubated you gastrically and started you on the Isocal. And to save time, to start nourishing your cells immediately, without waiting for you to metabolize the Isocal, I briefly piggybacked a filtered solution of it into your I.V. and changed you from straight saline to Ringer's.

"Fortunately, I had to answer Nature's Call myself at about that time, and that started me thinking: All that fluid had to go somewhere. You had stopped perspiring; logic offered but a single alternative: If your sphincter held, you would rupture your bladder.

"So I catheterized you. Yes, that's something else the servants didn't teach me. But according to the book, I probably did it correctly—you didn't bleed and haven't shown signs of infection.

"And you confirmed my suspicion promptly by filling the first container in a single nonstop gush. I had to mop the floor after fumbling the container change on the fly.

"You probably don't want to hear the details of how I coped with your bowels; but I can attest that you were marvelously regular until you emptied out what you had eaten before and were down to the Isocal residue; of which—I'm glad to say—there's almost none. But that's why you're in a diaper. And I've been transferring you back and forth between two beds as cleanup demands necessitated changing them. And you."

Shook head, almost shuddered, but music never wavered. "Ever since I attained puberty and learned what it implies, my primary ambition regarding girls has revolved around getting their clothes off. Et cetera. That has not been the case with you; I'm not into necrophilia, and a catheter is not conducive to romance: There was no 'et cetera.'

"And though I have acquired an exhaustively detailed, painstakingly thorough, unflinchingly intimate familiarity with your every tangible aspect—in fact I learned more about you physically than any girl in my experience—I must admit that I would have traded gladly every success I've enjoyed in the past in that respect at any moment during these six days for the privilege of getting you dressed. You have not been a fun date."

Can't say just when lost track of soliloquy; drifted off into own blissful, music-filled reverie. Didn't have to listen; details irrelevant—had *found* somebody . . . !

Months of accumulated desperate tension drained from soul like sand spilling from ripped sack, leaving slightly limp, giddy euphoria suffusing entire being. Wouldn't have been surprised had started glowing from head to foot. Was supremely happy.

And not without degree of justification—not leaping to conclusions; some data in already (sketchy, obviously preliminary, but [beyond mere fact of his *being*] encouraging): Appears to be good prospect. Hominem beyond doubt: obviously intelligent (piano talent alone points toward genius-level intellect; and when coupled with resourcefulness displayed in keeping me alive, plus syntactic evidence apparent from first words, leaves little room to doubt quality of brains). Further, demonstrated gentlemanly instincts. Additionally, sound physical specimen, apart from wounds (apparently healing nicely); with pleasant, well-bred features.

Finally, was good to helpless birdbrain, and idiot twin *likes* him (Terry spends bulk of waking hours rowing with only one oar in water—but is *never* wrong about people).

Not perfect, of course: Will be period of adjustment; may require gentle retraining (at bare minimum, driving habits need attention!).

But issue not impending. "Ever after" is long time, and too young now myself for twosome involvement; while boy (implied conquests notwithstanding) hardly year, two years older. Question resolvable at leisure, without deadlines.

Because *doesn't matter now* . . . ! Teacher was right—*really are other people out there* . . . !

Hominems—*my* people! Perhaps 150,000, according to Teacher. Maybe more, maybe less—who cares!—numbers immaterial. . . .

Are others!

And we're going to find them.

Together . . .

VOLUME III—Part I
Quest

Surprise, Posterity, here I am again . . . !

Gracious, who'd have thought, only months ago—still alive (knock wood) and everything.

Not crowing, mind you; must admit, have been lucky. Quite lucky. *Incredibly* lucky.

For one thing, ultimate war's bionuclear efficiency imparted breathtaking new scope to definition of "overkill"; for another, rigors intrinsic to existence in subsequent environment doing much the same for "unforgiving."

In fact, until quite recently your Humble Histographer brooded over eminently defensible, ever-deepening gloomy conviction that own small self constituted Earth's entire remaining sapient population. Under such circumstances, "mere" survival ranks as clearly epic achievement—whether due in any part to own feeble efforts or not.

No, certainly not crowing. Pleased. And not a little surprised.

But pleasure, surprise, now secondary to almost inexpressible relief: *Have found somebody!*

Finally—a real live *person* . . . ! That he happens to be intelligent, able-bodied, sensitive, not unattractive, brilliant musician to boot—all immaterial.

Quite suffices is *alive*!

For, therefore (*ipso facto,* and in conjunction with dogged faith in Teacher's opinions [as set forth in Final Letter], together with own unquenchable optimism), presence of *one* proves are *others,* too.

Must be.

Somewhere. . . .

However, have no intention of rushing headlong into romance, even if does turn out to be only game in town. Am only 11, after all. Shall indeed "carry out duty" for species' benefit when time comes, should ultimate necessity manifest; but much prefer relationship growing from mutual attraction, compatability, respect.

Not that would be all that difficult (apart from initial strain intrinsic to meeting under present coercive circumstances) to become attracted to new acquaintance. Possesses many good qualities, few (at first blush) unforgivable faults. Not bad specimen, viewed objectively.

Which is not to suggest totally lacks peculiarities, fair number of which would *not* be missed. For instance: Don't know his *name* . . . ! Won't give straight answer; merely offers sidelong glance, elevates near-side brow, smirks knowingly, replies, "Think of me as 'Adam.'"

Now, not prude, nor naïve, don't mind *entendres*, of whatever multiplication factor, but *that's old*! Bet Eve thought so, too.

(Wonder, sometimes, why always seems necessary to make so *many* allowances when dealing with 12-, 13-year-old boys [approximate real age, silly straight-faced assertion of 18 notwithstanding]. After all, I'm 11—is it *so* unreasonable to expect from boys of comparable vintage demeanor at least as balanced, reasonable, logical, dignified?)

Secondly, is genuine maniac behind wheel: Ambition, prior to End of World, was to become Grand Prix driver; campaign through Europe, world; win World Championship. Even days, that is; on odd days wanted to join NASCAR circuit, tour southern U.S., bumping fenders with "Good Ole Boys" at 195 miles an hour on superspeedways in Grand National stock cars—which nearly describes how we met: at downtown Baltimore street corner—avoided collision by hair's-breadth.

(What? Regard unlikely only two people in city would "meet by accident"? Think again—better still, ask neighborhood insurance-history buff about famous 1902 claim wherein only two cars in entire state of Ohio involved in intersection crunch.)

Adam's third peculiarity is he . . . he . . .

No. Can't say it. Excerpt from conversation at breakfast first morning posthibernation sufficiently illustrative.

Were bringing each other up-to-date on life stories.

Adam had distinct advantage of me: Read Vol. II while I lay in coma.

(Another indication of quality of boy's brains, incidentally: To decipher contents, necessary to teach himself Pitman shorthand theory—did so in *single day* [took me two!]).

Have, of course, exacted blood oath not to exercise newfound skill by violating *this* journal; thoughts immortalized in diary constitute—*must* be regarded as—privileged communication between writer, History.

Anyway, since my knowledge of Adam then quite meager (sharp as tack, clever at EMT work, good cook, brilliant pianist, and drives like mishap studying to become catastrophe) boy necessarily carried bulk of conversation. Was filling me in on high points of existence prior to Armageddon:

Parents unlikely pair: mother state senator, all-around busy, important person; father music director of Baltimore Symphony. Adam divided time between studying Muse, eavesdropping on Moving & Shaking within state government.

Determined early on art more fun than politics. And magnitude of talent soon emerged: genuine prodigy on piano; first public recital, age seven. "Father was so proud; mother, too. And I was tickled by all the adulation—amused, really, that something so easy should generate so much attention.

"But it didn't go to my head; I didn't have time for such foolishness. I was obsessed with perfecting my skill and committing to memory more and ever more selections. And while I did try to devote equal attention to all the great masters, I gradually found myself spending more and more time studying the works and methods of one in particular. In a remarkably short time I came to be known not so much as a prodigy but as a *Bach*ward child."

See . . . ? Down through centuries we women have put up with menfolk who caroused; stuffed faces without thanks; missed baths; littered floors with cigar butts, ashes, smelly socks; nobly marched off to war, leaving us to fend for selves (brought home loathsome diseases, often as not); beat us; and, not infrequently, simply abandoned families altogether, because responsibility proved too much trouble.

Okay. Can cope with that. If absolutely must. One way or another. Possibly with diplomacy; more probably to detriment of male in question. But can cope.

This, however, another matter entirely! Lad inexhaustible font of misused words. Delights in puns of every description, lower the better; also in perverting familiar constructions to own depraved ends: Assembling engine is "mantling"; accumulation of scattered components is "persion," competent person is "ept," etc. When I made mistake of suggesting words existed which did job more precisely, without requiring listener to perform involuted dissection, analysis, Adam replied was fond of *Bach*-constructions.

Truly is: Can dredge up Bach-related adjectives to mis-fit any occasion; more inapt or strained the useage, happier seems to make him. For instance, past girl friends' phone numbers listed in Little Bach Book; smug about Bach porches, his Bach-alaureate, skill at Bach-gammon; swimming Bach-stroke in Bach-waters during laid-Bach vacations at cottage in Bach-woods, etc.

But peripheral consideration; usually unexpected, often funny (sometimes over head), only occasionally irritating. A plus, generally. I think.

However, further problem exists, presenting complications of another order of magnitude entirely: Adam interested in initiating repopulation project. Immediately or sooner. Wants to get *me* on *my* Bach. (Actually, "obsessed with" probably more accurate descriptive than "interested in.") If, at given moment, somehow fails to be in midst of straightforward proposition, is hinting. Broadly. Constantly.

Initially broached (figuratively speaking) subject while describing rigors of growing up rich (still at same first breakfast—as I sat there, hardly 16 hours postcoma; barely alive; pale, thin ghost of former self).

". . . so even after both the grand jury and congressional committee absolved me of responsibility, the school withdrew permission to park the Lamborghini in the student lot, I had to be driven to class every day, everybody knew, it was terribly embarrassing, how long will it be before you're recovered enough to sleep with me?"

Paused; glanced from corner of eye, then quickly away; waited for reaction. And waited. And waited. . . .

Because object of affection having difficulty making mouth work. Reaction complicated: First, was dumbfounded; totally unexpected conversational turn, straight out of blue. Second, genuine no-foolin' *proposition* something with which, at my age, have had little—oh, all right!—*no* experience. Third, blasé expectation—nay; cavalier *assumption*—of automatic assent quite took breath away—*haven't even decided to keep him yet*...!

Went from startlement to shock, directly thence to offended feminine sensibilities; but hesitated momentarily, reflecting before venting feelings—all in space of single breath. Concluded, after brief deliberation, probably not Adam's fault. Entirely. From wrong side of tracks, after all; can't be expected to behave like normal person. Besides, is young, healthy; puberty in full cry, bursting with urges. Doubtless views me as Heaven-sent solution; perhaps even hard-won prize, considering effort invested in saving life—of which notion shall promptly disabuse him...!

(But consider parallel situation: If, when puppy does Terrible Thing in house, is immediately shot, replaced; is owner likely to end up with properly housebroken pet? Ever? Similarities existed here. Adam entitled to benefit of doubt during probationary/training period. Decided to let him live— pending....)

So closed mouth firmly; took deep breath, released deliberately; declined, with thanks.

"Oh, come *on*!" he coaxed heartily. "We're both healthy young adults..."

(Histographer's Note: Actually *said* "adults.")

"...we like each other, and it's just not *healthy* not to have a proper outlet for our tensions."

Now, recognize would be considered "old enough" in certain (now departed) cultures. Granted; not disputing point (nor implying *that* was reason departed). Further, addressing question from purely mechanical perspective, am very probably "big enough" as well.

However. Pragmatic as do try to be in every respect, find I cannot narrow down viewpoint; regard *this* question as solely practical matter—to say nothing of notion of debasing currency to point where becomes no more than casual recreation, temporary ennui remedy. True, not entitled to advance own opinion as expert—lack firsthand knowledge. Must rely upon instincts developed through exposure to Momma, Daddy, Teacher; their unvoiced opinions reflected in conduct toward selves, one another, world at large—and especially me.

No, can*not* put finger on precise dates, times, places; nor words, acts underlying own attitude. But do know that ingrained into very being is conviction that sex is small-but-important part of very complicated whole; blending liking-respect-tenderness-caring-need-love-coitus with implied life-long partnership-family commitment, babies optional.

Am *not* ready for babies: not physically, not emotionally—not *now!* Nor commitment. Yet. And if can't cope with package *in toto* (including deliberate election to proceed to motherhood or not), then strongly misdoubt wisdom . . .

Well, can work up to it, step-by-step. And undoubtedly will (if do keep him). But *not* beginning with *that* step. Period. No matter what "practical considerations" might seem to dictate!

So initially sought to counter Adam's enthusiasm with logic: Reminded him of age: Probably not fertile yet; and even if wanted to conceive at 11—and *don't!*—well-known amongst OB-GYN trade is fact that excessively young mothers produce generally frail, sickly offspring.

"I'm sure that was true of *Homo sapiens* women," Adam replied with irritatingly comfortable superiority, as usual ignoring objection's nontechnical aspect; "but how much data has been accumulated on *us?*"

(One of boy's less appealing qualities: Instantly pounces on flawed reasoning; zooms in for kill without hesitation; gives no quarter, takes no prisoners.)

"No, I don't know if it's true of us," I admitted. "How *could* I know? How could *anybody* know? Who would have had time to assemble a data base on us? Only a few hundred people knew about us at all, even before; and they didn't have time . . ."

"Besides," Adam interjected smoothly, "if you're not fertile yet, then what does it matter? The only question we need to consider is whether it's good for us; whether it will increase our chances of survival by improving our mental, emotional, and physical condition—which it will, you know; all the texts say so.

"But if even the *possibility* of conceiving, and the potential effect of your age on our child, really bothers you that much and you'd rather hold off starting a family, that's easily dealt with. So there's nothing to prevent us from enjoying the benefits of an active, healthy, satisfying physical relationship. See . . . ?"

Open mouth to reply. Stopped. Noticed bottom-line issue well on way to vanishing amidst mechanics of debate.

Quickly reviewed dialogue immediately preceding; concluded misdirection not accidental.

(Obviously Adam exposed to unsavory influences during impressionable years [perhaps too much time spent in company of mother's state government cronies]; had picked up verbal shell game skills—plus who *knows* what other tools comprising basic political arsenal.)

Realized then: Might be well to watch step around Adam conversationwise. Always heretofore considered concept of "promise" sacrosanct, orientation which may prove liability: Would rather not find have agreed to something which, through failure to understand, follow transactional semantics to proper conclusion, binds me to something contrary to expectations, intentions.

So switched to more direct approach: "I don't *care* whether it's true or not. That isn't the point. I'm too young— I'm *not* going to get involved in sex. Not *now*...!"

Like most *H. post hominems*, Adam has extremely sensitive hearing. But can be quite hard of *listening*: "Don't get your Bach up," he soothed. "I know, I know—this all has hit you pretty suddenly, and you haven't had time to think it through. But you know as well as I do that there're only the two of us. We don't have a choice—we *need* each other. And even though 'need' is an awfully broad term, the heart of it, under these circumstances, is sex—*I need you*...!"

"I don't *want* to," I repeated, somewhat more firmly (possibly because "need" touched nerve, eroded conviction). "At least not yet. I don't doubt that one day I *may* want to—at the very least, I will cooperate to the extent necessary to rebuild the population.

"But I *don't* have a need yet—and I bet you don't either; though I'll grant you've probably got a pretty urgent *want*, the same as any adolescent male. We're both too young— certainly *I* am. But even if we weren't, I've never heard of celibacy killing anyone, so I don't think we're in any immediate danger; at least not from that quarter. And if it's physical tensions you're bothered with, you know the solution to that just as well as I do.

"For Heaven's sake," I finished impatiently; "*look* at me—I'm almost still a *boy*...!"

"I have looked at you," he replied with a knowing grin; "in the most minute detail, for six long days while you were comatose; while changing your diaper, bathing you, and maintaining your catheter. No one would mistake you for a boy anymore. You are somewhat unfinished here and there, but you're very pretty. And I'm beginning to regret having been such a gentleman while I had you at my mercy. Did I miss my golden opportunity?"

"I thought you weren't into snuggling with corpses, and found catheters unromantic."

"I'm not, they are, so I didn't. But looking at you was very pleasant, in spite of your condition. And you aren't unconscious now, and there're no tubes in the way. Frankly, I don't understand your attitude—I'd think gratitude alone would be enough to motivate you, if not compassion for a suffering fellow survivor. . . ." This last delivered in tones of hurt puzzlement; wearing a trusting, wide-eyed, cocker-spaniel-puppy expression.

(Adam shrewd at picking apart others' arguments, but reckless about leaving opening for riposte. Always a mistake: No one who knows me would doubt willingness to snub slack once victim has rope enough to hang himself.)

"I'm glad you feel that way. That means you *do* understand how I feel about it, and you'll be happy to quit pestering me—if not from compassion, then out of gratitude."

"Gratitude . . . ?" Adam's expression fell. Belatedly realized he'd violated logic matrix, blown argument; but too stubborn to admit it, change tack, quit with grace.

"Yes, 'gratitude.' Who pulled you out of that fire and stitched up your leg?"

"Who got in the way and made me crash in the first place?"

"Who was driving like a lunatic?"

"Oh, yeah . . . ?"

"*Yeah!*"

(Have been several conversations like that since then; all revolving around oldest disputed topic; all concluding in same general vein.)

Apart from that, though, Adam seems pretty neat so far. Which is part of reason have not taken sterner line with him regarding nonstop campaign against my "virtue." Could, certainly, and would bring results. Knows my karate ranking from reading journal; knows am well able to enforce wishes, if so choose.

But don't choose. Yet. And truly hope never becomes necessary. Only five when Momma Foster died, but had

managed by then to impart to me her appreciation for
fragility of male ego; care required to preserve from unnecessary bruising. Have encountered nothing during subsequent
years to suggest wisdom of altering view (indeed, quite to
contrary).

Key word, of course, is "unnecessary"; would not hesi-
tate to warn of impending consequences, employ force as
required. But ever been possible for perceptive, intelligent
woman to avoid direct confrontation while still getting own
way: Merely question of discerning where buttons located,
cataloguing effect of each, pushing in proper sequence—without
getting caught at it. . . .

To that end, am studying Adam: Feeling out responses to
subliminal suggestions; learning what psychological knee jerks
exist, where kept, how triggered; reactions to my emotions,
etc.

But proceeding carefully. Not uncomplicated lad, nor at
all stupid (difficulty compounded by political psychology absorbed at mother's knee); will spoil everything if suspects
manipulation attempt in progress. At least two probable
consequences foreseeable: One, will realize am trying to
avoid controlling him by force; and two, thereby have nose
rubbed in very fact that I *can*.

Heart of problem, of course, is fact that Adam, while
surely hominem, *not* member of AA group—I know: All
names, addresses in Tarzan File. And *everyone* else alive
today on planet, by definition, must be considered AB—must
be regarded, absent substantial evidence to contrary, potential hazard to own life, limb, property. Wherefore, despite
uniformly favorable data accumulated to present—including
Terry's opinion—still reserving judgment; maintaining slightly
watchful attitude where Adam concerned.

(True, beginning to feel something of an ingrate by this
point; but learned through experience: Teacher *not* busy-
body; not in habit of volunteering superfluous suggestions.
On rare occasions when did go to trouble of offering advice
[particularly when so unambiguously phrased as to constitute,
unmistakably, Considered Opinion], proceeding notwithstanding recommendation almost inevitably followed by Consequences, usually regrettable in nature.)

Have known Adam (consciously) only two days. Most of
what have learned thus far limited to hearsay (his) or adduced
evidence (own conclusions, based on observations). Have not,

with own eyes, seen anything concrete enough to justify abandoning caution entirely—or confirm, for that matter. But preliminary impression favorable; rather suspect will cancel alert shortly; embrace (figuratively speaking) new acquaintance as companion, friend, partner—perhaps even (conceivably, someday, should events so devolve) mate.

Which will be distinct relief: Paranoia most wearing perspective for extended use; tiresome way to go through life. Trust more comfortable outlook—except when blows up in face, of course.

But doubt this apt to. Have often, during brief lifetime, entertained self by "people-watching"; plus always took advantage of opportunities to meet, get to know, as many people as possible. Thereby acquired something resembling competence at picking friends (at least those whom so labeled never betrayed trust). And while do perhaps weight Terry's judgment more heavily than should when forming own impressions of strangers, am not myself totally helpless in that regard.

And without being able to put finger on any specific event or reason why, feel *comfortable* around Adam. Have from first meeting postcoma. Almost as if have known him forever . . .

(Note to Significant Discovery Department: Just this moment realized—have felt this way with precisely three other people in whole life: Daddy, Momma, Teacher. Wonder what *that* means. Sounds like sort of question probably best not delved into too deeply just now. Or resolved in haste.)

Well, haste unnecessary; will have ample time to debate imponderables. Expect to be here several weeks at least, resting, eating prodigiously, exercising: Rehabilitation after physiological burnout amounts to substantial project; side effects no joke—not kidding when said almost died; did really bang-up job on self. Adam weighed me as part of initial diagnostic procedure; and, based on his data, had lost nearly 20 percent of total body weight, between water, tissue.

No, not sort of experience one bounces back from overnight. And still long way from even first bounce.

In fact, now that I think about it, this is quite enough for first effort: I'm *tired . . .*!

Good night, Posterity.

*   *   *

Help . . . ! Adam trying new approach: devious, insidious, unexpected—*fattening!*

Also wonderful: Who would expect servant-raised-and-educated, musically gifted, apparently hedonistic, smooth-talking young stranger to be competent cook—no, cancel that—inspired master chef? Can't imagine where he finds this incredible variety of makings—meats, fruit, vegetables, etc. All prepared with genuine magic touch. . . .

(Manufacture same dishes myself; results merely adequate. But let Adam walk through kitchen, stop at stove, sniff pots' contents. somehow Something Happens—something *wonderful!*)

And in present condition, trying to regain lost tissue, cannot begin to take objective view of offerings: Anything failing to bite me first goes to stoke fires (Adam has already used expression "feeding frenzy" [smiled when said it, but doubt really kidding]). In short, am ravenous; appetite running amok; not responsible for actions in presence of food—*any* food. But especially *this* food . . . !

Example, breakfast today: two homemade whole-wheat pancakes, dripping with real butter, drowned in clover honey; delicate two-egg/ham-cheese-mushroom omelette; four-ounce filet, crisp outside, medium-rare inside; hash-brown potatoes; ten-ounce orange juice, 16-ounce milk; megavitamin/mineral pills; huge bowl of *fresh strawberries!* (Where could he *possibly* have found fresh strawberries . . . ?)

Midmorning snack: half dozen hot, fresh blueberry muffins with thick pat of butter melted into each; big bowl of chocolate mint ice cream dripping with thick homemade hot fudge topping, sprinkled with nuts, buried under blanket of real whipped cream, capped with cherry; 16-ounce glass of homemade eggnog.

Lunch: large green salad covered with Adam's own *bleu* cheese dressing; two-inch-thick slice of rare standing-rib roast smothered in mushrooms, gravy; baked potato (skin crisped, suitable for crunching like cookie; insides removed, cream whipped, butter blended, then replaced); tender cauliflower swimming in exquisite cheese sauce; side dish of applesauce; fresh hot rolls; another 16-ounce glass of milk. Plus dessert: incredible *something* combining best features of angel food cake (laced with chocolate chips), vanilla pudding, covered with (so help me) miniature hot toasted marshmallows.

Midafternoon snack: two slices of completely egg-and-milk-saturated French toast, sprinkled with cinnamon, powdered sugar, liberally paved with butter pats, and dripping with maple syrup; colossal chocolate milkshake.

Whew... ! Isn't time for dinner yet; don't know what's planned. But doesn't matter; merely reviewing day's menu thus far imparts great sense of confidence for future (plus makes me hungry again): Know full well that whatever may be, will be work of sheerest culinary artistry. (Will *taste* good, too... !)

Obviously this is tough life: Gradually wake somewhere around midmorning to aromas wafting up from kitchen as Adam prepares breakfast. Ring to let him know am back among living.

Somehow puts preparations on Hold. Appears instantly in room to help me from bed (can walk myself, but balance not reliable yet; still awfully weak) to potty for morning dump. Thence into tub (which previously filled without waking me); turns on Jacuzzis, administers massage to get blood flowing again. Bathes me gently yet efficiently; impersonally, without "taking liberties" (either teasingly and/or in earnest), despite intimate contact necessarily involved (and notwithstanding undisguised libidinous ambitions). Assists me from tub, dries me with huge, thick, bath-sheet towels; dresses me to extent required by day's schedule (usually robe, slippers); dries, combs hair. Then, steadied by his arm, I walk to kitchen, where he completes breakfast, somehow picking up preparations where left off without even hint of difficulty.

After breakfast, again leaning on shoulder, I take quarter-mile hike (once around house, *inside*—no kidding!) for exercise; then lounge in library, reading while Adam practices piano. (In times past people world over paid *money* to hear poorer keyboard work than I get daily as private Muzak while enjoying fruits of most impressive book collection have ever seen.)

Adam wakes me when time to return to kitchen for midmorning snack (invariably fall asleep on couch); then back to library for more music, reading (as long as eyes stay open).

And then time for lunch. Afterward we repeat therapeutic hike; following which I nap until afternoon snack-time. Generally manage to remain awake thereafter, reading, until dinner.

After dinner Adam gets serious: Plays the Good Stuff; each work straight through rather than, as in practice, taking run after run at trouble spots. Makes it count. For that I stay awake. Don't even read.

Evening finally winds up with modest bedtime smackrel (no more than 1,500 calories or thereabouts); and so to bed, perchance to dream (generally of food).

Despite nursing schedule, Adam finds time to keep himself clean, groomed; kitchen spotless; do laundry; as well as housecleaning (dusting, carpets, etc.) for those areas of house I get to see; and still is as conscientious about taking care of Terry as would be myself if able.

Finally, manages—somehow!—to find, prepare that astonishing variety of wonderful food! (Where *could* he have found those strawberries . . . ?)

And throughout remains uniformly considerate, optimistic " . . . cheerful, thrifty, brave, clean . . ." etc. Having person like that around could get habit-forming. (Probably what he's up to—auditioning [*would* make some lucky woman terrific househusband]).

Only, if continue to let him wait on me hand and foot—never mind feeding me like this—in six months will be too fat to move. (Suppose *that's* what he's up to . . . ? Perhaps likes his women ample?)

If so, have long way to go. Only week since coma ended. Been eating, sleeping with remarkable devotion to duty ever since; and condition improving, true—color back to normal, no longer dehydrated, metabolic balance restored—but haven't begun to gain weight; still pretty puny example of Womanhood in Flower. If had any competition, doubt Adam would give me second glance. No, strike that; would look, but sympathetically: awfully nice person—for adolescent male, of course.

And *is* adolescent male, let's not forget. Far from perfect. (I mean—anyone who can be *that* cheerful in *morning* . . . !)

Further, he . . . No, can't go on. Quote from breakfast this morning (*breakfast*, mind you) quite damning enough:

" . . . was the loneliest summer of my life," he mused pensively. "Mother was seized by this notion that I should learn something resembling discipline involving areas beyond music. She decided that I should work mornings in her office. She reasoned, I suppose, that this would force me to get up early, which in itself would be Good For Me. Besides, discovering what it meant to work in a proper work setting, earning a minimum wage, would 'be good for your perspective.' That's what she said—I thought my perspective was fine just as it was.

"So I became an office boy. Not *just* an office boy: the *junior* office boy—the lowest of the low. I was given responsibility for sorting, storing, and checking in and out the innumerable little IBM type-balls, or elements, of the various sizes and fonts that Mother used in her official correspondence—it was a big office and there was a bunch of them.

"The work was boring and seemed without real value. However, I determined to put the best possible face on the situation and went about my duties cheerfully, earnestly, and doing my best to be nice to everyone."

Adam smiled, eyes going distant. "In particular, I did my best to be nice to the secretaries; of whom there was a considerable number, and each better looking than the next. True, some were slightly older than I; but that had never stopped me before—I've been out with many women in their twenties. In fact, some of my most interesting and, uh, productive dates have been with older, more worldly women. It looked as though the summer was shaping up nicely, apart from the job itself, of course.

"So you can imagine how disturbed I was when, after better than a week there, I had yet to get one of these ladies to respond to anything beyond the most businesslike inquiry: 'Thank you for returning that Orator-10 element, Miss Peach, and here are your Elite-12 and Italic-12. Have a nice day.' 'Thank you, Adam.' Beyond that—*nothing...*!"

Had no idea where he was going with this; didn't particularly care. Good company, diverting conversationalist; lived interesting life to date, related it entertainingly.

But didn't distract me from *food*.

"It was terrible," Adam continued plaintively. "I began to wonder if something was wrong with me: Maybe a postnasal infection had left me with an unspeakable variety of halitosis, of which only I was unaware. Or maybe I had deodorant failure. Or perhaps someone had circulated a vicious rumor that I had herpes—or worse, perhaps Mother had interdicted me...!

"I asked her about that and she denied it. Now, to my knowledge, she never lied to me. She was a fine lawyer and a consummate politician, true; and it was often necessary to listen closely to make sure that the words one heard carried the meaning they seemed to on the surface—but she never *lied.* . . .

"Well, by the end of the first month I was completely at a loss. I didn't know *what* to do; which way to turn. I had discharged my job duties flawlessly. I had kept track of all the elements without error; given them out, taken them in, ordered new ones from IBM; all in the most charming, helpful, personable manner possible—and I *am* my mother's son: I know my social psychodynamics.

"All to no avail, however: The ladies simply would not socialize with me, no matter what I did or didn't. My self-esteem was in shambles; my reputation as a roué was crumbling.

"Finally at wits' end, I sought advice from one of Mother's senior advisors. He was a wily old fox, versed in the intrigues of political life—but more importantly, he knew *people*.

"I told him my problem. He smiled paternally and patted me on the shoulder. 'Adam,' he soothed, 'don't let it get to you. It's nothing you've done, or can do; it's your *job*.'

"'My job?' Now I was more in the dark than ever. 'All I do is keep track of the—'

"'Elements,' said he. 'Of course they won't associate with you. Don't you understand? You're *taboo, the element boy.* . . .'"

Silence echoed through kitchen: Froze, glaring, fork halfway to mouth. Adam's expression a study in puzzled innocence.

Terry picked up vibrations; emitted long, low whistle; said, "How *'bout* that."

After counting to ten, slowly, again became aware of blended aromas rising from feast spread before me. Weighed benefits, liabilities. Carefully. Violence such a transitory satisfaction. Decided to let him live.

But just imagine: If do decide to keep him, will spend whole rest of life never knowing when something like *that* due again—but positive out there, somewhere. Waiting. With my name on it. . . .

Good *night!*

Surprise! Adam just *asked* to accompany us when search resumes for AAs—instead of baldly declaring intentions, per usual practice.

(This, standing alone, offers hope: May be making progress; perhaps housebroken status achievable within foreseeable future.)

So agreed. But with conditions. . . .

First: Must understand agreement embodies no implied secondary (read "sexual") acquiescence. Will be partners; sharing resources, proceeds, risks, hardships—period.

Second: Pooling brains, agreeing wherever possible on course to be followed—but with *me* ultimately setting policy. My decisions final. If time allows, prior discussions permissible; but if crisis looms, or events move quickly, orders must be carried out without hesitation.

Pecking order necessary: Present-day environment unforgiving; indecision, inexperience, lack of teamwork—all erode chances for survival. Despite Adam's slight age advantage, am more experienced in survival in world-as-is; been knocking about, self-sufficient, for months. Plus own education vastly broader, again despite age difference; for have devoted bulk of waking hours to emulating Rikki-Tikki-Tavi ("Run and find out!"); trying to learn something about everything, become "generalist" before settling down to specialty.

Adam, by contrast, has learned lots about very little; narrowed interests too early: From own observations, is unparalleled at keyboard, in kitchen; first-rate EMT; efficient domestic (Lord!—entire ancestry, along with ghosts of most of Baltimore's Upper Crust, must be spinning in graves at that summation!); plus shrewd student of people.

Clever also, according to hearsay, at mechanics, electronics. Demon inventor, tinkerer: Most stereo equipment throughout home product of Adam's handiwork; plus garage contains (says he; haven't been out there yet) numerous highly modified automobiles, none of whose designers would recognize, all of which boast performance, mileage, handling, durability far exceeding manufacturers' specifications.

But since Man's Passing, has existed (notwithstanding brash persona) as conservative stay-at-home, scavenging as need arises. Explorations limited to forays about already familiar (to him) city, suburbs. Totally unprepared to set off into wilderness.

Therefore, final condition: Must apprentice to me as karate student. Two reasons: First, we *will* encounter inimical ABs en route—utter certainty, this. Would be comforting to know partner competent to guard my back (plus will feel lots better knowing Adam able to take care of himself should something happen to me—certainly not least probable outcome in post-Armageddon conditions).

Second, instructing *him* good therapy for *me*: Am wreck; going to take weeks of rest/food/exercise to restore me to combat-readiness, and sparring only training better than *kata*.

Into second week now. Stronger; can walk unaided, bathe self—though in habit of sociable morning soak by now; luxuriating to Jacuzzi-driven hot water, massage, lazy prebreakfast conversation, laughing at Terry: Silly goose decided if we can, he can—and conducts most energetic baths imaginable at poolside (tubside—*tub*side [size blurs distinction!]); perched carefully on rim, grabbing huge beakfuls, slinging all directions, flapping violently, squawking ecstatically, drenching everything within ten-foot radius—all without getting more than tiniest sprinkle on feathers.

Have begun Adam's training. Initial work revolves around exercises to enhance balance, flexibility, coordination, strength, reaction time, speed; aiding student to recognize feel of own *ki*; learning to concentrate flow; focus, direct through body to attain instantaneous, automatic (preferably correct!) reaction, counterreaction, striking power.

Adam is, of course, quick study (suspect all hominems natural athletes, barring prohibitive physical defects). Mastered principles underlying balance in record time (yes, quicker than me here, too); same with footwork, physics governing striking power. Working now to establish basic group of hyperalert, hair-trigger reflexes which constitute foundation of martial art; "secret" of blindingly fast, shockingly violent, concentrated frightfulness:

Competent, well-trained student reacts without thought. Interlocking, interdependent, multiplex daisy-chain of yes/no decisions, once programed into subconscious, form automatic "combat computer." Conditioned reflexes evaluate degree of threat, determine quality of response. All takes place too quickly for conscious thought, formation of don't-hurt/hurt/hurt-lots/kill intent.

(Which explains why throwing surprise mock punch at karate student, especially relative beginner, such folly: Newly keyed-in responses imperfectly integrated; subconscious misjudges seriousness of threat, overreacts. Before playful intent apparent to cerebrum, foolish acquaintance has paid price.

Particularly risky game if done quickly—hurrying even most proficient of masters surefire ticket to own funeral.)

At this stage, however, all proceeds with deliberation, precision. Though weak, am able to perform necessary instruction. And drilling with Adam of immeasureable benefit to own condition: Each day can feel strength returning; body ever more ready to respond to demands.

And while lack even semblance of combat-readiness thus far, my response speed, accuracy, power have Adam's complete attention. Demonstrated in beginning that, slowed and weakened as I am, he cannot land blow of any kind; can block anything he throws, hand or foot; don't even look rushed. Yet can touch him anywhere, anytime, with any limb, despite his best efforts.

Brooded initially about effect on Adam's psyche (Momma Foster's caution again) of revealing how *far* beyond him I am in combat skills, but proved needless concern: If sensitive about being bested by "mere female," conceals it well; responds to challenge like Thoroughbred to touch of whip—most competitive soul have ever met! Uniform reaction to every demonstrated weakness (after eyes grow round) has been to knuckle down, do flat-out damnedest to match me.

And know from own lessons: Demonstrated superiority necessary for effective teaching: Student's appreciation of instructor's prowess *must* approach level of awe. Progress in karate matter of conquering own frontiers. Regularly necessary to issue outrageous pronouncements calculated to hype student's self-confidence (subliminal autosuggestion one of karate instructor's most effective tools) to enable performance exceeding then-assumed limitations. For as each new threshold crossed, matters little whether task once impossible (as well may have been, without overstimulated neuromuscular responses): Karate, at journeyman levels, hinges at least as much on psychology as finely honed physiology.

Felt good to get back into training. And better to have sparring partner. Doing us both good: Adam enjoying workouts; benefit to me simply incalculable.

Of disadvantages, only two immediately apparent: One, believe it or not, appetite actually increased (compounding Adam's awe!). And two, between meals, drills, sleep *constantly . . . !*

Good night, Posterity.

*   *   *

Preserve me from well-meaning innocents...! Naïveté on this scale can*not* be coincidental: Creator Himself must have planted Adam in my path together with circumstances mandating adoption.

Follow: "You know, Candy," he began this evening as we finished dinner, "I've been thinking..." (and cosmos trembled) "...you're going to be fit enough to travel pretty soon now."

"True."

"Well, I've been looking over your van..."

"And...?"

"It's small. Three of us living in that little thing will go *mad*."

"It's not so bad," I assured him. "It's certainly not as roomy and comfortable as living here, and it *will* be more crowded with you along; but it's adequate, once you get the knack of how to use what space there is, and when to spill outside for cooking, dressing, bathing, and whatnot."

"If you say so." Dubiously. "But,"—hopefully—"we do have an alternative, if you're interested."

Was; so Adam led way to garage. First time there since coma. Impressive as rest of home. Could have stored Daddy's house in there, too. Several times. With TV mast erected.

Also much taken with contents: astonishing variety of automotive toys. Lamborghinis are neat. Especially in red. Especially *that* red. Ferraris not bad either. Nor Maseratis. Nor Porsches. Never had much use for Lincolns, Cadillacs, limousines generally (bulky, clumsy, inefficient things—besides, who wants to be *driven* everywhere?); on other hand, Rolls (es?) could grow on one (*is* such a thing as elegance, after all).

But Adam brushed past four-wheel jewelry to far (perhaps "distant" more appropriate adjective) corner where stood what I took, at first glance, for garage wall. Wasn't. Goodness....

"This is how we traveled before," he announced, with proud sweep of hand. "Neat, huh? It's a converted Greyhound." Surely was; large, economy size; obviously capable of sleeping, feeding, entertaining regiment. Vehicle was Adam's mother's solution to visiting constituents statewide without having to (shudder) sleep in motels. Appointments bordered on sybaritic.

"And you *have* to see the kitchen," he enthused. "It duplicates the one in the house, in miniature. Anything I can cook there, I can make here: It's got *everything!*"

Telling point; mouth started watering at mere thought of Adam's cooking.

However. . . .

Silly thing was *40 feet long!* Twelve feet tall, not counting air-conditioners jutting from roof. Eight feet wide. Barely six inches ground clearance (got down, looked). And of three axles, obvious that only forward tandem driven; rearmost merely load-bearing idler; very front, steering only. Plus, GVW plate listed maximum weight at 16 tons!

Cast about briefly for means to pop Adam's bubble tactfully—was *so* proud of self, solution. Still merrily burbling on about juggernaut's wonderful qualities; taking my silence for enthusiasm, no doubt. Pondered variety of alternate approaches without satisfying requirements.

Finally concluded no help for it; might as well plunge ahead, rain on parade without sugar-coating—disappointments exist in present-day reality; must face sooner, later. Perhaps dose of disillusionment good thing; maybe yanking rug from under mobile Pleasure Dome's apparent usefulness helpful in conveying rational perspective of real-world conditions.

Opened with slow curve: "Boy, this is great!" Then fast break: "But something this size must have a really powerful winch to get across soft terrain. Where did they hide it?"

Adam ground to halt, looked puzzled, also faintly offended. "They don't put winches on a top-of-the-line *land yacht*," he explained, with slightly exaggerated patience.

"Oh, I see; all three axles powered then—must be just about unstoppable. Good thing; sure would hate to try to ford a stream otherwise—without a winch."

Adam hesitated, looked unsure for first time. So reminded him, while off balance, of tribulations set forth in Vol. II. Asked if cared to try balancing across railroad trestle in this, as I did van. Agreed was not enticing notion.

And that was that. Adam nobody's dummy. Chief failing consists of important gaps in background; ignorance of things obvious to anyone but cloistered genius reared amidst wealth, excess material advantages. Given hint, moves on quickly to grasp problem himself.

But *still* not satisfied with prospect of three of us living in van; determined to find solution. (Hope successful—really will miss that kitchen. . . .)

*   *   *

Hello again, Posterity. Please be patient; must proceed cautiously; maintain tight control lest emotional state bollix record through omission of pertinent, possibly vital, details.

Something Important happened today: *Found clue . . . !*

Happened like this:

Feeling pretty good past few days. Thinking seriously about resuming search. However, work undone right here in Baltimore: On way to examine Harpers' premises when originally bumped into Adam, got sidetracked. Logic dictated completing that before moving on.

Told Adam intentions; asked if familiar with area. Was; volunteered to take me there—correction—take *us* there:

(Terry *so* happy to have me healthy again; really bored during recuperation. Likes Adam lots but is *my* baby brother, knows it; expects to help *me* with daily chores, explorations, etc.)

Found Harpers' office easily; gained access (Adam as proficient at prybar locksmithing as self), commenced examination. I explained were looking for clues suggesting AAs' final destination, explanation for uniform disappearance; tangible or intangible—anything found, or deduction based on identification of something missing. Then went at it.

Adam proved quite good at fine-tooth search; was in fact he who found clue.

Took it calmly when he said, "Is there likely to be more than one Soo Kim McDivott associated with these people?"

"*What?* Where?" Adam tore sheet of paper from computer printer, held out. Snatched from hand, pored over it feverishly, and

. . . PAY DIRT!

Fragment of message to Harpers—*from Teacher . . . !* Content ambiguous, due to apparent computer malfunction. But faded print on remaining portion read:

> *. . . imple as it first appears . . . Telemetry . . . their* "*contingency solution*" *. . . already in place*
> *. . . oblem not resolved when it's "over."*
>> *The authorities still refuse . . . must be scrapped.* *Meet me . . . Palomar facility as soon as . . . and please bring everything!!!*
>> *Love to all, and good luck getting here.*
>> *Soo Kim McDivott*

That was all. But more than enough. To anyone who knew him, fragmentary missive shrieked starkest urgency. If had not seen with own eyes, would never have believed *Teacher* would end sentence with three exclamation points. Fabric of Universe hardly less flappable than Teacher.

Heard him express urgency only once. Happened perhaps six months before World Ended:

Though retired, Teacher still member in good standing of town's medical "reserves." Often baby-sat practices when Daddy, Jorgé Curaçao, G.P., (town's "other" doctor) needed time off. On one such occasion (genuine "must" seminar for every physician) Teacher volunteered services to enable both to attend. Set up shop in Daddy's office (front of our house).

Both gone less than two hours before hysterical truck driver arrived with flat-bed trailer carpeted with casualties from high-school bus capsize (ran over hog—basic rural no-no). Forty-some injured; ten, twelve critical; balance varied between minor broken bones, cuts/scrapes/bruises, acute self-pity.

And in keeping with rules governing such events (known in some quarters as Murphy's Law), Yours Truly only semblance of nurse/medical assistant available. Flitted about office, trying to be three of me: diving in, out of rubber gloves to hand instruments, operate retraction, tie off; fetch, install bandages; mop blood, etc.

But Teacher faster yet; moved quicker than ever saw outside *dojo*—seemed *everywhere!* Worked miracles: Sorted patients by degree of crisis; stabilized some critically wounded apparently by force of will while worked on others even more so. Somehow coped without losing anyone (and some critical really *were*) until reinforcements arrived from County General, 35 miles away in next town.

Was busy hour. During course of which urgency such that Teacher omitted saying "please." Twice.

So *three* exclamation points . . . !

"Important, huh?" Adam could hardly fail to note shaking hand holding paper.

Nodded wordlessly, thoughts churning.

He waited decent interval; then tried again, still gently: "I read it, but I don't understand the significance. Is this McDivott your 'Teacher'?"

"Oh..." Returned to surroundings with a start. "Sorry. Yes. This *is* from Teacher, I'm sure; telling the Harpers to meet him *somewhere*; probably just prior to the attack, though maybe right after. And he's worried about something—I don't know what, but apparently something that will be a problem even after Mankind is gone—even after he's gone himself, poor dear; Teacher was like that: Always worried more about others than himself."

"Any idea what 'it' he was talking about?"

"No. And 'Palomar' is pretty vague, too—unless he could mean Mount Palomar, near San Diego. But I can't imagine any connection between Teacher, the AAs, and an observatory. This doesn't furnish much information."

"Enough to get your hopes up, but raising more questions than it answers...."

"Exactly. Just enough to send us off on what will very likely end up a wild-goose chase and waste a lot of time."

"Not really; even if nothing turns up, there are plenty of AA addresses out there. You'll just be revising the order in which you visit them. You're looking at a potential gain, even if it's a long-shot. You can't lose, no matter what." Smiled beatifically. "I don't see the problem."

Adam never so irritating as when correctly stating obvious, particularly when I'm the one overlooking it (correctness always delivered with such cheerful assurance). However, took deep breath, swallowed retort poised on tip of tongue; agreed was little choice: Any course other than proceeding to check out "Palomar" manifest nonsense.

Should, however, conclude sweep of Harpers' office. No telling what else might surface.

Did so. Predictably, without profit.

And en route home afterward, Adam observed: "Seems an unlikely sort of coincidence. Are two of the Harpers married, and the other's their son; or is it a husband/wife/brother thing, or what?"

Glanced across at him. Engrossed in driving; expression devoid of clues usually accompanying deadpan teasing. Possible he didn't know? Had read Vol. II, glanced through Tarzan File, but perhaps missed that. Decided to accept question at face value.

"No, they're married."

"Who?"

"All of them."

"Oh," he replied disinterestedly; drove on. Several minutes later head snapped around, eyes narrowed in good-natured suspicion. Demanded, "*What?*" Then relaxed. "Oh, I see. It really *is* a coincidence: All separately married; no relation?"

"No, not related at all. Nor married separately. *Married*." Couldn't help smiling as watched Adam juggle possibilities. He noticed; grew truly suspicious.

Easy to tell when figured it out: Jaw went slack, eyes round. "All *three* of them . . . ?" Adam exerted manful effort to be debonair; but expression—indeed, total aspect from head to toe—very embodiment of shocked disapproval.

(Naturally, have no idea whether men's relationship extends beyond shared wife, but not about to let Adam off that easily.)

Smiled. Added helpfully: "Sure. Of course they're not the only ones; lots of AAs are involved in group marriages. You mean you didn't know?"

Didn't. Tee-hee. Wolf in wolf's clothing. Lecher, profligate, lady-killer, rake, debaucher, libertine, playboy. Swath-cutter amongst Baltimore's fair sex. Any and all of above. Says he.

Well, maybe. But just discovered mile-wide chink in macho armor: Adam dyed-in-wool, card-carrying, soapbox-standing, old fashioned *sexual conservative!* Face-to-face encounter with evidence of honest-to-goodness *ménage à trois* leaves him breathless with scandalized, bluenosed shock.

Hope exists for Adam after all. Gladder I found him by the day. Glad is coming with us. . . .

Adam not kidding about hating prospect of three of us living in small van. Nor about mechanical, electronic ingenuity, ability. Has been busy past few weeks; all to good.

Example: Now attached to van's rear by heavy-duty, load-equalizing hitch is lightweight, self-contained, 25-foot travel trailer. Clever notion: Enjoy luxuries without disadvantages intrinsic to vehicle unwieldy enough to carry them—in pinch, can drop trailer, proceed in van alone.

Adam sprung it as surprise: Went through Yellow Pages, visited dealers, located suitable unit; found, mounted hitch; hooked up, brought home. Then installed kitchen equipment matching that in parents' land yacht. (My taste buds thank you, my appetite thanks you, *I* thank you . . . !) Quiet, multi-kilowatt, 120/240-volt, engine-driven Honda alternator replaces LP tanks on trailer's A-frame tongue; powers everything.

Then he went through van with mad inventor's eye, determined weaknesses, corrected. Rebuilt engine, replacing nearly every moving part; all with what described as "competition specs" (sounds impressive, but don't ask *me*). Same for running gear.

(Whatever. . . . Bottom line, boy; don't care *how* watch built—what *time* is it? Speak *English*! [Verbal inquiry worded more politely, of course. Some.])

"Okay, okay," he agreed. Tone impatient, but eyes alight; clearly pleased with self. "What I've done will make the engine and drivetrain more reliable under load, and shifts the power range downward, which gives it more torque—makes it more powerful at low RPMs, and gives it much more traction so it can pull the trailer more easily and climb steeper grades.

"And it's more efficient now; goes farther on the same fuel. Since we have to rely on finding cars to siphon from, which may or may not have enough to bother with, or a gas station whose tank caps we can force, that's insurance.

"Sounds as if it was a lot of work."

"It was." He nodded. "But solving mechanical problems is fun; I've been doing it for years as a hobby—along with the electronic stuff."

"How did a well-bred, artistic type like you pick up such a physical sort of interest?"

"You mean 'rich and spoiled type' and 'filthy sort of interest.'" Adam grinned; displayed fine hands now covered with cuts, scrapes, bruises; embedded with dirt, grease. "It grew out of what you might call the 'flip side' of growing up terribly rich, with parents too wrapped up in their careers to spend time with me.

"I stayed busy. Even I could practice piano only so long; and I'm as quick a study as you, so academics took even less time. I whiled away a good bit of the rest following around my favorites among the house staff and learning their jobs. That's how I discovered that I love cooking—and where the EMT training came from, of course.

"But that still left a lot of time. Now, I'd gotten a taste for approbation from performing on the piano, and I'd noticed that people were impressed by fast cars and people who built and drove them. It looked like an entertaining hobby and a good way to show off. Naturally, anything *material* I wanted, all I had to do was ask; cost was never discussed. That's where the Lamborghini, the Ferrari, the Porsche, and the motorcycles came from—and, of course, the Trans Am I splattered.

"They hired Gus Wilson to take care of them. He was a proud old mechanic who used to run what he called a model garage. I became his shadow and he did his best to teach me everything he knew—it tickled him to discover that a rich, spoiled brat was genuinely interested in learning his craft, and didn't mind getting his schoolgirl-soft hands dirty doing it. Gus taught me my rule-of-thumb engineering, mechanical, and electrical skills.

"However, in the process, he taught me one of the most important lessons I ever learned: You can fix anything—*if you want to badly enough*. Sometimes what it takes is knowing where to find special tools and parts; sometimes it takes being able to figure out how to *make* special tools and parts." He grinned again. "Sometimes all it takes is a bigger hammer—you'd be surprised what you can accomplish with naked force.

"Back then, of course, all it took most of the time was to throw money at it. But *anything* can be fixed if you need to badly enough. *Somehow.*

"For instance—remember how you crossed the Susquehanna," he said abruptly, apparently out of blue.

Statement, not question. Do indeed; experience intrudes into dreams with regularity. Wish wouldn't: Wake up with racing heart, clammy palms. Balancing van on tracks on single-width railroad trestle at altitude barely inside Earth's atmosphere not fun.

"Look..." Adam squatted down, pointed to double-scissor-hinged frames bolted to van's, trailer's undercarriages; "...this is my masterpiece: I *fixed* it."

Perplexity must have shown on face.

Adam smiled, said, "Watch"; operated cranks protruding from underside of van, trailer, respectively—and additional sets of wheels lowered to ground. Tiny metal things, barely ten inches in diameter; located ahead of front, behind rear, wheels on van; just aft of tandems on trailer.

But even with demonstration, at first couldn't divine purpose—and really wanted to: Adam's expression appropriate for having solved Mystery of Universe. That he expected

praise obvious; but would spot bluffing, and understanding
nature of accomplishment prerequisite for intelligent head-
patting.

Then light dawned; indeed understood—and pretty darned
pleased own self: Wheels' flanges match rails' spacing, engage
inner edges—singlehandedly Adam devised, manufactured
rig permitting use of rails without drama, effort: Line up on
level crossing, lower guide wheels—unnecessary even to
steer.

"I reread that part of your journal after you pointed out
the problems with the land yacht," Adam explained. "I got
sweaty palms myself, just thinking about it. I figured there
had to be a better way.

"I remembered reading about railroads modifying cars
and trucks like this for their own use. I drove down to the
railyard, found a truck outfitted this way, and studied how
they did it. Didn't seem all that difficult a project, if you don't
mind getting out to crank the wheels up and down—the truck
had hydraulics; the railroad people wanted to be able to
deploy and retract theirs without getting rained on.

"After that it was just a matter of cannibalizing a couple
handcars, and a little fabrication. Anyone could have done it."

"*I* couldn't," I replied positively. "It never occurred to
me even to pull a trailer."

"You could if you were in my shoes." He grinned. "We
needed more room without incurring a permanent weight
penalty; a trailer is the obvious solution. And the rail-riders
are equally obvious: Without them, if we absolutely *had* to
cross a railroad bridge, we'd have to abandon the trailer. I
just couldn't see leaving behind all my best tools and music
and everything."

"Not to mention your kitchen!"

"And hot showers and a warm, clean, roomy bed."

"*Whose* . . . ?"

Daddy often voiced opinion that those in habit of giving
in to knee-jerk responses usually best described by omitting
"knee." Here was textbook example. Regretted immediately.
But too late.

Adam's smile unchanged, but no longer included eyes.
Realized, then, suspicion unfounded; sex farthest thing from
boy's mind. For once attention limited to demonstrating
fruits of own technical brilliance. Offended, no doubt about
it. And rightly so.

Without further comment, Adam led me to bedroom at rear of trailer. Accommodations consisted of twin-size bunks positioned fore and aft, one either side of room; dresser between at extreme rear; hanging closets on either side between door, foot of each bed.

Adam stopped, about-faced so abruptly almost ran into him. "I'm going to sleep in one of these," he stated loftily, with over-the-shoulder thumb indication. "You may have the other or you may, each and every night and morning, go through the trouble of making up the dinette or the couch in the salon—your choice; both convert to full-sized doubles. But when *I'm* tired, I'm going to go to bed, without going through the unnecessary nonsense of making it up. Suit yourself." Brushed past, started to walk away.

Already in throes of contrition; required little effort to appear more so. Pulled at lower lip with teeth; allowed eyes to fill, almost overflow; "impulsively" reached out to catch arm, stop him. "Adam, I'm *sorry!*" I blurted. (And found really *was*—astonished to discover how much!) "That was a rotten thing to say. I shouldn't have taken it that way. I've got a hair-trigger installed on that one subject, and I don't know how to fix it. I'm trying...but..."

Adam unexpectedly magnanimous in victory: Paused, took deep breath; then turned back, placed hand gently over my mouth, damming apologetic flood; said, "Hush, it's not your fault; I haven't said two words to you without one of them being a proposition."

(*That* much certainly true; but managed [for once!] to curb shrewish tongue, avoid getting in deeper. Fortunately. For Adam not through; further surprises in store.)

"Neither of us is at fault. Not really. This is hardly an ideal situation for comfortable boy-meets-girl-ing. We may be the last couple on Earth, and you are both intelligent and responsible; you understand the inevitabilities of our situation as well as I do: Unless we find someone else whom we like better, we're going to have to get on with making babies—in a primitive society children are *necessary*; they're our social security, all we'll have to take care of us in our old age.

"I've known all along that you feel pressured. It could hardly be otherwise, even if I never said a word about it.

"You know it, I know it, and I know you know it—and I haven't allowed you the courtesy of adjusting to the idea in peace. But I couldn't help it, and *I'm* sorry." Confession so sudden, caught me quite off balance. But looked, sounded really sincere.

Caught by surprise, then by intensity of affection suddenly upwelling in response. Hidden behind Adam's brash façade is genuinely likeable human being. Possibly even lovable. When lets himself be. . . .

Hey, Posterity. . . ! Vacation over: Back on the road again; we leave tomorrow morning.

And *about time*—though would have been madness to set off into unknown again with me in less than contest-ready condition. And of course will drill twice daily as we travel, both for physical conditioning and to continue Adam's training.

Speaking of which, progress confusing: Brilliant mastery of every technique demonstrated. Form excellent; power, speed, outstanding. Has assembled *kata* of unrivaled violence, grace. Have never seen such flawless performance in student below black-belt level. But . . .

Has not established basic reflex-matrix program. Plans, directs every step consciously. True, conscious reactions *very* quick—combined with execution skills, probably match for any two, three untrained opponents right now—but not as fast as correctly programed, subconscious combat computer. Perhaps problem is subliminal fear of letting go; perhaps doesn't trust reflexes to operate without cerebrum at helm. If so, don't know how to help him. Problem never arose during own training; programing took hold, settled in as if conscious mind wanted out.

Further, Adam's subconscious evidently resisting hysterical strength tap programing. Explanation obvious, of course: After nursing me through misuse sequelae, not eager for firsthand experience. But will never achieve full journeyman/Master status without; certain techniques possible only through at least momentary burst of focused preternatural power.

Remember clearly Teacher's induction formula; plus Adam good hypnotic subject: Achieves deepest somnambulistic trance state easily, first under my direction, later through own autohypnotic concentration. Listens quietly while in trance state; apparently absorbs programing formula. But posthypnotic triggering ineffective; available strength never exceeds norm.

Well, all I can do for now is maintain present training format: Continue *kata* critique, guidance; daily sparring; penetrate guard at will, while he can't lay finger on me. Perhaps subconscious will get message.

That's one problem; another is packing van, trailer for trip. Adam obviously graduate (*sigma cum load*) of school of scientific packing; only possible explanation of how managed to cram so much stuff into so little space. This, after several days' agonizing over what constitutes excess; boiling down to present two, three tons of irreplaceable possessions.

Actually, I exaggerate. A little. Maybe.

For example, managed to cram entire toolbox (five feet tall, four feet wide, two feet deep) and contents into heretofore unnoticed empty corner of van's interior (don't know how—certainly no room to spare before). Converted one living-room wall in trailer into electronics center: all-bands, two-way radio of own design; stereo system—plus thousand-plus cassette music collection, of course. And found room for much-modified Moog synthesizer keyboard and processor (plays through stereo speakers; amazing tone—can't tell whether hearing electrons putting on airs or genuine concert grand from library). Also stowed incidentals: food, clothing, Terry's stand, weapons, etc.

Plus final mysterious touch: 25-foot-long bundle of aluminum tubing wrapped in brightly colored cloth, secured to trailer roof rack. No idea what. Not only won't Adam say, but being smug about it: Says is surprise; something which, when need arises, will be indispensible. Probably; spends awful lot of time being right. But if keeps this up, may not live to announce "I told you so" when time comes!

Oh, something else—promise not to tell.... Serious business now—*really* promise! Requires hold-breath-and-spit, used-sweat-socks-on-your-tongue-if-you-tell oath. Okay. But into really dangerous territory—*have learned "Adam's" real name*.

Not surprised, of course—for first male encountered since end of *H. sapiens* really to be named "Adam" would require unlikely stretching of probability. And knew came from old family; knew parents influential. But never, in wildest imaginings, suspected depths of boy's dreadful secret. Didn't dream aristocracy willing to perpetrate such patent cruelty—to no apparent end beyond snooty continuity.

While prowling house, snooping into rooms heretofore

unexplored, on lookout for last-minute stuff (sort of thing one always forgets and later wishes hadn't), stumbled into what proved to be Adam's parents' bedroom. Not hard to identify: Walls, bureaus covered with pictures of them as couple, from wedding portraits on; plus baby pictures dating all the way back to wet, thoroughly dissatisfied, red face glaring from birth canal (family went at baby-picture-taking in big way!). Poked about until found album. Opened, looked at title page . . .

And there it was:

Melville. Winchester. Higginbotham. Grosvenor. Penobscott-Jones.

The *Fourth.* . . .

Can you imagine? Terrible thing to do to cute, defenseless baby! (And *was* cute baby, too, once pointy-headed newborn syndrome subsided, wrinkles smoothed out, expression moderated to one recognizable as ancestor of present calculated innocence.) No *wonder* chose new name earliest possible opportunity.

Well, identity safe as far as I'm concerned. Nor will "Adam" ever learn I possess truth from *me*: Some knowledge simply *too* dangerous . . .

On other hand, blackmail long a respected component of diplomatic toolkit.

And "never" is *long* time. . . .

Greetings, Posterity, from Beautiful East St. Louis. Having wonderful time; wish you were here. And other clichés. (Actually, trip quite dull [i.e., uneventful—may it so continue. . . .].)

Adam, reckless propensities under control, proving marvelously smooth, precise driver when not showing off (or perhaps satisfying show-off urges by displaying different aspect of motoring skills): Operates van-*cum*-trailer rig as though born with shift knob in mouth instead of silver spoon. Glides along roads without drama; slips through holes between obstructions where I would have *sworn* wasn't room. Possesses uncanny eye for solidity of terrain; plus flicks neatly in, out of four-wheel-drive, low-low range, without stopping, losing momentum: Haven't used winch at all—despite added load, trailer.

Must admit, however, fact we spent bulk of time slicing across continent in nearly straight lines, tooling effortlessly along railroad tracks at 60 mph, bypassing highway clutter altogether, may have bearing on ease of travel. Adam's invention works just as advertised: Line up rig on grade crossing, lower guide wheels, set speed control, select cassette, plug into stereo, lean back, relax, enjoy watching scenery unroll.

Terry delighted to be back on road. Does so love riding in cars. But for first few miles on tracks, wasn't at all sure he approved of no-hands driving. Stood uneasily on stand, shifting weight, bobbing head suspiciously, flitting to settle feathers. Peered out windshield with first one eye, then other. Occasionally muttered "How *'bout* that" in worried tones. Seasoned traveler; knows improper driving when sees it. . . .

Hard to believe, after own experience at post-Armageddon cross-country travel: Adam and I arrived in East St. Louis—just under thousand miles—only *three days* after leaving Baltimore! Could have made it in one, but not hurrying; rising when feel like it, eating well (love that kitchen!), performing *kata*, sparring, scrounging, quitting early, giving Adam time to practice on Moog, etc. But even at this rate we'll be at Mount Palomar in another week. Isn't that great?

Good night, Posterity.

Good morning, Posterity. Reality back—with a vengeance: Don't know how could have forgotten how much fun rivers can be. Evidence suggests Ole Man Mississippi took advantage of flood-control engineers' absence to flex muscles this spring. Must have been some thaw: One bridge left—clogged solidly with cars, trucks. High-water mark suggests crest wasn't all that high, but *something* sure took rest out. Perhaps river recruited help—string of fully loaded barges careening along in melt-swollen current would fill prescription, and plenty available. But . . .

Adam cut speculation short by pointing out that figuring way to remove obstructions from bridge more relevant issue on which to focus curiosity—please pay attention.

(Been unbearably pleased with himself since rail-riding rig proved successful—and "unbearably" surely operative word. Despite this, haven't destroyed him yet; treating situation as opportunity to strengthen character, exercise in self-control. *So far.*)

Good night, Posterity.

*   *   *

Bridge cleanup not so tough! Though surely looked as if might be to begin with: First vehicles in way all had dead batteries. Then refused to start upon being jumpered. Adam suspected watered gasoline—condensation from temperature changes, length of time abandoned.

(His reaction to frustration entertaining: Unaccustomed to failure [classes experience with me as "work in progress"]; regards even possibility might not triumph as personal attack on vaunted resourcefulness. Looks vexed. Grows a little defensive. Sometimes even pouts. But *never* gives up.)

Presently climbed onto commuter-bus roof, surveyed problem with hands on hips. Shortly got down, looking smug. Claimed had answer. But wouldn't tell me plan; wanted to "surprise me."

Located East St. Louis Yellow Pages, flipped through to "Machine Shops." Underlined half dozen addresses, visited in order. Found what was looking for at third stop: vitamin-fed forklift truck—really *big*.

Managed to get monster running; returned to bridge (not quick trip; shop some miles away). Adam directed me to follow in rig as he assailed blockage. Ran forks under first car, lifted, set to side, moved on to next.

Progress quicker once got up onto bridge approach: Adam simply hoisted, tilted forks, pitched over side. Didn't waste time, efforts: Cleared single-width path just wide enough for van, trailer. Soon into rhythm of forklift operation, drilled rapidly across bridge. Started crossing near noon; descended into St. Louis before dark.

Too late to continue then, so spending night on riverbank. Adam plans to locate railyard, pick up maps, get us "back on track" tomorrow (something about phrase seems to make him happy; wonder if be offended if I tore out his tongue....).

Goodness *gracious*—what a *day*! Whole complexion of travel now changed. Should have anticipated this; certainly would feel same way if were in their shoes. But shock, just the same.

All right—enough rambling; on to proper, orderly narrative while events fresh in mind:

Adam disappointed to learn St. Louis, despite (or because of) role as national-rail-network hub, impossible to get out of by rail. Same problem often encountered on roads near big cities: too much dead traffic. Endless switchyards, switch after switch set wrong; stopped trains, locomotives, isolated cars and/or car strings everywhere. Simply no room to move.

So found city map; began working our way out on streets. Not difficult, considering past experience, but not quickest travel thus far enjoyed. Adam's driving skills even more apparent here, as squeezed around, between abandoned cars, trucks; popped into four-wheel-drive, low-low, to climb curbs; bypassing obstructions down alleys, along sidewalks. Necessary to use winch only once; then only to haul another car out of way, not unstick us.

Not bad, by and large; and afternoon found us well into semiresidential area, past worst of downtown congestion. Adam finding this type of driving sufficient challenge even at low speeds; plus remains ever conscious of trailer contents' scatterability, fragility. Accordingly, were proceeding at entirely reasonable pace when, trotting in preoccupied manner from between two buildings, came *rhinoceros*...!

Prepoceros? Of course! But precise moment rhinoceros, size of house, discovered ambling across street directly in one's path, bad time to debate probabilities.

Adam reacted well: Cut hard left, tried to dodge behind—and stupid clot *stopped!* Nowhere to go—slammed on brakes, skidded to stop nestled intimately against beast's shoulder. No impact, just nudge.

"How 'bout that," said Terry in awed tones.

Rhino turned head, squinted disapprovingly down over shoulder with mean little pig eyes. Snorted. Horn about four feet long. Looked sharp.

Adam calmly, deliberately eased van into reverse; backed slowly away, concentrating intently on trailer, visible in mirror. Kept rig lined up. Kept going.

Rhino stared. Snorted again. Louder. Then frowned. Turned. Pawed ground. Lowered head.

Calm, deliberate sternway gained momentum, acquired salient characteristics of earnest retreat—then precipitous route as rhino took several quick, purposeful steps.

Fast reverse driving not easy with trailer; requires concentration. Covered perhaps 200 yards without jackknifing before rhino slowed, snorted, veered off between buildings, disappeared.

Adam stopped, sat immobile, breathing like Thoroughbred after crossing finish line. Encounter spanned perhaps 30 seconds, but was wringing wet. Eyes blinked rapidly. Knuckles white where hands gripped wheel. No sound emerged when first tried to speak. Had indeed been concentrating.

He took deep breath, held momentarily, released in tremulous sigh. Then tried again: "Wouldn't you think a city this size would have a leash law?" Grin unconvincing. "Where do you suppose that thing *came* from . . . ?"

And just like that, I knew answer. Obvious, really; should have anticipated. And amazing thing is this was first encounter.

Rhinoceros trotting down city street, two miles from St. Louis Zoo. Coincidence? *Haw!* Isolated, unaided breakout? Not likely.

Trade places with zookeepers—warm, conscientious people who, if didn't love animals, could make lots easier living, much better money, elsewhere. Utterly certain own deaths impending, how would react to animal friends' prospects, locked in cages? Do nothing? Ensure agonizing deaths through starvation, thirst?

Not in million years . . . !

Safe assumption, therefore, most—possibly all—zoo animals now at large throughout country, probably world. Suggested as much to Adam.

"'Lions and tigers and bears—*oh, my!*'" he quoted, with shake of head. "I'll bet you're right. Shall we detour and find out?"

Not keen on idea, but logic inarguable: Deliberately remaining ignorant of opposition bad strategy.

Proceeded to zoo. Conducted preliminary examination while driving, circling buildings. Exterior cages empty, but inconclusive: All connect to interior. Could be bodies inside.

Only one way to find out.

Reluctantly dug out, loaded M-16s, magnum pistols. Slipped holster belts around middles. Exited together, Terry on my shoulder (if failed to return, wouldn't want *him* locked in, either).

Not elegant performance; probably looked like Abbott and Costello, engaged in burglary: back-to-back, tiptoeing with exaggeratedly sneaky steps, spinning one way, then another, trying to cover all directions at once (*I* was; Adam maddeningly at ease). Cautiously we scouted every building, rifles at ready, set for fully automatic fire, safeties off—so

keyed up that, had even Daddy appeared suddenly, I probably would have cut him in half.

However, no untoward encounters; merely confirmed
my very worst fears: All—repeat *all*—enclosures open, empty. Even cobras. . . .

"Good grief, what kind of person can manage sympathy
for *cobras*. . . ?" I wondered aloud, trying to walk without
placing feet on ground.

"Nice people," Adam observed, peering around inter-
estedly. "Cobras have feelings, too."

"Well, yeah, maybe. . . ."

Returned to rig; departed immediately.

Discussed development en route: "The ecology of the
planet will never be the same," I ventured. "Lots of those
beasties will do just fine in their new homes."

"Do you think so?" Zoology not one of Adam's specialties. "I suppose animals from temperate climates will do all
right, but what about 'lions and tigers and bears' from the
tropics?"

Settled back in seat, took deep breath, delivered thumb-
nail zoological history/geography lesson:

Cobras (while notion makes my skin crawl) unlikely to be
enduring problem anywhere temperate or cooler. Poisonous
snakes in general not gregarious lot; solitary wanderers,
seeking food, shelter alone. Rodent population explosion
following *H. sapiens'* demise guarantees all species' small
initial populations' wide dispersal in totally strange environment: Ample food available wherever might roam. Further,
tropical foreigners incapable of lying dormant; never survive
winter.

Odds practically nil for compatible meeting, mating,
species' perpetuation before all dead of cold, old age, hunting
accidents. Even given warmer climes to south, threat exists
few years at most.

Warm-blooded predators, however, constitute distinctly
separate problem: General rule suggests anything furry capable of producing winter coat. Know for fact, tigers found from
rain forests to well above Himalayan snow line. One kitty
actually named "Snow Leopard." Lions roamed portions of
Europe mere centuries ago; disappeared from Turkish mountains since Ottoman collapse.

Besides, most zoos housed relatively large big-cat populations; and *are* gregarious, particularly lions: Band together in prides, breed like rabbits. Perpetuation assured.

But pussycats not only problem: Grizzlies, wolves, cougars all native North Americans; absent Man, make selves at home anywhere.

And what about Kodiak bears? Comforting notion: 1,800 pounds of appetite. And polar bears—11 feet long (not true bears at all; mink family—dispositions to match). Both regarded among deadliest carnivores on planet.

Vegetarians potential problem, too: Hannibal brought elephants across Alps; mammoths here before people. Doubt will enjoy winters, but most probably survive, multiply. Rhinos, too. Neither overtly aggressive; not truly dangerous per se (barring stupidity—not ideal subjects for teasing), but undesirable neighbors: To farmer visits equate with earthquake, flood, drought, locusts. Hope attentions dissuadable without bloodshed.

Sundry antelope types probably manage winters well as local ruminants—undoubtedly fare better in relations with new predator mix.

All of which certainly complicates outlook. Careful thought required for future. Must assemble projection of potential competition; learn strengths, weaknesses, formulate plans to cope.

During interim, M-16 probably adequate coper if cornered: Unlikely anything still standing after fully automatic setting empties 50-shot clip (expanding slugs) into ticklish spots. Other advantages: lightweight, accurate, reliable; spares, ammunition endlessly available; familiar now with teardown, maintenance drill.

Plus final advantage: Doesn't knock me down (petty detail, but personally satisfying). Basic physics, of course: Violence going *that* way usefully limited (given 70-pound shooter) by violence coming *this* way. Equation rules out .457 Weatherby Magnum Double, African guide's favorite equalizer.

"And if all else fails," offered Adam, when I paused for breath, "we can try a stern expression and an assertive tone of voice: 'Shoo!'"

Didn't dignify by responding. Said, "We need to tighten up our travel habits."

"Oh, yes, we're guilty of the French traveler's mistake."

"I think we should start wearing sidearms from now on, and keep the M-16s close at hand—*what*?"

Adam smiled. "You're right; we do need to tighten our travel security habits. We've committed the classical French traveler's error. You know: Too loose *la* trek. . . ."

Favored him with glare. "No more solitary wandering," I continued firmly. "We go everywhere together . . ."

"*Every*where?"

" . . . and we go armed."

"Oh. Pity."

"Be *serious!*" Adam's lack of concern more worrisome than newly discovered neighbors. How could be so casual, surrounded by slavering man-eaters . . . ?

"I am." Smiled again. Watched me, waiting expectantly.

Open mouth for scathing retort; then hesitated, closed again. Performed quick review of events since rhino hove into view—especially own conduct. Cringed at conclusion: Not once assembled, processed facts with brain switched on. Typical "fluttering, fragile ingénue" of worst gothic romance would be embarrassed to take credit for my performance past couple hours.

Ground teeth. Adam right. Again. Easily his most offensive habit.

Except for zoos' immediate areas, chances of adversary encounter with escapee compares favorably with odds on lightning strike. Possible, yes. But for first few years—until get spread out, established, build up populations, risk factor simply doesn't justify going to lots of extra trouble.

Yes, probably should carry M-16s whenever poking around inside strange buildings; yes, probably should cut out solitary explorations, period; yes, probably should take extra pains not to throw away food scraps close to campsite where smell might attract predators. Yes, should take commonsense precautions, in other words, practiced by *any* intelligent camper; but not lose head. . . .

Initial reaction doubtless based on too many Class-D movies—plus absence of rational thought. Product of small-town living: Every Saturday evening throughout summers, Town Fathers stretched sheet across one end of grassy natural amphitheater in park; ran freeshow for migrant workers' children: endless succession of marvelously bad old movies, always preceded by cartoons, oft-spliced old science-fiction/horror serials. Probably have seen every Johnny Weismuller Tarzan movie ever made; along with Bomba, the Jungle Boy; Sheena, Queen of the Jungle; Tim Tyler's Luck; Osa, Martin

Johnson's pseudodocumentaries about exploring "darkest Africa"; (plus Zombies of the Stratosphere; Flash Gordon, Buck Rogers), etc., etc. And *everyone* (freeshow attendees, anyway) knows jungle predators all live only to sink fangs into trembling flesh of heroine (nice girl, usually, most of whose problems brought on by disregarding instructions, behaving stupidly).

Almost as stupidly as self.

Spending night in outer suburbs. Judged proximity to zoo increases risk to point where additional security advisable. Adam concurred. Pulled whole rig into commercial garage; closed doors, windows. Verified (together, armed) nothing large enough to pose threat lurked in darkened corners.

Spending night with trailer door, windows closed, air-conditioning on. Structure probably sufficiently porous to eliminate CO threat, but Adam slipped hose over alternator exhaust, let out roof vent anyway.

This morning Adam checked Yellow Pages, located nearby burglar-bar service. Drove us over after breakfast. Dug through inventory, selected assortment of wrought-iron grilles, installed over van's, trailer's windows. Even windshield.

Over yesterday's jitters (all *right*, hysteria) and agree with Adam: Bars silly overkill precaution.

On other hand, intangibles difficult to evaluate. Bars' sturdy appearance reassuring when contemplating future possibility of looking out at something hungry looking in. Improved sleep quality, duration, might prove critical during future nonanimal-related crisis.

(Evaluation particularly difficult when consists largely of rationalizing decisions already made based on gut feeling rather than logic.)

Oh, Posterity, please be patient. Probably most difficult entry have ever faced. Emotional control fragile as crystal, unstable as if balanced on pinpoint. Forgive rambling if occurs. Will do best, but subconscious probably try to steer me away from subject.

Now camped on grounds of Mount Palomar observatory, southern California. Haven't kept up journal since leaving St. Louis, ten days ago. Inexcusable conduct for histographer, true. But couldn't write about what happened that day so soon after—and been unable to think about anything else.

First thing after bar installation, Adam identified rail line going proper direction. Soon on our way again, speeding cross-country, insulated from deteriorating road conditions, clutter. Interesting how rail system seems to have fared better than roads following Man's End. Perhaps essentially flexible nature of steel mounted on wood, laid on equally flexible fist-sized rock roadbed...

Well, didn't take subconscious long to start diversionary tactics. Sorry.

Were perhaps hundred miles from St. Louis, passing through small Missouri town, when heard eerie wailing sound. Adam, alert for defective track or open switch but otherwise relaxed, abruptly sat bolt upright, peering into mirrors. "What the *hell* ...!" he muttered. Braked heavily, bringing us to quick stop.

Equally quickly, was out door, running toward rear. I saw nothing in right-side mirror, but exited as well. Ran toward trailer's rear, intending to meet Adam, gain insight into curious behavior.

However, as rounded trailer, all became clear: Stopped behind us, lit up like Jefferson Starship stage, was state police car, driver's door open. Man—tall, thin, seedy-looking, long-haired/bearded, breathlessly wild-eyed, teary-but-very-happy man, age indeterminate—sliding from behind wheel. Stranger fell sobbing upon Adam's neck like long-lost brother, alternately hugging, pounding back, pumping hand as if never intended to let go.

(Proud of Adam then: Notoriously averse to emotional displays [even more so to long-unwashed B.O.], but accepted mauling nobly—remembered his own feelings upon first discovering not alone in world after all. Hint of long-suffering forebearance betrayed by posture apparent only to me—and only because know him so well.)

Presently man's eyes fell on me. Stared for long moments, then gasped, "You're a *girl* ...!" Took quick step in my direction, reaching out as if to sweep me into embrace also—and stopped short. Glanced down at self, abruptly conscious of grooming deficiencies. Released Adam; drew back. Looked embarrassed.

"I must present quite a sight," said in apologetic tone. "And smell," added with grimace.

Continued earnestly: "It's been quite a while since I've had anyone to dress up for. I'm afraid I'm out of practice. I'll shower, shave, and change as soon as we get home." Earnestness intensified, hysterical edge crept into voice: "I'm really a very respectable person once I'm cleaned up and wearing decent clothes. And I'll cut my hair. You *will* come home with me, won't you? We have so *much* to talk about. Please? *Please . . . ?*"

Unexpectedly then, suddenly as had aborted initial lunge toward me, man clamped mouth shut, cutting off accelerating verbal torrent almost midword. Closed eyes; took long, slow, deep breath. Drew himself up. Disreputable air wavered, then evaporated: Clothing notwithstanding, self-assured, dignified gentleman stood before us. Voice, when resumed, was low, well modulated; delivery cultured, articulate: "Sorry; I must sound like a complete psychotic, raving on like that. I've been alone a long time. I was sure I was the last man on Earth.

"I'm Rollo Jones. My house is about 20 miles back. I've been chasing you since I caught a glimpse of you going by the shopping center." Flashed sudden boyish grin. "You have no idea how uncomfortable a pursuit it was. Railroad roadbed is not made for high-speed driving in cars, even in something as durable as a patrol car.

"May I ask your names, ma'am and sir?"

Transformation amazing. By now could almost forget appearance, aroma—excusable anyway, under circumstances (though Adam hadn't let self go, nor I). Before our eyes, frenetic derelict metamorphosed into educated, refined, eminently likeable person.

Introduced ourselves; ran through briefest mutual biographies. Rollo listened attentively; displayed genuine interest. Then surprised us: Owned recordings of Adam in concert, though never saw him perform—and knew both Daddy, Teacher professionally: As small-town medical-school president, physician, prior to Doomsday, had rubbed shoulders with both during seminars, etc.

And had *never* been sick.

Caught Adam's eye, crooked brow. He nodded. On behalf of both I accepted invitation with thanks; agreed had much to discuss.

Continued on rails to next level crossing; retracted guide wheels (which Rollo admired extravagantly, to Adam's embarrassed delight). Rollo familiar with local roads' pitfalls; led way to his home. Drive took perhaps hour total.

Lived in big, comfortable-looking house amidst sprawling

grounds; once nicely landscaped, now gone to seed. Rollo apologized for condition; explained house, upkeep furnished by school. Wife's pride, joy; without her for inspiration, maintenance crew to do work, had little interest in appearance.

Met at curb by large, gaunt, battle-scarred, notch-eared, yellow- and black-striped tomcat, who greeted me with gruff courtesy but went into ecstasies over Adam: Head-dived at ankles, twined around feet until could hardly walk. Accompanied him to door, offered to follow inside. Rollo drew back foot; cat darted into bushes, favored him with unflattering personal remark.

"Sorry," he offered, noting my expression. "That's Tora-hōhi, my late wife's cat. Tora-hōhi means 'Tiger-breath' in Japanese."

Caught Adam's slight headshake, but couldn't spare attention to find out what he wanted. Sudden crisis in progress; required full attention:

As Rollo walked past, Terry growled deep in throat, hunched shoulders, fluffed plumage, bobbed head, narrowed pupils to pinpoints; then lashed out in great roundhouse swing, obviously with every intention of carving divot from whatever portion of man's anatomy he could reach. Was astonished at normally blithe sibling's reaction; first time ever saw him take dislike to obviously refined, well-educated person on sight. Probably the smell, raggedy appearance. (Couldn't blame him, really; *long* time since Rollo bathed, changed clothes.)

Intended victim hadn't noticed. Still apologizing for treatment of wife's cat: "I'm not a cat person myself, and it's never liked me, either. It considered us rivals over Sally ever since it was a kitten. The dispute never escalated to open warfare; we just settled, over the years, into a pattern of mutually respectful antagonism, which became a family tradition. That cat would be horrified by now if I displayed unseemly solicitude or affection toward it. It would view it as a clear violation of the armistice.

"And since Sally died, I haven't been able to allow it in the house, because it—well"—Rollo grinned ruefully—"it took to expressing its opinion of me—on my pillow . . . !

"Besides, I didn't think it would be fair to 'spoil' it in view of circumstances. If something happened to me, it would be better off already accustomed to foraging for itself." Rollo eyed the cat appraisingly. "So I booted it outside and tapered off feeding it. It's doing pretty well so far; I haven't fed it in months, and it's still in pretty good shape."

(Matter of opinion, I thought; but decided to keep lip buttoned for once. Also wondered at use of impersonal pronoun: "It" seemed unnecessarily rude.)

Really do like cats myself, though not rabid "cat person" per se: Terry comes first, period; and cats, birds uneasy bedmates—not that idiot twin afraid of, particularly at risk from, normal domestic housecat. Has encountered before. Generally clicks bill loudly, suggestively; settles feathers in menacing fashion; cat remembers pressing business elsewhere, departs unhurriedly. All very civilized. Has even been friends with one well-behaved neighbor cat over the years.

"I really can't imagine why it still bothers to hang around," Rollo continued. "Our relationship is quite limited. Whenever I leave the house it glares at me—no, amend that: Sometimes it sits on the window ledge and glares in at me, too."

Adam surprised me. Never had pets while growing up; no experience with cats. Last person would expect to be cat person. But blurted out then, "I don't know what 'good shape' means in a cat, but he looks awfully thin to me. Could we bring him in, just for the evening, and feed him? I'll watch and make sure he doesn't do anything he shouldn't."

Rollo debated momentarily, glanced at me, then smiled. "Sure, why not."

Once inside, Rollo disappeared to clean up. I returned to van briefly to fetch Terry's stand; set up in living room in unused corner. Then we waited for Rollo.

Tora-hōhi jumped into Adam's lap without hesitation. Adam looked surprised as cat butted him authoritatively in stomach, performed three formal turnarounds, then settled down firmly to accompaniment of soft, rusty-sounding purring. Volume increased by full order of magnitude when Adam hesitantly scratched under chin. Sounded like cement mixer.

(Knew then Adam genuine cat person; has "touch": One of those people who unerringly scratch right place every time. Tora-hōhi knew, too: Adam hooked.)

"'Tora-hōhi' doesn't mean 'Tiger-breath,'" said Adam softly. Expression, as scratched cat's neck, chin, stroked here, there, in response to unconscious clues, invited comparison with mother in Michelangelo's "Madonna and Child." "I competed in the Ozawa Competition in Tokyo a couple years ago. I never got fluent at Japanese; I just learned enough to get by—but we kids did learn all the *wrong* words. 'Tiger-breath' would be 'Tora-kokyū.' I think '*hōhi*' means 'fart.' I wonder if Rollo knows he's got it wrong. *I'm* going to call him 'Tora-chan.' That means 'Tiger-dear.'" Broke off to scratch particular spot behind cat's left ear. Tora-chan responded by snuggling even closer, stepping up already impressive volume, closing eyes as expression of total satisfaction overspread diabolical visage.

Smiled to myself: Adam unaware, of course, but had just announced intention of adopting crusty old warrior, regardless how relations might go with Rollo. Of course, had little real say in matter—such decisions belong to cat alone.

Rollo reappeared about an hour later, announced: "Is this better?" And received no answer because both Adam and I staring open-mouthed.

Had accomplished nothing less than transfiguration: Was clean, smooth-shaven, hair cut roughly but adequately; wearing clean, quietly stylish, casual clothes. Smelled good, too: aftershave (Coté's musk, I think).

Appearance now matched demeanor: Rollo poised, elegant; tall, slim, quietly handsome; perhaps mid-40s; touch of gray at temples; high forehead, cheekbones; firm, dimpled chin; astonishingly blue eyes; lots of laugh lines—cut singularly impressive figure.

Told him so. Looked pleased. Then suggested we adjourn to kitchen; intended to whip up festive dinner. Followed, bringing Terry's stand.

Adam fed Tora-chan, who ate until sides bulged. Rollo produced old litter pan from broom closet, filled, offered to cat. Tora-chan glared, but took advantage. Adam fascinated by performance: Had never known cats bury own waste. Also bury anything too spoiled to eat, garbage in general, Rollo added by way of information.

Then Tora-chan noticed Terry. Jumped up on counter next to stand; sat, stared. Twin clicked bill several times; fluffed, settled feathers; stared back without rancor. Tora-chan considered pros, cons; decided had better things to do. Returned to Adam's lap. Then pooled energies with bird, glaring as Rollo hustled around kitchen, making dinner, small-talking nonstop (over long months' isolation, had built up substantial conversational pressures).

Couldn't understand Terry's attitude; Rollo so *nice*—apart

from not being cat person, of course. And even there, had—well—not totally unreasonable justification for conduct. Perhaps brother's opinion based on initial appearance, smell; or spur-of-moment approval of cat—offended by Rollo's treatment of new friend at door.

But, though never known him wrong about stranger, inclined to be less conservative myself now that meeting Adam turned out well; now I had partner, reliable backup if crisis developed.

Besides, *wanted* meeting Rollo to turn out well; wanted for friend. Embodied most good qualities friend should have: intelligent, understanding, good-humored—funny (for five dreadful minutes he and Adam engaged in pun-ishing contest: Adam won, but issue in doubt right up to final groan).

Plus, as predinner conversation turned into dinner conversation, developed that Rollo had been *every*where, done *every*thing: Peace Corps physician for years in Africa, India, South America. Spent year traveling as resident physician with Ringling Brothers' Circus. Vacations included photo expeditions through Malaysia, Australia, Alaska. Had driven race cars in Europe (Adam's eyes bugged; already assembling list of questions), semis during summers while in school; flown sailplanes in Lee Wave over Minden, Nevada; snorkled Caribbean, South Pacific; climbed K2 in Himalayas. Wrote textbooks, had own TV show on local station, was two-term state house representative. Finally got into private practice, teaching, then administration. Both Daddy, Teacher had guest-taught at his school at one time or another.

This led to discussion of Teacher's work, *H. post hominem* theory, physical characteristics of new breed. Rollo listened intently to précis of events leading to species' discovery. Asked occasional questions. Finally shook head in amazement: "*Damn*, I wish I could have participated in that study. McDivott invited me to take part years ago, but I was just heading off to Save the World in the Peace Corps. Wonderful. . . ."

Then we got into my, Adam's survival, meeting; trip to this point, zoo-animal problem; clues unearthed thus far, purpose, hoped-for ultimate destination. Rollo impressed: Offered long, low whistle at narrative's conclusion. Opined were braver than he, out exploring by ourselves. His reaction to tragedy was dig hole, climb in, pull in after him: Withdrew, feeling sorry for self, grieving over loss of wife.

Rollo met her there at school. Twenty years his junior, she "...kept me young and interested—and our sudden marriage caused all kinds of entertainingly wicked gossip for first few months. When nothing materialized, it all petered out on a disappointed note.

"We never did have any children—much less that nine-pound preemie everyone expected. It wasn't a question of age; 25 would have been a fine age for Sally to begin bearing children; and, by microscopic examination, it looked as if I'd be fertile until they hammered down the headstone. We were waiting for me to retire so we both could be full-time parents. I had a bunch of investments that would have matured in another two years. We did take the precaution of freezing a quart or so of my semen, just in case my prognostications proved overly optimistic. . . .

"Which brings us to our next topic . . ."

Leaned back, sighed, patted his tummy, still amazingly flat despite quantity put away. "Golly, that was good. I wonder what I did right." (Adam stared vacantly at ceiling; Rollo hadn't noticed him sniffing pots during preparation.)

"...which is, of course, Candy." Rollo smiled fondly at me. Smiled back; such a nice man. Turning then to Adam, Rollo sat up straight, folded hands on edge of table, assumed serious mien.

"Sir," he began, "it appears that you are in sole possession of something we both want. In the absence of law, it becomes necessary to settle the matter between us personally. The question is: Shall we resolve it like the gentlemen we purport to be, or must we fall back on the time-honored method?"

Adam's expression the very picture of noncomprehension.

Rollo regarded him soberly. "In other words, will you share Candy with me or must we fight over her?"

Adam's eyes snapped open. Understood now—and *so did I* . . . !

Mouth open, retort quivering on tip of tongue; but Adam beat me to it. Did good job, too; covered every point would have raised myself, plus angles hadn't thought of (and language more diplomatic than I would have employed): "Candy is *not* my property. She is *no* one's property. I doubt if she ever will *be* anyone's property. I have no authority over her, nor is my permission required for any arrangement anyone might or might not reach with her. If you want to discuss sharing anything with her, you will have to talk to *her*."

Rollo pursed lips thoughtfully. Then nodded approvingly. "Fair enough, sir. And spoken like a gentleman. Thank you."

Turned to me. "I'm sorry; I misapprehended the relationship between you. I think I have it now.

"All right; are *you* willing to share *Adam* with me, or must *we* fight over him?"

If Adam startled before, completely dumbfounded now. Mouth flapped soundlessly. And surely doing no better myself.

Situation static for long moments. Rollo stared, aspect implacably serious, waiting for reply. Then eyes twinkled. Seconds later snickered, went directly thence to belly-laughing. Tears running down cheeks before managed to stop.

Personally saw nothing funny, but held counsel, pending explanation.

"Oh, I *am* sorry," he puffed at length. "I wish I had a picture of your faces just then.

"Okay. . . ." Rollo sobered finally; mood darkened, became almost somber. "I gave you both a shock. I did it deliberately to make sure that I had your undivided attention. I was teasing, of course; sex is the Oldest Funny Subject, and it's easy to get sidetracked. Besides, it sometimes helps to joke when the issue is serious. And this is *very* serious.

"You two are too young to understand just *how* serious sex can be in an adult world. But believe me when I tell you: No subject lies closer to the raw, untamed primitive in every man. Men have killed, and will kill again, over sex. Sex is *serious business*: That's a boiler-plate given; an unalterable fact of life. Don't forget it. Ever.

"Now, I don't know whether you two have become sexually involved yet or not—frankly, I don't care. That's history; it's none of my business. What *is* my business is the fact that I am a healthy adult male. I'm in the prime of life. I was married for five wonderful years to an equally healthy adult woman, whose sex drive was as well-developed as mine. We enjoyed an enthusiastic, extremely active, and marvelously fulfilling sex life. . . ."

Paused, eyed me bleakly. "I miss her—and *it*—very much."

Adam later reported was tossup whether my eyes or mouth open wider.

Rollo nodded sympathetically; continued gently: "Yes, that's precisely what I'm getting at. And yes, you *are* younger than anyone with whom I've contemplated sexual relations. But not by much.

"I got involved with a girl almost your age during the time I was stationed in Ujjain. She was a street child: no parents, no means of support, starving, regularly raped. I took her in to protect her—that's what I told myself. And for a good two months that's just what I did. Then one night she turned up in my bed and matters continued predictably from there. She claimed she was 14 when we first became intimate—I have my doubts. 'Love' was not involved on either side; we were merely very fond of each other and had complementary needs: Hers were for food, shelter, and protection; mine were for companionship, someone to take care of, and a sexual outlet.

"When I was transferred, two years later, I left her with friends, a good family, with a trust fund to take care of her—in India, back then, it didn't take much money to accomplish such things. Thereafter she married well and, by the time of the attack, had three children. I've never experienced any guilt at having 'taken advantage of a child'; and if she harbored any resentment, she never gave any indication of it—then or since, and we corresponded regularly.

"In fact, she brought the subject up herself once in a letter shortly after the birth of her first son—women's lib hadn't gotten very far in India by then; sons were *important*. She observed that she had me to thank for her happiness: her husband, her son—her very life. It bothered her that she would never be able to repay the debt she felt she owed me; it disturbed her even more that she could never make me understand the magnitude of that debt.

"I mention her as an example of the variability of the concept of right and wrong, depending on place and time. That was *there* and *then*: It was socially acceptable.

"Now, before the attack—*here* and *recently*—I'd have been leading the tar-and-feather brigade myself if I got wind of someone my age suggesting sex with someone your age: It would have been wrong within the social structure that existed.

"However, this is *here* and *now*. That social structure no longer exists—and with it have disappeared the laws and mores of which it consisted. Right and wrong no longer have meaning except where specific individuals meet and apply them to issues affecting them both. All that remains is the principle of enlightened self-interest, when dealing with reasonable people, and superior-versus-inferior force otherwise.

"One of the key elements of enlightened self-interest is the principle of supply and demand. Anyone possessing a commodity for which there is a demand is in a position to set her own price.

"But price is a very delicate question, and requires knowledge of all the factors potentially bearing upon the transaction. One of the more important of those factors is the presence or absence of competition, and the importance of your offering to the marketplace. If your commodity isn't particularly critical and there's plenty of other outlets, setting your price too high merely means no demand. However, where you have a monopoly, you can set any price you like; and if it's a really vital commodity, your customers will manage to scrape up the price, somehow.

"Or"—Rollo fixed me with gimlet eye—"if they perceive that you're taking unfair advantage of your position, they may simply take it from you. By force.

"I've started out discussing abstracts," he continued quietly; "but you know as well as I do that we're talking about two specifics: you and sex. Like it or not, to every male over the age of ten you represent *supply*—a *commodity*. It's not fair, I'll grant you, but it *is* a *fact*: Through no fault of your own, you are in the position of holding the key to satisfying a need—an extremely *urgent* need. Unless you administer that commodity in a manner perceived by your market as fair and reasonable, you're going to find yourself in frequent trouble, at best—at worst, and much more likely, you're going to find out what it's like to have control over your commodity taken from you. Yes, by force."

Rollo noticed me slowly edging chair back from table. Possessed no inkling of real capabilities, intentions, should events continue in direction indicated; probably thought was preparing to bolt. But immediately sought to quiet fears.

"Please don't get the idea that *I* would use force," he stated emphatically. "I wouldn't—*ever*. Sex with Sally was such a joy, so much just plain fun for *both* of us—I got at least as much pleasure from watching her enjoyment as from my own physical sensations—that I'd rather give it up entirely than have an unwilling partner, or even a grudging one."

Paused, then, eyes closed. Expression unreadable, but impression of an empty space somehow materialized next to him. Briefly Rollo looked terribly alone.

Moment passed. Opened eyes; shook himself all over. "*But*," he continued resolutely, "I am certainly in the minority in that regard. Hell, I'm probably unique." Smiled wanly.

Assurance had desired calming effect: Relaxed, settled back in chair, watching alertly. Never truly concerned over outcome had Rollo offered to supplement advocacy with violence, but happier knowing demonstration unnecessary.

However, still on guard. Lecture circular so far, but surely headed somewhere. Had feeling already knew punch line.

"Now, during the brief time I've known you I've come to several conclusions: One, you are the *de facto* leader of this little party, despite being a few years Adam's junior; because, I suspect, you know more about survival and life since the attack, and because you have specific goals in mind. Right?"

Adam nodded slowly, face a mask.

"Two, you're *terribly* intelligent—both of you are; you're at least as bright as I am. My advantage is limited to education and experience, and I wonder how much of an edge they really are. I'm pretty sure that you've already sized me up and you were thinking of asking me to join you in your search for the AAs—at least you were before this discussion began. Now you're having second thoughts. But you know I'm widely traveled; have a broad practical background in life in general and survival under primitive conditions. You also know I'm a doctor. You know how valuable I'd be as a member of your party.

"Now, I *would* like to join you and help. However..." Rollo paused, choosing words with care; "I *cannot* and *will* not endure your company on a celibate basis if, after speculum examination, it is my professional opinion that you are physically capable of accepting me as a lover. If you can't, fine; if you wouldn't enjoy it, neither would I. Then I'll take care of my physical tensions as I've been doing since losing Sally, and conduct myself as a member of the party anyway—and without reservation.

"But if you can and won't, the distraction of your presence, constantly near and unattainable, will simply drive me around the bend; and I'm not going to subject myself to that kind of frustration.

"Yes, I know: If I had a decent bone in my body, I'd wait a while. The fact that you met Adam, and now me, lends credence to Soo Kim's thesis: There are people out there, somewhere, and surely there'll be women my age among them; it's just a matter of finding them. But who knows how long that might take—I could be *dead* tomorrow. You, on the other hand, are here *now*; and I've been a disciple of the 'bird-in-the-hand' school for a very long time.

"I know that's not a chivalrous attitude, and I'm not proud of it; but I am a realist, and I know myself.

"Mind you"—he grinned ironically—"there's nothing particularly personal in this. Yes, I do like you, so far as I know you, and I admire you even more. Added to which, you're cute as a button and can only get prettier. But—and I'm sure this won't do your ego any good, and I'm sorry, but I'm not going to lie to you—under these circumstances any live, functional female would have the same effect.

Rollo paused again, fixed me with those earnest blue eyes. "So if, after due deliberation, you feel that my presence as a widely traveled, all-around experienced man-of-the-world, who has considerable background in dealing with the new wildlife problems, and my training as a doctor, would be of sufficient benefit to you in your travels to justify the cost, I'm yours—with all that implies: I'll come with you, and stay as long as you want me to—for life if you choose—and fight and die for you if it comes to that, or for Adam—but only as your invited, *wanted* consort. And I'll accept any reasonable time-sharing arrangement with Adam that you might dictate.

"Nor will I insist on assuming leadership of the expedition, merely because I'm oldest and, therefore, presumptively the wisest. I'm not at all certain that I *am* wiser than you. More experienced, better educated, yes. And I'll share it with you if you ask. But wiser? Insufficient data.

"Now, I would suggest to you that it is the right of every woman to establish the value of her consent. Every woman since Eve has. And I defy anyone to fault her for including practical considerations in the transaction. Down through the centuries numberless women have determined that a pledge of support, companionship, and security—which translates as 'protection' in primitive societies—for themselves, their children, and/or brothers and sisters, constituted a fair exchange. Many, if not most, assuming the man involved possessed even a vestigial sense of honor, lived happy, fulfilled lives. It was not uncommon for such women to come to love their partners in these marriages-of-convenience very much, and to find themselves ultimately quite satisfied with the bargain."

Could see Adam out of corner of eye, face expressionless. Probably mentally kicking himself—wishing *he* had thought of this approach . . . !

"I'll add one more thing; then I'll shut up and abide by your decision," said Rollo finally. "I'm good husband material: I'm gentle, understanding, and thoughtful; and nothing makes me as happy as making my woman happy, in or out of bed. As a single husband, I made Sally happy; as Number Two of two, I'll do my best to make you happy.

"As far as sex is concerned, if you come to me in good faith, you'll enjoy yourself. That sounds conceited, I know, but it's an honest opinion based on long experience—and if you *don't* like it, after a fair trial, I won't insist that you continue: That would eliminate half your attraction for me. And I'll stay with you anyway, as long as you want me to. But I'm confident that you will enjoy it: My specialty was gynecology and sexual counseling—there's very little that I don't know about evoking and satisfying the female sexual response."

Well!—how's *that* for subtle . . . ? Most outrageous proposition ever heard about, read, let alone encountered.

And how about "nothing personal" angle! Or "any live, functional" etc.!

(Though *is* better than being lied to. I suppose. Probably. Maybe. Hmm. . . .)

Well, consider matter logically: Was gentleman about it, under what must be profoundly trying conditions (could have hit Adam over head, had me all to self [surely thought so anyway]). But fact *did* think so made genteel approach all the more commendable. Yes, Rollo basically good person; possessed most qualities prefer in friend. Plus versed in survival skills; knew way around life-in-wilderness; bumped heads in past with immigrant carnivores. And *doctor*—presence invaluable, if not downright critical, in situations all too easy to envision.

But *hate logic* . . . ! What right had logic to butt in at time like this . . . ? *None*—that's what! Yes/no decision supposed to be matter of emotion alone, uninfluenced by crass realities. Logistics supposed to work themselves out afterward, as part of Happily-Ever-After scenario—*every*body knows that. . . .

However, "everybody" not faced with my problems, responsibilities. Nor this choice. Oh, dear, such *difficult* choice, too. If alone, would decline with thanks, without hesitation. But Adam to think of, with whom share Chinese obligation—mutual, true; but mutuality doesn't discharge debt; if anything, reinforces.

Debated question from every angle. Weighed pros, cons. Reviewed argument in detail. Had to admit was tidy, matter-of-fact, economical, pragmatic—and eminently correct, however offensive correctness might be in this setting! Looked for out—looked *hard*. But while couldn't quite bring self to agree with pat reasoning, neither could find anything to get teeth into to *dis*agree, at least not legitimately.

Presently realized question not really debatable; not for conscientious, responsible partner. Benefits potentially accruing to Adam of having intelligent, experienced adult (and *doctor*) join expedition placed personal reluctance in perspective: a bargain; no other conclusion possible. After all, no big deal—*every* girl does it.

Just a question of when.

And with whom. . . .

Well, having made decision, resolved to give it best shot. Simple question of equity: Rollo's commitment total; pledged time, efforts, plus contributing wealth of knowledge, experience. Doubtless find life in jeopardy before events reach dénouement. Entitled to fair return on investment.

(Harbored no genuine doubt as to physical ability to deliver own side of transaction.)

And never once considered possible out offered by suggestion would lose interest if I didn't enjoy. Cheap-shot evasion. Fair is fair; promise is promise. Would try to be as merrily enthusiastic a partner as fondly remembered Sally.

Maybe *better*. . . .

(Oh-oh . . . ! Occurred to me then [speaking of fair]: Could hardly accept Rollo's attentions, continue to exclude Adam, whom had known longer, and of whom, by this time, was very fond.)

Took deep breath, released slowly to establish control over emotions, voice. Stood, took another deep breath, opened mouth . . .

And before could announce decision, became suddenly, shockingly, horribly moot. Rollo, bustling about kitchen, cleaning up after dinner, got too close to Terry's stand. Twin's head shot out, huge bill halves closed, chopping golf-ball-sized gobbet from left tricep, shirt sleeve and all. Bobbed head gleefully, eyes glinting in malicious triumph, as flung bloody mess across kitchen; then crouched, wings half-spread, red-splattered bill gaping wide, poised to strike again.

Rollo gasped, eyes widening in shock. Spun, roaring with pain, rage. Drew back fist—containing heavy iron frying pan . . . ! Would crush fragile avian skeleton like eggshell— *Rollo about to murder my baby brother!*

"Time slowed" ancient cliché. But happens—and happened then: Suddenly everything happening in slow motion. Had ample time to study every tiny detail as situation developed. Enough time to notice sequential tensioning of Rollo's muscles, starting with abdominal, then chest, neck, shoulder, upper arm, forearm, as lethal swing began, pan accelerated in arc toward helpless sibling. Time to notice Adam's expression of growing horror; mouth slowly opening to shout warning, protest: *"No-o—"*

Enough time to realize own body suddenly in motion. But without conscious volition; moving of own accord: Combat computer, conditioned-reflex matrix, engaged, in control. Mere passenger now in own body; relatively sluggish conscious mind powerless to interfere, alter outcome during next few milliseconds.

Felt, then heard own *kiai* rip from throat; watched self cross nearly ten feet separating us midair, spinning counterclockwise. Left heel intercepted Rollo's forearm; limb folded in unnatural place, direction. Pan ripped from fingers, continued tangentially, well clear of intended victim.

Rollo's neck corded, beginning motion that would turn rage-contorted features toward me. Muscles governing still functional right arm twitched; hand slowly formed claw, started my direction.

Already wasn't there. Landed in stable cat stance, still passenger. Stepped under, past reaching limb; side-kicked spot just below hip. Femur broke with sound like snapping ax handle. Impact drove Rollo against wall, position from which could not fall away from blows.

Which continued as blocked still-reaching claw with forearm, ducked back under to front, unleashed hail of alternating lunge and reverse punches to clavicles, sternum, larynx, each powered to break bricks, driving through frail body tissues as if so much Jell-O.

Rollo began sideways motion to right, falling along wall toward damaged leg; but combat computer interpreted as flanking attempt. Clockwise spin-kick swept legs from under, sundering left knee at point of impact. Back-fist lashed out from continuing rotation, catching alongside jaw. Maxilla, mandible disintegrated with grinding sound.

Rollo hit perhaps another dozen times before conscious mind overtook events. Regained control as combat computer finished triphammer series of right-handed front-fist blows to upper thorax. Braced against rebounding from impacts by wall down which was sliding, Rollo absorbed blows' total force internally: Ribs snapped like balsa; underlying structures turned to pulp.

Time resumed normal pace. Tail end of Adam's cry echoed through kitchen: "—o-o-o . . . !" Rollo arrived on floor with mushy squish. Pan clattered against far wall, fell to floor.

Terry bobbed head, said, "How *'bout* that."

I uncoiled shakily, staring at ruin at feet. Looked up to meet Adam's gaze. Stunned expression mirrored my own.

Essayed speech: "I didn't mean . . . he would have killed . . ."

Tora-chan approached. Sat, surveyed body for long moment. Then stood, inspected mashed face; sniffed along broken length, head to foot. Moved off-side front paw along floor toward body, flipped upward: Same motion employed when covering mess in litter pan.

Tora-chan finished, glanced up with unmistakable cat smile. Purred. Performed luxurious head-dive on my ankle.

Next thing I remember is waking fully dressed following morning in own bed in trailer. Hugely depressed, but several minutes before remembered why. Adam supplied intervening details:

Went into shock, catatonia—whatever: nonresponding, physically inert, eyes-open stupor. Adam concluded immediate elimination of evidence, separation from scene best therapy.

Wiped Terry's bill, placed bird on shoulder. Picked up stand, called Tora-chan.

Then, moving cautiously, watching closely lest Weapon still armed, took me by hand, led to trailer. Stripped me, pushed into shower, washed off blood, adhering meat scraps. Dressed me in clean clothes. Debated old outfit briefly; judged icky beyond salvage, plus now probably haunted. Pitched *in toto*.

Placed me in van. Then drove as if demons pursued.

Continued far into night, until accumulated shock, nervous exhaustion, fatigue called halt—nearly conked out at wheel.

Put me to bed; started to get into own. But delayed reaction arrived then: Pitched such hysterical fit that Adam (hasn't said, but probably at considerable personal risk) sedated me. Finally climbed in with me, held me until asleep before adjourning to own bed.

Ten days now since killing. Beginning to come to grips with guilt.

Adam big help: Pointed out, and cannot disagree, am no more responsible for Rollo's death than unfamiliar firearm with which had managed to shoot himself. Am Sixth Degree Black Belt. And female. Terry my sibling/child-substitute.

Rollo's murderous lunge triggered maternal protective instinct, which in turn set off conditioned-response matrix at starkest level. Probably wouldn't have reacted with such single-minded, nonstop efficiency if merely swung at me—but my retarded *baby brother . . .*!

Besides, had hurried me.

Okay. Absorbed that; do believe it. Intellectually.

Problem is, haven't resolved it yet on gut level. Still hurts. Lots. Rollo nice man, basically good—certainly no saint, but frank about it. Made straightforward offer, value for value, yes or no, my choice. No doubt would have lived up to his end.

Adam thinks Terry sensed Rollo had violent temper; hence instant antipathy. Possibly. Equally possible: Just plain terribly painful bite—sure looked it. Adam disagrees; been hurt accidentally himself by people, once seriously. Managed without going *musth*.

Granted. But even if true, character flaw only; not capital crime. Nothing for which deserved to die. And could have prevented harm to Terry without killing, but for programed response.

Therein lies hard-to-swallow part: Killed innocent person—unnecessarily. No getting around it: *Unnecessarily*. Unavoidably, true, given circumstances; but still unnecessarily.

And still dead.

Worse, little nagging voice in back of head keeps suggesting may not have been *completely* unavoidable. Maybe subconsciously *wanted* to let programing run amok because had me cornered. Don't think so, but disquieting notion.

In any event, will *not* happen again. Been drilling past ten days with modified *kata*, sparring routine. Working to eradicate all automatically lethal responses. Programing deep-seated; will take time to effect changes. But am walking time bomb as things stand; waiting to explode, hurt, kill people upon cue—even inadvertent cue! Lots of work involved, and accomplishment not without risk.

But necessary: Intend *never to kill again* . . . !

Have gone through Mount Palomar facilities with great care. Nothing about contents to suggest AAs' presence in recent past. But sweep not entirely unproductive: Found Cal-Tech staff directory in one office—containing name, address of Tarzan File AA living in Pasadena! Will follow up on that tomorrow morning, unless . . .

Posterity, you simply won't *believe* what Adam did today. Remember bundle of tubing, cloth, traveling on trailer roof? Well, found out what it is.

I had complained, following search of observatory, that if AAs' secret rendezvous only hundred yards off road, would never find it in densely wooded, mountainous terrain. Suggested we track down U. S. Geological Service and Forest Service section maps; uncouple trailer, explore logging roads in van alone. Might turn up something.

Adam agreed in principle, but said had better idea—and *did* . . . !

Whereupon, removed mysterious bundle from trailer roof and, in space of probably 30 minutes, unfolded, unrolled, then assembled *airplane*—full-sized, man-carrying, aluminum-tubing-and-fabric ultralight. Disappeared briefly into trailer; emerged carrying breadbox-sized, metal-bound wooden case from which took miniature engine, propellor, snapped into place.

"Another benefit of growing up rich and neglected." Eyes twinkled as mixed gas, oil; filled tank. "'Mom, all the *other* kids have ultralights this summer!' It was an election year, you see; she didn't have time to check into the story—which *was* true . . ." continued impishly, squirming past fuselage tubes, settling into pilot's seat; fastening five-point harness; strapping on helmet; checking control surface movement as wiggled stick, pedals, " . . . depending on what neighborhood you canvassed and what numbers you considered a representative sample."

Yanked on pull-cord; engine snarled into life with literally deafening racket (started life as two-stroke motorcycle engine; Adam, per usual practice, modified for additional power, reliability; replaced muffler with "tuned" megaphone exhaust—result sounded like steroid-fed chainsaw). I jammed fingers in ears. Tora-chan dived under trailer; nothing showed but two orange-glowing spots of outrage. Terry's reaction, on other hand, surprisingly mild: Merely flapped wings to indicate disapproval—usually that much noise inspires featherhead to go for help.

"Actually," Adam yelled, pulling down goggles, "I think she thought an ultralight was about three feet long and flown by radio-control." With which he rammed throttle to stop, pulled back stick, acelerated to about human running speed, lifted gently from parking lot, soared out over Cleveland National Forestlands, leaving me standing wide-eyed, chin resting on toes.

Managed to follow part of flight with binoculars: Brightly colored midge visible for many miles from catwalk encircling 200-inch reflector's dome. Adam checked every logging road, cowpath, nature trail within 25-mile radius of observatory. Looked especially closely for indications of isolated structures— facilities *not* accessible by road, or whose construction and/or placement suggested attempted concealment.

Gone three hours, but eventually floated lightly from sky, touching down at walking pace, gently as falling leaf. Killed engine, removed helmet.

"If they're out there, they're well hidden," he shouted into silence; then added more softly, "Am I talking too loudly? I usually do after flying this. You're supposed to use acoustical earplugs, but I always forget."

Too close to dark to continue by time he returned, so spending night in observatory parking lot.

Adam glowing all over; simply irrepressible: bursting with puns, teasing, good humor—never seen *anyone* appreciate own cleverness so much. . . .

Oh, well, minor irritation, really. Of more concern is change in self: Since watching Adam fly ultralight, have felt unaccustomed longing, yearning, wish, want, desire, yen, attraction, need, craving—no-holds-barred patholgical *obsession*! For first time, understand Mr. Toad's reaction to initial sight of motorcar. . . .

Oh, Posterity, been such *exciting* two days . . . ! But shall adhere to histographers' discipline; set down events as transpired, without giving hints, muddling chronology—possibly losing later-important details in process.

So: Departed Mount Palomar early this morning; set course for Pasadena. Got as far as Riverside before routine shattered:

Adam rounded corner in usual gentle fashion—and small child on bicycle shot from behind abandoned car, directly into path, mere yards from bumper. Adam yanked steering wheel; almost simultaneously locked up brakes. Somehow missed child; stopped partially jackknifed on spot had occupied heartbeat previously.

Kid continued across street, darted between two buildings, out of sight.

As one we sprang from van, landed running. Adam, well in lead, covered good 200 yards, calling out reassuringly, before misjudging height of obstacle, snagging toe midvault, crashing heavily to ground. And since karate training still not implanted in reflexes, fell wrong: on left elbow. Bone's snap even louder than anguished gasp, curse.

Arrived on scene. Cautioned, "Don't move"; restrained bodily. Adam's karate discipline manifested then; late, but still useful: White, sweating but calm, lay still as examined. Explored as gently as possible, but still elicited grimaces, gasps. Upper arm visibly shorter, plus had grown extra elbow.

"Humerus," was verdict.

Even in agony Adam couldn't resist: "Not to me," he puffed through gritted teeth. Then spark faded, leaving only pain: "I thought so. Can you set it?"

(*Rollo could*, mocked little voice inside skull. But ignored it; concentrated on Adam [fixing broken arm challenge enough without compounding problems by indulging in guilt trip].)

"I *know* how to do it; I've never set one myself, of course. And you aren't going to enjoy it. The ends are overriding; you know what that means."

Adam knew. Grew even whiter.

Helped him to feet, supporting arm to immobilize. Returned to trailer. Strapped upper arm temporarily to torso; then adjourned to nearest hospital. Located plastic splint—and mouthpiece.

Helped Adam onto table, strapped down. "I don't know anything about anesthesia. I'm more likely to kill you than not if I give you anything." He nodded, staring at ceiling, already sweating in anticipation.

"Now, the only way I can overcome the muscle spasms holding those bone ends overlapped is by tapping my hysterical strength. Once I start, I'll have to forge ahead and finish in one pass, regardless how much it hurts. Otherwise I'll burn out and you'll end up with a short, crooked arm, or worse."

"I know," he replied tightly. Inserted mouthpiece, set teeth. Took deep breath, closed eyes, indistinctly grunted, "*Do it!*"

Placed knee in armpit. Grasped elbow firmly in right hand; clamped forearm under own armpit. Placed left hand over break, and . . .

Hesitated, struck by idea. Might work or not. Never tried before. But success depended on Adam believing: Positive attitude intrinsic to execution.

Assumed confident aspect, said, "*Whoa . . . !* Adam, we *don't* have to do it the hard way . . . !"

Adam opened eyes, peered up at me cautiously. Removed mouthpiece; bodily tension eased imperceptible fraction. "How else?"

"Hypnosis!" I announced in what hoped was triumphant tone. "I forgot—you're a great hypnotic subject. We'll just put you under and anesthetize your arm. You won't feel a thing."

Adam looked dubious. "It hasn't worked with the hysterical-strength tap."

"Of *course* it hasn't worked; you've been fighting it," I stated positively. "You *know* you have—you're scared of hysterical strength because of what happened to me. You achieve as deep a trance as I do, but you block the suggestion. If you *want* it to work, it *will.*"

Relieved to see hint of hope nudge in alongside pain in Adam's expression. Knew seed planted, taking root; but didn't give him time to think about it. Kept momentum building: continued sales pitch, preinduction psychology:

"Remember my telling you how Daddy did double duty, working as a GP as well as a pathologist? Well, he didn't like drug-assisted deliveries because of the effect on babies; he used chemicals only when a woman absolutely couldn't reach a useful trance state in classes during the months leading up to the delivery. Otherwise he used hypnosis exclusively. I often helped during deliveries, and I never once saw a woman evince discomfort during delivery under hypnosis—and childbirth is the standard against which all other pain is gauged, remember.

"Now, you're already past the hard part: You achieve a full somnambulistic-level trance. Unless you fight the suggestion, it *will work!*"

Adam visibly relieved. "You're right. But I don't think I can do it myself, hurting like this; it's hard to concentrate on anything but the pain. But I can follow your voice. Will you put me under?"

Of course would. And did. Adam responded immediately to preprogramed induction code; slid into profound trance state as promptly as if session merely another in regular series dealing with focusing *ki*, tapping hysterical strength. Pain-drawn features eased even before turning attention to anesthesia: Total concentration characteristic of deepest trance state precluded sparing attention to notice pain.

However, could hardly count on incidental effects to protect against bone-resetting agony. So proceeded with anesthesia induction: Reminded Adam how sleeping in wrong position sometimes puts arm "to sleep": complete sensation lack, plus motor paralysis. Explained acupressure point just under armpit responsible. Placed finger on supposed location; told him 30 seconds' firm pressure there would put arm to sleep for minimum of two hours; repeatable as necessary.

Pressed firmly and—no wonder primitive societies regarded hypnotism as magic—whole body sagged as relief from pain canceled subconscious adrenaline alert.

More importantly, spasming muscles in damaged arm went limp; perhaps could perform resetting without triggering own hysterical strength. Only one way to find out.

Replaced knee in Adam's armpit. Took elbow in right hand, left hand over break; again clamped forearm under own armpit. Then pulled firmly but with control. Stretched limb until felt broken ends grind clear of each other, opposing bulges disappear beneath left hand. Eased tension, allowed ends to settle into what hoped was apposition.

Studied result. Reduction apparently successful: arm grossly straight, same length as right. But palpation ineffective in final determination, and no knowledge of x-ray. Hoped okay. Best I could do.

Slipped plastic splint halves into place. Strapped upper

arm to side; bent elbow 90 degrees, strapped forearm across abdomen.

Gave wake-up code. Adam sighed, stirred—then froze, body tense, apparently awaiting pain's resumption. When failed to materialize, opened eyes cautiously, looked around. "Done?"

"Uh-huh."

"Fixed?"

"I think so. It's straight and they're both the same length. Ask me again in six weeks."

Adam regarded me searchingly. "Are *you* all right? After what happened the last time you used hysterical strength. . . ." Assured him metabolic supercharge unnecessary; had not suffered.

Unstrapped him from table; let sit on edge for while, waiting for residual dizziness, nausea to pass.

Presently shuddered. "That was *not* fun. It doesn't hurt now, but it sure did before." Eyed left hand where protruded from strapping. "This *is* like waking up after sleeping wrong. But it's scary—I assume my hand will work again once it's worn off?"

"As soon as you *want* it to wear off. You can keep it numb for as long as it bothers you by renewing the acupressure block. But you'll be playing piano again as soon as the splint comes off."

Adam nodded; then looked up abruptly. "We've got to find that kid. He was *clean*—that means he's not alone: A kid that size doesn't bathe except under duress."

Good point. (Does have unique talent for isolating essential details.)

"I suppose we can drive up and down the streets, blowing the horn and yelling until we find them."

Adam shook head. "A kid on a bike covers more territory than a tomcat—it would take forever.

"If it weren't for this"—he indicated splinted arm—"I'd fly a search pattern. That would bring them out—I doubt if planes are a routine sight these days."

Felt heart miss beat, but tried not to let elation show. Asked nonchalantly, "Does it take long to learn to fly?"

Adam regarded me thoughtfully. "No; flying is almost instinctive—though the 'almost' is important; the differences can kill you. But with your brains, reflexes, and coordination, you shouldn't have a bit of trouble."

Thought briefly. "We should find someplace wide and flat. Most parking lots are roomy enough for ultralight operation, but an airport would be better for instruction."

Checked couple gas stations, found Riverside city street map; then drove to airport.

With one-armed coach's advice, assistance, unfastened bundle from trailer roof, assembled toy plane in about an hour. Adam explained, demonstrated controls, radio helmet (didn't bother to point out base-station transceiver amongst goodies on trailer's electronics wall when *he* flew; just let me worry!), verified operation. Strapped me in, started engine. Then coached by radio, step-by-step:

Slow taxiing first, gradually increasing speed to learn steering transition from differential braking to rudder; then high-speed taxiing to get feel of all controls biting airstream. Followed by more high-speed taxiing; lifting, lowering, alternate wings to acquire feel of aileron/rudder interaction. Then still more high-speed taxiing; raising, lowering nosewheel to learn elevators.

Big Moment finally arrived: Allowed me to increase power fraction beyond setting used for high-speed taxiing. Main gear lifted from runway—was *flying* . . . !

Not high, of course; Adam kept me skimming up, down runways, yard above ground, for hours: lift-off, touchdown; shallow right, left turns—endless repetition. Never exceeded 30 knots. Slow-flight practice continued until could detect imminent stall power on or off; whether normal or gee-induced, accelerated variety (cute phenomenon, that: stalling speed mounts as gee forces increase aircraft's effective weight); ease in, out of stalled condition without height, control loss.

(Fascinating, wrong assumptions otherwise well-educated person can harbor: From exposure to cars, had assumed knew what controls do. Not so. For instance: Fore-and-aft stick movement governs pitch, thereby airspeed—period. Had heretofore assumed increased, decreased altitude. *Throttle* setting does that. Likewise, did not realize ailerons initiate bank, then back pressure on stick causes actual turn. Rudder's sole function is to prevent yaw (skidding) caused by aileron drag—or induce deliberate yaw in sideslip when attempting to descend steeply without building up airspeed for short-field landing.)

Adam finally satisfied: For past hour had executed all maneuvers to perfection, plus performed "unusual attitude recoveries" (with more altitude under wheels) without incident. Gave me news by radio as concentrated on flying circles about point. (Tricky: To keep radius constant, necessary to increase bank angle when downwind, ease off upwind—adjusting constantly all the way around.)

Landed grinning ear to ear (Mr. Toad correct: "Glorious, stirring . . . poetry of motion . . . only *real* way to travel!")

We spent night at airport. Next morning I topped up fuel; Adam inspected ship minutely. Finally I launched to fly search pattern.

Adam navigated from ground: I reported landmarks below; he plotted position on city map, gave headings to fly. (Alternative was wrestling with three-foot-square sheet of paper in open-bodied aircraft—'tis to laugh.)

Flew at perhaps 300 feet; low enough to spot signs of current habitation: smoking chimney, laundry hung out, crop cultivation in midst of residential area, etc.

And flying is, as knew would be, marvelous ("Here today—in next week tomorrow . . . O bliss!"): In absence of Man, California skies now clear, crisp; visibility unobstructed, breathtaking ("Always somebody else's horizon! O my! O my!"). Yielded to impulse; essayed snap roll.

"'O *stop* being an ass,'" Adam snarled, patience exhausted. "I read it, too. Pay attention now; if you kill yourself I'll never speak to you again." Promised to behave. Leveled off, headed for initial search area, where had almost run over child.

Adam's map ruled off in grids. Examined each methodically, flying slowly, giving anyone on ground ample time to drop everything upon hearing rackety engine (loud, indeed—acoustical earplugs genuine necessity), run outside, be seen.

Covered about six grids before happy discovery. Person ran from house as I passed, waving violently (do mean violently: jumping up, down, shrieking—actually heard faint cries at altitude, through engine noise, helmet, earplugs).

Circled back; pinpointed location for Adam, who jumped into rig, set off by road.

Then scouted landing conditions. Let down to 100 feet, performed slow flyby, studying surface; noting presence, absence of wires, poles, fences, ditches, etc. Detected nothing prohibitive; looked safe.

Set up approach assuming same wind direction, speed as at airport. Drifted down gently, skimming low over house at end of block, slowed to near stall, let big fabric wing float us down. Touched down 50 feet from very excited person—*two* excited persons: one large, one small.

Killed engine, unstrapped, extracted head from helmet, pulled out earplugs, stood . . .

And promptly swept off feet by hug-attack, replete with cryings, incoherent wet sobbings—more huggings, cryings, etc., etc. Managed to discern assailants both female. Happy to see them, too; but of course third, fourth encounters (respectively) with Somebody Else Alive: Old hat, you know; retained semblance of control.

(Oh, all right; did get *slightly* teary. . . .)

Eventually emotions subsided enough to swap preliminary information: Bigger one Kim Melon, age 25; smaller, daughter Lisa, age six. Family survived depopulation intact—husband, too, but accidentally killed shortly thereafter. Small boy seen earlier *was* Lisa ("*I'm* not a *boy . . .* !").

Adam arrived; greeting hysteria resurged briefly. Adam bore up bravely. . . .

(Have I described Kim yet? No? Perhaps summary helps shed light upon Adam's fortitude. Kim could serve as Judging Standard for California Golden Beach Girls: "five foot two, eyes of blue." Slim, willowy, long-legged. Waist-length natural Swedish-blond mane. Pretty face—correction, beautiful face—double-correction, movie-star face. Plus last name describes salient physical characteristics with unintended hilarious accuracy. Pact with Devil not uncommon result when mortal female encounters Kim's type. Heck, probably feel that way even if *weren't* eleven; but as things are. . . .)

Effect predictable: Adam suddenly very tall for his height; gained inches in chest expansion between one breath and next. Aged years demeanorwise in eyeblink. Casually mentioned is 18 (straight-faced) about half-dozen times during first five minutes: " . . . the same age my father was when he met my mother—she was a few years older, too." Etc.

Would have been proud of me, Posterity: Smile never faltered; not once offered to help by reminding of stray facts somehow omitted during suave repartee. Not even when, during one of those casual mentions of his age, managed to drag in mine, and that I was " . . . a wonderful *young* person, incredibly talented in so many ways, but of course not old enough for a serious relationship. . . ."

Glad chose path of forebearance, however: Later that evening, as Adam, beaming each time caught her eye, slaved away in trailer kitchen (invited to dinner first thing), preparing culinary triumph calculated to inspire wonder, dazzle palate (melt heart, dissolve inhibitions), Kim leaned close and, without moving lips, whispered, "I wish Adam would quit trying so hard. I'm sure he's really a nice boy, but it's awfully hard to tell. Any ideas?"

Several possibilities came to mind right away. Kim got giggles listening. Then offered own suggestions, most of which better than mine. Best of lot impractical at moment: Where would we get whoopee cushion on such short notice...?

Think I'm going to *like* her.

Know I'm going to like her, Posterity! We fit like peanut butter, jelly. Never had sister; never realized what was missing. But have one now. And doesn't try to be *big* sister; not know-it-all; treats me as equal. Most *comfortable* person have met outside immediate family—but knew right away would work out: Terry adored both on sight. Tora-chan approved, also.

Especially Lisa: Tora-chan spends as much time lap-sitting with, purring at, following her around as he does Adam, his official new daddy. And Terry thinks she's neatest thing since frozen pizza. Watches every move whenever in view. Already picked up several phrases from her; letter perfect, too, complete with lithp in right platheth. Unusual: Normally requires couple months to polish up, tack on new word, phrase.

On other hand, baby brother may be turning into idiot savant: Not sure when this started, but recently noticed vocabulary expanding. Just this afternoon, for instance, produced brand-new, quite elaborate word string, startlingly apt for circumstances—and can't imagine when, where might have heard it.

Was inspecting Adam's splint for proper fit, position, etc. Terry, on my shoulder, said, "Not too tight? Not chafing? How're your fingers? Warm? Pink?"

Really amazing performance. And so appropriate. Always has had elephantlike memory for phrases, voices, related situations, of course. Maybe dredging past; perhaps something heard Daddy say.

Whatever source, am thoroughly impressed—practically took words right out of my mouth....

* * *

Been here about a week now, getting to know one another. Happy interlude, pleasant company.

Adam finally relaxed to point where presence isn't embarrassing—and surprised to learn makes no difference to Kim: Likes him just as is (or perhaps despite). Treats as equal, too.

Finished basic history exchange; low-key story-swapping sessions as days passed. Adam told approximately same story I got; but sticking to age-18 bit. Kim accepted with earnest, wide-eyed gravity; so sincere, may even really believe him. Hard to tell.

But doubt it. Kim nobody's fool. Top electrical engineer specializing in computers Before. "Show me *proof*!" her unspoken motto. Cheerful, optimistic soul, expecting best in everyone—but without shred of naïveté; enters into relationships with eyes open, missing nothing.

Both only 17 when married, still in high school. But continued education, with only briefest Hold for Lisa's arrival two years later. Achieved prominence in complementary fields (Jason master programer); worked closely together whole professional lives.

Neither ever sick.

Lisa, therefore, presumptively double-hominem—whatever that means...! And according to Kim, been raised, albeit unwittingly, in purest AA fashion. Results predictable: terrifyingly precocious child.

Fundamentally too trusting, however—though slightly less so after brush with disaster. Stranger appeared one day not long ago while Kim out scrounging. Delighted to see someone new after so long, Lisa invited in. Proved, judging by subsequent behavior, classic AB sociopath:

Kim returned Just In Time—Lisa screaming, clothes off, man just at Point of No Return.

"I don't know how I did it." Amazement showed in voice. "Other than the War, and then losing Jason, I had led the most tranquil existence you could imagine up to that point; I never even had to raise my voice as a child! This guy was a foot taller than I and outweighed me by a good hundred pounds. But I saw what was happening and I grabbed him by the hair and threw him across the room—literally!

"He jumped up—I've never seen such an expression on a human face—and charged me. It was obvious that his intentions were the same; he'd just found a new victim—*first* victim...!

"I sidestepped his rush without thinking. And while he was turning around, I picked up a poker from the fireplace and hit him over the head with it. He fell and I kept hitting him until he was dead. It took a week to get the mess out of the carpet."

Kim completely untroubled by lingering doubts. Eminently satisfied with cause, result of her killing. Wished own case so clear-cut. Told her so. Then related incident.

Kim listened quietly, thoughtfully, sympathetically to facts. But cut off subsequent breast-beating soliloquy: "Stop that—stop it *right now*! You have nothing—*nothing*!—to feel guilty about! With your training you could have done nothing else—

"*But*...!" Blue eyes flashed impatiently. "If you *could* have—if you had it to do over again and the only way you could save Terry was by killing Rollo—or someone else you knew no better—and you had time to plan every single action in advance, what would you do?"

Mouth opened, then closed without reply. Whole universe shifted on moorings. Most disturbing perspective, but question in that form completely self-answering, of course: *Yes!*—in hot millisecond would kill to save baby brother—*dozen times over*...!

"You don't have to shout," Kim remonstrated, smiling. "You're only three feet away."

Felt *so* much better! Killing weighed on me, even though had rationalized intellectually with Adam's help. But Kim, with unerring instinct for bottom line, spotted flawed reasoning underlying residual guilt; skewered with single question; fixed it on gut level, where really counts.

Future resolve unaffected, however: Intend to do level best never to kill again. Still working to eliminate lethal automatic responses from combat computer. Rough stuff still available if circumstances mandate, but want use contingent upon conscious evaluation, decision. No more accidental discharges.

Kim disagrees. Stated emphatically, upon adding her (Lisa, too) to training schedule, wants entire arsenal, undiluted. Feels minuscule accident risk inadequate justification for blocking instant access to most potent techniques. Haven't argued; teaching them same program I learned originally, as requested. Even Lisa working on baby drills targeted (once acquires sufficient mass, strength, coordination) at unthinkingly lethal potential.

But *I'm* not.

Wish party included animal behaviorist. Perhaps could furnish simple, reasonable explanation; thereby preserve my sanity: Terry's vocabulary still expanding in exponential increments: words, phrases, sentences—*paragraphs*—few of which could have heard often enough to implant in memory. Don't know what to make of it. Always been good talker, of course (for Hyacinthine Macaw; not best-talking psittacines, just one of most loyal, loving, intelligent). And recent performance nothing short of phenomenal, no question. Maybe even anomalous.

But hardly justifies Adam's present reaction: Has convinced himself is in on ground floor of major Unnatural Happening (as distinct from minor Unnatural Happening?).

Latest speculation: Terry and I mind-linked—"It's the only possible explanation; he says almost *everything* you do half a breath before you get it out."

Nonsense began day Terry spouted relevant new word string as I checked Adam's splint. Observed patient's awed expression then, but failed to recognize significance. If had, would have nipped in bud. Explanation obvious, reasonable, logical—mundane:

Of *course* anticipates me regularly: Been with me almost every waking moment since egg: developed sophisticated conditioned-reflex matrix based on my behavior. Picks up clues too subtle for observer lacking long-term close association; achieves fair degree of accuracy guessing what I'll do, say next.

But missed boat; no letup since.

And driving me *mad*. . . .

At least Adam more at ease with Kim now. Signs unmistakable.

This morning she related experience with gasoline generator upon utilities' collapse: Located, hooked up to house wiring; enjoyed benefits for two weeks—until failed. Checked, noticed oxidization buildup on commutator surfaces; attempted to clean with alcohol to no avail.

"Of course not," Adam interrupted; "no generator will work after being doused with alcohol."

Kim looked puzzled; advice clearly at odds with training. "Why not?"

"Because," he pontificated, "a *potched watt never toils*."

Kim joined me in retaliatory tickle attack without moment's hesitation.

We (Kim and Lisa, too; somehow inclusion into party never in doubt) proceeded to Pasadena, located AA address from Palomar Cal-Tech directory. Site examination produced sketchy clues pointing to Jet Propulsion Laboratory.

Adjourned thence, invested several days searching. Results ambiguous. Fairly recent activity evident, certain areas only: Footprints in deep dust contain shallow dust; elsewhere coating undisturbed. Plus Kim says much equipment she saw during recent touristy-style visit missing.

Oddly enough, only relevant information found by Lisa. Scrap of paper crumpled on office floor: Apparently someone's crib notes of meeting at secret (ah-*hah!*) AA facility sometime after attack—meeting attended by all available AAs, families.

Attack no surprise to AA community. Knew how would be conducted but not when. Informed Defense Department to no avail. Though knew mechanism possible (Daddy's research), and Other Side undoubtedly possessed technology, officialdom judged probability of use—and attendant implication that goal was worldwide elimination of everyone not within own ranks—incredible: "That's not war; that's *insane!* We can't base policy on that—*nobody* would do that . . . !"

AAs living out of suitcases for weeks prior to attack; irreplaceable belongings either already in shelters comparable to Daddy's, boxed, ready to load, or lined up in orderly fashion, ready to snatch-and-run on moment's notice. Instant missile phase ended, all on way to retreat—

(All but self . . . ! Daddy never hinted—other than How-Bad-Things-Are lecture, shelter checkout shortly before went to Washington. Likewise, Teacher knew attack would find me home alone—wonder why let me rot in shelter, and months afterward. Surely could have told someone, left message. . . .)

Per usual, nothing in document suggested location of AAs' retreat. Apparently putting in writing contrapolicy. Frustrating, but makes sense: Is *secret*, after all. . . .

Contents little more than summary of regretful broodings about events leading to that point; checklist of writer's immediate duties in data-, equipment-gathering expedition to certain installations about Cal-Tech campus, outlying research facilities, collecting stuff hidden When Balloon Went Up (to protect from random looting and/or vandalism). Plus intimation that booty awfully useful when things quieted down after "poor old H. sap" gone, and certainly critical during "instant emergency."

But not a clue concerning *how* useful. Or *where*.

Adam still at it: Watches Terry like Rhine Institute test monitor—or first-time séance attendee. Anytime baby brother utters anything unexpected, relevant, clever, complicated— whatever—Adam pounces immediately, blows all out of proportion. Has everybody else doing it now, too—i.e., Kim.

But Lisa to blame for current intensity of Terry-watching fever: All sitting around living room one evening, chatting about nothing in particular. More particularly, Kim and I ragged Adam as attempted to spin improbable yarn about past. Terry observed antics beatifically from stand while Tora-chan drowsed in Adam's lap. Lisa ostensibly paying no attention, reading book.

"... was the loneliest summer of my life. If I worked for him, Father would allow me to solo occasionally or play with the orchestra during concerts. I got paid for performing, but not for the office work. I didn't mind *too* much: As a performer, I was known; and most of the young ladies in the vicinity could be considered my groupies."

Kim rolled eyes heavenward; Terry offered raspberry just as about to myself. Lisa giggled.

Adam continued unperturbed: "Unfortunately, I was assigned to conduct an inventory of the physical properties belonging to the orchestra—everything in the building. A lot of legwork was involved, but I had access to the computer so it didn't look too difficult to list, categorize, and account for everything."

"Have you read any good books lately?" Kim asked sweetly.

"*NOOO-nooo*-no-nonono...!" yelled Terry, bobbing head delightedly.

"Good stories are hard to come by," I replied, controlling expression firmly: Intended beginning own response with "no."

Lisa giggled again.

"After counting everything," Adam continued, eyeing us severely, "and inputting the whole monumental collection into the computer, I started up the analysis and cataloging program. The system processed it; then suddenly erased all the data."

"Gaw-awl-ly . . . !" quoth Terry. I blinked, closed mouth: Beaten to punch again.

Noted Lisa trying *not* to giggle.

"I called service; they came right out. The hardware man checked and pronounced everything healthy. The programer analyzed the system's behavior, reloaded the software, rechecked everything, and assured me that all was well."

"Well, well, well . . ." intoned bird. Didn't attempt to conceal reaction this time: Glared at featherhead; prefer to kibitz for myself.

Lisa engrossed in elaborate study of fingernail.

"I reinput the inventory, started the program—and exactly the same thing happened again!"

"How 'bout that . . . !" offered Terry. Adam, ostensibly staring preoccupiedly at ceiling, now watching bird out of corner of eye. Kim paying attention, too. All of which very funny: Terry's reply that time his own for sure; hadn't intended to comment.

"I called the service people back, and they did exactly what they had done previously, then left. I re-reinput the inventory and—"

"The same thing happened again!" Kim and I chorused— again half a breath behind Terry.

Kim's, Adam's eyes met momentarily. Lisa giggled again. I affected indifference.

"It happened six times in a row," Adam continued distractedly, attention now wholly fixed on bird. "And I was getting pretty tired of it. But finally the analyst announced he'd identified the problem.

"Our system was running on their third-generation software, which apparently contained a glitch that only surfaced under certain conditions. Our inventory provided them.

"They'd just finished writing their *fourth*-generation software, and they decided to try it on our system. After loading it, they hung around and watched while I input the inventory one last time—I hoped."

"*Then what?*" Chorus this time included only Foster twins, Terry still half a breath in lead. Kim sat this one out, watching.

Adam's hesitation visible; almost lost track of story. Almost.

"That did it—or very nearly. It processed the inventory electronically and didn't erase it, but wouldn't print it.

"The programer displayed an incomprehensible screen full of numbers and symbols, studied it for a few moments, then nodded.

" 'That's it,' he gloated. 'You see'—he highlighted a section—'this is assembly language, our fourth-generation software, and here's the *print* program.'

"He went back into the third-generation program briefly and displayed the *sort* section. 'Here,' he said proudly, 'is where that glitch resides that's been wiping your library. It's this command right here.' He pointed to a single symbol.

" 'We intended to use that command, updated to fourth-generation, to order *send-to-printer*. But somehow we left it out when we actually wrote the program.' "

Adam radiated air of malicious anticipation. "I'm sure by now you've all figured out what the problem was."

Had, embarrassed to confess. Kim hadn't, though; result of gentle upbringing: Basically nice person; thought processes unaccustomed to such depravity.

Adam smiled cherubically, savoring moment; then began: "We needed the . . ."

"*—heir of the byte that dogged us!*" shrieked Terry, as I opened mouth. I glared as bird exploded in manic laughter, head bobbing gleefully, dancing back and forth on perch.

Adam's expression went from wicked delight to outraged disappointment—then genuine startlement. Kim's eyes grew round, as well. Both stared at bird as if suddenly had started ticking. Lisa passed "giggle"; went straight to "belly laugh."

"*That* didn't come from memory," Adam stated flatly.

"Nor from random word-string assembly," Kim added apologetically.

"You guessed the punch line," Adam continued darkly. "He got it from *you*."

"He has been taking the words right out of your mouth a lot lately," Kim offered uncomfortably.

Adam pressed on resolutely: "It hasn't happened with

me or Kim; you're the only one he anticipates—or speaks in stereo with, often as not. *That bird is reading your mind!*"

"He is *not*," I protested, probably somewhat peevishly. Explained again how years of close association had given baby brother private insight into clues pointing to imminent actions, words.

Adam began scathing retort; Kim placed hand over mouth. "But even if he had heard it before," she said gently, "doesn't it strike you as unlikely that he would pick just that moment to say it?"

Opened mouth to reply; then closed thoughtfully. Kim asks hard questions! "That's kind of difficult to explain, I'll admit," I began. "But I'm sure . . ."

"This is silly," interrupted Lisa, hands on hips, expression radiating undisguised impatience with stupid grown-ups. "*Every*body knows Terry knows what Candy thinks. And if Candy thought about it, she'd know what Terry thinks, too."

Palpable silence descended, broken, finally, by Terry's comment: "How *'bout* that."

Adam now staring at Lisa: "*'Too' . . . ?*"

Lisa snickered; suddenly lost interest.

"*'Too' . . . ?*" repeated Adam. Glanced at Kim, whose expression showed sudden disapproval of new conversational direction. "You don't suppose . . ."

"No, I don't," she responded firmly. Tone suggested wisdom of dropping subject.

But Adam on scent now; not deflected by subtlety: "She is a double *hominem* child." Paused dramatically; then continued in hushed tones: "Who knows what talents might be lurking behind those huge, fathomless black eyes. . . ."

Lisa glanced up, sighed, returned attention to book. Kim snorted inelegantly.

"That's dumb," observed Terry—as I opened mouth to say that very thing.

Well, trail's end: Treasure hunt fun while lasted. Nothing left for short term but fall back to Plan A: Resume address-by-address examination of AA homes, work settings.

Between Kim, Adam, self, have dreamed up bunches of alternative approaches for locating AA headquarters in long run: For instance, Adam and Kim putting heads together over trailer's electronic wall innards; plan to hoodwink some innocent component into serving as band-searching beacon.

Device to dial endlessly up, down spectrum, pausing briefly to spout message beseeching reply on specific wavelength, to which, of course, receiver tuned, with relay-actuated recorder poised in case nobody listening when response comes in. Are confident of success. Lack only couple more transistors, chips, whatnots.

But immediate options exhausted.

Have decided, following discussion, to follow AA trail up West Coast, loop over northern end of Rockies, touch base throughout Midwest, finally concluding initial search back home...

Shucks, by this time, after posting all those leaflets, lovely little town, surrounding area, probably completely repopulated—with AAs themselves, likely as not, having stumbled across advertisements. On arrival will surely find thriving, industrious, cheerful little farming community—all wondering what's keeping me. . . .

Here we are in Fresno—what's left of it—and here we seem to be stuck. Despite distance from San Andreas Fault, earthquake must have been humdinger: Roads—even open country!—impassable north and west. Terrain broken, fissured, stepped, generally messed up something awful. Unless backtrack, loop all the way around Rockies, seems to be no way to get from here to San Francisco, Sacramento, etc., next AA addresses.

Kim keeps looking around, Giving Thanks lived no closer to epicenter—ride was quite rough enough 300 miles away in Riverside. Assuming managed to survive immediate tectonic violence (slim odds, judging by conditions hereabouts), unlikely would have had place to live. Not much left standing.

We poked up every road on USGS map, even set out across open country, cutting fences as necessary—got nowhere. Repeatedly. Every road and/or off-road compass bearing blocked by fault damage. Major displacements involved, too: Haven't found passage for even van alone, never mind with trailer. Rock shelves jut 50, 100 feet high; bottomless fissures gape 100 yards wide or more—both running miles across terrain, usually intersecting with others to form impassable barriers, culs-de-sac.

Adam started grumbling about finding bulldozer, making own road; quit when couldn't find one sufficiently intact to operate.

All of which finally led ("O bliss!") to scouting by air. Just returned from second survey flight. News to west, north, all gloom: Simply no way through. Devastation astonishing. Would be difficult even afoot. Tomorrow will head east; perhaps find logging/fire road around mess through Sierra Nevadas.

This is Kim reporting: Candy is missing. She was close to eighty miles out, having traced a series of apparently usable fire trails well into Sequoia National Park, when she reported that her engine had lost power and she was losing altitude. She triangulated her location for us as well as she could by taking compass bearings on landmarks in the few moments before intervening mountains cut off her signal. Adam managed to get a bearing on her, as well, during that time, using the RDF processor incorporated into that amazing electronics wall of his, so we have a fairly good fix on her location.

However, if the coordinates are correct, she went down in an area that is both rugged and heavily forested with mature sequoias.

Jason was a Civil Air Patrol volunteer and participated in many high-country air searches. I have seen the CAP's film on recommended techniques for ditching in trees. The theory is that if you land in the treetops in a full stall, impacting at about a forty-five-degree nose-up attitude, you touch down at the slowest possible speed, and present as broad an area as possible to the foliage, so that kinetic energy is used up in smashing through the branches on the way down. It is not uncommon for trees' resistance alone to stop the descent, the ship ending up trapped in the branches. This is preferable to falling all the way to the unyielding ground, which entails a substantial impact even after deducting the retarding effects of the foliage. But either way, chances for surviving such a landing are better than one might expect.

Unfortunately, the film dealt with normal forest conditions, with trees between fifty to eighty feet tall. A mature stand of sequoias ranges between two and three hundred feet in height. Sequoias generally resemble enormously outsized pines: Trunks are massively thick, as much as forty feet in diameter, and lower halves are usually bare of branches. Top halves are sparse Christmas-tree parodies, with gnarled limbs immensely thick for their length, and little secondary and tertiary branching.

The structure of a sequoia forest offers little hope for a successful treetop ditching: There is nothing resembling the approximately level "roof" of an ordinary forest; a stand of sequoias is a sea of huge, upward-jutting cones. And as bigger trees crowd out lesser neighbors by blocking their sunlight, victors in the competition are usually less closely spaced than normal trees. Foliage generally overlaps, obscuring the sky from the ground and vice versa, but only down in the mid and lower reaches; and the branches which accomplish this are far too thick to break and absorb energy from impact with so light and fragile an object as a falling ultralight, except out at the very tips.

If Candy manages to locate a relatively closely-spaced stand of sequoias and achieves a letter-perfect pancake landing in the upper-middle branches, and if they slow and trap her plane without undue damage—and they might, as light as it is for its size—she has a chance.

Of course, that will strand her at least a hundred feet above the ground, at whatever point the branches cease. Her survival kit includes many things; but rope is heavy, and when dealing with ultralights, compromises must be made. So even if she is uninjured, getting down will be a challenge.

If she did not succeed in remaining in the treetops, however, I see no likelihood that she could have survived the passage through the branches, or the final free-fall to the ground. Repeated collisions with those huge, unyielding limbs on the way down would have demolished her miniature airplane like a balsa model. What remained would have plunged the last hundred feet like a stone.

I don't know how much of this Adam is aware of. I have not discussed it with him yet. I can't even think about it without crying.

Besides, this has not been a good time to discuss anything with Adam. Since this morning I have helped where I could and remained quiet and out of the way otherwise. Adam has been an absolute wild man: I have never seen anyone so quietly, intensely, efficiently, and constructively hysterical.

In the space of two furiously busy hours he located a generally undamaged private airfield, found an old Cessna 180 still intact, and, working like a one-armed tornado, with my small assistance, got it running.

During the next hour, operating the control yoke with

his good arm and the rudder pedals with his feet, with me serving as his other hand to operate the mixture, throttle, prop-pitch, trim, and flap controls, he taught himself to fly the big old taildragger, accustoming himself to the considerable handling differences between it and the tricycle-geared ultralight. Then we assembled provisions, medical supplies, and survival equipment, including lots of rope, loaded it aboard, topped up the tanks, and took off—all five of us; we couldn't leave the animals.

We found the location that Candy had triangulated for us. From that point we extended a ten-mile radius, and within that area we began a careful search, flying slowly only a few hundred feet above the treetops.

At the outset I risked suggesting to Adam that he not waste time trying to make out anything on the ground. Chances of spotting her there were minimal to nonexistent. From the air we could see only a fraction of the actual surface; the trees were just too thick. More likely was picking up a flash of color from that brilliantly rainbow-hued wing fabric snagged in a treetop.

Adam nodded absently. He was flying by conditioned reflex, his entire concentration below us, but I think he heard me.

We crisscrossed the area repeatedly, the three of us scanning the terrain until our eyes smarted, endlessly trying to raise her on the radio. After scouring the initial twenty-mile circle without detecting a sign of her, we doubled the radius. Later we tripled it.

I think Adam would have had us out there yet, peering down through the darkness, had we not begun to run low on fuel at about the same time that we ran out of daylight. As it was, even I forgot that it was going to take close to half an hour to get back to the field, and that sunlight lasts longer at altitude than on the ground. It was still possible to make out landmarks below us, but I was glad the old plane's landing lights worked. We touched down in a gloom hardly distinguishable from dead of night. Utilities are out in this area so the runway lights no longer work, even if someone had been here to turn them on.

While I made dinner, Adam sat and glared unseeing into space. The intensity of his feelings was almost palpable. I have never seen an expression so bleakly, ragingly frustrated. His features contained no remnant of boyishness.

He ate what I put in front of him without, I think, knowing that he did so, and with no change in expression.

After dinner, Tora-chan vaulted into his lap and butted him in the stomach. When that failed to produce the desired chin-scratch, the cat upgraded his effort to a full formal head-dive. Still nothing. Then he sat down in Adam's lap, gazed up at his face with a puzzled expression, and said, "Mee-*ow*-oo...!" But the boy never twitched; he remained where he was, immobile, unresponsive to outside stimuli.

I debated jolting him out of it physically, and was on the verge of giving it a try, when suddenly, unexpectedly, he stood and, in a firm, decisive, completely rational tone, said, "Come on, let's break camp. We can be at park headquarters by midnight, if those roads Candy reported really are passable."

I was caught completely by surprise. I thought he was in shock withdrawal, but he was *thinking*, furiously, accurately; evaluating every facet of the situation, together with our options.

Almost incidentally, as we prepared to leave, he brought me up-to-date on his thinking: "Searching by air is a waste of time. It would take a miracle to spot her in those trees. And even if we did, we couldn't help her from the air, anyway. So we'll save time by getting there on the ground as quickly as possible. The landmarks she used are unmistakable, and my RDF line hits the intersection of her compass bearings dead center, so we have an accurate fix on where she went down. We'll get right up there and conduct a ground search.

"We'll get some bullhorns at a police station—there are bound to be some still operational—and pick up trail bikes from a motorcycle shop. We'll pull the trailer in as close as we can get it; then push on in the van. If necessary, we switch to the trail bikes. Or we walk—

"*Oh*..." Adam broke off, looking concerned in a preoccupied sort of way. Obviously this was the first time all day that my presence had even partly registered, beyond my potential usefulness in prosecuting his search-and-rescue mission. "This is going to be rough. I can't drag you and Lisa into it. I'll leave you at the park headquarters in the trailer, and come back for you as soon as I find her."

He was still only half-aware of whom he was talking to or he never would have suggested anything so stupidly sexist. My reply put a stop to that right then, and got his full attention, as well:

"You and what SWAT *team are going to leave us be-hind ...!"* I snapped.

Adam's eyes focused suddenly. He *saw* me. I heard Lisa giggle behind my back.

"What...? Oh, no-no, I didn't mean—"

"I know you 'didn't mean,'" I replied more gently. "But Candy's my friend, too. I'm entitled to help."

"What about Lisa?"

Adam tends to be a little conservative, not to say naïve, when judging the fragility of those whom he considers "children." Lisa was only slightly less forthright than I was about correcting him. "You'll never find her without me," she announced solemnly.

Adam stared. Then he smiled wanly. He interpreted her declaration to mean that he'd better not try to leave us behind, and thought she was trying to cheer him up.

But I know my daughter. That was not bravado or sloppy syntax; Lisa meant it literally. I found myself studying her thoughtfully. She pretended not to notice. She and I will have to talk about this, very soon.

We did arrive at the park headquarters shortly after midnight; Candy's advice about the roads was accurate.

I ordered Adam to bed as soon as we stopped. He didn't argue, and he let me put him under, using the trance-induction formula that Candy had implanted. Once the trance had taken hold, I converted it to normal, deep sleep.

I wish someone could do that for me. One reason I'm making this entry is that I can't sleep. I keep seeing Candy, riding that gossamer-and-toothpicks ultralight down into the sequoias, the airframe breaking up into smaller and smaller pieces as it bounces off those huge upper branches, one after another—finally plummeting unimpeded to the ground.

Another reason is that I write a pretty fair Pitman....

But the main reason I'm doing it is common decency: Adam can hardly be allowed in Candy's journal while a chance remains that she's alive. It wouldn't be fair to let him peek at her intimate reflections, especially her opinions of him, when she may have to face him again. Yes, he would swear never to violate her confidence by looking anywhere but the page on which he's writing, and he'd mean it and believe it himself as he promised. But I'm curious myself about what she's written about me, and I'm not In Love with her; though I doubt if I could feel any closer to my own sister, if I had one.

Dear God—*please* let her be all right ...!

VOLUME IV
Destiny

Hello, Posterity...! Great life, isn't it?

Sorry; being silly. Please excuse. Euphoria betrays intensity of relief on *finding* self still alive.

Quite unexpectedly so: Surviving events of this morning brings new depth to expression "cheating odds."

Granted, details of flirtation with Grim Reaper, viewed objectively, probably of interest to participant only (was indeed; heart surely stopped couple times from thrill factor alone). But data valuable to Adam; understanding cause of problem key to preventing repetition—and truly in favor of that: Airplane engine failure contains potential for more than passing inconvenience!

Shan't bother with introduction, history review this time around. Don't anticipate spending much time on this volume: Shall merge with Vol. III immediately upon rejoining party (tomorrow morning, with luck). Could make record then; but events best recorded while fresh in mind.

(Originally planned to use this pen, pad to make notes, draw map en route. Instead, will discharge duty to history during twilight hours, plus entertain self.)

Trap sprung during this morning's first reconnaissance flight while heading generally east over Sierra Nevadas, studying roads *en passant*, reporting back via helmet radio.

USGS map suggested possible logging/fire-trail pass over mountains, through Sequoia National Forest. Overflight confirmed hard-surface and/or graded roads intact to ruts' jump-off into wilderness. Passable trail led thence into forestlands, over mountains. Barely discernible as break in solid forest cover, through which could observe ground here, there; verify no landslides, earthquake damage existed on scale likely to block rig.

Intended to follow, inspect tracks until fuel limitations necessitated turning back. Never got that far.

Lacked probably 15 minutes of turnaround point when engine went sour. One moment howling merrily, as good ex-motorcycle engine should; next moment sputtering, tachometer dropping toward idle; total shutdown threatening, imminent.

Until then reveling in sheer joy of flight ("O bliss!"); mindlessly wallowing in freedom of motion, endless visibility. Occasionally essayed snap roll, or some other aerobatic excess, just for fun of it. Having wonderful time, with never a thought toward potential consequences of mechanical failure.

Sudden power loss restored focus on reality. Jarringly so. Nothing in sight to raise hopes for safe emergency landing: Nothing but endless sea of conical treetops stretching uninterrupted every direction to mountainous horizon and beyond.

Abruptly conscious of chill fingers tickling pit of stomach.

Cut back power immediately. Knew from lawn mower, outboard motor experience: Sometimes possible to keep distressed engine running by nursing throttle; often continues operation under partial load, even though won't take max or cruise settings.

Relieved to note similar response from ultralight engine: Exhaust note smoothed out as revs dropped. Quickly edged throttle forward again, feeling for critical setting. And found it

Lower than hoped, well below point at which altitude maintainable.

Felt cold fingers tighten grip on liver & lights.

Fiddled with throttle again, trying to learn more about problem. Soon assembled picture: While only about quarter throttle available for sustained use, could get as much as five seconds' full power or about 15-18 seconds at minimum cruise after idling just shy of full minute.

But positively engine's best offer. Increasing idle time produced no further change in power-on duration.

Even as explored parameters of problem, already on radio, alerting Adam; banking, searching for mapworthy, recognizable landmarks. Relevant chart section sandwiched between sheets of plexiglass these days (Adam so clever), mounted to fuselage tubing over knees, edge-on to slipstream. Took only seconds to match peaks in vicinity with those on chart, pass on bearings by radio.

Adam acknowledging, reading back coordinates, when voice, already weak from distance, faded entirely as I dropped below mountaintops.

Well, would have been nice to have company on way down; feeling pretty lonely just then. But upcoming forced landing promised to demand full attention; likely too busy for idle conversation anyway: Terrain below really rugged; nothing visible but solid treetops as far as eye could see—emphasis on "solid."

Unbidden, characteristics of forest's namesake came to mind: Have heard sequoias described as industrial-grade redwoods. Plus saw photograph of General Grant tree in old set of Time-Life books Daddy kept around house: 260-odd feet high, trunk alone 40 feet in diameter—considered only "pretty big" by local standards.

Debated chances of achieving successful treetop landing. But already apparent, even at this altitude, that big trees' foliage skimpy in proportion to overall bulk; also that major limbs thick, visibly unyielding. Attempting to find, manage touchdown amidst, branches springy enough to absorb impact without damage to self, yet strong enough to trap airframe, hold tightly, prevent fall to forest floor, surely constituted unreasonable demand on luck. And failure meant *long* fall.

Barely 500 feet above tallest treetops when spotted opening through foliage. Not big hole, but ultralight wingspan only 25 feet; maybe big enough.

(Not that ducking through hole automatically eliminated risks. In fact, only in sequoia forest could question arise at all; trees much too close together in normal woods even to think about trying to dodge between, around trunks long enough to reach ground intact. No idea what might find down there; from this altitude, in bright sunlight, details invisible in shadow.)

But losing altitude steadily; decision imminent, clearly of either/or nature. Would have to make up mind. Soon.

Question proved self-answering: Once down at treetop level, true scale, scarcity of limbs, evident. Successful landing in those branches not question of mere luck; would take no-holds-barred *miracle*.

With decision made for me, turned full attention to opening. Down this close, could make out some details with certainty—and news not all bad!

Portal lay probably 150, 200 feet below treetops, at bottom of chimney created by missing foliage, broken limbs. Horizontal clearance inside shaft limited to perhaps 100 feet in tight spots, but usually more. Hole itself about 50 feet across, roughly circular; framed by lowest tier of branches projecting from surrounding trees.

Pretty close quarters, even at ultralight's minimum controllable speeds (22-knot level-flight stall), but not impossible.

Enough woolgathering; moment of truth at hand.

Tried to ignore damp palms, suddenly racing heart; set up short-field landing configuration: Carb heat on, engine back to idle, flaperons full down in maximum drag/lift setting, nose-up trim (extra tug on harness, helmet chin strap). Turned radio volume all the way down to eliminate possibly distracting static.

Slowed to 30 knots; eased into spiral, radius dictated by trees' spacing; alert for preliminary aerodynamic buffeting, warning of incipient accelerated stall induced by steep turn's gee forces (even experienced pilots occasionally trapped that way). Then in shaft, committed to descent.

Hard to tell, as trees rose on all sides, whether sink-rate really gentle as felt (or perhaps time-sense perception again listening to own drummer) but seemed to take forever.

Tried to divide attention as descended: Vital not to allow hitherto-unnoticed projecting branch to snag wingtip; but also needed to see what lay below, catch earliest possible glimpse of conditions below foliage. But shadowed details still undiscernible; would have to wait, see; rely upon native resourcefulness, inborn determination, vaunted *H. post hominem* reflexes—plus yeoman-caliber assistance from old friend Luck.

Cracked throttle briefly about halfway down to clear spark plugs of potential fouling after long minutes' idling (Adam says two-strokes touchy that way); then again about 30 feet above opening itself to provide moment's crisper response to controls: Necessary for final steeply banked turn, dive-and-duck squeeze through shaft's narrow bottom.

Plunge from early midday sunlight into relative gloom beneath foliage precipitated only momentary pupil–accommodation crisis, but blindness persisted long enough to supply genuinely ugly thrill before vision returned.

Looked around quickly; simultaneously raised flaperons to 50 percent, reducing aerodynamic braking effect without substantially affecting lift. Also brought power back up to maximum available. Amounted to maybe 25 percent, but not complaining; appreciated every little bit: Even partial throttle improved glide characteristics; and every second remained airborne boosted odds on spotting safe landing site.

But not encouraging picture: Beyond small glade in which found self, dimly green-lit cavern beneath foliage extended out of sight in all directions; roof supported by massive columns, fairly regularly spaced; most closer together than would prefer under circumstances; by and large offering just about enough room for ultralight's passage. Alert, skilled pilot might stave off disaster for several whole minutes before inevitable caught up. Dyed-in-wool ultralight freak probably wax ecstatic over challenge.

And welcome to it! Own interests much simpler, more basic: Just wanted to get down in one piece—and immediate outlook less than reassuring: Lesser trees obscured forest floor between sequoias, plus intermittent underbrush furnished dense ground cover.

Became, therefore, engrossed in feverish search for any approximately level, unobstructed surface on which stood remote chance of setting down relatively intact before unwinding altimeter closed off debate.

Search not instantly productive. Nothing visible beyond what already described. Nothing anywhere but vast, unyielding sequoia trunks above; smaller trees, bushes below, all capable of snatching fragile plane from air, smashing to ground out of control.

Finally looked straight down and—*behold!*—Heaven-sent solution . . . !

If pilot enough to bring off.

(Heaven apparently not big on sweeping, all-encompassing fixes. Maybe concerned that doing too much for supplicant erodes self-respect, destroys incentive, is somehow demeaning. Perhaps. But at that moment trading self-respect for tangible assistance would have seemed bargain.)

Hole through which descended, plus clearing, both created when enormous sequoia toppled sometime in recent past. Carcass sprawled along ground for hundred yards, splintering smaller trees, crushing other vegetation beneath incredible bulk. Resultant clearing possibly 100 feet wide at crown end, 50 at root.

Trunk diameter uniformly at least 35 feet from base halfway to top; first 150 feet unobstructed by branches. If could line up approach, would be ample room to land flying flea on fallen giant's curved upper surface...

If could line up approach:

Room to circle available in widest portion of clearing only: over crown, lowest, most massive branches of which projected upward, blocking glide path to trunk from that direction. Impossible to descend steeply enough after clearing branches without building up prohibitive velocity before touchdown. Never get stopped before colliding with gnarled roots.

However, to land other way along huge log required approach from out amidst trees: First entering forest, completing 180-degree turn amongst Brobdingnagian sequoia trunks, reentering glade on final—all without becoming oversize bugspot on tree trunk....

Hoped Adam would take good care of Terry.

Well, no point dwelling on possible unpleasant side effects; obviously only solution at hand.

Eyeball reconnaissance, strategy review, subsequent conclusion, occupied only couple plane lengths after clearing opening; greenery still almost in reach overhead as juggled what probably would be last relatively unhurried decision before reaching ground: Selection of left- or right-hand approach pattern—euphemistic description of brief-but-agonized nail-biting over where trees more closely spaced.

Bore off toward monster tree's root end. Intended to set up basic 180-degree approach. Hard to beat for simplicity, plus should minimize exposure time in forest. Would parallel log; penetrate forest just far enough to execute 180-degree turn; emerge from trees on final, right over root end, ready for flare-out, touchdown, routine quick stop.

Debated briefly, unhappily, before settling on airspeed of 35 knots, 13 over normal stall. Would have proceeded even more deliberately if had druthers; but cushion essential safeguard against accelerated stall should circumstances require sudden high-gee vertical bank or the like. As well might.

But ought to be all right. Only about twice flat-out running pace, after all; slow enough to permit noting trees as approached, evaluate separation, make deliberate go/no-go decision, take evasive action as necessary. Sure. Probably. (*If* alternate route accessible.)

Besides, 35 knots efficient airspeed: Optimum glide angle; maximum flying time available before ground intersected glide path. Maybe several whole minutes.

Had time for single deep breath as exited clearing; then learned whole new meaning for word "busy":

Glided between first two massive columns with room to spare. Bore slightly right to clear still another monolith; then initiated gentle left bank to circle it—when bark-covered wall unexpectedly materialized in path, appearing suddenly from behind one already using as pylon.

Huge trunks separated by 12-15 feet. Barely.

Slammed stick against left stop, then yanked back hard. Craft jerked upright on wingtip, warped violently into turn, structure trembling under gee loading. Skimmed inner tree so closely, wondered briefly why rudder tip didn't drag. Shot through slot like watermelon seed; then leveled, angling toward wider gap visible ahead.

Considerably lower now, of course. Elementary aerodynamics: Only so much lift produced at given airspeed. Turn increases induced drag, causing speed loss. Lower nose to get speed back, sink-rate increases. Turn steeper, sink faster. Straightforward energy exchange.

High-gee maneuvers grossly wasteful. Couple more episodes like that, find self on ground ahead of schedule.

Plus noted compass now useless: Violent maneuvers had it spinning merrily.

Glided straight ahead between two other trunks, watching compass with peripheral vision to see if might stabilize in time. Apparently not; dead-reckoning time for Kamikaze Kid—assuming own orientation not equally scrambled by now, as well could be.

Grazed safely past, between several conveniently placed trees, trying to get headed back toward where thought clearing lay. But before completed turn, had to duck around still another bole.

Suddenly mere passenger: Combat computer spotted impossibly closely-spaced cluster of gargantuan trunks immediately ahead; engaged. Sat helpless; watched as plane
. . . stood vertically on left wingtip, tore through left-hander between first two trees, thence instantly—without reversing bank—into subsequent right-hander, pulling nega-

tive gees; reversed control inputs coordinating what amounted to inverted turn. Then

. . . airframe bucked, buffeted, shuddered on verge of accelerated stall, as sliced left again between two columns so close together that actually felt bump as main gear grazed bark beneath fanny. And

. . . emerged on final in clearing, wings level, lined up with log, heading straight for massive roots bulging from lower end—*now too low to clear.* But

. . . throttle already jammed forward, stick back; engine howling deafeningly at full power. Plane ballooned upward several yards, clearing roots by fraction; staggered for timeless instant on brink of stall as engine sputtered again; then stick forward . . .

And suddenly back in control, easing stick back, yanking flaperons down to full drag/lift position, closing useless throttle, flaring out, feeling pounding as wheels bounced on rough, corrugated bark paving log's upper surface. Braked to stop in matter of feet. Killed engine.

Silence echoed through forest.

Sat unmoving for indeterminate span, blinking fast, breathing hard, disbelieving.

Reviewed past 30 seconds' events; speculated odds on anyone surviving. Concluded *never* find room to write all those zeros.

And suddenly in grip of giggles: Terry would have loved wild ride. Could almost feel manic twin clutching shoulder as careened amongst sequoia trunks, inches from disaster. Would be crouched, wings half-spread, bobbing head, yelling, "Wheeee-e-e-e . . . !"

Giggles intensified; shortly indistinguishable from hysteria. Shakes set in soon after. Quite some time before able to unlock quick-release buckle, shrug off harness. First attempt at standing garnered predictable results: Jell-O knees not useful when planning serious legwork.

Decided better deal with physical, emotional condition first:

Removed helmet. Extracted canteen from emergency knapsack mounted behind seat. Poured water on head, shook excess from hair, mopped face with sleeve. Leaned back against seat, closed eyes, took deep breath, held, released slowly. Triggered relaxation sequence; felt body gradually unwind as emotions subsided.

Sat for long moments with eyes shut, breathing regularly. Then opened, looked around.

And fought off momentary resurgence of hysteria. Time-Life photos failed to communicate how *big* sequoias are. Scale of surroundings distorted reality: They looked normal; *I* felt small. No one could stand in clearing without reevaluating own importance in Scheme of Things. Example: Can walk better than ten feet laterally from centerline on top of log before encountering important grade—*log*, for Heaven's sake...!

And looking up ... Opening through foliage almost vanishes in distance, against background. *Nobody*, viewing this scene, would believe airplane gotten in here via own wings! Even miniature airplane. (Almost don't believe it myself—combat computer *one hot pilot* ...!)

Okay, enough awe, philosophy; places to go, things to do, people to meet. Stranded by sick engine nearly 100 miles from anywhere, with lightweight minimum of supplies, tools—and no mechanical background. (How's that for promising scenario...?)

Looked around, evaluating surroundings with eye toward eventual departure. Quickly apparent that, while probably no more fun than arrival, flying out possible, assuming can get engine running: Ultralight designed for passenger weighing 250 pounds maximum; own weight a third that. Resultant angle-, rate-of-climb far better than manufacturer's specifications. No problem anticipated climbing back to, through opening in greenery overhead, ascending chimney beyond to open sky.

Takeoff, however, potentially every bit as hairy as landing; reasons identical: Have to launch into forest, return; then circle wide end of glade, spiral up to, through opening.

Only "into forest" part gives pause. Done that already, thank you.

Return trip bound to be less thrilling, though. Ample time to scout route first; won't be improvising second by second.

But no point worrying now. Becomes consideration only after manage to fix engine....

And background or no background, logic (and time spent looking over Adam's shoulder [lectures almost as compulsively as Daddy]) dictates infernal combustion engine operation dependent on three primary requirements: gasoline, oxygen, spark. As side issue, needs correct gas-air mixture. Spark timing critical also.

No, too basic; engine runs fine—but loses oomph after few seconds' brisk operation. Now what easy-to-find, easy-to-repair-without-tools-or-specialized-knowledge failure could cause that?

(Sure *better* be something like that; only class of problem falling within expertise. Otherwise might as well be total.)

Pushed plane along trunk with some difficulty due to rough bark. Arrived at first tier of branches; turned ship about, nose toward roots. Employed light nylon line included in emergency kit to effect tiedown, using branches as anchor.

Yanked pull-cord. Came out by roots. Said bad word. Then prop-started engine gingerly—first time ever handled propellor with ignition on. Uncomfortable sensation: like violating parents' warning about sticking fingers in electric fan.

Ran up, timed failure. First try produced full-throttle run of almost 20 seconds; then held consistently at five through five more tests.

Good; at least failure mode consistent. Nothing worse than trying to diagnose intermittent problem.

Now all had to do was figure out *why*. . . .

Shut down engine again. Then realized had forgotten acoustical earplugs; Adam not kidding when remarked unprotected flight left him half-deaf. Exhaust note even louder, standing next to craft, than when flying; helmet offers degree of protection, plus some noise carried away by slipstream. Curious sensation: Yelled experimentally; felt voice in throat, but almost inaudible via ears.

Not particularly worried. Deafness following loud noises usually temporary; results when ears' defenses cut in: Short-term paralysis of ossicles insulates inner ear from overload. Hearing probably return to normal soon if not further abused. (Of course, repeated exposure results in permanent loss, as rock concert aficionados often learned in past. Resolved to use earplugs faithfully hence.) Besides, even if permanent, deafness not treatable here, now. So ignored it; had other problems. Stared at engine, thought.

Problem with troubleshooting two-strokes is are so *simple*. Too simple: two pistons, two connecting rods, one crankshaft. Five moving parts. What can go wrong . . . ? (Also had solid-state ignition, but if problem lay there—never mind . . .)

Ran through obvious rituals first: Replaced spark plugs (new this morning; unlikely to blame); checked for loose spark lead, condenser wire; clogged fuel pump, carburetor screens, etc.

Inserted earplugs, restarted engine, ran up, confirmed problem still present. Shut down, glared impotently.

Think: What demand increases with power setting? Gasoline, of course. Well, how about partially blocked fuel line? Perhaps allowing sufficient flow for lower output but starving engine above certain point? Sounded promising; theoretical failure matched real-life symptoms.

But how to test without wasting fuel? Certainly shouldn't dribble on log. Nearly half gone when problem arose; none to spare.

Thought for moment; weighed priorities. Surroundings' appearance suggested no dearth of water in area. Okay. Uncapped canteen, inverted, propped up; turned attention to fuel line.

Required strong fingers: Secured by stiff spring clips. Once clips removed, engine end came off without too much difficulty. Canteen empty by then so held line over opening, let flow.

Almost abandoned investigation before fairly begun; flow strong, steady, clearly adequate. But already invested water in experiment; might as well follow through. Continued, watching closely.

Bingo . . . ! At ten-second mark flow suddenly dropped to trickle.

Smug thrill of triumph, self-satisfaction coursed through soul: So *there*, Adam—experience not everything; logic works, too . . . !

Okay, now problem isolating cause of blockage. Probably something floating around inside tank. Anything big enough to block outlet surely visible to naked eye.

Momentarily plugged line with fingertip. Unscrewed fuel cap with other hand . . .

Tank hissed as cap loosened, like vacuum-packed jar. Detected immediate fuel-pressure increase against fingertip.

No—couldn't be *that* simple! Or could it . . . ?

Reinstalled fuel line on carburetor inlet. Poured fuel trapped in canteen back into tank (all but last drop, lest any water remain).

Removed cap all the way, peered down inside tank. Inlet

four inches across; tank nicely crafted, bright light-alloy cylinder: Entire bottom visible if moved head around. And, as suspected, absolutely clean; nothing but gas/oil two-stroke mixture.

Then turned attention to cap. Was indeed vented, but *cleverly* so: intricate compound-leverage float-and-counterweight valve designed to plug breather during brief negative gees. Observed valve closely as inverted cap, then turned upright.

And there it was, big as life! Valve remained in closed position, sealing vent tightly. Textbook physics demonstration: Fuel not replaced by air as used; resultant vacuum resists further delivery, engine loses power.

Noted, without surprise, country of manufacture: German designers notorious for overengineering, obsession with excess gimmickry. Dieter Heinz, resident madcap mechanic/ social critic at small VW dealership back home, possessed in ample measure practical field-worker's contempt for Ivory-Tower theoreticians; opined most warranty recalls result of factory engineers' insistence on devising ingenious solutions to nonexistent problems. Referred to resultant debacles as "chooting zemzelves een ze voot."

Dieter speculated was real explanation of how Nazis lost war. Took particular delight in satirizing defect bulletins, highlighting technical overkill. Remember one in particular:

TO: All Noncommissioned Officers and below.
FROM: Blitzkrieg High Command Quality Control Center.
SUBJECT: Hand-Grenade Repair Bulletin Follow-up.
MESSAGE: In a previous bulletin, ZVP–111000WUB–827–D, it was reported that certain hand grenades manufactured by subcontractor Sturm & Drang between 3 June 1943 and 8 October 1943, bearing Serial Numbers 87A000–112498BZQ148 through 87A000–112498BZS157 in one-millimeter-high characters on the inside of the release lever, have detonated in 4.91465 seconds instead of the specified 4.97771 seconds. This variation exceeded manufacturing tolerances.

Bulletin ZVP–111000WUB–827–D described how to correct this defect. However, it has been learned that this bulletin contains a typographical error. If

*Step 3 is followed as written, hand grenades so
modified will detonate in .07331 seconds and could
pose a hazard to the user.*

*All copies of bulletin ZVP–111000WUB–827–D
must be corrected as follows: In Step 3, the word
"left" in the third line should be deleted and the
word "right" inserted. If the corrected instructions
are followed properly, the hand grenades will perform satisfactorily.*

*However, if any hand grenades are observed to
detonate in .07331 seconds, even after being correctly
modified, safety pins and release levers of such hand
grenades must be returned to Blitzkrieg Warranty
Center. Upon receipt of safety pins and release
levers, together with Quality Control Follow-up Report Forms filled out correctly, credit will be issued.
Credit will not be issued if forms are filled out
incorrectly.*

Dieter posted above on service-department bulletin board
during scheduled zone man inspection. Zone man German-
born, -raised; ex-Reichwehr foot soldier. Was reported
unamused.

And, as studied mechanism further, found was not all
that amused myself. Simple reverse-acting needle/seat float
valve would have done job without failure-prone complications.

However, Adam says he never met gadget too complicated for Shadetree Engineering fix. Secret usually is big-enough
hammer. Or in this case pliers: Held breather open with
fingers; mashed, mangled clever device until couldn't move
again even if received Summons From On High.

Screwed cap down on tank. Placed mouth over vent,
blew; felt, heard air hiss through opening.

Prop-started engine again. Advanced throttle to full,
timed run with wristwatch. Two minutes later still going
strong.

Then, to satisfy scientific curiosity, placed finger over cap
vent hole—stumbles set in hardly 20 seconds later. Released,
engine ran smoothly again.

Men have hung on flimsier evidence.

Okay. Engine fixed; now to get out of here. First step:
Reconnoiter takeoff route. Roomy, undramatic takeoff route.

Selected root leading downward from log's base; employed

to reach ground. Spent hours surveying loop from log into forest and return, plotting safe course. Took no chances: Manufactured wingspan go/no-go gauge from sapling; physically verified separation between each pair of trees through which must pass, marked route.

(Sounds as if contemplating major trek through woods. Not so; out and back, shortest possible distance. But hard work, hindered every step by environment. No problem solo, but 25-foot sapling not ideal hiking companion amidst underbrush, smaller trees, etc.)

Finally done. But too late to venture aloft; darkness approaching. Ultralight not equipped for night flying; no lights, rudimentary instruments only. Certain to get lost. Plus landing attempt in dark doesn't bear thinking about (infrared perception isn't *that* good). No choice: Must wait for morning.

Not looking forward to spending night here, but will manage: Made up only moderately uncomfortable bed beneath wing; consists of moss, leaves, etc. C-rations filled belly, though hardly in style to which accustomed—nothing like Adam's cooking. Located cold, fast-running stream for water. Filled canteen, shook, drained; repeated endlessly until only hint of yummy gasoline flavor remains.

Then sat down to make present update. Which have. That's where things stand now.

Time to try to get some sleep.

If possible.

Know am acting like fool, jittering like this. Physically verified trees' separation, marked route clearly. No possibility of getting lost, encountering trees too closely spaced for plane's passage. Nothing to worry about.

But can't help it.

Do so *hate* waiting . . . !

Oh, Posterity, *Posterity* . . .

If get through this without blowing punch line will surely validate claim to histographer's mantle. So much to tell; so little time. . . .

However. Remember histographer's creed: Unemotionally, deliberately, chronologically. Therefore:

Woke next morning at sunup, stiff, sore, cold. Night spent curled into fetal position on pile of moss no match for cozy trailer bed, clean sheets, warm blankets. Guess am spoiled.

Hearing back to normal: Ringing gone; could hear birds calling, insects humming, etc. Quite relieved, despite confidence affliction only temporary. Doubt deafness much fun—besides, countersurvival: What if failed to hear immigrant carnivore's approach?

Stumbled down from log to stream; sloshed water on face, shrieking, gasping, sputtering in reaction—couldn't have been warmer than 33 degrees! Did clear away cobwebs . . . .

Performed morning elimination. (Amazing how few people grasp importance of emptying bladder, bowel, before risking possible injury. Daddy occasionally served as trackside physician for local quarter-mile stock-car racers. Pet peeve was heroes who, despite oft-repeated warnings, started race without first making personal pit stop. Lost count of those whose only injury following minor shunt was ruptured bladder, bowel. Daddy often remarked on dearth of repeaters: Burning, urine-filled void between thigh muscles, under skin, and/or peritonitis, both followed by otherwise unnecessary surgery, quite educational.)

Performed abbreviated *kata* to loosen up musculature, hone reflexes; followed by scant breakfast of C-rations.

Then was time. Removed tiedowns; coiled, stowed line; resecured emergency kit behind seat.

Inserted earplugs; pulled on helmet. Started engine, settled in seat, fastened harness.

Checked all controls; performed two-minute full-power test; during which relaxed; expanded consciousness, alertness. Combat computer assumed control.

Released brakes. Only peripherally aware of wheels' pounding over rough bark as ship accelerated.

Lifted nosewheel before 50-foot mark; popped 50 percent flaperons as airspeed hit 22 knots. Total takeoff roll less than 75 feet. Zeroed in on first pair of sequoias framing entrance to in/out plunge through forest. Pegged airspeed at 30 knots for best angle-of-climb; watched trunks loom large ahead, pass on either side—then into woods proper, concentrating on remaining centered in premarked corridor.

But no surprises, no stark maneuvering (trees hadn't moved since yesterday). Pylon dodge'em game without drama this time; plenty of room all the way in, around, back. Emerged from forest already halfway to lowest branches.

Flying level, almost within reach of greenery, by glade's

far end. Performed steeply banked 180; leveled, headed for opening, building speed.

Going almost 60 when yanked back stick, shot up through small opening into chimney. Immediately lowered nose, stabilized airspeed at 35 knots (best rate-of-climb speed also); rolled into endless climbing turn.

Breathed huge sigh of relief as emerged from shaft above treetops—then inexplicably giggled again, wishing Terry were here. Would have enjoyed ride so much, even if less exciting than yesterday. Could almost see twin now, bobbing head, wings half-spread, wearing expression of utter delight. Missed him dreadfully.

Missed Adam, too. And Kim, Lisa. Tora-chan, too.

Missed family.

Climbed toward cruising altitude. Reached for helmet radio switch, intending to try to raise them once above intervening peaks—only to discover already on; batteries stone dead, apparently left on yesterday.

Oh, well. Irritation, not problem.

(But *major* irritation . . .)

Settled down on return course. Resisted urge to push throttle to max. Unsure of fuel situation, but knew was tight. Gritted teeth, cut back to efficient minimum cruise.

No sweat; arrived at departure point with fuel to spare— but *nobody there* . . .

Landed, looked around for note, clue to whereabouts. Found nothing—fine quandary!

Indulged in moment's self-pity; then thought matter through: Put self in Adam's, Kim's shoes. Of course: Gone to look for me—exactly what would have done were positions reversed.

Well, easily enough solved: Obtain fresh radio batteries, return to area where forced down, fly around until family notices, switches on own radio (surely will; exhaust note probably audible for five-mile radius). Once in contact, arrange location to meet.

Okay, problem solved.

Restarted again, lifted back into air, flying slowly, low. Looked for, found gas station. Buzzed, inspected; apparently in good shape. Landed in street, taxied up apron. Access to station no problem; standing wide open. Rummaged briefly; found hose, pump, couple cans of two-stroke oil. Mixed up formula, refueled.

Located electronics store next. Managed to find carton of appropriate 9-volt radio dry cells, plus tester with which to determine condition. Replaced helmet batteries with best of lot; stuffed extras in pockets.

Stepped outside just in time to feel ground tremble, hear concussion. Looked up, motivated by ancient habit; noted barely visible, fast-moving contrail splitting sky, heading south-southwest. Continued toward ultralight without breaking stride. Donned helmet and...

Contrail?

CONTRAIL . . . !

Went briefly out of control then, Posterity. Must have. How else to explain certified genius running back, forth in street; dancing up, down; waving, screaming—at aircraft five miles up....

Hysteria ended abruptly as begun: Winds aloft shredding vapor; evidence rapidly dissipating.

Moved quickly; probably set record for ultralight engine start, takeoff, climb-out. Aligned own craft with contrail as cleared ground. Maintained course, watching compass, as continued maximum climb. Needed sufficient altitude to ensure local magnetic anomalies (ferrous accumulations, etc.) not affecting reading.

Five minutes, 3,000 feet later, contrail's last fleecy wisp lost in distance, heading unchanged.

Leaving Junior Birdwoman again dangling skewered on dilemma's needle-pointed horns:

Pacific 150–200 miles ahead on present course, according to memory. Unless headed overseas, jet's destination lay somewhere within three and half hours' flying time at ultralight's peak cruise.

But following up would cost at least eight hours' round trip; add full day to separation from family—cruel to leave Adam, Kim, et al., in doubt, combing sequoia forest, searching for own tattered remains.

On other hand, at least day's work involved in locating, rejoining them. Even if landed somewhere ahead, jet could be on other side of globe before found family, returned.

(Leadership sure is lonely business sometimes!)

But some decisions easier than others, though not necessarily pleasant: *Had* to chase jet while trail still warm. Simply no alternative.

So ignored anguished little voice worrying about family;

concentrated on course, terrain ahead. For next three and half hours.

Embarrassing, really, how completely by surprise otherwise well-informed person can be taken. Despite own keen interest in things scientific, substantial knowledge of geography, never suspected jet's destination until loomed out of distance, so huge, size alone misled perspective.

Not until very close did recognition set in. First experienced pang of disappointment as perceived coastline; feared had missed landing site, or perhaps jet continued out over water.

Only after blunt-nosed, moth-shaped silver barnacle—adhering halfway up huge, sharply dome-topped, dark beige tower rearing amidst cluster of even larger structures—caught eye, held it, did I recognize Vandenberg Space Shuttle Launch Complex.

But technical wonders held attention only briefly: Moments later, could discern moving vehicles scurrying about shuttle's base . . .

And people . . .

People everywhere—*lots of people* . . . !

Don't know how managed to land in one piece. Certainly in no condition to fly by then: senses reeling, heart racing, breath coming in sobs, half blinded by tears. Only know that presently ultralight bumped to stop in shadow of monster spaceship.

People converged; helped me off with harness, helmet; pulled me to feet.

Strangers all, but reminded me somehow of Daddy during first moments. Men, women both; mostly young; kindly features, concerned expressions; vital, handsome people.

Hardly anyone uttered intelligible word at first. But no need: Even with everyone laughing, crying, passing me from hug to hug like stuffed toy—never doubted for instant!

Had found AAs . . . !

Managed, finally, to blubber name in response to inquiry from gentle young Adonis in charge. Reply caused odd metamorphosis to pass across features; stir ripple through crowd.

But recovered quickly. Smiled, said: "Then here's someone you'll be happy to see again."

Felt pair of hands take me by shoulders from behind. Was turned around.

Then looked up—not very far up—into well-remembered, wizened, elflike features. Inexpressible love, joy beamed from dark, slanted, gently mischievous eyes as, streaming tears himself, Teacher said: "Candidia, my child, the sight of you makes an old man..."

Never learned what sight of me did. Voice broke. Teacher enfolded me in arms, held very close.

Whereupon, for very first time in entire life, Candy Smith-Foster—plucky girl adventurer; most promising preadolescent intellect yet discovered amongst *Homo post hominem* population; youngest ever holder of Sixth Degree Black Belt; resourceful, unstoppable, never-say-die superkid; conqueror of unthinkable odds, who searched out, found AAs across length, breadth of North American continent...

Fainted.

Evening when awoke. Lay in narrow bed, alone in small, tidy, unmistakably "military-looking" room. First thing to greet eyes was note taped to headboard. Stretched comfortably, pulled down, began reading.

From Teacher: apology for startling me; promise to explain everything at tonight's meeting...

Teacher...! Memory flooded in. Sat bolt upright—in process discovering attire limited to birthday suit—stared at note as if might bite. But *how...* what...

Saved from further blithering by gentle knock on door.

Pulled sheet up around chin; managed, "C-c-come in."

Door opened, woman entered. Perhaps 15 years older than self; tall, marvelous figure; carriage bespoke flawlessly fine-trained physique: Moved with unconscious power, effortless grace of panther. Richly glowing dark hair, bangs in front, rest in waist-length ponytail. Startlingly beautiful features radiated intrinsic warmth; currently wore tentative, gently concerned smile. Reminded me of Kim. Liked her on sight. (But would *kill* to look like that!)

Bundle under arm proved to be my clothes, now clean, dry, neatly folded—badly needed attentions after two exciting, sweaty days.

But sight of completed laundry started wheels turning in head: Must have been out of circulation for several hours minimum; which deduction led to remembering shameful fluttering-ingénue performance upon seeing Teacher; which

in turn again recalled incredible shock of *seeing* Teacher—
alive...!

Woman took in expression, posture, paper, trembling
hands, all in single glance; correctly evaluated problem.
Smile broadened, became infectious grin, as placed clothing
on bed. "My guess is that you haven't had much experience
meeting ghosts," she offered by way of greeting. Scooted
bedside chair close; settled in for cozy chat.

"Teacher asked me to apologize for him," she went on, as
I stared blankly. "He knows he gave you quite a shock, and
he's terribly sorry. But he's been totally immersed in the
project, and your arrival so startled him..."

(Quickly bit lip; stifled momentary impulse to burst out
in hysterical laughter—she thought *he* was startled!)

"...and he was so overjoyed to see you, that he forgot,
in the excitement of the moment, the impression you must
have gotten from the letter he'd left for you with the Tarzan
File—at the time, of course, that's pretty much the impression he had himself.

"I'm Gayle Kinnart, by the way," she continued sociably.
"I'm one of Teacher's official AA guinea pigs. Until you
turned up I was one of his prize exhibits."

Flashed engaging grin, evoking image of mischievous
eight-year-old tomboy—then looking *nothing* like Ph.D.-five-
times-over rebel who met American Bar on own turf, stomped
into ground in head-on clash before Supreme Court!

"Your test results created quite a stir among our little
group," she added cheerfully. "No one had an explanation for
you. Your upbringing wasn't even close to AA standards; your
intellectual development violated all the rules. Of course,
Teacher always has said that you never had much use for
rules.

"I'm supposed to bring you to the meeting, incidentally.
Teacher wanted to be here when you woke up, but he's *so*
busy..." Expression clouded briefly. "We all are, actually,
and time is so short—but Teacher's been doing the work of
five of us. I'm just coming on duty and I promised to bring
you along. I gather you just this minute woke up?"

Nodded vaguely. Things moving too fast; having trouble
keeping up. Most of all, having trouble focusing on discussion: Single unanswered question kept intruding, clamoring
for answer, derailing extraneous thoughts. Took deep breath,
stilled emotions long enough to regroup faculties, assemble

something resembling coherent thought: "Wait a minute! I didn't think any *Homo sapiens* were left; how did Teacher survive?"

Grin returned. "He was more surprised about that than anyone. He was so desperately ill immediately following the attack that he thought for sure he'd contracted the plague along with all the rest of *H. sapiens*. We *all* thought so: He certainly had all the symptoms; it seemed the obvious explanation. But you'll never guess what it turned out to be . . ."

Gayle paused, eyes dancing. "*Food poisoning . . . !*" she marveled. "Not a disease entity at all; merely ingestion of a toxin. To that even we aren't immune.

"For three days he was hardly able to hold up his head—and of course he still insisted upon working nonstop, expecting to run out of time any second. We did our best, of course, treating him, trying to make his final hours comfortable. But we were as amazed as he was when he started to show improvement.

"Peter's the one who figured it out. Teacher had been at it for about 80 consecutive hours by then; and he was a little punchy, muttering to himself as he worked, wondering what on Earth was keeping him alive. Peter looked up from his own console, did sort of a double take, stared thoughtfully for a moment, then asked him if he'd ever been hominem-screened himself.

"I was there, and I'll never forget the sight of Teacher's face at that moment. Can you believe that, after working on the hominem study for close to 30 years, it never once occurred to him to wonder why he'd never been sick himself?" Gayle had nice laugh; reminded me of Momma Foster's.

"It was difficult, as busy as we all are, managing to squeeze in time to run even a few preliminary tests, but they all turned out positive. Which weakens the case for the 1918–19 flu pandemic theory, though surely that bug has been around, in isolated cases, for . . ."

Interrupting is rude, I know. But with gun at head couldn't have held tongue just then. Obvious which direction explanation heading even at outset; mind already racing ahead, remembering *someone else* whom had never seen, heard of, being sick: "If Teacher's one of us, how about *Daddy*? You know, Dr. Foster—is he here? Has anybody heard anything from him? Could he be . . ." Voice trailed off at Gayle's expression.

"I'm sorry, Candy. No one I've talked with has seen or heard of Dr. Foster since about two hours before the attack. He was at the Pentagon. And they used surface-targeted missiles on Washington, you know."

I nodded. Hadn't really expected. Just hoped.

And *still* hoped, dammitall! Daddy much too smart to get caught like that, with everybody expecting attack from moment to moment. Two hours ample time to get out of range. Just matter of finding him. If alive. As well might be. As *very* well might be.

And *is*—I *knew* it! Would *find* him. Someday. Somewhere. Somehow. . . .

"I hope you do find him, Candy," Gayle said softly. "I haven't given up hope either. My fiancé was at that conference. But there hasn't been time. . . ."

Decided to change subject: Can't dwell on Daddy's possible fate without emotional complications; and Gayle's expression betrayed need for distraction as well. Besides, consumed by curiosity enough to get dozen Elephant's Children in trouble—and Gayle's apparent ability to answer unasked questions seemed good place to start digging.

"No, I'm not reading your mind," she assured me as I stared open-mouthed—again before could ask.

(Well, if she said so, all right. But dandy imitation; downright spooky.)

Gayle explained: Observation of unconscious facial, body muscle patterns a longtime hobby. Founded in, extension of, so-called "body language" beloved of popular-psychology cultists of earlier day; results more reliable, accurate. Indeed, not mind reader; *muscle* reader: astute observer of subtle clues.

Threw back covers, jumped from bed into shower, turned on. And as scrubbed at two days' accumulated grime, raised voice to be heard above water's drumming: "What are you all doing here? What's going on? That message we found at Harpers' mentioned something about a continuing problem, and led us to Palomar . . ."

"*What message . . . ?*" Gayle's voice suddenly so sharp that I jumped. Face appeared over shower-stall door, white as proverbial sheet.

No idea what triggered panic; but related search of Harpers' offices in Baltimore, discovery of computer-to-computer message fragment from Teacher notifying of AA assembly at secret hideaway, containing vague mention of Palomar.

Gayle listened intently, without interruption; then said, still almost fiercely, "Where is it now? Did you bring it with you when you left the office?"

Thought briefly as emerged from shower, plied towel. At first couldn't remember; finally recalled stuffing into pocket when left office. Probably still at Adam's parents' house, or somewhere in van, trailer. Gayle's relief almost palpable.

Fixed her then with what hoped resembled gimlet eye; suggested she brief me. Obvious from her reaction: Something scary afoot. Bad joke if somehow I knew something vital, perhaps learned by accident on travels, failed to pass on to proper person through ignorance of relevance.

Gayle eyed me appraisingly. Appeared to think it over; then nodded. "You're right," she said slowly. "But 'scary' isn't the word. 'Nightmare' is more like it:

"Those friendly, fun-loving folks who brought us the End of the World didn't expect to lose the war. They planned carefully. Over a course of many years they conducted thorough intelligence studies of America and every other military power of any consequence. By the time they struck, they were confident that they had allowed for every contingency.

"Fanatics in the truest sense of the word, they could hardly conceive of the possibility of failure. But even that minuscule chance was unacceptable; they couldn't *stand* the thought of someone else winning—even if they lost. So they laid in some 'insurance,' just in case."

Gayle shuddered; but recounted facts quickly, efficiently, without omission, exaggeration, as I dressed.

And if anything, "nightmare" understated proposition: Even in nightmare would have difficulty envisioning people fanatic enough to carry out murder on such a scale. And to conceive so implacable a revenge after own deaths would require thought processes far removed from anything heretofore recognized as human.

Aggressors known as *Bratstvo* (translating as "Brotherhood"): select cadre of ideological zealots recruited from all over behind Iron/Bamboo curtains; cabal pervading bureaucratic/military hierarchies at highest levels, using governmental resources for own purposes. Fanatics all, dedicated to proposition that ideologically pure, totalitarian communism destined to achieve unopposed sway throughout world. Scorned as ideologically lax even limited wrong-mindedness, free expression, capitalist ambitions tolerated by own governments.

Regarded established methods of achieving objective—subjugation through propaganda, sabotage, terrorism, military force, etc.—as soft-headed, inefficient. Hit upon notion of cleansing planet of unbelievers in single bold stroke; starting afresh, without competition.

Would have worked, too, but for unanticipated effectiveness of Free World's intelligence agencies (enhanced, unbeknownst even U.S. leaders, by AAs' subtle contributions—in which effort *Teacher* prime mover!); plus unexpected targeting accuracy, sheer firepower contained in retaliatory arsenal. *Bratstvo's* headquarters designed, constructed, anticipated proof against even direct, near-direct hits—but not so many; became 40-mile-wide, 15-mile-deep crater; all outlying facilities vaporized as well. Cleanup, according to satellite reports, total. Many targets still glowing.

But same Free World authorities who refused to believe zealots' ultimate goal elimination of everyone not sharing beliefs, until warheads, plague, exploded across planet, also discounted AAs' evidence of contingency plan; took no steps to gather up loose ends.

Leaving fledgling hominem population with problem: Parked heretofore unnoticed in geosynchronous orbit over central Asia is Doomsday Machine, strontium-90 bomb, programed to commence reentry upon failing to receive periodic coded signal—next of which due in 11 days; frequency, content known only to long-dead fanatics.

Big strontium-90 bomb: genuine multi-ziloton planet-wrecker, if intelligence reports correct; explosion comparable to asteroid impact. Targeted for deep waters overlying Murray Fracture Zone, 700 miles west-southwest of San Francisco. Programed to sink to ocean floor before detonating.

Blast effects threefold: First, will puncture Earth's crust like balloon (less than three miles thick at that point), sending massive lava tsunamis radiating out across upper mantle's molten surface, cracking tectonic plates, resulting in catastrophic worldwide seismic convulsions. Accompanying seawater tsunamis, though hundreds of feet in height, of negligible significance by comparison.

Second, will hurl uncountable cubic miles of vaporized sea water, mud, rock into stratosphere, where will circulate with planetary atmospheric convection, showering strontium-90 fallout first across North American continent, eventually whole world.

Strontium 90's half-life 29 years—if bomb not stopped, Earth uninhabitable by unprotected humans for something like next *two centuries*!

Finally, resultant atmospheric pollution will trigger real-life Fimbulwinter, destroy what little may remain of biosphere.

"But the *Bratstvo* were no slouches at intelligence work either; it was even money that they knew as much about us as we did about them. We had to assume that they had traced back along our intelligence line and knew where most of us lived and worked.

"We also had to assume that they would have operatives here during the attack to try to ferret out our plans—suicides, possibly; or, perhaps more probable, they might have succeeded in concealing the fact that they had a vaccine for the lethal virus. In either case, they would have searched our homes and offices as soon as we left and couldn't have missed that message.

"We normally destroyed such communications immediately after reading them; and I doubt if any of the Harpers would be guilty of such a basic oversight. More likely, the computer somehow retained it and burped part of it back up, due to the electromagnetic side effects of all those bombs going off at once.

"We expected terrific electromagnetic pulse effects, and had our stuff well shielded against it. But their catalytic warheads emitted in a peculiar region of the spectrum and generated hardly any normal EMP at all; that's why utilities and so forth continued to work for a while afterward. But they did generate *something*; and whatever it was, it had an interesting, if temporary, effect on some computers.

"But if *Bratstvo* agents *had* found that message, the destination alone would have enabled them to deduce our plans. They would have been able, during the initial confusion, to beat us to the launch centers and sabotage the shuttles, which would have ended our hopes for good."

"Well, apparently they didn't see it," I observed; "or there weren't any agents after all. Anyway, now I see why you almost jumped out of your skin when I mentioned finding it.

"Meanwhile, you said 'shuttles'? What *are* we doing about the bomb?" Spoke without thinking; without considering relative ages, backgrounds, educations; participation, contributions to date. But Gayle registered, accepted "we" in spirit offered; no hint of condescension.

"Once we learned what they'd done, we started laying plans of our own," she said thoughtfully, as I finished dressing, followed from room, down corridor, outside. "We pooled our money—there turned out to be quite a lot of it—and built a large, totally self-contained shelter complex in a salt mine located in a theoretically seismically-stable area in Kansas. But we needed to ride out the attack close enough to JPL and Vandenberg to protect those facilities from looting and/or vandalism, so we built a smaller shelter under Mount Palomar. It's nowhere near as geologically stable, but we weren't expecting much in the way of earthquakes unless we aren't able to stop the bomb—in which event, of course, we don't know if even the Kansas shelter will hold up."

"Why did you need to be close to JPL and Vandenberg?" I prodded.

"Patience; I'm coming to that.

"Both shelters are well concealed and very heavily shielded. We were as concerned about stray outbound radiation, which might give our positions away, as we were about incoming hard stuff from bursts and fallout. You wouldn't have found the Palomar shelter unaided.

"We also organized a plan to find and qualify surviving hominems as quickly as possible as to mental and emotional stability and useful skills. Radiation levels dropped to safe levels within a week after the attack, and *H. sapiens* were gone, so we went to work.

"In the course of only two or three months we found and enlisted over a thousand people. We were pleased to learn that, in practice, general-population hominems turned out to be only about 20 percent unstable. The rest are hard to tell from AAs: likable, well-adjusted, intelligent, highly motivated overachievers. Quite a few of even the minority are all right, given a challenge and intelligent supervision.

"Of course we ended up with many more than we anticipated, and we don't have room for them all in the shelters. If we can't stop the bomb, we'll face some difficult decisions or, more probably, decide who goes into the shelters with a lottery."

"I'm going to hold my breath until you get to the point," I warned.

Gayle smiled. "Your original question was, 'What are we doing about the bomb?' Happily, some 30 or so of us—the expanded us, not just the AAs—were key NASA people. I say 'happily' because our only hope of escaping two centuries of underground living—assuming we survive the earthquakes—is to launch the *Nathan Hale*..." We rounded corner and Gayle indicated monstrous assembly poised on pad with casual wave surely more appropriate for discussing weather than *H. sapiens'* ultimate technological achievement. "... rendezvous with the bomb in orbit, and deactivate it."

(Something in statement tugged fretfully at psyche, but instantly forgotten in rush of amazement over scale of plan.)

Briefly reinforced hoary, naïve-ruralite stereotypes by stopping abruptly, gawking openmouthed in unfeigned wonder at monstrous spacecraft looming overhead. Television doesn't come close to conveying scale. Bigger close-up than appears on tube. Lots.

Proximity to technological marvel stimulated imagination, triggered inspiration; conceived possible solution, far less complicated: "Gayle, if you can launch a shuttle, why not send up a big thermonuclear ICBM—oh...." Realized, even as spoke, couldn't be that easy, or already *fait accompli*.

Gayle apparently still reading mind—or whatever—nodded approvingly as reached proper conclusion. "The *Bratstvo* thought of that and took precautions. First, the entire vehicle in which the bomb is housed is constructed of a new lightweight, long-molecule material that seems to be sort of a metallic polymer.

"Becky Chamberlin, one of our best metallurgists—plastics are her second love—had a chance to play with a sample shortly before the attack. She says it's so strong and such a fabulous insulator that, in space, that bomb could probably ride out a multimegaton, near-direct hit without damage—depending on how well the components are packaged, of course.

"But it doesn't have to; it mounts quite capable defenses: the latest analytical radar, a sophisticated computer, and lasers capable of destroying any missile long before it gets close enough to constitute a threat. Finally, it's programed to initiate reentry the moment it's attacked."

"How did we get the sample?"

"One of our number was a quadruple agent..." Gayle paused, noting blank expression; elaborated: "One of us, pretending to them to pretend to us to work for us while actually spying on them as well as a fourth party—got that?"

"This spy business sounds unprincipled, deceitful, and entirely too complicated," I replied with mock disapproval.

"Of course it is." She grinned. "That's the way things were in the old days: All professions cloaked themselves in as much mystery as possible—spies were nowhere near as bad in that respect as, say, real estate appraisers.

"Anyway, Wallace Griffin allowed himself to be recruited by the *Bratstvo* while he was in Russia, supposedly undergoing training with the KGB for his work in the U.S. Quite a few of the KGB were members, and they were always on the lookout for likely prospects. Wallace is good at his job: While ostensibly helping program the on-board computer, he managed to microfilm the bomb's entire schematics package— warhead, drive, guidance system, software, and all. He's the one who brought back the material sample.

"Then, only days before the attack, everything Wallace learned was confirmed when one of the *Bratstvo*'s people tried unsuccessfully to defect and warn the world. His name is Kyril Svetlanov; he was an inner-circle figure among the fanatics. But his story wasn't believed any more than ours was; so *we* took him in, and he's been helping us ever since. He's our resident strontium-90 bomb expert: He was involved in its design, construction, and launching, and works harder than anyone here, with the possible exception of Teacher. But that's understandable: In his place, I wouldn't be able to *live* with the guilt!"

Cast sidelong glance at Gayle. Did not appear type to believe in Santa Claus. She noticed, grinned, addressed unspoken doubt: "Yes, we *did* find it suspicious that a highly placed member of such a fanatical organization should suffer so convenient a change of heart, turning up just when we needed the specific information on which he was a leading expert. But we investigated his story from every possible angle, even interrogating him under drug-augmented, deep hypnosis, and everything checked.

"We've assigned him to the bomb deactivation phase of the project. And since then we've tested him further: At various times we produced data which we knew was erroneous, and led him to believe that we believed it valid and were going to include it in our planning. They were reasonable errors, of the sort which might have been introduced through faulty translation from Russian or even data missing due to incomplete intelligence-gathering, but which almost certainly would have scuttled us in the end.

"Each time he caught and corrected the mistake. Once, when we *insisted* that we knew what we were doing, he threw up his hands and was on the point of quitting, stating that we had doomed the project and further effort was pointless. He's passed every test with flying colors.

"I've studied him myself as closely as I know how, and I've never spotted even a suggestion that he's not sincere. And finally, he's going along on the *Hale* to make sure everything goes all right, which is in itself pretty convincing evidence of his sincerity and desire to atone. Even so, of course, he's *never* alone."

(That disquieting *something* nudged psyche again, but still couldn't put finger on cause.)

Gayle continued as we rounded building's corner. "You'll see him at the meeting—there he is now, and here we are," she finished, pointing out young man as we arrived at meeting site.

Populace assembling in bleachers arranged in semicircle before elevated platform outside launch control center, near huge payload preparation room; everyone present who could be spared even momentarily from duties: numbered in hundreds...

And at stage center was *Teacher*!

Undignified shriek, run-and-hug, probably disrupted proceedings, if any in progress; but didn't care, and nobody else seemed to mind—Teacher least of all. Long time before he let go. Finally held me out at arms' length; scrutinized head to foot. "I think you're in better shape now than when I last saw you in Wisconsin," he said approvingly.

Smile wreathed features, eyes sparkled; but strain, fatigue, perhaps even something which might be mistaken for desperation (in anyone besides *Teacher*) showed in features. And as watched, light died, lines deepened, shoulders sagged.

Voice somber as stated, "I'm astonished that you found us."

"Just lucky," I replied. "I was in the right place at the right time. I heard a sonic boom, looked up, and saw a contrail. If I hadn't run into trouble the day before, we'd have been probably 200 miles from there."

Teacher looked up thoughtfully, momentarily distracted from problems. "With the whole of the North American continent to search, you 'just happened' to see, and be close enough to take advantage of the return of, the first supplies-gathering expedition we've sent out in two months, which will be the last for quite some time to come." Regarded me quizzically. "Coincidence on that scale is difficult to credit, and we hominems are a largely unknown commodity. I wonder where a study of the mechanics of that sort of phenomenon might be commenced, and in what direction it might lead. . . ."

Strain returned to features as Teacher continued. "I had planned to take you with me. But I returned to find you securely locked in your shelter, with both telephone and computer terminal unresponsive—for what reason, I can't imagine.

"I wanted to tell you in the letter where we were going—where the AAs were going, that is; at the time it did not appear that I would be a lasting consideration—and why. But I could not; I hope you can understand why I could not. The best I could do was introduce you to your heritage and suggest that you start looking for your peers.

"I intended to send someone back to search for you as soon as it became possible, but so far it has not: For an amateur group as small as ours to modify and prepare for launch a shuttle, normally groomed by an army comprising several thousand intensively trained experts, in the time allotted, is no modest task. We have not been able to spare *anyone*."

"I guess that answers my next question." I sighed. "My family—my adopted family—is searching the Sierra Nevadas for my body. I'd like to go find them and bring them here. You can't spare a crew, maybe with a helicopter . . . ?"

Teacher shook head slowly. "No; I'm sorry. If you can wait until we've launched the *Hale*, then certainly. But that will leave precious little time in which to find and warn them, should the mission fail, won't it?

"Though . . ." Teacher's eyes closed briefly in pain, ". . . of course in that case they'll just have to go into the lottery with everyone else. They'll be among those for whom the question of whether there is room will be decided by chance.

"Mind you," he added quickly, "the lottery applies only to adults; you children are included automatically."

Teacher blinked then, as if suddenly remembered whom talking to. "I don't mean to sound patronizing, Candy. If it should come to that, it boils down to a question of racial survival. We must attempt to save the young and those possessing the knowledge and skills which will improve their chances. Where possible, those with knowledge will *be* the young. No one in my age bracket, whose skills are duplicated by anyone younger, will be eligible for the drawing."

Understood that. And mortally ashamed at depth of relief I experienced on learning own place in shelter assured, along with Adam, Lisa.

But what if Kim left out . . . ?

Or Terry!—*surely Teacher wouldn't exclude twin!* After all, doesn't take much room, eats like a . . .

No. Now neither time nor place for that discussion. Question probably never arise anyway; *Hale*'s mission surely successful. No benefit to increasing Teacher's burden prematurely, perhaps unnecessarily.

Immediate problem was locating family. Wanted to get them back here soon as possible; be on hand myself, make limited talents available in any manner planners might deem helpful (as well as family's talents—Kim's, Adam's not nearly so limited).

Only extraneous body in vicinity clearly mine; would have to go myself. Decided to leave first thing in morning. No idea how long search might take, but sitting ducks up there for earthquake, fallout; had to try to get them to AAs' shelters before scheduled bomb fall, just in case.

Then worry about lottery.

Noticed Teacher looking over crowd; wondered if missed anything while woolgathering. "I think everyone able to attend has arrived. I must call the meeting to order. Why don't you sit up here with us? There is plenty of room." Stepped toward podium, gathering notes; cleared throat, switched on mike.

I looked around at stage. Consisted of raised platform some 30 feet wide, ten deep. Easel at stage center, just behind podium, held large presentation board. One end of stage littered with odd-looking machinery.

On ground beyond stood large, complicated sculpture with one curved wall, many convolutions, interior open on side toward crowd. If let imagination wander, could easily have been pie slice from cutaway aircraft mock-up. Or giant 3-D rat maze. Bracing crowded interior; one inside surface covered with projections, knobs, dials, tangles of wiring gathered in messy looms. Looked like awkward place to get around in. Small oblong opening in intermediate wall peeked through at wall to which majority of découpage affixed.

Settled in chair near enigmatic artifact; tried to look inconspicuous. Gayle took seat next to me, smiled reassuringly. Grateful for presence; felt very much out of place.

Teacher opened meeting with brief, forced-sounding pleasantries; then discussed progress to date in preparing *Nathan Hale* for launch.

(And suddenly identified source of subliminal itch bothering me since Gayle's first mention of shuttle: Familiar with names of NASA's shuttles; *Nathan Hale* not among them. Apparently AAs rechristened. Well, sure; why not? Previous owners unlikely to object. Besides, had heroic sort of ring to it; sounded neat [though *not* as neat as *Enterprise*—cheapest of evasions to pretend to honor lobby's request; then waste name on mock-up intended for glide tests only!].)

Teacher praised collective efforts to date: Group had faced, overcome immense, unprecedented challenges. Among most pressing: Fact that shuttles never intended for geosynchronous orbit work. Designed, constructed as low-orbit ferries, operating no higher than about 700 miles.

But hominems worked miracles: Devised fittings to mount four solid booster rockets in place of usual two. New trick liquid fuel mixture boosted main engine thrust efficiency several critical percent, improved consumption picture. Cargo bay now accommodated huge custom-built orbital maneuvering system tank (much larger than earlier OMS kits).

Ship also lightened substantially; almost gutted, in fact. Everything extraneous to mission ripped out: Air, food, water storage cut down to irreducible minimum. Storage cabinets, noncritical instrumentation, crew's "amenities" discarded. Landing-gear system removed *in toto*. . . .

(Good thinking: Shuttle expendable after mission; parachutes adequate for crew.)

Aerodynamic control surfaces permanently locked in neutral; related hydraulics, computers, sensors, control sticks, pedals, etc., gone . . .

(Goggled when heard that; couldn't imagine how expected to manage reentry.)

. . . along with all exterior insulation.

(Say *what?*)

Calculations showed *Nathan Hale* now capable of attaining desired orbit.

Just.

Chin dropped; heard own voice involuntarily whisper, "*Oh ...!*" as finally caught on.

Now understood shuttle's new name: *Nathan Hale*—"My only regret is that I have but one life..."

One-way trip.

Volunteers all, three-man crew would attempt to reach bomb, disarm...

And die!

Vision blurred. Felt tear start down cheek. Others followed.

Gayle noticed; divined cause. Leaned close, whispered that crew selected from entire population at launch center—every person involved in project volunteered; AAs, ABs alike.

Shook head; tried to envision what must feel like to step forward, with full knowledge of facts; make rational, intelligent, premeditated decision to give life so others might live.

Couldn't.

Spontaneous, unthinking heroism understandable; bravery in heat of battle, excitement of moment, not uncommon (been known to yield to occasional rash impulse myself); but this—courage required simply defied comprehension...!

Blinked away tears to gaze out over crowd in awe. And as stared, felt unfamiliar stirring: undefinable, comforting. Source eluded identification; but awareness of assemblage somehow expanding, deepening. Vaguely realized was perceiving bond extending beyond present mutual predicament, project, goals. Shared warmth, togetherness almost tangible: Glow slowly pervaded, suffused entire being. Heart swelled, soul thrilled to sudden, absolute knowledge that sapiency's new standard-bearers well chosen.

Slow tears resumed, but proudly now—my people worthy inheritors. Earth in *good* hands....

Kyril stood, joined Teacher at board. Regarded him with new awareness, appreciation; understood Gayle's comment now about how insistence upon inclusion in *Hale*'s crew lent credence to change of heart, penitence. Tall, handsome man, but wore same dejected air as Teacher.

Unveiled large multiple-overlay transparency cutaway drawing of bomb, missile in which housed. Launched into discussion of vehicle's weaknesses. Of which, turned out, were damned few!

Equipped with sophisticated computer, detection/analysis equipment; mounted lasers capable of crisping approaching missile like moth in oxyacetylene flame; structurally invulnerable, in practical terms; everything but propulsion nuclear powered—rocket engines conventional, but more efficient: next generation development permitted by new material, capable of ten gees.

Fanatics planned, built well. Doomsday machine no pushover.

But not omnipotent. Planners mortal men. Achilles' heel of every computer-controlled mechanism is software written by selfsame mortal men, trying to anticipate, cope with hypothetical future problems—forced by memory storage limitations to choose which, amongst whole spectrum, most likely to materialize—determine appropriate responses. Programing limited bomb's awareness of, response to, stimuli likely to be missiles: high-speed metallic objects exceeding certain mass, approaching within hundred-mile spherical perimeter, whose plotted trajectories come within five miles.

Kyril not personally involved in detection-package development, but opined, from general knowledge of project requirements, that slowly moving men in spacesuits, even if picked up by radar, probably ignored by computer. Probably.

Teacher's experts, after poring over liberated drawings, software, over period of weeks, in substantial agreement: Components resulting therefrom unlikely to care about indistinct signals returned by small, slow, essentially nonferrous targets.

Therefore, strategy arrived at called for parking *Hale* safe distance back, proceeding to bomb in spacesuits, using manned maneuvering units; forcing launch service access hatch, entering vehicle; sending robot equipped with TV cameras, powerful waldos, through inner shell hatch (too small for man in spacesuit) to pull plug.

However, project in trouble. Big trouble. Quite possibly insurmountable trouble: Robot development not progressing as anticipated. . . .

"In the months during which we have been working on this problem," sighed Teacher, shoulders slumped, "we have advanced the field of robotics well beyond the point at which we found it. We have accomplished amazing things; but unfortunately they have not been the amazing things which we set out to accomplish. We are now at a dead end."

Couldn't believe ears, eyes! *Teacher*—sounding, looking, *acting* as if defeated!

"Which is why we've called this meeting," he continued more resolutely. "We need fresh input and we need it *now*.

"You all were furnished copies of drawings as you arrived. They depict the attempts we have made so far to come up with a usable design."

Noticed everyone but self had sheaf of paper. Nudged Gayle, elevated brow. She nodded, passed me extra. Glanced through quickly, noting salient details.

Teacher continued without pause: "The first sheet is a list of design criteria, beginning with the initially limiting factor of the inner shell access hatch size, 9 inches by 14; and going on to detail grip strength required of waldos, forces necessary in push, pull, and torque functions; and drawings of the machine's anticipated route from the hatch and working environment inside the bomb, illustrating all known handholds and obstructions.

"Those of you with suggestions are asked to come up and view the full-scale mock-up of the bomb's interior..."

Oh, so that's what this thing was. Stood quietly, stepped down from stage, compared drawings to replication. Clearly drawn; easily matched up. Curved wall was outer hull, with main access hatch. Tiny inner shell access hatch mounted on next wall in. That bulge indicated warhead location, buried near center of nose cone. There was umbilicus plug, last thing disconnected before launch. On-board computer behind that panel there, etc.

And there, at center of cobweb of wiring, all needing to be removed in correct order first, was detonator, accessible only after squeezing through tiny bottleneck hatch, climbing past maze of structural bracing. Would take boneless, acrobatic midget to get in there in first place.

But disarming didn't look too complicated: Remove wiring in proper order, unbolt cover, extract shaped charge by seizing shaft ridges, pulling out. And—oh, yeah, shaft/socket tolerances finely machined, snug fit; 400-500 pounds of force required for extraction, twisting as emerges to clear obstructions. Midget better be husky sucker.

Could see problem now: Complicated, overlapping, multiple functions involved in basic task placed heavy demands upon small machine lacking both tactile feedback for operator guidance and joint flexibility of human hands, wrists, elbows, shoulders. Robot's need to stabilize self while working in weightless environment posed additional problems. As did necessity of finding room for high-resolution, closed-circuit color television camera to enable operators to maneuver unit along tortuous route from hatch to detonator site, carry out assignment.

"No one has ever attempted to extract so many functions from a single machine of such small size," Teacher went on.

(Certainly believed that!)

"We have managed to duplicate each function called for separately, but have not managed to combine them all in one machine of the requisite size. It is beginning to seem probable that we will not succeed before time runs out: The latest possible launch date is only seven days off; and it would be better not to delay until then, in case we run into last-second glitches.

"I don't think anyone here misses the implications: This problem *must* be solved, and within seven days. If our pooled inventiveness fails to come up with a solution by then, our efforts here will have been in vain; we will have no choice but to abandon this work and hasten back to the shelters.

"We all know, however, that the shelters are capable of supporting a maximum of 500 people. A lottery will be held to determine who goes in and who stays out.

"Those remaining outside have virtually no chance of survival: Earthquakes, vulcanically generated airborne toxicity, and fallout will see to that.

"Even the survival of those inside the shelters is questionable, hinging upon whether they emerge from the period of seismic violence sufficiently intact. Our seismologists and engineers hold out little encouragement. In fact, were it not for the fallout and poisonous emissions, it might be safer to attempt to ride it out on the surface."

Teacher winding down; other speakers queuing up to augment presentation. People already converging on mock-up, scanning drawings, examining robots, conversing in muted tones. I resumed seat to keep out of way.

Meeting dragged on for hours. Endless succession of hopefuls approached, put heads together, offered suggestions, argued, compared notes, eventually left, shaking heads. I passed time chatting with Gayle, Teacher too, when neither occupied.

In between, to degree possible without being pushy, I eavesdropped. And of course bent own thoughts to problem at hand. But not mechanical or electrical engineer or programer—nor much of anything else useful for that matter. Generally kept mouth shut; self out of everyone's way.

And worried, of course: With room for only 500 people split between two shelters—one even less likely to come through quakes than other—something on order of 6-, 700 people out in cold if mission fails. And beginning to look as if might: Robot problem no closer to solution now than when meeting began.

Wished Adam, Kim here; no idea whether might contribute or not—just missed them. And Lisa. And especially Terry. Even Tora-chan—bet he wouldn't be allowed in shelters either: Too old; mousing, purring, lap-sitting probably not adjudged "useful skills." Or if so, possessed by someone younger.

Despairing atmosphere infectious; reinforced own self-pity, worry over family's, friends' chances. Gloom deepened as person after person, expert after expert, approached with varying degrees of confidence, gave it best shot, resuming seat shortly thereafter, looking glum. Presently trickle slowed, stopped.

Teacher looked around for more. Expression betrayed depth of disappointment as realized think tank dry. Glanced at Kyril. Russian shrugged, shook head; returned to chair, sat heavily, head hanging.

Teacher rotated slowly, searching faces hopelessly. Our eyes met at exact moment—

Oh! Of course. How . . . *obvious!*

Conclusion, decision, accompanying shock, must have shown on face; for Teacher's thoughts paralleled own, arriving at identical solution merest fraction thereafter. Have never seen anyone look so stricken. For endless seconds old Chinese gazed into, through my soul. Then set jaw, drew himself erect, eyes shining with love, pride, tears. Nodded imperceptibly; watched in silence as I rose jerkily from seat, suddenly nerveless fingers cascading stage with papers, soft-drink can, remaining munchies.

Own slow tears resumed but interfered with vision hardly at all as retrieved diagram, tucked into pocket, stepped down from stage, forced unwilling feet to propel me to mock-up.

Stepped through outer door, strode to tiny inner hatch opening, poked head through, looked around for handholds. Inserted shoulders, first one, then other. Grabbed convenient truss, pulled torso through. Hips, fanny snug fit; harbinger of Better Things To Come (pity will never find out).

Ignored suddenly buzzing audience visible through cutaway's open side. Wormed way between hull braces to detonator site. Wiring complexity immaterial just then; yanked loose *en masse*.

Then produced diagram, studied briefly. Positioned self carefully on back, planted feet on either side of detonator shaft. Took firm grip. Drew long breath, released slowly; took another, whispered hysterical-strength tap trigger, and
...*PULLED!*

Didn't even require major effort. Audience gasped as shaft slid easily outward. Shortly encountered obstruction. Experimented, turning one way, then other; pulled again.

Moments later stepped out through cutaway, carrying detonator in one hand. Stunned hush marked progress back to center stage where Teacher waited, tears streaming down wrinkled cheeks. Own tears still flowed but control holding otherwise; breathing almost normal, hands steady.

Carefully set down detonator, stood, put arms around dearest friend. Marveled again how solid he felt, despite years. Held him tightly for long moments; wishing could do something to ease silent convulsions wracking him. But cause obvious, situation inescapable; we both knew it.

Released him, put hands on his shoulders, stood on tiptoes, placed kiss on wet cheek.

Stepped to podium, pulled mike down within reach. Felt curiously at peace as looked out over all those people. All *my* people.

Surprisingly easy to get words out; voice clear, firm, unwavering as took deep breath, said, "Does anybody know how to take in a spacesuit?"

Well, not quite that simple, of course. Even after predictably outraged debate over including 11-year-old in suicide mission faded before dearth of alternate suggestions, practical difficulties remained:

Among which, spacesuit more complicated to "take in"

than pair of jeans. Principal challenges: one-piece plastic bubble helmet; neck, waist sealing rings; portable life-support-system package; aluminum frame surrounding chest, hips—all rigid; all products of elaborate engineering, exacting manufacturing procedures; all exceeding 9-by-14 hatch dimensions by substantial margins, even in smallest of three available sizes.

But given no opportunity to follow tailors' progress; had own problems: Rushed immediately into astronaut training (*immediately*: that night—only six days remaining in which to master necessary skills).

See: Launch one of mission's more critical stages; process rife with opportunities for sabotage. Original crew consisted of one seasoned NASA shuttle pilot, one experienced civilian test pilot, one *Bratstvo* defector. Assigning two most experienced pilots to do flying permitted tactfully glossing over fact that Kyril, still not entirely trusted, was being kept away from vital equipment. My presence unavoidably sundered gentlemanly façade: Minimum personnel boiled down to one pilot, one bomb expert, one husky midget. Retaining original copilot not fuel efficient: only valid criterion.

Which left rosy-cheeked grammar-school refugee (big-time ultralight jockey) sitting in simulator's right-hand chair, reading off checklists, updating on-board computers, responding to CRTs, flipping switches right and left, watching gauges—trying to ignore fact that eminently qualified engineer/computer-scientist/jet-pilot cooling heels in deactivated mission specialist's chair just aft: patently so much dead weight.

Bothered me so much at first, finally took Kyril aside at break, planted foot squarely in mouth trying to apologize for being promoted over him. However, Russian promptly set mind at ease, using charming, sideways-fractured social English (love listening to him, though sometimes wonder if deliberate [technical syntax flawless]).

Kyril completely in agreement with assignments as posted; understood hominems' reservations about sincerity—would insist upon same precautions were positions reversed. Bore absolutely no resentment toward me for "usurping" role, nor anyone else for that matter. Suggested I forget disparity in ages, backgrounds; concentrate on job—predicted would find quite enough to occupy attention without manufacturing needless concerns.

Might have had trouble buying sincerity even then had not he broken off pep talk midword, startled me by impulsively taking my hands in his, expression desperately earnest, saying, "Candy, Harris is being ex-Marine pilot fighter: chubbyhearted, compellsive hero. He goes consequencely he knows he is best; could not be living with himself should mission boom out through flub of one less adequate sitting in his shoes. My justify are resembling: My proficiency of bomb is excelling. And I am at culp.

"But *you . . .*" Swept me into brief, intense hug; then released, holding at arms' length, gazing intensely into eyes. "I am astonish of you! I say without exacerbation: Inside little-girl window-condiment is most prodigal woman have ever had glad accident to meeting."

Now, emotions running pretty close to surface these days, as can imagine; I vacillate between forced cheerfulness, depths of despair. Naked admiration shining from Kyril's eyes at that moment far exceeded stimulus threshold necessary to loose floods.

Instead, horrified to detect genuine giggle born deep inside; growing, gaining impetus with each passing second, working inexorable way upward despite every effort to suppress—because didn't *want* to laugh: Kyril sure to take wrong—no; there lay problem: Sure to take right; and laughing at accent in class with poking fun at physical defect. Kyril really nice person; last thing wanted to do was hurt feelings. So forced features into rapt, wide-eyed smile; bit lip, tried to weather storm.

But Russian's enthusiasm still gaining momentum: "I think what I regret most-secondly about this kettle of grubs is not knowing you ten years awayer—hell's jingles, I would accommodate for meeting you four, even *three* years subsequentially. What you looking like then isn't mattering; outside would being old enough for getting to know you without raising flatulent vibes of moral torpitude. Would never want you predicate of false scandal . . ."

At that, final vestige of restraint popped like soap bubble: Sputtered first, noble intentions to contrary; then whooped uncontrollably, noises moderating thereafter to helpless belly laughing—situation made even funnier somehow by heartfelt guilt over puzzled expression momentarily overspreading Kyril's face.

But as I held aching ribs, puffing for semblance of

restraint, he grinned wickedly, said, "That's better. To beginning, I despond you turning up to be humorless. And you don't *looking* Russian." Which, of course, added fuel to laughter.

Grin turned to warm smile. "Telling me: Did you really thinking I have noisy intestines over such applesoup as who sits where? We have imperative jobs to do; I do mine, you do yours."

Then smile faded. Brushed my cheek with gentle fingertips; said tenderly, "But making no misconstruings: I meant exactly how I said: I *proudly* to being sat alonghind you."

That did it, of course: Dissolved wetly into Russian's arms; useless for next 20 minutes.

Been truly frantic week; busy every second. Spent ten hours every day practicing on shuttle simulator, employing hypnotically augmented concentration to absorb duties—greatly reduced, fortunately, from load normally carried by right seat's occupant, due to elimination of systems, related controls, instruments. But Kyril correct: Still plenty left to keep me out of trouble!

However, shuttle training only part of schedule; followed each day by further drilling: getting to know bomb inside out; acquiring basic smattering of Russian, sufficient command of appropriate software assembly language (turned out both hard-, software started life American), requisite programing skills. And really had to knuckle down; both computerese, Russian lots harder than Pitman shorthand—*and so little time*!

AAs concluded long ago bomb too dangerous to have around, defused or not. But daren't risk setting off in orbit. Warhead *magnitudes* bigger than anything ever detonated on Earth, and strontium 90 really nasty stuff. While preliminary figures suggest only small fraction of fission byproducts likely to make it into atmosphere during next 200 years, sheer volume of output guarantees borderline-hazardous level of fallout. Further, one school of thought amongst AA astrophysicists suggests possibility that blast on that scale could have adverse effect on Van Allen belt.

Wherefore, AAs came up with complicated, but hopefully effective, procedure which should eliminate problem for good, while avoiding side effects. Vehicle's own awesome power, fuel reserves, form heart of disposal scheme.

Bratstvo anticipated possible need for all-out departure

from orbit, minimum-time reentry. Designed, constructed vehicle with ample fuel, power to do job. If attack detected, brakes go on at ten gees. Takes slightly more than 30 seconds to kill orbital velocity, but engines scheduled to operate for full minute, thrust alignment shifting throughout: Acceleration at burn's conclusion almost straight down; massé shot with only slight easterly vector, producing high-speed cometary graze. Engines fire again just before perigee: Remaining fuel blunts awesome velocity; adjusts speed, course, to dead-center reentry window.

Pointed in proper direction, however, vehicle capable of delta-V boost ample to leave Earth's gravity well entirely. Which amounts to pretty thorough disposal.

First step is physically disarming warhead (*very* first step, lest something go awry during succeeding stages; result in unscheduled reentry with live warhead, or, almost as bad, detonation in orbit). Suitcase-sized terminal with liquid-crystal display screen then unfolded, plugged into on-board computer's umbilicus; ballistics program wiped, new one loaded; engines fire up on schedule, end of problem.

But AAs didn't feel right about merely pitching ghastly device out into space for someone else to bump into sometime in unguessable future; destination of new ballistics program is Sol's interior—programed for dive into sun: When AAs get rid of something, stays got!

(Obviously my people intrinsically tidy bunch: I like that.)

Well, this pretty well wraps up journal, I guess; not a lot more to say. We launch tomorrow morning. Find prospect of shuttle flight thrilling, if narrow perspective sufficiently; view carefully, without thinking beyond.

But made interesting discovery during course of week: Oddly enough, am *not* afraid to die.

Oh, apprehensive, of course. And perfectly willing to hold off for century or two. But not really, truly, personally frightened of death per se. Not sure why, but true. Perhaps partial consequence of horrendous weeks immediately following attack. Possibly that, coupled with subsequent episodes, has toughened psyche. Maybe fear of death something to which, through repeated exposure, one can acquire degree of immunity.

Don't know. But thinking back, can remember several previous occasions where prospect of trying something new, unknown, brought on appreciably higher anxiety levels. For instance, present attitude toward death nothing compared to heebie-jeebies briefly inspired by decision to accept Rollo's bargain. (Never would have admitted it to him, but contemplated prospect of initial session with same enthusiasm as root canal without anesthesia.)

Hmm... Thinking of Rollo makes me wonder if should have said "yes" to Adam. Feel sort of guilty about dying with issue unresolved. Viewed in retrospect—maybe.

Once heard "love" defined as condition in which own happiness dependent upon happiness of other. Makes sense, except literal interpretation covers parent/child, sibling/sibling, etc.; relationships which usually don't lead to sex. And while feelings toward Adam surely different from those for Daddy...

Hold on there. Oh, really? *Adopted* father, after all: No genetic bar; no reason shouldn't. Just never crossed mind before; never viewed Daddy from "female" perspective; never thought of him as "male."

Perhaps *should* have gone ahead with Adam. Then at least wouldn't be dying as virgin (I know, I know—wouldn't be dying as virgin if went ahead with *anybody*). But only 11, after all. Had expected to become functional, functio*ning* female in own good time; derive same enjoyment books all prate about—but haven't *wanted* to yet, with Adam or anyone else.

(Still don't, actually.)

But mighty curious, and time running out. Well, too late now—unless perhaps vamp Harris or Kyril (or both?) on way out to rendezvous, or after completing mission, before life-support runs out.

But no, not Harris; regards me as likely prospect for sainthood. Apparently feels my age somehow makes my sacrifice more creditworthy than his. Don't understand reasoning myself, but he means it. Also thinks I would have made good Marine.

Besides, considers me cutest thing since invention of puppies. "Fathers" me for all he's worth—half the time absent-mindedly calls me first by one of several daughters' names. Even if managed to convince him offer not irrational behavior brought on by approaching end, would never take advantage.

In fact, as ponder matter further, probably be mortally offended that anyone would think for second *he* could be interested in someone my age. No; much too fond of him to take risk.

And Kyril—uh-uh, don't think him either. Granted, genuinely beautiful man, and quite fond of him, but—well, don't *know* why; somehow notion makes me uncomfortable. Hate to admit it after contributions—giving life same as we, after all—but somewhere down in deepest, darkest corner of soul, perhaps share AAs' unresolved doubts about Russian's ultimate sincerity.

And apart from that, is so incredibly intelligent, perceptive (along with sweet), would probably deduce real motive; cooperate out of desire to satisfy childish scientific curiosity, acting as one friend helping another. Doesn't sound much like formula for making Earth Move.

Never mind; maybe have better luck next time around.

Speaking of which, would be nice to know for sure What Comes Next. Suspect main reason not afraid of death is Momma Foster's attitude as own end approached. Things like that stick with five-year-olds; settle into, become part of basic makeup, foundations. No doubt in my mind whatsoever Momma went to Heaven; and find myself looking forward to reunion—maybe with Daddy, too? Hope so. . . .

If get there myself, of course. . . . Whole life has yet to "flash before my eyes," but difficult to resist occasional furtive glance over shoulder as time approaches. Have attempted to live "good" life: Always tried to help where could; never hurt anyone on purpose when could avoid it.

But occasionally good intentions didn't pan out.

Wonder how killing Rollo looks on Record in Big Book. Accident? Yes. Unavoidable? Under circumstances, yes.

But as Kim pointed out, if had known in advance that that's what would take to save twin's life . . .

There. Now getting down to real pain locus—never suggested facing imminent death easy; or knowing manner, hour of arrival, fun.

No. Hurts. Hurts lots. Hurts *awful!*

Thinking about loved ones' pain. Counting own losses—never again holding serious "grown-up" philosophical discussions with Lisa; no more whispered, giggly huddles with Kim on subject of Men, Women & Life; never again holding nose over one of Adam's puns, or watching him glow with pride as I wax lyrical over product of culinary genius. Never again to learn from Teacher; or dig up own data, make own discoveries—and *so* much to learn . . . !

And nevermore to chat, play, share contented silences with Terry. . . .

That may be most distressing thought of all—everyone else rational, intelligent; understands circumstances, reasons; will grieve, heal, remember me, go on.

But innocent birdbrain incapable of understanding circumstances; doesn't reason. Only knows is happy with me, miserable without. Only knows I left him, never returned. May recover, may not. But will hurt for long, long time and *never* know reason why.

No. Nothing fun about knowledge of impending death. For first time in months have experienced resurgence of bleak, terrible loneliness; horror, nightmares; depression that so paralyzed me during weeks following attack: Feelings of helplessness, futility; cornered feelings. Granted, predicament voluntary—but circumstances leading to stepping forward *not*.

(And homilies about spilt milk may be apt, but sure not very comforting.)

Well, might as well wrap it up, go to bed. Launch scheduled for 6:00 A.M.; means 3:30 reveille: Must be aboard *Hale* by T minus one hour 50 minutes; lots to do before lighting fuse.

Plus big breakfast scheduled first; traditional astronauts' steak-and-eggs pig-out—especially critical this time because weight considerations preclude taking much in way of consumables with us: Every ounce left behind frees that much more fuel for maneuvering as we rendezvous with bomb—promises to be near thing as is.

And apologies for neglect, Posterity. Have wanted to update journal, honest; but these few minutes before bed this evening literally first opportunity have had since landing here six days ago. Wasn't dodging responsibility; well understand importance: If mission succeeds, future generations of teachers will want to bore students with inspirational Life & Times of Candidia Smith-Foster, Plucky Girl Savior of Our People.

(Of course being sarcastic; but also stating fact. National heroes—nay, racial heroes, more important yet—really should try to leave accurate, intelligible [did my best] record of How I *Really* Did It and Why. Failure to discharge responsibility spawns inevitably inflationary folklore—and can't bear thought of future generations hearing how I crossed Susquehanna on crumbling trestle's single remaining rail, van balanced on two wheels, thereby eluding marauding band of sex-crazed mutants; or that I stupidly chopped down cherry tree in youth and even more stupidly admitted it.)

Will leave journal on table tomorrow morning for Teacher to find. Has promised to make locating family crash-priority project first thing after crisis; invite them into burgeoning hominem community. In due time he or they—someone, surely—will merge this volume with previous three.

(And must say, resulting tome disappointingly slim. Had planned on, hoped for, much more substantial monument.)

Really must be getting to bed now; 3:30 horrendous hour. (And do *not* understand necessity: Geosynchronous orbits, like gibbets, available 24 hours a day—so why must astronauts, condemned prisoners alike, always get up before dawn? Doesn't make whole lot of sense.)

Well, good-bye, Posterity. Take care of future for me.

And good-bye everybody else. Good luck—I'll do my best.

I love you.

VOLUME III—Part II
Portents

It's been four days now, and still no sign of her.

A fire trail enabled us to haul the trailer within about two miles of the point where Adam's RDF line and Candy's compass bearings all intersect, so we're base-camped right in the middle of the search area. We've got a lot of supplies; we'll be able to stay for weeks before having to go back to restock.

The sequoia forest is absolutely magnificent. Just being here in the heart of it should be wonderfully, spiritually fulfilling. It's very quiet: The only sounds are a blend of the breeze sighing through the treetops so far above, and bird calls, insect noises, and small animals rustling in the underbrush. Natural lighting way down here on the ground, almost shut off from the sky and direct sunlight, is diffuse and soothing. The trees are so immense that you tend to forget that they *are* trees; the trunks extend upward out of sight like vast pillars supporting a green ceiling, and lend an almost cathedrallike quality to the scene. It's so very peaceful; and if it were not for the constant awareness of what brings us here, I would love every second of it.

As it is, I see it only through Candy's eyes: envisioning what it must be like for her, probably injured, with only a few pounds of dried rations, a canteen of water, and no shelter—it gets cold up here at night. It's hard not to feel guilty, sleeping in a warm, comfortable bed, eating solid meals, while she's lost out there.

There's ample room to get the van between the sequoias, but often that space is clogged by smaller trees of various descriptions and underbrush. Adam is confident that he can get through to pick her up when we find her, if she's too badly injured to ride out behind one of us on a trail bike. But until then he prefers not to risk the van unnecessarily; if we cripple it, we would have to abandon the trailer when we leave, and come back for it if we can. That would be inconvenient.

For that reason we've been using the bikes to search. They're Hondas, lightweight and easy to ride. They have eight forward speeds, automatic clutches, and big, high-traction, off-road knobby tires. Adam brought along five bikes, providing double redundancy in case one or more should fail under the pounding. So far none have, and they've been given every excuse. We search from sunup to dark, covering probably seventy-five miles a day or better, under conditions which range from smooth going on firm, dry, level, leaf-covered soil, to scrambling and bouncing over logs and boulders.

Adam wrapped a thick towel around the handlebars of Lisa's bike to provide secure footing, and Terry spends the day riding with her. His presence is quite helpful: I always can tell when Lisa starts getting too enthusiastic by Terry's sound level. He loves jumps, wheelies, and going fast; the more fun he's having, the louder he gets. When he becomes audible over my bike's exhaust, I point the bullhorn in that direction and speak sternly.

Lisa had an uneasy relationship with her bike in the beginning. She couldn't reach the ground from the seat; and because it outweighed her by at least four to one, she had great difficulty bracing it upright with one leg. So she has learned not to need to: She stands or sits, depending on how rough the terrain is, feet always on the pegs, never quite stopping, and *never* touching foot to ground. Her effortless progress through or over virtually anything Nature puts in her path is simply amazing to behold.

It's even more amazing from my perspective: I often drag one or both feet for stability and usually have to maintain my balance, when going very slowly over rough ground, by pushing with one foot or the other. Not uncommonly, I simply get off and walk it over the very worst conditions. Adam is better at it than I am but is in awe of Lisa.

We conduct the search by riding through the forest on a compass course, three abreast, Lisa and Terry in the middle, Adam and I keeping her barely in sight, all three of us studying the ground in front and on both sides, and trying to remember to keep an eye above us as well, in case Candy might be trapped in a tree. Periodically we stop altogether, shut off the engines, call through the bullhorns, and listen for a reply. We've been keeping track of the areas we've searched by chopping blazes on tree trunks as we proceed and marking our progress on the sectional map.

Because the bikes provide such speed and mobility, Adam reasoned that one of us might find him- or herself out of even bullhorn range in only a few minutes. So when shopping for the bullhorns, he picked up several sets of police personal radios, with belt-mounted battery packs and speakerphones designed to be clipped to the wearer's collar. We carry two each; one worn, one in reserve on the bike. They're a great comfort when I look in Lisa's direction and can't see her for minutes at a time.

An odd thing happened the day before yesterday, by the way, unrelated to the search: We had an earthquake. It wasn't much of one; we probably wouldn't have noticed if we hadn't been stopped for lunch, sitting on a log, watching Terry chin himself upside down from a creeper. For the briefest instant the log and ground both trembled, and we heard, or perhaps felt, a faint, distant, rumbling sort of boom.

Adam says trucks passing his parents' home in Baltimore were more noticeable. I guess that means he wasn't impressed.

But I was: This isn't really "earthquake country" up here. For us to have felt it this far from The Fault, it must have been a fairly respectable tremor.

Which means we could be cut off up here. We came up the only open road in a hundred-mile radius; if it's blocked now, we'll never get the trailer out, and probably the van as well. Both are replaceable, of course, but we'd have to replace so much equipment, as well. I haven't mentioned this to Adam; he has quite enough on his mind.

Incidentally, I wonder if I might have discovered an unsuspected partial explanation for the amount of time and effort Candy spends on these journals: Sitting down, reviewing a day's or week's events, and composing a clear, concise summary provides an unequaled opportunity to see things in perspective. Details which seemed trivial at the time often acquire significance upon reflection, or vice versa.

For instance: Years ago I had an Aunt Becky who had a charming Panama parrot named Ellery Green. They were very close. And when she died, they almost lost Ellery, too. He refused to eat or drink or take an interest in anything; he just sat in his cage and pined. They force-fed him for weeks. He probably would have died anyway had not one of my cousins overcome his grief through sheer intensity of love.

Now, Terry and Candy are *much* closer than Aunt Becky and Ellery were, and at first I worried that Terry might react similarly. But he hasn't. The only hint of change in his behavior is that he's reverted to his original vocabulary; he's stopped using those long, convoluted, totally inexplicable sentences. In fact, apart from that, if it *is* significant, I can't see that he's even noticed that she's gone! He's entirely content, and I don't understand why.

True, Terry likes both Adam and me. He lets us feed and water him and clean his stand, and he's obviously grateful when one of us offers him a head-rub. But his attitude toward us remains more a matter of courtesy and friendliness than love.

Lisa falls into a different category, of course. Before we lost Candy, Lisa was his second-favorite playmate: If she was around and Candy wasn't, he wasn't happy unless he was either on her shoulder or close enough for frequent, mutually reassuring physical contact. That's still the case; they play riotous games, laugh uproariously, and "converse" for hours.

But Lisa isn't Candy, and his relationship with her is very different from that which he shares with his "twin." For instance, only with Candy has Terry ever participated in hours-long Rapt Silences, snuggling quietly in her arms, both content just to be together.

There are other distinctions as well, of course; but the point is that, no matter how satisfactory we three are as baby-sitters, the center of Terry's universe is Candy, just as Aunt Becky was for Ellery, and I find it strange that he's taking her absence with such aplomb.

But what bothers me most of all is the fact that Lisa isn't worried either. I attempted to explain that Candy has had an accident and may be hurt, or may even have Gone To Heaven, like Daddy. I know she feels the same way about Candy that I do, but she was completely unconcerned. She told me not to worry; that Candy is fine. I've probed this as deeply as I dare, considering her age and the potential for trauma, and I don't think that what she's doing is refusing to face facts. Lisa is serenely, utterly confident that Candy is all right—no, correct that: Lisa *knows* that Candy is all right. But she doesn't know how she knows.

And then there is the curious thing that happened the morning that we lost Candy and early the very next day.

We were sitting around the living room, listening to Candy report road conditions. Adam was at the radio; I was on the couch. Lisa was in a chair in the corner, Terry on his stand. Things happened very quickly after Candy's distress call, and neither Adam nor I had time to pay attention to Lisa and Terry, consciously anyway. Since then, however, I've had time to assemble a composite of what they were doing by retrieving memories of peripheral glimpses of things I saw but which didn't register.

Lisa sat, staring glassy-eyed into space, holding both arms of her chair with white-knuckled hands, smiling enigmatically. Terry was crouched, his body level, tail extended. His expression was even more gleefully vacant than usual. His head bobbed, his wings were half-open, and both he and Lisa swayed unevenly in unison. A short while after we lost the signal, Terry suddenly flapped violently. Both he and Lisa weaved and bobbed back and forth, squealing, "Wheee-e-e-e...!" until either Adam or I snarled at them to shut up. They did; but I heard Lisa whisper to Terry, "That was *neat!*"

Then early the next morning, as Adam guided the rig swiftly but smoothly along the fire trails toward the search area, they did it again! The silence echoing from the rear of the van attracted my suspicions—that's something mothers learn early.

Terry again wore that silly, delighted, not-here expression; crouched on his stand, tail slightly elevated, wings half-spread. Lisa, too, was staring vacantly into space again, holding the arms of her chair tightly with both hands, and smiling. Both leaned and shifted their weight in unison; Terry's movements especially were reminiscent of an aircraft banking for turns.

I watched surreptitiously in the sun-visor mirror until it was over. As before, both returned to an awareness of their surroundings simultaneously but apparently independently. Lisa blinked a couple times and then sighed happily. Terry resumed his normal upright posture and shook himself briefly to settle his feathers. Lisa glanced at him and grinned. The bird bobbed his head in reply.

Now, I'm an engineer. My training deals with concepts

capable of mathematical proof, and their relationships to tangible objects or provable intangibles. I have an imagination, but it's under control. Thus far I've never had trouble differentiating between fantasy and reality. Nor have I had difficulty keeping *what I want to be* separate from *what is*.

But now I'm not sure. Events of the past few days hint at things beyond my training and experience. Sometimes I wonder if I'm letting my imagination run, fed by Adam's previous speculations, and seeing more than is there. At other times I wonder if even his suspicions fall short of the truth; if perhaps we're seeing surface indications of a phenomenon operating on a level we're not equipped to perceive.

However, I've always prided myself on an open mind. I've never ruled out something without hard evidence and/or math to justify my opinion. I've always believed in, and tried to practice, the scientific method: When faced with an enigma, I've always deferred judgment until completing a proper study of the available data. Mere absence of positive data does not prove the negative. In fact, several times I have refused to venture a professional opinion when I judged that the data, while unanimously pointing to a certain conclusion, was insufficient to support it.

Nor have I ever allowed my own involvement to influence my observations and/or conclusions. So far, that is. I wonder if I have this time. I'm very uncomfortable about this. Lisa is my baby, my first born, all that remains of the love I shared with Jason. I may, in fact, be guilty of resisting the conclusion that a growing body of evidence increasingly suggests:

Lisa or Terry, or both, *may*, through some unknown mechanism, be in touch with Candy. I can't imagine how they could be, but neither can I prove that they aren't. If they are, they're not any clearer about how it works than I am—and *whatever* it is, if anything, it's not directional; Lisa has no more idea where Candy is than I do.

I've tried to question her about how she knows whatever it is she thinks she knows, but I haven't had much luck with it. I don't think she's being deliberately evasive, but somehow every conversation ends up back where it started, with no identifiable information changing hands. When I tried to find out what she and Terry were doing right after we lost Candy's signal, for instance, it went like this:

"Lisa, what were you and Terry doing? Were you playing a game?"

"We were going *fast*."

"But you were sitting in a chair. How could you be going fast?"

"Candy was going fast."

"But Candy wasn't here."

"No; she was going *fast*."

"But if she wasn't here, how do you know she was going fast?"

"It felt fast."

"What felt fast?"

"Candy."

"But she wasn't here?"

"No; how could she be here and go fast?"

"Well, where did the feeling come from?"

"From Candy."

"Oh. What did it feel like?"

"Fast, it felt *fast!*"

"What felt fast?"

"Candy did."

"How did you know she went fast?"

"By feeling it."

"But how could you know that, sitting in a chair?"

"By feeling it."

"Feeling what?"

"We were going fast."

An alternate ending to this conversation is a blank look and "I don't know."

I'm beginning to suspect that part of the problem is that Lisa and I don't share common referents to describe what she's trying to tell me. This could give the term "generation gap" a new lease on life.

A week now, and still no sign of Candy.

We're not a happy group: Adam's determination has taken on overtones of desperation. Lisa has been uneasy this past couple of days as well. She still insists that Candy is fine, but admits that she's "awful busy, and kind of scared." Which describes my own feelings in a nutshell.

Even Terry is no longer his usual carefree self. He's still eating enthusiastically, so I'm not worried that he's working on the Ellery Green syndrome, but he's growing more subdued day by day.

Apart from that, he's just plain driving us mad! His vocabulary has shifted back into high gear. He's talking absolutely nonstop again, employing words in combinations that none of us have ever used in front of him, forming sentences that he simply can't have heard before anywhere.

His behavior defies rational explanation. When Candy was here, we could speculate that he was taking it from her thoughts somehow. But she's not here; and even if she were, her presence would hardly explain *this*, delivered in fits and snatches over the course of several days:

". . . yellow stripe on green first, then black stripe on green, *then* solid red. Right? *Stupid cam-latch . . . !*"

". . . if the total is larger than sigma, colon; go to sub-YBVD. If larger than lambda, colon; go to sub-YBVE. If less than sigma, go to sub-YBVF . . ."

". . . twist right and pull. I mean *left!*—I'm sorry, I'm *sorry!*"

Lisa says she knows where he's getting it, but her explanations haven't shed any more light on this than they have anything else.

Lord, I wish we *knew* something. The only thing worse than uncertainty is—probably the truth. . . .

This has been a bizzare day. Unproductive and disturbing, but especially strange!

There's still no sign of Candy after nine days—unless you count the inexplicable conduct involving Lisa and Terry, which I find very difficult to credit.

Adam doesn't believe it at all. He's quit putting up a brave front; he hasn't smiled practically since we got here, and now he's almost stopped talking. He continues to search, grimly, determinedly, refusing to admit the possibility of defeat, but without hope.

Lisa isn't very cheerful anymore, either. She says that Candy is frightened and has been growing more so daily. She doesn't know why, but it scares her as well.

Actually, none of us are too spritely. It's as though some sort of pall has settled over the forest. I've been having this growing sense of impending doom for days now. I try not to let it show around Lisa, but every day it gets harder.

And Terry's behavior steadily becomes more unusual.

This morning he launched into a monologue before sunup. I heard it from the beginning—ever since having Lisa, any unusual sound wakes me instantly. And this, even compared to his normal behavior these days, and apart from the hour he started, was *unusual*.

It began with a singsong voice in the darkness: "Control, this is *Nathan Hale*. Radio check."

"Wha—huh? *Now* what?" muttered Adam sleepily from the bedroom.

"Roger, loud and clear," came the disembodied reply.

Adam grumbled something about "dumb bird!" I heard his feet hit the floor. "I guess he means it. Well, the sun will be up soon. Might as well get up and eat so we can get going at first light." He stumbled from the bedroom and turned on a light; I shielded my eyes against the sudden glare.

Terry perched on one foot on his stand, eyes squinting, head tilted back slightly and sunk between his shoulders. He looked rather grumpy, as if *we* had waked *him*. "Inertial measurement unit alignment in progress," he said, yawning.

"This is a new wrinkle." I yawned back, stretching, standing, then folding the bed back into a sofa. I didn't wake Lisa, asleep on the converted dinette; at her age, she needs all the sleep she can get. Time enough when breakfast was almost on the table. "But sounds familiar somehow, doesn't it?"

"Uh-huh, I *have* heard this somewhere before," Adam replied, fumbling out cooking utensils and dishes. "But I can't think where. You want in the bathroom first?"

"Boiler control switch on. Nitrogen supply switch on."

"No; you cooked yesterday. You go first; I'll start breakfast."

"Hey . . ." Adam called from the bathroom after a while; "I know why that sounds familiar. Have you ever watched a shuttle launch on television?"

"You're right. Golly, doesn't that bird ever forget anything?" Something tugged at my memory. For a moment it eluded me. Then I had it: "Adam, I don't remember a shuttle named *Nathan Hale*, do you?"

"No."

A brief silence ensued, interrupted as Terry continued: "APUs powered up."

"Me either. This is his eeriest performance yet."

"Amen."

Adam emerged from the bathroom and regarded the

bird in perplexity. "I hate it when he does stuff like this. It's positively scary." He smiled faintly. "But he certainly has the patter down perfectly. He makes me want to rush to the nearest television and watch."

"Me too." I could have kissed the silly goose; that was the first time Adam had smiled in days.

Perching relaxed on one leg, eyes half-closed, head tilted back slightly and sunk between his shoulders, Terry droned on: "Main engine gimbals nominal."

Adam sat on the couch. "What's for breakfast?"

"Oh-two vents closing. H-two pressurization okay—going for launch. . . ."

"Pancakes, bacon and eggs, cocoa, and orange juice," I replied.

"APU start is go," said Terry.

"Nectar of the gods," Adam approved.

"The on-board computer is on the job."

"I wonder how long he's going to keep it up," Adam mused. "He's just about through the launch sequence, if memory serves."

"Five, four—main engine start—two, one . . ."

"That long." I grinned.

". . . *zero*—solid booster ignition—*LIFT-OFF* . . . !" Terry shrilled the last two words, voice cracking, flapping violently.

Lisa shot bolt upright in bed and screamed. Her eyes stared, round and unseeing. She clutched at the bed as if to steady herself.

"*Wow* . . . !" Terry was bobbing his head now; even I could recognize the manic delight in his expression. "*Wow* . . . !" he squealed again; "we're *boldly going* . . . !"

Lisa's eyes cleared and focused as I reached her. She looked around dazedly. Then she closed her eyes again and—I swear!—she looked around *inside* the lids. "Gee," she breathed. "I thought I was dreaming. This is *neat!*"

Adam caught my eye. His brow crooked.

"Instituting roll," offered Terry.

"Lisa, honey," I said gently, "what's happening?"

She didn't answer for whole minutes. Finally I shook her gently. "Lisa?"

She opened her eyes. The faraway look was back.

"Main engine throttle-back," said Terry.

"Lisa?"

"Max Q.," said Terry.

"We're going *fast*," came the dreamy reply.

"*What* . . . ?" said Adam, eyeing her sharply.

Now I regretted not having discussed with him my previous conversations with her on this subject. I shook my head quickly and intensely, indicated Lisa behind her back, and caroled, "We can talk about it *lay*-ter."

"Main engines back up to one-hundred percent."

Adam caught on but didn't look pleased. He stared across at Terry, still bobbing and flapping, and then down at Lisa's closed eyes and entranced expression.

"Solid booster separation," said Terry helpfully.

Adam's expression was a study in confusion and misery, untouched by hope. "We sure will," he muttered darkly.

VOLUME V
Revelation

Damn!—hope this turns out legible. Easier things to do than trying to write Pitman shorthand while floating weight-less in dark, scared to death, sole illumination furnished by flashlight wedged between hull braces, hand gripping pen encased in bulky EMU glove and possessing every reason to shake.

Never been so terrified in whole short, violence-prone life. Still not afraid of death per se—though if guessed wrong (as well may have, with limited data on which forced to make decision) impending demise promises to be painful enough to satisfy fantasies of even most demanding masochist.

No; fear based upon possibility might have guessed even wronger; in which case probably won't be physically painful at all: Instead will have several hours in which to dwell on consequences sure to befall family, friends—all my people.

Would accept eternity of physical torture to keep that from happening.

Yes, Posterity, it's me again: Candidia Maria Smith-Foster, adventuress, aviatrix, heroine at large—*would-be* Plucky Girl Savior Of Our People—at your service.

So what's nice girl like me doing in place like this? Kind of thought that might be next question. Sweating, that's what—and trembling like leaf.

Plus working feverishly to complete account of past four days in wan hope that at least this record will survive next few hours; alert hominem community to continuing existence of implacable threat to species' very survival.

Modest enough ambition; and from cursory inspection of

problem, odds slightly encouraging, given precautions now in works: Shall encase completed volume inside one EMU; place that inside another, stick that inside third. With thermostats turned down all the way, triple insulation should keep paper below magic 451-degree mark.

And EMU sandwich *better* protect volume; because if gets anywhere near that hot, as probably will, record inherits sole responsibility for passing on warning—Your Obedient Servant will have been parboiled in own juices long since.

(Don't like to think about that part—but important thing is this record *must* reach Teacher . . . !)

Suspect am rambling. Partially deliberate, partially self-indulgent: First, good therapy—trying to reestablish semblance of control over writing hand; reduce shaking to point where penmanship legible to someone besides own (probably, by then, dearly departed) self. And does seem to be working. Somewhat. Spastic scribbles clearing up perceptibly as necessary concentration on task blanks out distraction of surroundings, past horrific events, future possibly worse ones; pothooks starting to look purposeful again.

Self-indulgence therapeutic, too: Fair idea how much time remains before fate determined. Need to keep psyche occupied between now, then. Sure to lose control otherwise. And last thing need up here is screaming, arm-flapping, hysterical crazy. Particularly when crazy is self.

Okay, shaking under control now. Mostly. On with show:

Wakened at 3:30 A.M., morning of launch, by Gayle, obviously trying not to cry. Felt sorry for her; pretended not to notice, engaged her in idle conversation, avoiding The Subject. Took advantage of opportunity for final luxurious hot shower—with *Nathan Hale* stripped of amenities, would be last opportunity. *Very* last. . . .

Pushed bleak awareness of impending doom into remote corner of mind; sternly told stay there, shut up; went to breakfast/farewell party. Harris Gilbert, Mission Commander, and Kyril Svetlanov, Russian bomb expert, both there already, together with everyone who could be spared from countdown duties.

My breakfast consisted of medium-rare filet; fluffy scrambled eggs on toast; pancakes with maple syrup; orange juice, milk; huge slab of rich, moist chocolate cake with thick, dark, almost-bitter chocolate icing. Wonderful . . . !

Not exactly USDA-recommended breakfast menu for

11-year-old girl, granted. But weight-saving considerations precluded taking much in way of food on mission; big last meal important—plus was, symbolically at least, Last Meal in other sense as well, so damn well ate what I *wanted*.

(Curiously, knowledge of approaching death affects appetite only during first couple days after notification; loses effect thereafter. Had no difficulty stuffing face to repletion.)

But then came farewells from those able to attend. That *was* difficult. Teacher, emotions under most tenuous control, made short speech; expressed gratitude of entire hominem community; assured us would not be forgotten. He shook men's hands, embraced briefly. Then hugged me long, hard, our tears mingling; kissed lips gently—left room abruptly.

Others lined up along route to launch complex. Got hugged, cried on *en passant* by people hadn't even met yet. Finally found ourselves strapped to seats atop *Nathan Hale*, beginning crew-participation phase of countdown.

All three wore spacesuits (very latest models; theoretically Van-Allen-radiation-proof [as if mattered!]) to preclude pressure drop imperiling mission—this was one shuttle flight that *had* to continue, regardless what minor glitches might arise.

Both men wore standard-issue EMUs. But mine product of heroic postproduction reengineering of smallest available size: Had to fit through 9–by–14 detonator access hatch inside bomb, plus still leave room for own four-foot-ten-inch frame. And does. Just.

Rigid aluminum upper-torso frame on which shoulder constant-volume joints mount leaves precious little room for secondary sexual characteristics. But fortunately (narrowly circumstance-limited usage!) am not stunning example of physically precocious 11-year-old girl; assets compressed, but not uncomfortably so. Likewise with hip/fanny development: Were another half-inch of me, doubt could stuff into corresponding lower-torso/hips CV-joint attachment frame.

My portable life-support-system package not physically mounted on suit's back as with other two's suits, and as have been since shuttles' introduction. AA engineers debated whether easier, more reliable, to reconfigure PLSS components into 8.5 by 13.5 package or detach from suit, couple with lines long enough to allow me to reach detonator while PLSS remains outside; settled on latter.

Helmet solution classic example of back-alley mechanics'

triumph over engineering sophistication: Excised broad strip
from spherical one-piece Lexan bubble; rejoined edges by
drilling bunch of tiny holes along edges, slipping edges into
slots in narrow, bent-H-shaped strap fashioned from titanium.
Tightening myriad small bolts compresses H's legs together,
forcing gaskets against Lexan, forming strong joint, positive
seal. Resultant helmet normal size laterally; much shallower
fore-and-aft: With occipital hair firmly pressed against rear,
nose has about one inch clearance at front. Don't know how
they regained circular shape at neck for attachment to upper-
torso sealing ring, but did.

Waist sealing ring, on other hand, doesn't even pretend
to be round. Sealing involves assembling, tightening bunches
of bolts, washers, wing-nuts; compressing ring halves together. Lots more complicated than other suits.

Well, launch proved every bit as thrilling as advertised.
Countdown smooth, no Holds; managed to perform own
assignments without irreversible error. . . .

And then LCD clock was flashing last few seconds:
". . . main engine start," I puffed, restrained from bouncing
up and down in chair by harness; ". . . two, one, *zero* . . . !"

Half wondered, during training, whether concentration
on rapid-fire copilot duties might keep me too busy to
experience, enjoy excitement of launch. But not to worry—
missed nothing: Adrenaline surged through veins; palms grew
damp, breath rapid; heartbeat pounded inside skull until
drowned out by wondrous, swelling, all-encompassing roar
which took form, grew until pervaded entire universe, seemingly unto my very bones.

And then: ". . . solid booster ignition—*LIFT-OFF* . . . !" I
shouted, voice cracking with excitement.

And we *did*—though disgraced myself by squealing
"Wow . . . ! *Wow* . . . ! We're boldly going . . . !" as gee forces
drove me back into seat cushions.

Momentarily wished Terry could be here; would love
rush, acceleration, sensation of power throbbing in very
air—could almost feel baby brother's toenails gripping shoulder as bobbed head, yelled approval.

Caught briefest glimpse of Harris's private superior smile
before voice of Ground Control dragged attention back to
task at hand: "*Nathan Hale*, you're clear of tower. All engines
look good."

"Roger," I replied, trying to sound as if did this sort of

thing every day (not easy while in throes of ultimate fantasy-gratification); "instituting roll."

My instruments, CRTs, etc., continued to show optimum readings as we reached, exceeded Mach One. Control announced computer-instituted main engine throttle-back (earlier, deeper than usual, due to combination of doubled SRB thrust and to need protect now-vulnerable, easily melted aluminum skin)—redundantly, far as I was concerned: Reduction in gees quite perceptible.

Max-Q arrived on schedule; engines throttled up to 100 percent; I informed Control. SRB separation came about one minute later; gee forces abated slightly. But a few minutes thereafter computer again throttled back main engines to avoid exceeding three gees as fuel load lightened.

After running external tank dry on schedule (resultant mixture-imbalance flame-out totaled main engines [Harris cringed, but reuse not contemplated in mission profile—and needed *every* drop]), we fired up orbital maneuvering system. Some time later Harris announced we had sufficient delta-V to reach geosynchronous orbit; shut down OMS. Everything had worked like clockwork.

We took care of final housekeeping details necessary to put *Hale* on hold for next three days; assumed belly-sunward attitude to keep heat off cargo bay fuel tank, opened bay doors . . .

And finally had time to breathe. Shed EMUs with relief. Grouped around windows, admiring beauty of Earth Seen From Orbit, pointing out familiar landmarks. Chatted animatedly a while thereafter, rehashing launch, generally unwinding from intense concentration involved.

Hard to say just when pendulum started back. But presently noticed three of us drifting around cabin, trying not to meet each other's eyes. And could have cut silence with shovel.

Understandable, of course: Letdown following excitement of launch, coupled with knowledge that we had absolutely nothing to do during three days would take *Hale* to complete long outward parabola, together with trying not to think about what would happen within single day following mission's completion, combined to lay pall on company.

All well on way toward satisfying wallow in melancholy by time Harris recognized own symptoms, those of others; roused himself sufficiently to call halt: "This will never do,

people. I don't like what's happening here. If we keep this u
for three days, we'll all be in catatonic withdrawal when th
time comes to do our jobs."

Kyril blinked, looked around momentarily as if startled
Felt much same way myself. But, tending more towar
assertiveness (i.e., spoiled brattiness) than gentle Russian
fought for my right to become zombie; snarled, "Leave m
alone. I don't feel like company right now."

"Neither do I," Harris replied sternly. "But I'm going t
have it—*and so are you.*"

Harris doesn't have to raise voice to make point; ha
Command Presence: lot like Daddy in that respect.

Already snapping out of incipient depression before prop
erly finished resenting intrusion. Performed quick self-inventory
found Commander right as usual. Apologized for rude tone
Harris accepted with grace.

We turned to find Kyril grinning at us. "Shucks . . ." h
teased; "chumps again, just when things getting engrossable
Was processed to grieve for absenting of popmaize and fellov
random numerologist with whom to collate speculatings
Mutiny's outcome providing abstruse handihatting. Absenc
of gravity outsetting size to broadness extant, but thinking m
trove still on Commander."

Corners of Harris's mouth twitched; fixed me with pene
trating eye, shook head imperceptibly. "Just don't bet to
much 'trove' on me," he advised. "I'm getting too old to mi
it up with anyone as young and flexible as Candy."

Kyril's grin broadened; appreciated self-deprecating hu
mor: As if little girl could pose a challenge to tough ol
ex-Marine.

(But exchange left me regarding Harris with bemusement
Suddenly realized that, while no one had ever said anythin
to me on subject, neither had anyone ever mentioned m
martial-arts ranking in Kyril's presence. Russian obviousl
still in dark about nature of my strength—equally obvious
Harris preferred to keep it that way; apparently my capabili
ties Top Secret for time being where Russian concerned
Attitude seemed extreme, but respected unspoken wishes
kept own counsel.)

"There, that's better," Harris approved. "Everybody'
smiling again. Now the question is: How do we stay this wa
for three days? We couldn't bring a damned thing to occup
our hands and minds—not even a pack of cards. So how d

we stay interested and alert and avoid getting lost in terminal introspection?"

Kyril's face lit up like kid's at Christmas. " 'Terminal,' you are saying? How about we programing BFS computer's unused memory to do video gaming on CRT? Is being lots of capacity."

Harris looked thoughtful; could see him mentally reviewing backup flight-system software interfaces for boobytraps potentially affecting mission. Then face brightened. "Good idea. I'll block off a couple of files to keep us out of trouble; then we can start writing the programs.

"Only"—eyes danced at prospect—"instead of emulating just another video game, let's write an interactive orbital-mechanics simulator for Candy—that's more fun than Space Invaders." Kyril rubbed hands in agreement. Both fell to.

Took them better part of first day to write, debug program. Kept me in stitches whole time with gleeful deadpan technical sophistry, arguing nonstop about respective programing skills, techniques, etc. Was like watching Laurelovich & Hardy Olde Tyme Comedy.

But finally complete; proud creators placed me before terminal, explained keyboard basics—then sat back to watch (laughing fool heads off, offering contradictory advice), as attempted to master deceptively simple-appearing, diabolic complexities of orbital relationships.

CRT display consisted of two-dimensional representation of orbital problem: Small circle in middle represented planet, gravitational source; two objects circled primary, one oblong, one triangular. Hypothetical shuttle orbited close-in, at high speed; target satellite, located two-thirds of way to screen's edge, moved much more slowly. Shuttle's fuel status presented in lower right-hand corner; figures updated continuously as power used, whether reaction control system (attitude control) or thrust. Control inputs (vector, feet-per-second; whether RCS, OMS) displayed at lower left.

Object of game was orbital rendezvous, docking. Operator keyed in delta-V changes, trying to alter vehicle's orbit, effect rendezvous. Once orbits very closely matched, screen shifted to large-scale display; enabled close-in maneuvering, docking.

But quickly discovered orbital mechanics *ain't easy*—in fact, ran out of fuel 13 times back-to-back before discovering basic principle by accident: Farther out the orbit, slower the

orbital speed (everybody knows that)—but to *overtake* target
ahead in same orbit, necessary to *slow* vehicle! Speeding up
forces you out into wider, slower orbit—*never* catch up.
Reducing delta-V drops you into lower, faster orbit. Short
burn necessary to circularize new orbit. After overtaking
target on inside track, *add* delta-V, which moves you back out
into wider, slower orbit; then circularize again.

Only after positions, orbits, practically identical do maneuvering inputs produce results compatible with reasonable
expectations.

Took me 26 tries to achieve docking. And wasn't until
then that I noticed how quiet cabin had become; realized
teasing, needling, good-natured, boyish laughter had died
out quite some time back. Looked up to meet Harris's gaze.

"Ordinarily," he observed wryly, "I let my students learn
how incredible they are from someone else. However, these
are rather special circumstances.

"Candy..." Harris paused, shaking head slowly, "...you're
making me look bad! I'm not going to tell you how many tries
it took me to manage my first rendezvous and docking on a
simulator like this—and I didn't have to figure out the theory
first...!"

Kyril's grin was ear-to-ear. "You sure you not Russian...?"
he prodded. "I knowing you not looking Russian, but..."

"But now I'm going back into the software," interrupted
Harris firmly, "and I'm going to install the antisatellite-missile
launching program."

"Oh, that's being a really toughie," approved Kyril.
Turned to Harris: "Trying again?"

Harris shook head. "Uh-uh, I'm not betting against *her*
again. I didn't get where I am today by repeating mistakes...." Paused, looked around cockpit; then grinned ruefully.
"Let me rephrase that."

Too late by then for additional computer horseplay; time
for bed. Time also to nibble at unsatisfyingly small store of
high-protein, high-energy foods which, together with Tang
(ick), comprised total nutrient inventory.

Then time to perform *other* necessary function—truly
distasteful business: God obviously had gravity in mind when
designed Man's bowels.

(And have I mentioned? Tidy, odor-free, NASA-designed
unisex waste-collection system deemed excess weight; removal, viewed with cold practicality, no more than passing

annoyance for those involved—inconvenience over in few days anyway. Meanwhile, am paying price for bladder-dumping logistics less conveniently arranged than males': Wearing my old friend, Foley catheter. Again. For "rest of my life." Whee.)

Close of long, exciting day. Experienced no trouble going straight to sleep; tied myself down with blanket, muttered posthypnotic trigger phrase, dropped right off.

Woke in middle of night just long enough to realize: Adults' slapstick enthusiasm, while surely mutually therapeutic, intended primarily for *my* benefit; Harris, Kyril spending all that energy to keep *me* from getting depressed. Discovery gave me warm, cozy, "loved" feeling, even though neither in hugging range at moment. Good boys, I thought drowsily; good stock—hoped passed on lots of genes while had chance, before getting mixed up in this. Knew Harris had three grown daughters; didn't know about Kyril.

Snickered sleepily to self: If only *little* bit older, would see to it they both died smiling.

And resolved to devote equal energy to keeping them cheered up as well: Who knows—might set up loop effect, positive feedback, mutual reinforcement. Be good for all of us.

Second day much like first, but slept later.

Earth visibly smaller; still heartstoppingly beautiful.

Harris, Kyril juiced up orbital-mechanics game as promised. Took me bulk of morning to score first hit. But success did me no good; once I got hang of it, they turned up wick still further by equipping target with antiantisatellite-missile missiles, plus dodging ability. Didn't score again that day.

But did notice C-rations even less filling.

And some things do *not* improve with practice: Found self hoping Heaven boasts gravity, sit-down commodes.

Third day repeat of second.

Crew's spirits held up well.

Scored intermittently during morning on orbital-mechanics game; didn't miss once during early afternoon, so boys put heads together to complicate things further. Wouldn't say what had in mind. Could hardly wait; wasn't video-game addict before, but this was *challenging*.

Hunger on way to becoming serious annoyance. (And

became necessary to watch boys carefully to verify eating own rightful portions; both had this sweetly distressing tendency to want to treat me as Damsel In Distress. Caught them working shell-game variant to see I got lion's share.)

Still hated lack of toilet facilities; though output dwindling in proportion to intake—plus C-rations probably low on residue.

Nathan Hale arrived at rendezvous point on fourth day at 4:57 A.M. (Pacific Time Zone), just seven hours before bomb scheduled to start down, which meant up at 3:30 (again!). But did get to eat up bulk of remaining C-rations on waking ("Eat, drink, be merry, for tomorrow..." etc.).

Warming up ship's systems, preparing for OMS burn to circularize orbit, took about an hour. OMS burn short, sweet; start, stop, both on money.

Harris looked up as OMS shut down. Glared out windshield, face suddenly hard. "All right, let's find the bastard," he grated.

Activated pulse radar. Antenna covered 90-degree cone straight ahead, centered on ship's axis. Screen lit, remained blank.

Harris rotated ship on RCS thrusters to bring new section of sky into focus. Radar pulsed—and bingo!

Harris took careful range, bearing readings. Recorded figures, shut off radar with emphatic snap.

Smile wreathed face as unstrapped, pushed away from controls. "If you've *got* to do it for the last time," he breathed, "it sure feels good to do it right! We're just six miles behind it. Our orbit is so nearly identical that I can't read the difference. We're well within MMU range. Let's go *get* that mother before something goes wrong."

Kyril unstrapped, drifted free. "Is it visible from here?" he asked.

Harris unshipped expedition's sole pair of binoculars, pulled himself to windshield, peered in appropriate direction. "Yes, it's clearly visible through these," he replied. "Very low albedo; must be almost jet black. Wonder if the color's paint or that new material. Ominous-looking beast...."

Unstrapped myself at that point. Started to push gently away from seat; changed mind, but hand slipped—found self hanging immobile, out of reach of everything. Smiled as realized had just committed science fiction's favorite neophyte's standard error. Glanced up to let boys tease me about it. And . . .

Blood froze in veins.

Suddenly everything happening in slow motion.

Eyes focused on Kyril, just drifting past, knife in hand.

Was perhaps two-tenths of second during which could have latched on, torn into him with everything have ever learned about fighting; ample time for even modestly-skilled karate student to save day . . .

But *couldn't move!* Could only hang there, mouth open, futilely trying to draw breath, scream warning, as reflexes warred within body.

Had been drilling for weeks with modified *kata*, sparring routine, working to eliminate lethal responses. But my system acquired intact from Teacher: his own—balanced, efficient; painstakingly developed by generations of greatest Masters over centuries; weaknesses long since discovered, rooted out. Now learned penalty for tampering. . . .

Conflicting responses held me immobile during fraction of second it took Kyril to glide out of reach, plunge weapon under Harris's left scapula. Commander went limp so quickly, doubt even felt it.

Then managed scream: "Kyril—*NO* . . . *!*"

Russian turned quickly, bloody knife still in hand; motion sent tiny quivering scarlet globules drifting across cabin to squish wetly against bulkhead.

Our eyes met; his contained wild look. No more than six feet separated us. Kyril firmly anchored to command seat with empty hand, both legs; poised to spring. I hung midair, out of reach of every handhold, turning almost imperceptibly about longitudinal axis—already sideways to him; soon would be completely backward to expected attack. Flailed arms, legs, trying to check, reverse spin—added tumble component instead.

Tactical situation growing less promising by the moment.

On point of triggering hysterical strength, turning job over to combat computer with instructions to give it best shot once Kyril within reach, when sanity returned to Russian's eyes. He glanced at knife, shuddered, flung it from him.

Felt surge of relief. But didn't lower guard.

Kyril smiled ruefully at me; then looked away quickly, shook head as if in pain. Shocked to realize sparkling beads drifting outward *tears*. More where those came from; Kyril dabbed at them absently. "Your General Sherman was right, Candy." He sighed; "'War *is* hell.' I hated doing that."

He drew limp form downward, settled it in left seat, secured harness almost tenderly. "*Hale* was his last command; this is where he belongs," he explained, voice unsteady.

He turned back to me. "I wish there had been some way I could have kept you from seeing that," he continued, still speaking with difficulty. "I know that you were very close to him. But Harris was a good marine, an experienced old campaigner. I knew that I would be lucky to catch him with his guard down even once. I had to strike the moment the opportunity presented.

"Now"—Kyril turned back to instruments—"I don't think that it lies within the realm of reasonable possibility that a radio message sent from here would be heard by anyone listening at Vandenberg; that's clear on the other side of the world, after all. However..." tore open communications panel fascia; extracted circuit boards, gazed at them thoughtfully, then deliberately began breaking them into small pieces, "... I cannot take the chance. And fanatic though I am, I do not want to have to kill *you* in cold blood. ...

"I said earlier that I wished I could have met you after you grew up. I meant it. I still mean it. I have never met a woman of any age whom I hold in higher esteem. Our children are educated from birth to understand, as I do, that we exist only to discharge our guardianship; that to sacrifice one's life in that endeavor is the sacred duty and privilege of every one of us—yet I doubt whether any one of them, at a comparable age, would have volunteered as you did. I do not exaggerate when I say that I was more stunned than McDivott when you stepped forward."

Kyril turned back from ruined radio. "There, that takes care of that. We both know that I could never watch you every second; this way I don't have to—nor do I have to kill you. There is no possible way for you to warn your friends."

Only then did situation's gravity sink in: Responsibility for mission's success, failure, now rested solely with me—no advice, no help, no backup. Survival of all but tiny handful of my people hung in balance (and earthquakes meant chances slim even for group in shelters); would be decided by my actions during next few minutes. Never in short, busy life have I felt so totally alone, inadequate, helpless.

Forced attention back to here/now. Realized Kyril speaking flawless, accent-free English; conclusion sent goosebumps up, down spine: To play rôle so convincingly, over so long a timespan; to get past AAs' drug-assisted hypnotic interrogation; to deceive Teacher, Peter, all those AAs—even muscle-reading Gayle—Kyril *good* at job. Faced first-class opponent.

Now understood why Harris kept lid on my karate skills. And grateful. Opponent still in dark, thanks to him; thought of me as ordinary child, apart from freakish strength. Experienced old campaigner, indeed—*crafty*: After working with him all this time, old marine still mistrusted smiling Russian's sincerity; held back final trump card—*me*.

Sure hoped Harris knew his business; awful lot riding on outcome—and now would be really bad time to learn was given to excess optimism regarding associates' talents, capabilities. Intended to do very best, of course; but wouldn't have bet penny on own chances at that moment.

But even as thoughts raced—searching for solution, weighing alternatives, evaluating risks—was already laying groundwork for *whatever* action might decide on: Feigned horrified, wide-eyed helplessness (didn't take that much feigning!); encouraged tears to come (damned nuisance in free-fall, too; stayed right where formed, pooling, growing deeper; interfered dreadfully with vision); plus began wailing in heartbroken tones.

"Bu-but *why*, Kyril?" I blubbered, swiping ineffectually at eyes. "This is crazy. Your people are all blown up. What good will it do to kill everybody now? What are you accomplishing? It's meanness for meanness' sake. It's dumb—it's just being a Dog-In-The-Manger. It's—*Kyril! Don't ignore me . . . !*"

"I am not ignoring you." Response came in unexpected whisper. Looked more closely. Russian in midst of deep-breathing exercise, apparently fighting for emotional control. "I would *never* ignore you. But becoming a hero of the people is not without cost. Just how much cost I had not realized. I had accepted death for myself. But Harris was the best friend I had among your people. He was brave, intelligent—'noble' is not too strong an adjective.

"He would have made a great *Khranitel*," Kyril finished mournfully. Suddenly he added, "No, Candy, *my* people are *not* all dead."

Heart skipped beat. "*What . . . ?*" I blurted; "how could anybody . . ."

"None of *us* died in the holocaust. Many of our subordinates did; but it was necessary to leak their locations to create a convincing illusion of our total annihilation. It seemed poor strategy to have you genetically superior hominems aware that we survived your retaliation."

"'*You* genetically superior hominems'?" I parroted, not believing ears. "But—aren't you a hominem, too? What *are* you then? Who are you people . . . ?"

"No, I'm not one of you *Homo post hominems*," Kyril continued obligingly. "None of the *Khraniteli* are. Your people subjected me to a remarkable variety of tests in their efforts to prove or disprove the sincerity of my defection, but that one never occurred to them. Fortunately I was able to remain healthy and they never suspected.

"Because of my regard for you, I will tell you who we are and how matters have come to this sorry state. It can do no harm now.

"We are a small, meticulously screened, rigorously trained group of true humans—*Homo sapiens*, rightful owners of this planet. We discovered you and yours even before Dr. McDivott did. We studied you thoroughly. We learned your strengths, your weaknesses—we learned your genetic imperative. . . ."

Voice grew resonant; took on edge. "And we decided that we did not *want* to be replaced. *Homo sapiens* is a mighty race. We are not as easily brushed aside as was Neanderthal by Cro-Magnon."

"But we wouldn't . . ."

Kyril cut off protest almost midsyllable: "Not from malice," he said sternly; "nor by force. You wouldn't have to; you *breed true*: Sapiens/hominem breedings produce only hominem offspring; we have proven it. In a few generations you would have replaced us completely.

"So within the framework of the *Bratstvo*, but unknown to them, we formed the *Khraniteli*, the 'Guardians,' in English: a secret society within a secret society, dedicated to the preservation of *true* humans. Naturally, given the genetic realities of the situation, the only means of doing that was, and is, to eliminate you before you eliminated us.

"The *Bratstvo*, at the time we infiltrated and took over its direction, was working efficiently toward eventual world domination for ideological reasons, a goal with which we were in complete accord. But it was only a beginning; we encouraged their natural impulses and broadened the scope of their thinking. It didn't take too much psychology to bring them around to believing that they had invented for themselves the idea of starting over, unopposed, on an otherwise uninhabited planet.

"There were quite a few hominems in the *Bratstvo* already—though none ever realized that they were different from the rest of us. All were first-generation hominems, raised by human parents unaware of their potential. All were angry, disturbed antisocials, the type your people have labeled 'classic AB sociopaths.'

"But they *were* brilliant, so we put them to work in areas where their brilliance would be most effective. That new alloy that your scientists are so fascinated with was developed by our hominems. They were also responsible for most of the breakthroughs that led to the final design and construction of the vehicle which houses the strontium warhead."

Kyril smiled coldly. "They thought that what they were building was the ultimate ideological housecleaning tool. They never knew that they were creating the means of their own species' destruction. Naturally, we stationed them in locations known to your intelligence people during the attack. American missiles solved the problem for us.

"We were amazed at how many of you there proved to be after the plague eliminated all extraneous humans. Our studies suggested nothing like the figures that McDivott's group extrapolated, which seem to have been borne out by experience. But no matter; isolated hominems around the world are not a problem: Even if a few somehow manage to get under cover in time to avoid fatal overdoses at the outset, strontium-90 fallout is patient. It takes planning and preparation to survive two centuries underground; only we and McDivott's people are ready.

"We knew that he and his organization would come through the attack and plague intact—I was amused to learn that he hadn't known he was a hominem himself. So we leaked enough details about the strontium bomb's existence, and what it would take to stop it, to guarantee that he would have no choice but to try to launch a shuttle. We knew that he would have to gather every single member of his group there to accomplish it.

"I was planted on them both to keep an eye on their

progress as well as to make myself an indispensable part of the mission. I was quite taken aback, upon being admitted into their organization, to learn that they had acquired far more information through their own efforts than we had leaked. Which meant that I had to watch my step; I had no idea how much they might know in addition. So I played absolutely straight, relying upon being able to stop the mission at the very last moment, as I have done.

"Now, there were only three facilities in the entire world equipped to launch an expedition of this type. The one in Russia, of course, is gone; that left the two in America. I anticipated that they would use the Vandenberg facility; being a military base, it is more completely, independently equipped than Cape Canaveral. And I was right. But it made no difference: In either case the outcome would have been the same.

"You see, the Murray Fracture Zone is not the target. It never has been. The warhead is less powerful than McDivott was given to think; but even so, if it exploded there, the resultant quakes would reduce much of the Earth's crust to rubble. That would be too sweeping a remedy even for us—though it would have been a satisfying revenge, had that really been our intention. No; we would not destroy the Earth's surface; we need it for ourselves.

"The bomb is targeted to impact about 25 miles due west of Point Arguello. The crust is thicker there. The explosion *will* generate earthquakes, massive ones; but it won't ruin the planet, not permanently anyway—at least not our part. We'll ride it out; our shelters are constructed of the new alloy—yards thick.

"However, Vandenberg lies inside the fireball, within the radius of total destruction. McDivott's group will still be there, to the last man. They will be eliminated at a single stroke; they literally will never know what hit them.

"There never has been a cancellation signal, by the way; only a retargeting signal, in case it might have been necessary to shift impact to, say 25 miles out in the Gulf Stream, just off Kennedy. That was false information, deliberately leaked to confuse the issue. The bomb cannot be stopped other than by physically boarding and disarming it. Preventing that from happening was my mission. It was not difficult.

"Now, I am sure that you must hate me at this moment more than you have ever hated anyone in your life, and I don't blame you. But I want you to know that meeting you has been one of the greatest privileges of my life. I wish that you were human. Even though you are not, I salute you."

And, so help me, actually *did* salute.

But Kyril wrong: Didn't hate him. Didn't hate anybody—didn't have time for peripheral distractions. (Maybe would hate him later.) But for now, had *job* to do: suddenly expanded, desperately important job—this changed *everything...!*

Disarming bomb no longer adequate solution. Still necessary, yes—vitally! But *Khraniteli* would just try again, using different approach; probably succeed next time around—hominems didn't even know threat existed; would get no warning!

Simply *had* to warn my people!—*that* was mission's primary goal now! Disarming bomb, then dying nobly, exercise in futility unless got word back in process.

Had no choice. Simply must. And would.

Somehow.

But Kyril between me and next step—*whatever* might prove to be. Had to do something about that. First. Immediately.

Debate over options took only seconds; limited, as practical matter, to single course of action. Hoped acting skills up to challenge.

Responded to Kyril's explanation, salute, with total flood: surely most abjectly pitiable performance since Bambi calling for Mother in forest fire. Covered face in hands (peeked between fingers, gauging effect), curled into fetal position. Sobbed as if world coming to end—which, unless managed to do something about it, pretty well summed things up!

(Now, awfully fond of Kyril—before—and Russian well aware of feelings. Likewise, as top-level *Khranitel* operative, held probably justifiably high opinion of own physical prowess. Unlikely to fear assault from 11-year-old. Plus was awfully fond of me, too. Finally, was very well educated; certain to have read same child-psychology theories I did: knew abusee usually turns to abuser for comfort once attack over. [Irrational? I'll say. Own approach would be to wait until adult asleep, take baseball bat—*stop*; getting sidetracked.] Point is that dependent child normally turns to nearest adult of whom is fond for comfort *regardless* what atrocities said adult may have just committed.)

Looked up through tears, held out arms, wailed, "Oh, *Kyril...!*"

He bought it: Expression softened; propelled himself across cabin, catching me gently in passing.

Redoubled weeping, threw arms around neck, buried face in shoulder. He sighed unhappily, put arms around me, held close, patted clumsily on back, murmured soothing noises. Didn't notice legs closing around waist until too late. If at all.

Snuffled, bubbled, then wiped eyes with right hand; which brought forearm across beneath Russian's chin, left still around neck.

Whispered hysterical-strength tap trigger, closed trap in single motion: Legs tightened about torso, ankles locked. Left hand seized back of head, left side; right hand closed on chin, right side of face; both in unbreakable grip. Kyril barely had time to register surprise before I

. . . TWISTED!

Don't know how might have made out against Russian in fair fight—particularly in free-fall. As top *Khranitel* agent, probably one of very best. But will never know: Hysterical strength rotated head beyond vertebrae's yield limit in briefest fraction of second. If live to be 100, will never forget that noise.

Body convulsed momentarily; subsided gradually to consistency of Jell-O. Maintained grip until, pressing ear to chest, heard heart sounds slow, stop. Then released, shrugged free of corpse's embrace, pushed off for wall. Landed, took firm grip on handhold; watched as body drifted across cabin in slow-motion sprawling tumble.

Realized, then, at least part of solicitude impelling Kyril to strap Harris into command chair was elementary tidiness: Would be in way constantly otherwise under weightless conditions. Jumped across cabin, grabbed body by belt, propelled toward copilot's chair, secured with harness.

Then looked purposefully around at surroundings. Over which now held undisputed sway.

Would have been easy to let emotions go: Had just killed someone of whom had become very, very fond. Had watched him kill someone else of whom had become very, very fond. Was more alone than anyone in human history—nearest human at least 22,300 miles away. And own lifespan now measured in hours . . .

Yes, would have been *very* easy to let go. But couldn't afford luxury. Bomb departing from orbit less than half day hence; must be disarmed first. Much work remained undone in preparation—plus still didn't know how was going to get message back to earth. . . .

Well, logical first step in solving any problem is inventory of available assets: Familiarity with gear confined to that intrinsic to own once-limited responsibilities; surely Harris, Kyril brought along equipment relating to their jobs. Spent solid hour scouring *Hale*'s entire pressurized demesnes; confident would turn up something to solve, or suggest solution to, communications dilemma.

But didn't.

Boys brought even fewer personal articles than self (my toothbrush no less likely to figure in solution than theirs). Mission equipment limited to three adult-size EMUs, four MMUs (one spare of each), single toolbox, two plug-in briefcase terminals. None of which triggered spontaneous inspiration.

Returned to cockpit, growing more worried by moment. Debated briefly returning after disarming bomb, attempting OMS retroburn to drop *Hale* from geosynchronous orbit. Perhaps could jury-rig heliograph-type device from shiny interior panel, flash warning to hominems as passed over California (pretty good at Morse; only member of scout troop to qualify for merit badge). Pretty sure could get RCS, OMS running (tried to memorize Harris's duties as thoroughly as own during endless simulator run-throughs).

But gave that up moment saw fuel gauges: Could drop from geosynchronous orbit with remaining fuel, but not far; be lucky to achieve even shallow parabola. Plus initial progress very slow; *Hale* would be ghost ship by time got around to far side of globe: Life-support due to run out barely 18 hours hence; even without boys' added consumption, no chance still alive by then to send signal.

Worrying in earnest now. Unless managed to get word back, *Khraniteli* surely successful in wiping hominems off face of Earth, sooner or later.

But *how*. . . ? Here I sat (okay, floated), stranded in orbit—in fuel-depleted ship stripped of exterior insulation, aerodynamic controls, landing gear—everything necessary to get down. All of which immaterial: Even were everything in 100-percent flightworthy condition, most unlikely that 15–plus hours in ultralight qualified me to power up, accomplish solo reentry, landing—in single most complicated vehicle ever assembled by *H. sapiens*. . . !

But always have had this tendency to keep beating head against wall when situation hopeless—even more so when *obviously* hopeless. Just not the giving-up kind. Mind kept dodging, weaving, bobbing, looking for solution. Didn't discard any idea without scrutinizing thoroughly first. Not even silliest conjecture dismissed out of hand; retained long enough to see how looked in conjunction with all the rest.

Got so bad, even started wondering whether bomb's computer, lasers, would hold still for slow, close approach by *Hale* on RCS thrusters. Certainly enough fuel in bomb for reentry, after all. If somehow could transfer fuel from bomb to *Hale*, maybe could extend retroburn long enough to put me over California before life-support ran out. Knew would get only one shot at signaling, of course; be days before *Hale* returned to perigee again.

Hominems *better be looking!*

Only, how does one go about transferring monomethyl hydrazine and nitrogen tetroxide in quantity from one vehicle to another in vacuum? Without proper high-pressure equipment. . . .

Doesn't, of course. Scratch another idea.

Scratch *Hale*, really: "All the King's horses and all the King's men" couldn't prepare shuttle for reentry without full resources of Space Transportation System crew, facilities. Simply no way lightened, stripped—gutted—ship could survive plunge into atmosphere as result of anything *I* could do.

Pity bomb carrier not designed for cargo, I thought wryly. Could just—

Blinding flash. Soundless concussion. Universe bucked, rocked, shuddered.

Of course!

(Suddenly felt very stupid.)

The *bomb* . . . ! Mounted in vehicle eminently capable of reentry; already programed, equipped—scheduled, in fact—to do just that, commencing in less than six hours. So what if not designed for cargo; ample structural dead space around warhead; same dead space through which would be crawling when entered to disarm.

No reason couldn't leave message in there . . . !

Except that missile presently targeted for impact some 25 miles offshore; to deliver message would be necessary to reprogram computer's ballistics software (disarming warhead *first*).

Well... during one of those rare quiet moments during
otherwise hectic week at Vandenberg, noticed yellowish pa-
perback titled *IFR Supplement of the United States*. Contained longitude, latitude, time zones, etc., plus other pertinent data, for almost every airport on North American continent.
Thumbed through; spotted couple familiar names. One was
Vandenberg; remember it well—together with coordinates:
34 degrees 44 minutes north longitude, 120 degrees 35
minutes west latitude. Not launch facility, of course; nearby
Air Force base.

Further, despite fact that mission profile (assuming everything went as scheduled) called for straightforward ballistics software wipe, reloading with AAs' bomb-disposal program, did avail self of opportunity to scroll through Russians'
software during programing portion of training. Distinctly
recall seeing submenu titled *Ballistika*, inside which was
fill-in-blanks subsubmenu headed *Koordinaty Prizemleniya*,
with words *Dolgota, Shirina*, followed by two strings of
numbers.

Now, according to my crash-course, bush-league knowledge of Russian, *Ballistika* translates loosely into "ballistics";
Koordinaty Prizemleniya into "coordinates of touchdown";
Dolgota, Shirina, into "longitude," "latitude." If subsequent
numbers really longitude, latitude, retargeting probably involves no more than straightforward substitution. Probably.

AAs surely still there; could hardly miss descent—so few
objects arrive these days on huge multiple parachutes. AAs
would swarm over bomb like ants at picnic, first hurrying to
ascertain warhead disarmed; then scientists gleaning data
guaranteed to keep them happy, busy for next ten years.
Somebody would find message taped to detonator-chamber
bulkhead. Bound to.

Longer deliberated question, better idea sounded: Surely offered best odds on getting warning delivered.

(AAs probably not thrilled to have all that plutonium on
hand, but would cope—and scientists would go quietly mad
studying breakthroughs, etc., embodied in reentry package
structure, warhead itself. Plus knowledge gained would stand
them in good stead during upcoming war against *Khraniteli*—
of whose existence, intentions, now would be warned.)

Turned thoughts to safeguarding message. No idea how
well *Khraniteli* protected computer, warhead, detonator, from
reentry heat, but probably get pretty warm in there (forget

taping to bulkhead). Well, surely easier to keep paper belov
mythic 451-degree flash point than to protect human, with fa
lower performance envelope. Could wrap message in EMU—
maybe two EMUs, with PLSS thermostats turned down a
the way. Three extra EMUs on hand now that Harris, Kyr
had no need. Plus own spare—

Oh . . .! Realization came as almost physical shock.
(Stupidity getting to be habit.)

For solid week had been psyching self up to die. Ha
accepted necessity, inevitability.

But maybe didn't have to. . . .

Could ride down in bomb!

Have no clear memory of next few minutes. Suspec
intensity of relief exceeded capacity for rational appreciatior
Vaguely remember bounding around cabin, ricocheting o
walls, ceiling, floor; shrieking, crying, laughing like ma
thing. Next event of which have firm recollection is crouchin
on Kyril's lap, gripping flight suit lapels, shaking him violentl
(albeit ineffectually, in zero gee), screaming into dead face
"We'll beat you yet, you cold-blooded, censored son of
bowdlerized, unprintably expurgated deletion! We'll wip
you out to the last man, woman, and grub! We'll . . ."

(Had come long way from Candy Smith-Foster of yore—
firmly resolved never to kill again.)

Didn't so much regain control as run down. Spewe
rage, hate, frustration at uncaring corpse until gone, leavin
me limp, trembling, teary-eyed.

At which point coherent thoughts again intruded. Ur
pleasant coherent thoughts. Whole string of unpleasant cc
herent thoughts which totaled even less pleasant sum: Chance
for living through reentry slim to nonexistent. At best.

Odds steeper for own person than those facing message
For instance, had no idea what sort of gee forces migh
encounter en route. Missile's cargo included computer, detc
nator mechanism, warhead, etc.; all potentially delicate, sen
sitive. But vehicle powered for ten gees—at what point di
Khranitel engineers draw line, say, "Anything above this leve
is excessive stress"? Unanswerable question, of course. Bu
likely well beyond what *own* designer considered acceptable

In addition, original plans called for water landing. Ow
destination dry land. Unyielding dry land. Probably quite
bump.

However, above concern nowhere near as scary as reentry

heat question: Prospect of slowly burning to death not something can just shrug off.

Have seen it done.

(And will *never* forget: Two days after tenth birthday was
riding in car with Daddy, returning from Oshkosh after TV
show on which Daddy appeared as guest physician. Observed
car accident on lonely stretch of highway around midnight:
Drunk in Corvette wandered off road, bashed tree. *Old*
Corvette; equipped with competition gas tank—36 gallons.
Ruptured on impact, flooding interior with flaming contents.
Victim staggered out, blazing from head to foot. Daddy
doused with own car's extinguisher. But victim already 80–
percent third-degree case. Daddy ordered me to stay in car,
call for help on CB. Did *not* want me to see burn damage
close-up. But soon realized needed more hands; had to
involve me. Will *never* forget that man: Charred, cracked
skin. Cooked meat bleeding through raw, inches-wide, exploded deep blisters. Dangling flesh. Incinerated tissue.
Scorched bones showing through barbecued muscles. High,
thin, nonstop screaming. The smell.)

Now, if descent profile anything like NASA's, dive from
atmospheric interface at 400,000 feet to slowing below mach
two at 60–, 70,000 feet takes about 15 minutes. Heat build-up
inside vehicle progressive, implacable: Grows steadily hotter,
hotter, hotter still, until imperceptible threshold crossed;
discomfort suddenly becomes agony; blisters form, crisp, pop;
tissues roast, char; own superheated greasy cooking smoke
inside EMU sears lungs.

Quarter hour under those conditions could be very long
time indeed. . . .

No. Decision whether to risk burning to death not
casually made.

Horsefeathers!—chopped off self-flagellation impatiently;
issue never in doubt for second: While chance remained, no
matter how slim, would go for it. Am constitutionally incapable of giving up.

Well, now *that* foolishness over, done with, were steps
could take to improve chances; preparations above, beyond
those necessary for originally planned bomb-disarming, -disposal
EVA. And time to get to work regardless; just five hours to
bomb's scheduled deorbit burn.

Fell to, assembled gear in airlock: all three adult-size
EMUs, both of mine; all four MMUs, both terminals, tool-

box, etc. Strung everything together with wire (plenty available from communications panel); would tie into snug bundle once outside.

Retrieved binoculars from Harris's dead hand; employed to scan darkness beyond cockpit windows. Bomb not easy visual target; but presently made out tiny, indistinct, deeper black spot against jet sky. *Hale*'s longitudinal axis still lined up on it.

Okay, knew bomb ahead of us in same orbit. Using shuttle, Earth, bomb as references, was oriented as to orbital plane, direction. Knew which way had to. go—critical, because at first would be unable to resolve destination with naked eye, and binoculars useless while wearing helmet (though intended to take outside, have look-see; maybe helpful after all [try never to burn bridges unnecessarily, prematurely]).

Donning EMU took good half hour (mine more trouble than most, due to endless array of tiny bolts, washers, wing nuts holding waist sealing ring halves together), but finally checklist complete: suit airtight; PLSS operational, secured by straps to back, life-support lines neatly coiled at waist.

(Folded sleeping-station blanket into makeshift, multi-layered cushion; taped to inside of helmet at rear. Hoped would distribute pressure of head's contact against Lexan bubble during anticipated heavy gees. Pad's bulk left barely room for nose in front. Looked forward to accumulating many greasy nose prints before day over.)

Herded gear into airlock; closed, sealed inner door. Dumped air, opened outer hatch, exited gingerly, moving one handhold at a time, drawing equipment behind me with wire attached to utility belt.

Glanced at complicated watch on EMU's wrist: Three and quarter hours remained before bomb commenced descent, according to countdown timer. My PLSS standard issue; good for seven hours with full-sized astronaut; hard to say how much own lesser consumption might affect duration.

(Likewise hard to say how long descent will take. Totally dependent upon how much straight-down acceleration incorporated in reentry program. If employs descent profile called for upon detection of approaching missiles, should be on ground roughly two hours after deorbit burn. But couldn't *know* that. And if exceeds four, five hours, won't matter much. Certainly not to me.)

Did best to ignore urgency, surroundings, scenery; focused on job at hand: Moved deliberately along hull's upper rim, at cargo-bay door hinge, paralleling huge extra fuel tank. Paused at rear end of bay. Gathered equipment into bundle with additional wire loop; secured to belt in front on both sides.

Then backed into first MMU, shrugged between armrests, secured latches. Closed EMU glove around right-hand control handle. Ignored inner conviction that long fall awaited. Took deep breath, let go left hand; placed on control handle.

Now. Bomb six miles ahead. Distance sufficient to involve orbital mechanics.

Sure wished Harris alive; navigation during "quick hop" across to bomb amongst his mission specialties.

Not mine.

Knew theory, of course: Drop into lower, faster orbit, circularize; reverse procedure upon arriving in bomb's vicinity. Did it bunches of times on boys' home-grown video game on way out.

But fundamental difference exists between understanding theoretical principle on intellectual level and believing it at core of tightly knotted stomach. Performing operation with computer terminal push buttons, watching results on CRT, does not prepare one for hanging in *real* space, lining up *real* thrust axis, then *really* accelerating out into limitless void on course leading, obviously, *away* from destination.

Every instinct shrieked "Madness!" Took every ounce of will power to force hands to operate controls.

MMUs powered by compressed nitrogen; charge sufficient to impart roughly 66-feet-per-second total velocity change to normal-sized astronaut before poohing out. That translates to accelerating to about 45 miles an hour. Once. Or boosting to 22 miles an hour, then stopping. Also once. Own mass slightly more than one-third that of normal astronaut. However, extra gear probably more than made up difference.

Aligned thrust axis with right hand, applied power with left. Drifted toward rear, between wing, vertical stabilizer.

Looked around as cleared ship's stern. And froze, transfixed. Not even mortal anxiety over impending intraorbital transit, consequences of failure, could prevent first unimpaired sight of Earth, heavens, from filling spirit with awe, joy, reverence. Much of planet dark from this perspective; but suddenly realized was at imminent risk of going blind again

due to thickening lens of tears forming over eyes—with no
means of wiping them away inside EMU.

Which reminded me: Not out there to enjoy sights—life
of every hominem on pearlescent bowling ball dependent on
me. Had no business wasting time rubbernecking; had *work*
to do.

Blinked eyes furiously; shook head to clear vision. Twisted
MMU's tail.

Consumed about half fuel load during initial retrosquirt.
Then coasted five minutes, watching *Hale* slowly dwindle.
Inexpressibly relieved to note gradual shift in apparent attitude: Had left shuttle's RCS attitude control on automatic;
apparently really *was* dropping into faster orbit.

Reversed thrust at end of five minutes; used up balance
of fuel on circularization (I hoped!) maneuver. Released MMU,
pushed gently away. Untangled second from bundle, latched
into place, rested hands on controls.

Then waited.

Waited while *Hale*'s aspect changed from distant rear
view to more distant belly view to even more distant nose
view, steadily foreshortening in ever more remote distance.

Tried to estimate speed from changing relationship between self, shuttle; couldn't. So played with numbers in
head: If relative velocity 15 miles per hour faster than
shuttle/bomb train overhead, could expect to cover distance
in something like 15–20 minutes. Wished had had better idea
how far below original orbit was riding, but couldn't tell that
either. Estimating astronomical distances freehand slippery
business.

Meanwhile, scanned heavens intently for dark spot that
would indicate bomb's location. Could still make out *Hale*
well enough to use as pointer; knew where target supposed to
be—but *couldn't find it*.

Tried binoculars without success: Eyepieces' distance
from eyes hindrance but not major problem; merely reduced
field of view; worked fine otherwise.

But couldn't identify bomb.

Then had inspiration: Looked back at *Hale*; tried to get
handle on distance by comparing relative size of shuttle with
bomb as seen through binoculars *from* shuttle.

By that yardstick, seemed should be closing in on target.
Decided had no choice but to act on assumption; add back
delta-V, see if Gods Smiled.

About to implement when struck by doubt: Total package now massed less by one MMU. Wondered what effect reduction might have on response to thrust. Then realized would have opportunity to compensate with circularization shot, assuming bomb somewhere in vicinity. Deferred worry until then.

Looked back at *Hale* through binoculars, lined up thrust axis with direction of travel, consumed half fuel reserve in replacing delta-V.

Then waited again, looking desperately where bomb *ought* to be. And still wasn't.

Getting really, no-foolin' worried by this time. Orbital juggling performed as Harris taught me; bomb should have been in sight.

Waited another five minutes; circularized orbit again, using all but last whiff of nitrogen. Then looked around with earnestness not unmixed with, distinct from, panic. . . .

And there it was (I'll be damned!) no more than couple hundred yards away!

Resumed breathing.

And, in retrospect, diagnosed problem: Vehicle dead black, nonreflective; visible only through occultation under best of conditions. Spot over which hung on Earth's equator approaching sunrise line; bomb almost between me, Sol; background glare obscured.

Then took first good look at bomb: *huge* thing—carbon copy of *Hale*; lacked only cockpit, cargo bay doors, etc. But where shuttle essentially friendly looking, bomb *not* (visceral reaction; don't ask why). Harris correct: ominous-looking beast. Hung in void looking like modern Charon's ferry.

Used up last puff of nitrogen from current MMU; kicked loose, mounted third. Lined up thrust axis on bomb, used five percent of remaining reaction mass accelerating. Two-mile-per-hour approach speed ample: Still two and a half hours to bomb's departure; no point losing head, rushing. Would feel foolish during final seconds if, when so close to success, lost head, hurried; built up too much speed, split helmet on hull.

Braked to relative stop only yards from nose. Then realized hadn't faintest idea where on monster access hatch actually located—training involved only cutaway sectional mock-up; drawings studied encompassed only specifics of own job. Engineering logic suggested had to be somewhere near bow, of course. Just matter of jetting around, finding it.

But now learned how limited MMU skills really were. Operation heretofore limited to straight-line thrusting; examining bomb carrier involved full range of maneuvering operations: yaw, pitch, twist, start, stop—and damned thing insisted on doing what I *told* it to do instead of what I *wanted* it to do. Frustrating in extreme.

Finally managed to stabilize self. Checked MMU status: about 50 percent gone; mostly wasted curing pilot-induced tumbling. Transferred to final MMU, left equipment bundle parked against what would be belly on *Hale*; set out to reconnoiter solo—maneuvering much more easily.

Drifted gently back along starboard side to wing's leading edge without encountering hatch. Checked motion; moved toward topsides, headed back toward nose. Still nothing.

Eventually found hatch almost exactly where *Hale*'s crew hatch located: short distance up from belly, back from nose on portside.

Returned for equipment; maneuvered cautiously, with only occasional miscue, back to hatch.

Studied locking mechanism. Appeared similar to that on drawings, mock-up. Operation proved identical.

But not easiest gismo to operate under weightless conditions: Breathing pretty hard, faceplate partially fogged, by time got it open.

Parked MMU; secured with wire tie to latch handle. Drew self, equipment in through opening. Switched on flashlight.

Looking around produced sense of *déjà vu*: What could see of interior corresponded perfectly to training aids.

Headed for inner shell access hatch. Wriggled amongst, between structural pieces without difficulty (one aspect of task made easier by zero gee). Located, unlatched, swung open.

Wedged toolbox in convenient angle between trusses adjacent to hatch. Unstrapped PLSS from back, squirmed through 9–by–14-inch opening, trailing life-support lines.

Drew PLSS close to hatch; pulled entire coil of life-support lines through with me. Reached back, retrieved toolbox.

Maneuvered through complex of structural members to

detonator, carefully paying out lines en route, watching for, avoiding, tendency to kink.

Studied exterior components; verified everything as represented on drawings, mock-up. Opened toolbox, set to work.

Actual warhead defusing anticlimactic. After week of intensive training amidst ever-mounting tension, operation proved simplicity itself: Snipped wires in correct order, undid four bolts, removed one plate; planted feet on bulkhead on either side of detonator, gripped shaft firmly; triggered hysterical strength, pulled, twisted, pulled again. Ta-dah.

Retained grip as shaft slid free; preferred not having 150 pounds of high-explosive bouncing around inside closed compartment with me.

Hour and half remained before deorbit burn.

Returned to hatch, carefully gathering life-support lines as retraced route amongst structural members. Brought toolbox, detonator shaft.

Squeezed back through hatch, resecured. Remounted PLSS on EMU back; coiled lines neatly, resecured to belt.

First act upon returning to outer hatch: Pitched detonator shaft into space. *Hard*.

Then reeled in MMU; snuggled between armrests, closed latches. With briefcase terminals tied to belt in front, set off for electrical umbilicus hatch, some 15 feet forward.

Prevailed upon MMU to halt inches away after brief, seesaw discussion. Got hatch open without difficulty. Scrutinized multiple-prong socket, identified computer port.

Unshipped briefcase, opened (keyboard in one half, LCD display in other). Unfolded solar-cell array, positioned in direct sunlight. Deployed extension arms; snapped into appropriate EMU belt/shoulder fastenings to hold terminal in proper waist-level typing position.

Flipped main switch to *on*; waited while baby mainframe disk spun up to operating speed, read/write head deployed. Queried system as to state of health, spirits; received affirmative reply (bulky EMU gloves no advantage on standard keyboard).

Unwound coaxial cable from pouch at belt; inserted plug firmly into port, wiggled. Felt click as seated even through gloves. Plugged other end into terminal.

Offered cheery "good morning" to IVN. (no kidding;

acronym derived from actual Russian name [three guesses
how pronounced]); waited, holding breath.

And waited.

(Not complaining about delay, mind you; understood
IVN pretty busy with deorbit countdown, sundry prereentry
chores. Probably didn't have lots of time to spare for small-
talk.)

After about two minutes (during which debated wisdom
of repeating access demand, but didn't for fear duplicate
commands might confuse issue) IVN welcomed me in. Greeted
appearance of primary menu with heartfelt relief.

(And unspoken prayer of thanks to Whomever arranged
for *Khraniteli* to incorporate stolen American disk-operating-
system virtually intact, retaining logically daisy-chained menus-
within-menus-within-menus software format. Child could operate [child *thanks* You!].)

Selected *Ballistika*. Waited some more.

Just how much of IVN's capacity tied up in countdown
activities increasingly apparent: Took almost four minutes to
locate, display submenu. Took another three minutes to pull
out *Koordinaty Prizemlenia* fill-in-blanks programing display.

Thought hard for moment, confirmed Vandenberg's figures in head; plugged in numbers, reached for *execute* key...

Stopped dead—horrified at how close had come to falling
into trap.

Have known all along bomb intended for water landing.
But to me, "water landing" conjures up images of old *Mercu-
ry*, *Gemini*, *Apollo* capsules splashing down in Pacific on
parachutes. Assumption settled in quickly, took hold. Not
even sight of winged behemoth penetrated hell-bent fixation,
set off warning bells.

Obviously this vehicle designed for conventional shuttle-
style approach: high-speed glide to flare-out, touchdown.
Builders clearly intended vehicle's 120-ton momentum (multiplied by 200-plus-mile-per-hour touchdown velocity), together with new alloy's incredible strength, to add up to
can't-miss, unmanned, midocean landing technique—rain or
shine: Would punch through storm waves, if necessary, as if
not there, deceleration remaining within design limits (at ten
gees, after all, takes only *one second* to stop from *Hale*'s
215-mile-per-hour touchdown speed).

But Vandenberg not ocean. Dry-land Air Force base. Set
into, amongst craggy coastal hills. Almost low mountains.

Now, *Khraniteli* copied almost everything else about NASA shuttles while designing, constructing bomb-carrier; probably copied good stuff from Terminal Area Energy Management system as well: IVN undoubtedly programed to come in high, hot; feel for ground with radar altimeter; set up approach pattern, glide-slope calculated to touch down on precise point called for in *Koordinaty Prizemleniya* order blank.

But coordinates in *IFR Supplement* usually for given airfield's geographic center. Maybe high-speed touchdown (in whatever direction) at 34 degrees 44 minutes north longitude, 120 degrees 35 minutes west latitude, would place me in middle of lovely, wide, two-, three-mile-long runway, with lots of room to dissipate speed...

Or maybe not—and doubt new material strong enough to withstand dissipating speed in mountainside (or if so, not apt to matter much to me; would be thin red film on forward bulkhead).

Realization came very close to triggering total panic as wondered what else had overlooked. But time growing steadily shorter; watch showed little better than hour remaining before deorbit burn.

Clamped down, blocked out emotions; refused to permit access to transaction. Forced brain to *think*—constructively; not wordless, nonstop, fearful keening that lurked just beyond fraying edges of control.

Willed mind's eye to recall, display tattered yellowish *IFR Supplement*. Mentally opened cover, began thumbing through, looking for familiar names, as had last week. Remembered seeing Oshkosh, Colorado Springs, Los Angeles, Chicago...

Edwards Air Force Base ...!

Of course—original shuttle landing site! Perfect: miles and miles of flat, unobstructed desert in every direction...

If only could recall coordinates. Hadn't specifically noted at time; would have to reconstruct page from memory of peripheral observation.

Ought to be possible: Always have had good memory; almost eidetic at times. True, occasionally lose names, places, details, appointments, etc.; but only temporarily—have *always* been able to retrieve when necessary. Just matter of time...

Of which didn't have any! frantic little voice shrieked inside head.

Bore down instantly, cut off emotional outburst; focused total attention on completing picture in head. Knew details in there somewhere, *had* to be; just matter of digging out—*dig . . .*!

I dug. And suddenly numbers stood out from page. Quickly, before doubts could blur outlines, copied figures into *Koordinaty Prizemlenia* menu: 34 degrees 54 minutes north longitude, 117 degrees 52 minutes west latitude.

Paused briefly; mentally tried for close-up to confirm. Nothing happened. Apparently best could do.

Okay. Took deep breath, stiffened resolve, pushed *execute*. IVN mulled instructions for endless minutes; finally responded with *Peremena Prinyata* (change accepted).

MMU operation while returning to hatch appreciably less smooth than on way out: Shaking hands, near emotional collapse, serious impediments to efficient operation.

But final details remained undone before deorbit burn. Among which, closing hatch—never intended to be operated from inside (naturally enough). Cycled exterior latch handle several times, peeking around edge, studying workings of bits, pieces on inside. Functions seemed obvious enough; didn't think getting closed, locked, would pose insurmountable problem. So pulled self in through opening.

Turned back, gave MMU hearty push; likewise with terminals—suspected would have trouble enough without large, heavy, unyielding objects bouncing around interior with me at Moment of Truth.

Swung hatch shut; employed tools (retained toolbox; would need during next several minutes) to secure latch. Then adjourned to preselected passenger area: lateral bulkhead just aft of warhead chamber, as near to hull's central axis as could find suitably flat surface close to struts, braces, trusses.

Brought along cushions, harnesses from *Hale*'s three remaining seats (had to disturb Harris, Kyril, briefly to remove). Cushions consist of several pieces per chair. Combined (sticking together with tape) into full-length, double-thick mattress; taped firmly to bulkhead between two stiffeners.

Combined various harness, toolbox components to construct semblance of body restraint over top of makeshift acceleration couch; anchored to structural members. Final product unlikely to pass FAA inspection; attachment strength not even close to that inherent in strap material itself. But harness created for limited purpose of keeping me from being dislodged from cushions by intermittent lateral RCS jostling during periods of major gees. If still conscious after reentry, can attempt to reposition self against forward bulkhead before touchdown.

If not...

Well, won't have to worry about it then, will I.

Employed still more tape, wire, to tie four spare EMUs in place.

Toolbox disposal final chore: Once couch assembled, wormed across to infamous inner-shell access hatch, opened, pushed toolbox through, resecured.

Then unfastened PLSS from back; secured to adjacent bulkhead truss. Positioned self against couch. Fastened straps with trembling hands, lay head against intra-helmet pad, placed helmet firmly against cushions.

Glance at watch showed three minutes to deorbit burn— nothing like cutting it close...!

Closed eyes, breathed deeply, triggered relaxation sequence. Mentally reviewed physical condition: better than expected after events of day, including tapping hysterical strength twice (but only briefly; twisting Kyril's neck over in hundredths of second, detonator shaft came out easily).

Hanging within web of straps, helmet touching cushions which in turn contacted bulkhead, became aware of activity within structure: thumps, clicks, beeps; taut, powerful humming; occasional muted bang accompanied by barely perceptible shove as RCS thrusters completed final preburn alignment. Background sounds conveyed impression of enormous, humorless, very hungry beast gathering to spring.

Countdown timer showed 57 seconds to go. Placed arms carefully under straps at sides. Began breathing deeply, rapidly as possible; wanted to hyperventilate, carry oxygen surplus into deorbit burn: No idea if breathing possible under ten gees.

Counted off seconds in head. Discovered internal clock needs adjustment: Heard APUs (or whatever *Khraniteli* call theirs) start up at minus 30 seconds; then detected heavy vibration, deep rumble at about minus 15 as main engines fired, built up to operating pressure...

And suddenly very glad hyperventilated: Had time for

single final inhalation as gees mounted; then could *not* breathe. Or move. Or do anything else beyond wishing ghastly, crushing pressure would end.

Experimentally tried to move finger. Any finger. Could. Just. Didn't try to move anything else.

Terrible ride seemed endless: Pressure, noise, vibration went on and on and on and...

Suddenly floated up against straps as compression of cushions, own tissues, released. Deorbit burn *over*...!

But quickly squelched rising jubilation: Gee forces least of worries.

And had work to do—most vital work of all: writing this record. Spent roughly last hour and quarter scribbling feverishly by light of now-dying flashlight, hurrying to finish before bomb completes dive, arrives at cometary orbit's perigee where main engines cut in again.

Dragging heels at ten gees chops 320 feet per second from velocity each second. That's 19,200 feet, three and a half miles per second, slower per minute. To stop ship entirely, drop into atmosphere without reentry-heat problems, would require braking for roughly minute and half. Very much doubt will happen that way.

However, preparations made (to extent possible): My spare EMU already inside Kyril's EMU's lower torso, lacking only helmet. Kyril's unit's lower torso already in spare adult EMU's lower torso. Both adult suits' upper torsos already assembled: helmets, gloves, etc.

Life-support lines from my spare's remote PLSS lead in through small slits in adult torsos. Stripped PLSS from Kyril's EMU: Of no benefit inside outer suit; any heat it extracts from interior only has to be removed second time by outer suit's PLSS.

After final braking, before atmospheric contact, will place record inside my spare, install helmet; assemble Kyril's around it, uninflated; then assemble adult spare around both. Pretty squishy, but fits (already tried it for practice).

Once record tucked inside innermost EMU, all three buttoned up, appropriate PLSSs activated, record should be safe (safe as anything likely to be under circumstances).

For own protection, have already donned Harris's EMU over mine, helmet included. Lack only outer gloves, work of seconds (hard enough to write through *one* pair). Am ready to close up, grit teeth, at moment's notice.

But perhaps better call halt, for moment anyway, compose self for engine braking. Getting caught unawares, with arm unsupported over body in writing position, could result in broken bones. Or worse.

Probably have few more comments after final burn—not because expect to have anything important to say, but helps keep mind from dwelling on atmospheric braking side effects.

Damned *Khraniteli* double-crossed me! Have to hurry now, Posterity—*was no engine braking prior to reentry . . .!*

(Or perhaps my fault? Could attempted retargeting have screwed up software?)

Whatever—was already wondering if braking sequence might be overdue, whether something amiss, when perceived first hint of returning gravity; detected faintest, shrill whining sound transmitted through hull, cushions, helmet— already entering upper atmosphere . . . !

Sure wish could ride out reentry inside inner shell with computer, detonator, other tender components; but adult suit won't fit through hatch, and have no way of securing remote PLSS reliably. Would be in bad way if started bouncing around out here; could wreck internal workings, sever lines.

Damn . . . better hurry—starting to get *warm* in here!

Please, God—*don't let me burn . . .!*

VOLUME III—Part III
Finale

This isn't funny anymore—not that it ever was....

Something is going on. Something spooky. Something downright eerie, in fact. Whatever it is, I think it may be coming to a head.

And I'm scared. I can tell Adam is, too.

Terry's "launch soliloquy," with Lisa's related sudden upset, was bad enough. But this morning was *crazy*. And if it continues much longer, I'm positively going to lose my mind!

It started at exactly 5:30 A.M., just moments before we would have been getting up anyway to get an early start and take advantage of every minute of daylight. I was already awake, staring unhappily into the dark; worrying about Candy, wondering about Lisa and Terry; and about this creeping sense of foreboding that weighs increasingly upon all of us.

There was no warning; it's a good thing I've got a sound heart or it would have stopped right then and there.

Simultaneous with Lisa's inarticulate scream came Terry's high, thin shriek: "Kyril—*NO*...!"

Adam is not troubled by indecision: He was on his feet with the bedroom light on before the echoes died away, and he had the living room light on even as I sat up and looked around.

Lisa was sitting straight up in bed, trembling; eyes wide, empty, and horrified. Terry was on the floor, looking around with a confused, frightened expression.

Leaving Adam to retrieve him, I went immediately to Lisa and took her in my arms and held her. She gave no sign of knowing I was there. Her every muscle was rigid and trembling. She panted like a winded fawn and her heart raced wildly.

Adam replaced Terry on his stand. The bird was hunched, head down, plumage fluffed—the very picture of abject misery.

Adam stood silently, gazing back and forth between the bird and my trembling daughter. "*Dammitall!*" he exploded, turning away, "I'd give my left arm to find out what's going on! I *hate not knowing!*"

I "shushed" him and tried to calm Lisa. I rocked her gently, the way I did when she was little, and stroked her hair.

Finally her eyes cleared; she noticed me. "That was *mean!*" she whimpered.

"What happened, baby?" I murmured, glaring a warning over her shoulder at Adam, who, hearing her response, had already wheeled around, ready to administer the third degree. "Who was mean?" I continued. "Who? What did he do?"

I might as well have saved my breath. Lisa pulled away slightly and met my gaze. She opened her mouth to reply, then hesitated. She pulled at her lower lip with her teeth. Finally she shook her head in perplexity. "I dunno, Mommy." She sniffled. "But he was *mean!*" she added emphatically.

"What did he *do* that was mean?" prodded Adam, despite my warning frown. "If you know he was mean, you must know what he did."

But she didn't. At least she was unable to explain it to either of our satisfactions. Or, I suspect, her own.

And suddenly it was happening again: Terry was growling softly, blood-chillingly; he crouched, bill wide, pinpoint pupils staring into space. Lisa withdrew again, her expression going blank, her entire body tensing, muscles gathering.

"Lisa . . ." I began.

She cut me off: "*Shh-h-h-h!* Quiet, Mommy; he'll hear you. We have to be careful not to warn him . . . ."

"Oh, *Kyril . . .!*" wailed Terry.

"Warn *who?*" demanded Adam in exasperation.

"Shh-h-h-h!" was the only reply. Beneath my hands she coiled perceptibly, then started abruptly . . .

"*Haiee-AHH!*" shrieked Terry, flapping violently, this time without quite losing his grip.

Lisa brightened. "All right!" she gloated. She pulled away from me and shook herself. Her sweet baby face wore a positively savage expression. "All *right* . . . !" she repeated with grim satisfaction.

Terry subsided; so did Lisa—into tears.

". . . have to *warn* them!" muttered the bird. ". . . but how? *How? HOW* . . . ?"

Adam exhaled a sigh of repressed wrath and stalked off to the kitchen to make breakfast. It was a noisy process: Pans, dishes, and utensils paid the price for his frustration.

And all the while Terry continued to mutter intermittently in a *sotto voce* undertone, only portions of which were intelligible:

". . . never hear me way around here even if I *could* fix it!"

". . . idea was it, anyway, to put short-range sets in EMUs?"

". . . isn't even a *mirror* in here . . . !"

Apart from the running commentary, breakfast was a quiet affair. Adam ate in stony silence. Lisa moped, dripped tears, and sniffled by turns, and only ate because I threatened reprisals against her stuffed Pooh-Bear.

Both were too preoccupied to recognize the development of a genuinely terrifying omen: *Terry didn't want his scrambled eggs* . . . ! Not since the dawn of time, according to Candy, has he *ever* rejected scrambled eggs—not even during the terrible three days, two years ago, when he almost died of pneumonia!

That's when I started to get a cold feeling in my stomach.

But it was as we were cleaning up the dishes that the Last Straw landed: "Of *course!*" Terry whispered excitedly.

Adam's eyes met mine: Who ever heard of a bird *whispering*?

"I can send it down in the damned *bomb* . . . ! All I have to do is retarget the computer. I can do that—I think . . . What were those coordinates? Remember-remember-*remember*—I *remember!* 34 degrees 44 minutes north, 120 degrees 35 minutes west. Damn—that's almost twenty miles from the launch site; sure hope somebody's watching. *Please,* please, somebody—be *watching* . . . !"

Adam looked suddenly thoughtful. Seizing a pencil, he scribbled on the countertop.

"I give up," I said; "what're you doing, and why?"

By way of answer he went to the electronics wall and pulled open the map drawer. He rustled through the contents for a few seconds; then pulled out a USGS section map. He labored briefly with dividers and parallel rule. "There . . . !" he grunted under his breath. "I would have bet money on it."

He turned to me. "Look here!" he said, in mounting excitement. "Just look where those coordinates lie."

I glanced at the map; Adam had drawn an X on it. I glanced up. "What coordinates?"

"Didn't you hear Terry? That was longitude and latitude he quoted. And look where they cross—Vandenberg Air Force Base!"

My confusion must have been apparent.

"Don't you get it?" he demanded. "They've never landed a shuttle at Vandenberg Air Force Base; they have their own three-mile strip right there at the launch complex, almost twenty miles away—Terry *couldn't* have heard those figures on television."

"Well, he had to get them from somewhere."

Adam eyed me cautiously. "I think he got them from Candy."

"Well . . ." Whatever reply I might have planned was swept away by Terry's next interruption:

"*Oh . . . !*" he exclaimed. "Of *course!* How did anyone so stupid manage to live eleven whole years—*I can ride down, too . . . !*"

Adam stood silent, head down, thinking; his expression was almost a prayer. Then he straightened, eyes hard. He took a deep breath, faced me, and said, "That's *Candy*. Terry is relaying her thoughts—don't ask me how, don't ask me from where. But he is. And she's going to try to get to Vandenberg and it's important and she's afraid. I'm going to be there to meet her. I'm leaving right now. I know it's crazy. Are you with me?"

I, too, hesitated, thinking hard. I reviewed the events of the past several weeks: the innumerable occasions on which Terry clearly anticipated Candy's next statement and beat her to it or said it in chorus with her; his recent incredibly scholarly eloquence, coupled with Lisa's related behavior.

The evidence *in toto* was substantial and convincing. But for our (and Candy's) ostrichlike reluctance to face facts, we would have accepted the obvious conclusion some time ago: Candy and Terry, and Lisa too, *are* in communication—call it ESP or whatever—and we *have* been eavesdropping on Candy's mental processes, wherever she is and whatever she might be doing.

"If we're wrong," I cautioned, "we'll have lost several days' searching up here."

Adam nodded tensely. "I know. But we've covered at least a ten-mile radius so far. If she were here, we'd have found her by now."

I sighed. "I think so, too."

"Right; let's go." Adam was getting into almost as intense a state as the day Candy went down. He swept through the trailer like a whirlwind, gathering various tools, equipment, foodstuffs, and the like. When I asked why, he replied that the trailer would slow us down—he didn't know what the problem might be, but Candy was frightened; he was *not* going to be late.

Adam often talks about his pre-Armageddon ambition to compete professionally in Grand Prix and Nascar, and describes his efforts (uniformly illegal) to acquire the high-speed motoring skills necessary for such a career. The stories tended to begin with "It was the loneliest summer of my life," and I dismissed the bulk of them as exaggeration, wishful thinking, and tall tales spun to entertain us.

However, if there is one thing Adam has not exaggerated, it is his driving skill. For the first few minutes I was terrified; I expected every second to end in a crash. But I knew there was no point in trying to get him to slow down as long as he wore *that* expression. I gritted my teeth and held on—and for once I didn't have to remind Lisa to fasten her seat belt. I held Terry securely in my arms; Tora-chan clung to a seat cushion in the rear, looking annoyed.

But soon I noticed that Adam's driving actually was as smooth as ever; only the speed was different. He was completely relaxed behind the wheel as he hurtled us along the twisting fire road through the sequoia forest.

He cornered *very* quickly—but under perfect control; every turn was executed in the same precise manner; it was like watching a machine drive: He approached each corner from the outside, braking late and heavily with his toe on the brake, using his heel to punch the accelerator as he double-clutched, downshifting to the appropriate gear. He twitched the steering wheel just before releasing the brakes, which put us perceptibly sideways going in. He fed in power, increasing it steadily as we cut across the width of the road, clipping the inside verge just past the geometric apex, accelerating out on an expanding radius. The slide angle tapered off to zero as we accelerated down the ensuing straightaway. There was none of the wild, time-wasting, back-and-forth broadsliding that one sees when Hollywood attempted to depict fast driving; I don't think I saw him cross-control the steering three times during the whole hours-long dash.

And we certainly did go *quickly!* We pulled out of the search area in the deep sequoia forest around seven; Adam got us to the hard-surfaced park roads by about ten. We went even faster on pavement.

Terry continued to mutter intermittently as we traveled: "... cooling longjohns' connected to the backpack, shoulder ring's connected to the helmet ring, glove ring's connected to the arm ring, neckbone's connected to the..."

"*Oh*—God *bless!* What a *sight!* That's *beautiful....*"

"Where *is* it...? I did everything right—I'm *sure* I did..."

"*There...!* Oo-ooh, damn, it's big. Okay, board and storm—no, let's not be greedy; boarding will be quite sufficient."

Adam glanced across at the bird occasionally and shook his head. Once he said, "This is crazy. If we accept this premise, then Candy must have gone up on a shuttle; she must be in space *right now.* What's an eleven-year-old kid doing in space?"

"Would you rather go back and keep searching?"

He kept driving.

Terry continued to "keep us posted." Briefly he repeated some gibberish we'd heard previously. But by quarter to eleven, he got excited: "No-no-no; stop here! *Oh*—must the damned thing *always* go where I *steer* it instead of where I *want* it...!

"Okay, wake up, all you little transistors; Momma wants to talk to Ivan. Ivan, *Ivan*—talk to me, you ideologically deficient collection of cowed chips!

"There, that's better. Okay, now let's have *Ballistika.*"

"Adam," I ventured, "that sounds like Russian."

Adam concentrated on his driving. His jaw muscles worked but he didn't reply.

"*Dear Lord...!*" Terry burst out abruptly. "Did you make me this stupid originally or have I picked it up on my own! I can't put this thing down at Vandenberg—I don't want to wind up inside a mountain . . . !"

Suddenly Terry had our undivided attention. Adam braked to a quick stop.

"*Now* what . . . ? What other coordinates do I remember? *Think*, dummy—or do you *like* it up here! Think harder! We're running out of time! Think! Think think*think*! Picture the IFR Supplement in your head—certainly there ought to be room for it; we know there's nothing else in there. What did you see—whatwhat*what*? Of *course* . . . ! Perfect!

"Now the coordinates. *Think*—the clock is *running* . . . !

"Ah-*ha!* 34 degrees 54 minutes north longitude, 117 degrees 52 minutes west latitude . . . ! Damn, what a memory! And . . . *execute!*"

I hadn't had to be told; I copied the numbers as Terry uttered them. Adam was already unfolding the chart. We didn't have the dividers and parallel rule, but it wasn't difficult to make an approximation . . .

"Edwards Air Force Base," breathed Adam. "Of course, perfect."

"She said that," said Lisa from the back seat. We spun and stared. "She's awful scared," she continued solemnly. "I think we better hurry."

We arrived back at the little airstrip outside Fresno a few minutes after noon. Lisa's soft-spoken observation was all it took to revert Adam to a full-blown wild man. He fueled and preflighted the Cessna; and by 12:30 we were accelerating down the runway. Adam banked almost the instant the wheels cleared the ground, and seconds later we were on course for Edwards.

He climbed us to about seventy-five hundred feet; the operator's manual suggests that altitude as the ideal compromise between lessened air resistance and engine-power loss due to reduced oxygen. He fiddled with the mixture, manifold pressure, and propellor pitch until he was squeezing out the absolute maximum speed of which the plane was capable.

We've been in the air for about an hour; just under a half hour to go.

I'm not a compulsive histographer like Candy. I've been keeping her journal up-to-date in her absence because I know she would rather not have any significant gaps. But today's record is being made in hopes that keeping busy will enable me to retain what little remains of my sanity.

This is *crazy*, what we're doing—it simply is *not* rational!

But we're doing it anyway; and I think Adam really expects to find her at Edwards when we get there, or shortly thereafter.

I think I do, too.

But...

Sorry for the interruption. We're in the midst of a crisis; it's panic time among our little group. And justifiably so, I'm afraid.

All doubts have vanished; we *know* that we're listening in on Candy's thoughts through Terry—however he's doing it. And it doesn't take much imagination to figure out what's happening.

A few minutes ago Terry gasped (I *know*—whoever heard of a bird gasping?), "What the *hell* ...! That's *atmosphere*! What happened to the brakes! Oh, damn, this is going to be *hot*!"

"Mommy," said Lisa unhappily, "Candy's awful scared."

I wasn't much of a mother just then. I said, "Yes, dear, I know. Be quiet now and let us hear what's going on."

"Knock it off," snapped Terry. "Let's get that record wrapped up and safe first. Then be as hysterical as you like. Okay. In through the neck, snap on the helmet; now Kyril's waist ring, now the spare. There. Both PLSS thermostats cooling at max. Good, maybe it'll come through okay.

"Now me—oh, Lord, I'm scared...! Pay *attention*!—right glove—stop *fumbling*; you've done this a dozen times in training! Oh, yeah?—with another pair of gloves on already? Okay. Left glove. Good. Now turn PLSSs down all the way.

"Whoa—gees building up already. Better get up somewhere near the middle of the transverse bulkhead, away from the hull. That hull's going to get hot!

"Idiot!—*don't forget the record* ...! Maybe I can wedge the EMU in between those bulkhead stiffeners. There. EMU—*stay*!

"Hey, where's my PLSS? Oh, that's no good; I better ...

"What was that! What are they doing; firing the laterals in the atmosphere? Boy, that's thorough; what a paranoid bunch! I bet nothing in the Free World's entire defense arsenal could keep *this* sucker from completing its appointed rounds. Not at—what?—seven miles per second . . . ?

"Oh, damn—how high will I be when I pass over Vandenberg? Why didn't I think of that before? Too high and the shock wave won't reach the ground at all; they won't notice—they'll miss their only chance! The record can't warn Teacher *if he never finds out about it* . . . !

"No; they're bound to have radar looking west—watching for the tsunami, if nothing else; that would be their first indication that we failed. Yeah, they'll notice—they *have* to notice! And it'll take an Act of God to keep them away after that. Okay, the warning will get through—if it gets down intact.

"Wonder if I'm going to get down intact—damn, it's hot in here! I wish they'd quit banging away with those lateral thrusters; it's hard to hang on.

"Whoo-ee . . . ! Aerodynamic dodging! Wonder if that's programed at ten gees, too. Got to admire somebody that determined. Those people—"

Suddenly Lisa screamed shrilly and clutched at her upper arm.

"*Ouch* . . . *!*" coughed Terry. "Lord, my *arm* . . ."

Adam's head jerked around, his face ashen. Our eyes met in helpless silence.

"Mom-*mee*-ee . . . !" wailed Lisa, rubbing her arm. But there was nothing I could do for her: Sometimes it's not much fun being a Corsican sister.

"*Oh, that hurts* . . . *!*" continued the bird. "Now Adam and I match. Surprised it didn't smash the inner helmet, too! How am I supposed to climb back up there with *this*? Hell, how could I hang on even if I—"

Lisa screamed again.

"*Jees-sus* . . . *!*" panted Terry, "I feel like a pingpong ball in a doubles match! Good thing I'm wearing two—"

Lisa grunted as if the breath had been kicked out of her, then moaned inarticulately.

"*Uh* . . ." said Terry. "Where am I? My arm hurts. It's so hot. Oh, I remem—"

Lisa shrieked, then sobbed in silence.

"*Oh!*—wonder how many ribs that was. It *hurts* . . .

"What's that—*my PLSS line* . . . *!* Quick, crimp it off—stop the lea—"

Lisa "oofed," her sobbing momentarily interrupted; then she continued. I felt so *helpless!* For both of them.

"Oh, that was a *good* one. Wonder what broke that time. Where's that life-support line? There, crimp it again—*crimp* it! Not that it matters—it's getting so hard to breathe. So hot.... Oh, damn, I thought maybe it would work; I *wanted*—"

Lisa hardly reacted at all that time; only an added moan on top of her crying.

"What a choice—cook, suffocate... beat to a pulp...."

"Mommy," whimpered Lisa, hands at her throat, "I can't breathe...."

"God... bless Mother and Father... Smith, and Momma and Daddy Foster and... Teacher... and Adam and Kim and Lisa. And Terry... oh—*please* take... care of Ter—"

The bird fell silent. He fluffed, hunched. His eyes went blank. He began to make a soft keening sound. Lisa stopped crying. I started.

"Terry can't *feel* her, Mommy," whispered Lisa in stricken tones. "She's not scared anymore."

That's when Adam slammed the throttle forward and lowered the nose. Our airspeed indicator is now pegged at the red line. In theory, the plane can break up if we go any faster. In practice, the exhaust-gas temperature readings are over the limit already.

But the dry lake is in sight. We can glide from here if we have to.

Only a few minutes more...

There it is ...! Whatever it is. It looks something like a shuttle, but bigger. It's dead black. It's a threatening-looking machine somehow. It's well above us, approaching from the west, descending rapidly. There are no lights or windows. There are no markings.

Adam is diving the plane to pick up even more speed. It's right at our height now, crossing in front of us. Adam is turning to follow, losing ground.

We're over the dry lake bottom now. There's a good five or ten miles of smooth, flat surface ahead. It's well ahead of us now, beginning its flare-out. It's only feet above the ground. There's no sign of landing gear yet—it's *down*; it touched down on its belly. It's sliding smoothly along the lake bottom, trailing an immense plume of dust, slowing gradually.

We're overtaking it, skimming along just above the ground, bleeding off our dive-induced excess speed.

We're alongside now, and Adam is slowing us, maintaining formation.

Our wheels are down—isn't that thing *ever* going to stop . . . ?

Lisa is becoming agitated. She's begun to whisper, "Hurry, Mommy; hurry, Mommy," through her tears.

Terry just began to moan.

Adam glanced across at him, his face an absolute death mask. "That's the noise he made before," he remarked in a controlled, brittle, horribly offhand manner, "when her heart stopped after she pulled me out of the fire and stitched up my leg."

We're almost *stopped*—I don't know what's going to happen, but Adam is still wearing *that* expression.

Hello. Mommy can't write now. She's hurt. Adam is too. I know Candy would want somebody to tell what happened. I'm the only one who knows what happened who isn't hurt.

I'm writing in squiggles too. I don't know why they call it shorthand. I learned how to write this way three years ago. Mommy doesn't know. I haven't been telling Mommy all the things I can do for a long time. I could feel her worry when I told her stuff sometimes. So when I felt her worry about something and she asked me, I pretended I didn't understand. She feels different now. Maybe I can tell her everything.

There was a book on the living-room shelves. It showed how to write shorthand. I already knew how to read and write English. I had to read fast while Mommy was taking a bath. She thought I was too young to read books without pictures. Candy writes this way in her books too. I practiced reading them. Nobody knew I could read them. I never wrote this way before. It feels funny.

I felt Candy hurt real bad. It hurt a lot. Then I almost couldn't feel her and she almost stopped being in Terry's mind. I got awful scared. Then I couldn't feel her at all and she wasn't in Terry's mind anymore. Then Terry got real scared too.

The spaceship came down like on television. Adam landed next to it. We got out. Terry wanted to go to Candy. He knew she was inside the spaceship. I couldn't feel her, but he could. He flew at the spaceship. It was very hot. He

burned his feet and feathers. I pulled him away and held him
so he wouldn't. He screamed and tried to get away.

Adam and Mommy ran to the spaceship. They opened
the door. They burned their hands. They climbed inside.
They got burned more. They found Candy. They carried her
out. She was wearing a spacesuit. It was smoking. The glass
thing on her head was full of smoke too. You almost couldn't
see her face.

They tried to get the spacesuit off. It was too strong.
Adam was crying and said bad words. Mommy was crying
too. I could feel how scared they were. I was scared too. I
couldn't feel her even that close.

Then Adam said the word that makes you strong. I didn't
think it would work. It never made him strong before. But it
did work and he was strong and he tore the spacesuit apart.
There was another spacesuit inside that one. He tore it apart
too.

Candy was asleep. They tried to make her wake up. She
wouldn't. I couldn't feel her at all. Then Terry screamed
because he couldn't feel her in his mind anymore. He wanted
to be with her. I put him down. He couldn't walk because his
feet were burned. I put him right by her head. He put his
head against her cheek and cried.

Adam started kissing Candy and pushing on her chest.
He did that a long time. He was awful scared. Mommy tied
sticks to Candy's legs and arm and put bandages and needles
and tubes and stuff on her.

Then the helicopters came and people got out. They
were nice. One of the people is named Teacher. That's a
funny name. He has nice eyes and lots of wrinkles and feels
nice inside. He took Candy's wrist in his hand. He put his ear
on her chest like Adam did. Then he got scared too. He
looked at the bandages and tubes and stuff that Mommy put
on Candy. He said Mommy did a good job. I don't understand why he cried if Mommy did a good job.

They tried to wake up Candy too. She wouldn't wake up.
They put more bandages on her. They put bandages on
Mommy too. They put bandages on Terry. They had to put
them on him right by Candy because he wouldn't leave her.
They wanted to put bandages on Adam. He wouldn't let
them. He kept kissing Candy and pushing on her chest. He
wouldn't stop.

Then I felt Candy wake up part way. I could feel her

hurt. It wasn't as bad as before. Adam didn't know she was awake yet. She put her good arm around his neck. She kissed him back. He was surprised. Kissing like that feels funny.

Then Candy woke up all the way. She opened her eyes. She was surprised too because she was kissing Adam. That was funny. She said, "Hello, Melville" to Adam and he was more surprised. Mommy laughed. I never saw anybody laugh at the same time she was crying. I wonder who Melville is.

Candy wanted to talk to Teacher. Her voice was very weak. I couldn't hear what she said. Teacher didn't want her to talk. She said a bad word. Her voice wasn't weak that time. Then Teacher got down on his knees and put his ear close to her mouth and she talked to him.

He was surprised. He talked to some of the other people then. They went inside the spaceship and came out with somebody else. I thought it was somebody else. It was a book inside three spacesuits. Teacher thought it was very smart of Candy to put the book inside three spacesuits. I don't understand why that's smart.

I like Teacher. I like the way he feels. He likes Candy. He was glad to get the book. He said now everything will be all right. I am glad.

Teacher is glad Candy is back. I am glad Candy is back. Mommy and Adam are glad too.

Terry is gladdest of all.

VOLUME III—Part Four

Epilogue

Pay attention now, Posterity; do not intend to repeat myself:

Positively last time I travel coach . . . !

Finally out of traction, thank you; and burns healing nicely. Haven't required I.V. in better than month. Yesterday morning doctors (*crème* of AA medical community; all hand-picked by, working under direction [gimlet eye] of, Teacher) even let me try walking—for first time since reentry. (Three, four months ago, I think. Maybe longer.) And no more Foley catheter; can go potty myself again—*at last!*

Truly was a mess:

More bones broken than intact. Epidermis essentially one large hematoma—which underlay widespread first-, second-degree burns. Also concussed. Etc. (*Lots* of "etc.")

Pretty well out of things during initial weeks. Fortunately. Memory of that period consists primarily of impressions:

. . . Pain.

. . . Darkness.

. . . Intermittent awareness of intruding kindly hands, gentle for most part, but often doing things that hurt; fleeting hazy glimpses of faces; nearby voices speaking occasional hearty encouragement—frequent muffled sobbing in background.

. . . Adam. Swathed in bandages at outset. No idea when slept, if ever; but seemingly there every minute, quietly performing endless little chores required by intensive-care patient, or sitting at bedside, holding hand.

. . . And, of course, Terry. Don't think twin slept any

more than Adam. (That's one possibility; other makes me
nervous—Teacher promises study of phenomenon soonest
possible opportunity.) Anyway, never opened eyes without
finding brother peering intently from bedside stand, reaching
out gently to nuzzle cheek, offer greeting: "Hello, baby!
What'cha *do*in'... ?"

Though personal universe limited in beginning to Pain,
Presence & Absence of, vaguely remember gaining impression baby brother moving more cautiously than usual—plus
seemed to be wearing fuzzy white slippers. By time own
condition improved to point where data registered as anomalous, footwear gone, irrepressible sibling madcap self again:
dancing back and forth on, chinning upside down from,
perch; wrestling endless with bell (lifelong obsession: clapper
got in there; *must* come out); chattering merrily, singing,
whistling, laughing, etc.

As well, once my recovery status permitted such, enjoying
visitors (Terry so loves company). And we had *lots*: Vandenberg
community census approaching 2,000—must have seen each
at least once during past months.

(The lengths some girls will go to, to be popular....)

Prognosis suggests complete recovery; no sequelae: no
physical impairment, no motor/sensory dysfunction—no scar-
ring from burns; not even hypopigmentation. (Was *awfully*
lucky.)

Nor, happy to report, psychic trauma over killing Kyril....

Yes, regret necessity. Very, very much.

Sweet man. Bright, fun, good company. Also cuddly.

Dear friend.

Gallant foe.

Miss him. Intensely.

But his job conflicted with mine. Mortally: Under circumstances, "him-or-me" synonymous with "them-or-us."

Chose us.

And would again, thousand times over. Million times
over! Along with entire tribe, root and stock...!

Genocide ugly concept. Not arguing point. But *Khraniteli*
chose ground rules, set stakes. In no position to complain
when plans backfire.

Teacher will do best to avoid massacre, of course. But
equally certain: Will *not* expose tiny hominem population to
slightest risk of another brush with extinction. *Khraniteli* who
survive next encounter will be product of most careful screen-

ing imaginable—plus can expect to spend balance of days under tightest supervision.

Goodness... That's enough for now. Suddenly it's kind of tired out.

(Been sick, you know.)

Good night, Posterity.

Progress! Teacher studied x-rays, conferred with colleagues, pronounced repairs complete: skeleton intact, skin whole. Sent me home to family.

Which now includes Gayle. Kim, with Adam's concurrence (*ha!*), asked if wished to move in with us. Did. So now have *three* sisters. Cozy, homey, fun. (More fun still: Adam badly outnumbered; stays rather distracted....)

Lisa has another new friend, by the way: small boy, approximately same age. Nice lad—despite growing up under handicap: Parents named him Leslie Vivian Sweet. But not teased about it. Possibly because first showed up several weeks ago—*riding full-grown male Kodiak bear...!*

Charming beast; answers to name of Baloo.

Leslie's father zookeeper in San Diego. Baloo born at zoo but fell sick; had to be taken home for special nursing. Became Leslie's constant companion for whole year. Attempted return to zoo utter failure: Both pined inconsolably for weeks. Zoo authorities, father finally yielded to inevitable: Baloo remained family member until Armageddon; protected small charge thereafter until stumbled onto hominem community.

No one has slightest fear of shaggy giant, despite obvious horrific potential: Gentle as puppy, affectionate toward everyone; does everything boy says—plus everything he *doesn't* say....

Positively uncanny: As responsive to thoughts as to spoken commands.

Teacher promises to include Baloo in study as well.

Terry says, "How *'bout* that."

Everybody wears variety of hats these days: Gayle serves part-time as martial-arts instructor. Took me under wing immediately; and wasted no time getting after damage done by well-intentioned tampering: Together with continuing therapy directed at physiological restoration, most drills center on reintegrating lethal responses. Progress heartening: Strength, coordination, reflexes, speed returning; endurance building toward preinjury levels. Building rapidly—sparring with Master does bring out best in student.

Kim, Adam, Lisa numbered amongst students also. Gayle complimentary about progress to date; told them in front of whole class—and me—could tell had learned basics from true Master. Embarrassed me to death. Especially when all turned, applauded.

Hominems have predecessors' mistakes clearly in mind; intend no repetition. Planning to restore, preserve planet; concentrate upon research, education, individual development, etc.

Approve of that; parallels own ambitions for organizing Wisconsin hometown community as people wandered in after reading leaflet I posted all across continent, had circumstances required fallback to contingency plan. (*So* glad didn't!)

As for own plans... Well—are in considerable disarray at moment: Adam never party to forced cheerfulness during incapacitation. Eyes, on occasions when managed to focus both mine on him at once, were intent, watchful; reflected worry, strain—and Something Else (something new, gentle, confident; devoid of any hint of previous leer; patient, but conveying intentions every bit as direct, purposeful, unmistakable—and unexpectedly welcome!) which, detected in someone *much* older than 13, would be difficult to distinguish from way Daddy's eyes always shone when looked at Momma. Meeting gaze makes me feel all quivery inside.

(Would have sworn [before all this happened] Adam too young for such depths [not to mention self!]. But—well, not so sure now.... Both *lots* older [calendar years surely very minorest component].)

However, though find myself in substantial agreement—*just not ready yet*! At least, don't think so. But not sure. And don't know how to find out (short of empirical research).

Asked Teacher. But no help at all. No matter how I phrased question, merely smiled benignly; expressed serene conviction that, whatever decision I make, will turn out for best.

And big sisters worse. Kim grins wickedly; Gayle smiles archly. Both profess to envy problem: Regard Adam, age difference notwithstanding, eminently catchable (for sport or long-term, singly or double-team!); only respect for my amusing, old-fashioned, all-or-nothing, provincial morality, coupled with recognition of implied prior claim, keeps them from taking run at him themselves.

Kidding, of course.

(I think.)

Fortunately, not facing deadline; Adam applying no pressure. Of course, forebearance clearly due to opinion that he doesn't *have* to push; that quarry solidly hooked; that bringing matter to resolution only matter of time.

All of which quite frustrating—only thing more vexing than suspicion that everybody around you knows you better than you know yourself is *ever-deepening conviction they're right . . .!*

Well, maybe are. But have to find out for self. Shall take advantage of Adam's newfound maturity, patience: Continue present relationship (with addition of occasional CPR practice as medically indicated [cardiopulmonary system already shut down three times in only 11 years, after all—prudent person plans ahead]) until sure of own motivations, feelings.

Both still young; have all the time in the world to explore question. In whatever depth necessary.

Research promises to be interesting.

So does future.

ABOUT THE AUTHOR

DAVID R. PALMER was born in the Chicago area in 1941 and grew up there. He has worked at an amazing variety of jobs over the years (mail clerk, bookkeeper, junior accountant; VW mechanic, assistant service-manager, service manager, car salesman; appliance, furniture, and insurance salesman; school-bus driver; pet-store owner and manager; gravel-truck driver, intra- and intercity bus driver; typesetter, legal secretary, court-reporting transcriber—to mention only a few).

His pastimes have been equally varied, and have included (apart from *lots* of reading) flying, motorcycling, sailing, skin-diving, photography—and racing (he was a Formula Vee champion in the 60s, in a car designed and built in collaboration with a friend).

Currently he is a certified shorthand court reporter (the term "court stenographer" is held in very bad odor among practitioners of the profession) working in north central Florida with his wife, also a court reporter. Their family consists of (at latest count) four cats, two dogs, a parrot, and a horse.

Emergence is his first novel. Parts I and II appeared in the January, 1981, and February, 1983, issues of *Analog*, and were his first and second sales. His second novel, *Threshold*, will be published by Bantam in December, 1985.

OUT OF THIS WORLD!

That's the only way to describe Bantam's great series of science fiction classics. These space-age thrillers are filled with terror, fancy and adventure and written by America's most renowned writers of science fiction. Welcome to outer space and have a good trip!

☐	24709	**RETURN TO EDDARTA** by Garrette & Heydron	$2.75
☐	22759	**STAINLESS STEEL RAT FOR PRESIDENT**	$2.75
		by Harry Harrison	
☐	25395	**STAINLESS STEEL RAT WANTS YOU**	$2.95
		by Harry Harrison	
☐	20780	**STARWORLD** by Harry Harrison	$2.50
☐	20774	**WHEELWORLD** by Harry Harrison	$2.50
☐	24176	**THE ALIEN DEBT** by F. M. Busby	$2.75
☐	25261	**MASTER OF THE SIDHE** by Kenneth C. Flint	$2.95
☐	25251	**INFINITY'S WEB** by Sheila Finch	$2.95
☐	05090	**THE DREAM YEARS** by Lisa Goldstein	$13.95
		(A Bantam Hardcover)	
☐	24710	**A STORM UPON ULSTER** by Kenneth C. Flint	$3.50
☐	24175	**THE RIDERS OF THE SIDHE**	$2.95
		by Kenneth C. Flint	
☐	05089	**CHILD OF FORTUNE** by Norman Spinrad	$16.95
		(A Bantam Hardcover)	
☐	25061	**THE MIND GAME** by Norman Spinrad	$3.50
☐	24543	**CHAMPIONS OF THE SIDHE**	$2.95
		by Kenneth C. Flint	
☐	25215	**THE PRACTICE EFFECT** by David Brin	$2.95
☐	23589	**TOWER OF GLASS** by Robert Silverberg	$2.95
☐	23495	**STARTIDE RISING** by David Brin	$3.50
☐	24564	**SUNDIVER** by David Brin	$2.75
☐	23512	**THE COMPASS ROSE** by Ursula LeGuin	$3.50
☐	23541	**WIND'S 12 QUARTERS** by Ursula LeGuin	$2.95
☐	22855	**CINNABAR** by Edward Bryant	$2.50
☐	22938	**THE WINDHOVER TAPES: FLEXING THE**	$2.75
		WARP by Warren Norwood	
☐	23394	**THE WINDHOVER TAPES: AN IMAGE OF**	$2.75
		VOICES by Warren Norwood	

Prices and availability subject to change without notice.

Buy them at your local bookstore or use this handy coupon for ordering:

Bantam Books, Inc., Dept. SF, 414 East Golf Road, Des Plaines, Ill. 60016

Please send me the books I have checked above. I am enclosing $_____
(please add $1.25 to cover postage and handling). Send check or money order
—no cash or C.O.D.'s please.

Mr/Mrs/Miss _____

Address_____

City_____ State/Zip_____

SF—9/85

Please allow four to six weeks for delivery. This offer expires 3/86.

FANTASY AND SCIENCE FICTION FAVORITES

Bantam brings you the recognized classics as well as the current favorites in fantasy and science fiction. Here you will find the most recent titles by the most respected authors in the genre.

☐	25260	THE BOOK OF KELLS R. A. MacAvoy	$3.50
☐	25122	THE CHRISTENING QUEST	$2.95
		Elizabeth Scarborough	
☐	24370	RAPHAEL R. A. MacAvoy	$2.75
☐	24169	WINTERMIND Parke Godwin, Marvin Kaye	$2.75
☐	23944	THE DEEP John Crowley	$2.95
☐	23853	THE SHATTERED STARS Richard McEnroe	$2.95
☐	23575	DAMIANO R. A. MacAvoy	$2.75
☐	25403	TEA WITH THE BLACK DRAGON R. A. MacAvoy	$2.95
☐	23365	THE SHUTTLE PEOPLE George Bishop	$2.95
☐	24441	THE HAREM OF AMAN AKBAR	$2.95
		Elizabeth Scarborough	
☐	20780	STARWORLD Harry Harrison	$2.50
☐	22939	THE UNICORN CREED Elizabeth Scarborough	$3.50
☐	23120	THE MACHINERIES OF JOY Ray Bradbury	$2.75
☐	22666	THE GREY MANE OF MORNING Joy Chant	$3.50
☐	25097	LORD VALENTINE'S CASTLE Robert Silverberg	$3.95
☐	20870	JEM Frederik Pohl	$2.95
☐	23460	DRAGONSONG Anne McCaffrey	$2.95
☐	24862	THE ADVENTURES OF TERRA TARKINGTON	$2.95
		Sharon Webb	
☐	23666	EARTHCHILD Sharon Webb	$2.50
☐	24102	DAMIANO'S LUTE R. A. MacAvoy	$2.75
☐	24417	THE GATES OF HEAVEN Paul Preuss	$2.50

Prices and availability subject to change without notice.

Buy them at your local bookstore or use this handy coupon for ordering:

Bantam Books, Inc., Dept. SF2, 414 East Golf Road, Des Plaines, Ill. 60016

Please send me the books I have checked above. I am enclosing $_____ (please add $1.25 to cover postage and handling). Send check or money order —no cash or C.O.D.'s please.

Mr/Mrs/Miss_____

Address_____

City_____ State/Zip_____

SF2—9/85

Please allow four to six weeks for delivery. This offer expires 3/86.

SAMUEL R. DELANY

Hailed by *The New York Times* as "the most interesting writer of science fiction writing in English today," this Hugo and four-time Nebula Award-winning author is one of SF's most insightful and dazzling talents.

☐	24856	**Flight From Neveryon**	**$3.95**
☐	22842	**Tales of Neveryon**	**$3.50**
☐	25391	**Dhalgren**	**$4.95**
☐	25149	**Stars In My Pocket Like Grains of Sand**	**$3.50**

<u>Prices and availability subject to change without notice.</u>